I0590970

JANE DE LA VAUDÈRE

THE WITCH OF ECBATANA
AND THE VIRGIN OF ISRAEL

TRANSLATED AND WITH AN INTRODUCTION BY
BRIAN STABLEFORD

THIS IS A SNUGGLY BOOK

ISBN: 978-1-64525-052-4

THE WITCH OF ECBATANA
AND THE VIRGIN OF ISRAEL

JANE DE LA VAUDÈRE was baptized Jeanne Scrive and was married to Camille Gaston Crapez, who began styling himself Crapez de La Vaudère after inheriting the Château de La Vaudère from his mother. Her prolific literary work is very various but she was assimilated to the Decadent Movement firstly because of two scandalously scabrous Parisian novels, *Les Demi-Sexes* (1897) and *Les Androgynes* (1903), and, more pertinently, because of a series of accounts of *moeurs antiques*, some of which—notably *Le Mystère de Kama* (1901)—set new standards of excess in their exotic eroticism and fascination with torture.

BRIAN STABLEFORD'S scholarly work includes *New Atlantis: A Narrative History of Scientific Romance* (Wildside Press, 2016), *The Plurality of Imaginary Worlds: The Evolution of French roman scientifique* (Black Coat Press, 2017) and *Tales of Enchantment and Disenchantment: A History of Faerie* (Black Coat Press, 2019). In support of the latter projects he has translated more than a hundred volumes of *roman scientifique* and more than twenty volumes of *contes de fées* into English. He has edited *Decadence and Symbolism: A Showcase Anthology* (Snuggly Books, 2018), and is busy translating more Symbolist and Decadent fiction.

His recent fiction, in the genre of metaphysical fantasy, includes a trilogy of novels set in West Wales, consisting of *Spirits of the Vasty Deep* (2018), *The Insubstantial Pageant* (2018) and *The Truths of Darkness* (2019), published by Snuggly Books, and a trilogy set in Paris and the south of France, consisting of *The Painter of Spirits*, *The Quiet Dead* and *Living with the Dead*, all published by Black Coat Press in 2019.

CONTENTS

INTRODUCTION

This is the last of six projected volumes translating fiction by Jane de La Vaudère (15 April 1857-26 July 1908). Five of those volumes each contain two of her short novels, while the second in the series, *The Double Star and Other Occult Fantasies*, contains a selection of her short fiction. The first volume, *The Demi-Sexes and the Androgynes*, contained translations of *Les Demi-Sexes*, originally published by Paul Ollendorff in 1897, and *Les Androgynes, roman passionel*, originally published by Albert Méricant in 1903. The third volume, *The Mystery of Kama and Brahma's Courtesans*, contains translations of *Le Mystère de Kama, roman magique indou* (Ernest Flammarion, 1901) and *Les Courtisanes de Brahma* (Flammarion, 1903). The fourth, *Three Flowers and the King of Siam's Amazon*, contains translations of *Trois fleurs de volupté, roman javanais* (Flammarion, 1900) and *L'Amazone du roi de Siam* (Flammarion, 1902). The fifth, *Syta's Harem and Pharaoh's Lover*, contains translations of *Le Harem de Syta, roman passionel* (Méricant, 1904) and *L'Amante du Pharaon, moeurs antiques* (Jules Tallandier, 1905). The present volume contains translations of *La Sorcière d'Ecbatane, roman fantastique* (Flammarion, 1906) and *La Vierge d'Israel, roman de moeurs antiques* (Méricant 1906).

Jane de La Vaudère was baptized Jeanne Scrive; both her parents died when she was still a child, and in the social class to which her family belonged, which might be described as the "upper bourgeoisie," the standard practice when a young girl was orphaned at an early age was to put her in a convent, where she would be educated until her teens, and then marry her off as soon as possible. That appears to be what happened to Jeanne Scrive and her elder sister Marie. It is necessary to say "appears" because almost nothing is now known for sure about Jane de La Vaudère's personal life and death, presently-recoverable data being sparse save that derived from the statements she made in a few newspaper interviews and a few objectively determinable facts.

In one such interview La Vaudère said that while in the convent of Notre-Dame de Sion she seriously considered remaining there permanently, the idea of living as a nun having a certain romantic attraction, but she soon abandoned the idea. Not long after leaving the institution, when she apparently went to stay for a while with Marie, by then married to a military surgeon, she was married to Camille Gaston Crapez (1848-1912), who inherited the Château de La Vaudère at Parigné-l'Éveque (Sarthe) from his mother and styled himself thereafter Crapez de La Vaudère. The name with which she signed her books was not, as many sources report, a pseudonym, although she deleted the Crapez and anglicized her forename.

The Crapez de La Vaudères had one child, Fernand, who apparently stayed with his father when his mother went to live in Paris, where she seems to have lived alone. Although she was never divorced, and her body was taken back to Parigné-l'Éveque for burial after her death in Paris, the separation appears to have been complete, no newspaper reports of her appearances at social events or interviews conducted at her home mention the presence of her husband. Nothing was reported about the circumstances of her death, and neither her husband nor her son appear to have been with her at the time; the unusual brevity of the death notices and the conspicuous absence of the customary post-mortem eulogies suggest a diplomatic silence, but we can only speculate as to what it was that was deliberately not being said about her sudden death at a relatively young age.

The circumstances of Jane de La Vaudère's early life evidently had a profound impact on her literary work, to which she turned a trifle late in her career. Before she began writing, in her thirties, she had attempted to make a career as an artist and exhibited at the Paris Salon; when she decided that her real vocation was literary she first began writing poetry, and then wrote for the stage. Her first collection of poetry, *Les Heures perdues* [The Lost Hours] (1889) appeared in the same year as the production of her one-act comedy *Le Modèle* [The Model]. Her verse is Romantic and might have seemed a trifle old-fashioned at the time of its publication; she was certainly not unaware of contemporary tends in Symbolist poetry, since she was a very voracious reader and her influences were eclectic. *Le Modèle* was the first of many frothy one-act comedies, usually in verse and often performed with musical accompaniment—fifteen of them were collected in *Pour le Flirt! Saynètes modernes* [approximately, Just For Fun, modern satirettes] (1905)—but she also wrote longer comedies and dramas.

She continued to write poetry and plays alongside her prose fiction, but there are very striking differences between her work in the three genres, and her prose work also shows sharp generic divisions. It is not unusual for writers to manifest seemingly different world-views in their prose fiction and work for the stage, especially if the latter mostly consists of vaudevilles written as pure entertainment while the former is more earnest and intense, but in La Vaudère's case the difference is extreme, even in her contemporary Paris-set novels, which often feature female characters not unlike those routinely featured in her stage comedies—young socialites, actresses and artists' models—but very markedly in the remarkable series of exotic novels set in far-flung places and times that make up the last four volumes of the present series of translations.

La Vaudère's first novel, *Mortelle étreinte* [Mortal Embrace] (1891) is the story of a young orphan brought up in a convent who then goes to live with a relative, where she continues to live in virtual seclusion, in the psychological environment of her vivid imagination and the books she reads in abundance. She knows nothing about the real world and is utterly unready to cope with her own hectic emotions when she is first attracted to a man—a man who is also greatly attracted to her, but who is, from every other viewpoint, quite unsuitable and incapable of providing her with the existential anchorage and security that she needs and desires.

The basic features of that story-line were to recur again and again in the author's work, sometimes transplanted to exceedingly bizarre décor. Its melodramatic intensity is inevitably restrained in *Mortelle étreinte* by the conventions of the society in which it is set, but when it is removed to ancient India or ancient Babylon, in the author's accounts of *moeurs antiques*, such shackles no longer apply, and the pitch of that intensity is then turned up to a level unequaled in the work of any other writer of the era. The sensation of having been brought up in an artificial environment, with little or no parental guidance, and then thrust into a world equipped with hopes and expectations that are certain to be betrayed, is developed in story after story, in variants that are extraordinarily wide-ranging, often wildly exaggerated, and almost always brutally tragic.

Much of La Vaudère's early short fiction, beginning with "Amour Astral" (1890-91) in *L'Univers illustré*; tr. as "Astral Amour") and the references in those stories reveal that she had become intensely interested in contemporary research in physiological psychology, especially hypnotism, and the possible connections between hypnotism and the magic and mysticism of the occult revival. La Vaudère probably attended spiritualist séances in the 1890s, and probably continued doing so until her death. In an interview with Madame Louis Maurecy published in the 15 June 1906 issue of Gaston Mery's propagandistic periodical *L'Écho du merveilleux* she claimed that she had witnessed strange phenomena in her childhood, that the séance described in the preface to *La Sorcière d'Ecbatane* was one that she had attended, and that she had actually seen the phenomena described therein—although she stopped short of claiming that the novel really had been dictated to her by the spirit of an ancient Assyrian mage.

Although La Vaudère might only have been telling the credulous Madame Maurecy what she wanted to hear, there is no doubt that her interest in the occult and its secret history was real. We can only speculate as to how closely she was acquainted with Camille Flammarion, the brother of her principal publisher, whose weekly salon played host to many of the most celebrated mediums of the day, as well as writers and scientists, and often included experiments in "automatic writing." Her visionary fantasy "L'étoile double" (1893; tr. as "The Double Star") is clearly based on Camille Flammarion's ideas. La Vaudère had surely read his bestselling *Uranie* (1891) and might well have picked them up from there. The question is of some interest because La Vaudère's fiction sometimes does give the impression of having been written in a self-induced alternative state of consciousness. One could, of course, say that about all fiction, but La Vaudère's more exotic work, which often shows little sign of advance planning in its story development, frequently has a quasi-hallucinatory quality, and often gives the impression that the author is narrating her fantasies, including her sexual fantasies, with a rare lack of self-censorship. Key passages in both *La Sorcière d'Ecbatane* and *La Vierge d'Israel* seem to invite interpretation in that fashion, and Sigmund Freud would surely have found them fascinating had he had the opportunity to study them.

The direction that La Vaudère's later work took seems to have been largely defined by the success of her first best-seller, the controversial *Les Demi-Sexes*, whose *succès de scandale* she tried hard to repeat in one of the strands of her subsequent work, to considerable effect. She also took evident inspiration from the success of Pierre Louÿs' flamboyant fantasy of erotic obsession in ancient Alexandria *Aphrodite, moeurs antiques* (1896), which sold three hundred thousand copies and launched a bandwagon chased by many Parisian publishers, including Ernest Flammarion, and especially Albert Méricant, the publishers of the two novels of *moeurs antiques* translated in the present volume.

La Vaudère's first venture into exotic erotica, the Java-set *Trois fleurs de volupté* (1900) is not set in the distant past, and owes something to the French genre of "travelogue" fiction, but its successor, *Le Mystère de Kama* (1901) pulled out all the stops in a remarkable extravaganza of eroticism—Kama is the Hindu god of amour—which is also remarkable for some gruesome scenes of torture, further exaggerated in *L'Amazone du roi de Siam* (1902), *Les Courtisanes de Brahma* (1903) and *Le Harem de Syta* (1904). Depictions of physical torture were omitted from the next novel in the *moeurs antiques* sequence, *L'Amante du Pharaon* (1905), but returned in force in the two novels published in 1906, incidentally in *La Sorcière d'Ecbatane*, but of crucial and central importance in *Le Vierge d'Israel*.

That recurrence is more suggestive of psychological obsession than a straightforward repetition of a narrative move that had proved capable of generating sales, and the same is true of certain other recurrent features of La Vaudère's accounts of exotic mores, although the accounts of childhood sexuality featured in the earlier novels in the series are conspicuously absent from the later ones, perhaps having been dropped as a measure of editorial prudence. The heroines of both 1906 novels are still in their early teens, however, and the stories retain the author's preoccupation with dancing girls, only slightly marginalized; *La Vierge d'Israel* also makes much of the notion of females raised and kept in closed religious communities dedicated to the worship of female deities. The last novel in the sequence, *Les Prêtresses de Mylitta* (1907; tr. as *The Priestesses of Mylitta*), is set in the same milieu as *Les Vierges d'Israel* and brings female characters of that kind into closer focus.

The images of young women featured in the series of novels are highly fanciful, often bizarre, but it is obvious in retrospect that their imaginative bedrock is the author's own experience of having spent her childhood and early adolescence in a convent. It is possible, of course, that La Vaudère's frequent depiction of barely-pubescent girls who are naively obsessed with sex is completely imaginary, as is her frequent suggestion (but not depiction) of the brutal sexual exploitation of those same young girls by the priests of various religions; nothing like those depictions features in her novels of contemporary French life, in spite of occasional ventures in pushing the envelope of the conventionally-unmentionable. On the other hand, it would perhaps be surprising if such imaginations, and their frequent coupling with the threat of torture, did not have psychological roots of some kind.

There is an inevitable temptation to charge writers describing scenes of gruesome torture like those featured in *La Sorcière d'Ecbatane* and of central importance in *Le Vierge d'Israel* with "sadism," and it is necessarily the case that they credit sadistic motives to the characters responsible for the described torture, but that skips over the crucial question of whether the author is inviting the reader to identify with the torturer or the victim. Invariably, in La Vaudére's case, and very obviously in *La Vierge d'Israel*, her narrative voice shares the distress of the victims and witnesses of torture, and offers the same facility to her readers. The most extreme deployment of atrocious imagery—the repeated torture of Kali-Yana in *L'Amazone du roi de Siam*—is certainly a compassionate nightmare, not a sadistic one, and the same is true of the ordeals to which Phédyne is subjected in *La Vierge d'Israel*. *La Sorcière d'Ecbatane* is, however, an exception, in that Nysista does not witness the torture scenes featured in the novel and is not manifestly threatened with physical torture herself, although in her case, her treatment by the author does seem exceptionally vindictive, given her complete innocence of any wrongdoing, even of the reckless stupidity manifested by Phédyne.

Nysista and Phédyne are the most exaggerated examples of the most evident pattern of evolution in La Vaudère's exotic novels, that of the increasing impotence of her heroines. In spite of her extreme youth, Soakia in *Trois fleurs de volupté* is an active character who takes her fate firmly into her own hands to the extent that she can. Viamalah in *Le Mystère de Kama* struggles hard against the spell cast upon her by Nassudamy, and if she fails to escape from it, it is not for lack of trying. Kali-Yana in *L'Amazone du roi de Siam* is an ineffectual disgrace to her vocation, but she is nevertheless an amazon, and she does take action in pursuit of her goals, albeit inappropriately. Assilinia tries to do likewise in *Les Courtisanes de Brahma*, but fails dismally, and Syta in *Le Harem de Syta* makes a belated effort, but fails even more dismally. Zelinis, however, in *L'Amante du Pharaon*, does not even attempt to take positive action in her own interest, allowing herself to be led meekly wherever stronger characters guide her.

Nysista and Phédyne both continue that trend of increasing impotence to graphic conclusions, which become utterly bizarre in Phédyne's case, where the manner and intensity of her fascination with "Warka," and its persistence even after she discovers his actual identity, seems positively pathological, and the extent to which La Vaudère dwells on her heroine's strange state of mind—more extensively and more intensely than in any of the other novels in the series—is surely quite remarkable. It is, of course, conceivable that the relevant trend in her work and the climax of sorts it reached in *La Vierge d'Israel*, did not reflect any development in the author's own state of mind, but if it did, the fact of her sudden death in 1908 might seem slightly less surprising.

It is not at all surprising, of course, that almost all of La Vaudère's literary work focuses intently on the literary mythos of amour—the idea and the ideal of an exclusive, omnipotent, all-consuming and indestructible passion, which surely has no existence in reality—because that had been the focus of most literary activity by female writers since Mademoiselle de Scudéry had invented commercial fiction. What is surprising, however, is that her work represents that ideal with such an extraordinary intensity and strange extremism, which might have been impossible of imaginative attainment for someone not brought up in remote isolation from the real word, feeling acutely that she was bereft of useful guidance, in an ambience of assertive religious pretence.

For Jane de La Vaudère, perhaps to a greater extent than any other writer, the idea of extreme amour, at least in the works she published in the last few years of her life, seems to embody both the idea of Paradise and the idea of the Inferno; it is simultaneously the most sublime exaltation and the ultimate torment, the only really worthwhile desire there is, but an essentially deceptive and self-destructive desire, opening a gateway to damnation and eternal, inextinguishable fire—literal, in the case of *La Sorcière d'Ecbatane* but perhaps even more forceful in its metaphorical development in *La Vierge d'Israel*. She was by no means the only twentieth-century female writer to pen tragic love stories, but no one else ever did it as repetitively and as graphically as she did, deliberately and insistently flying in the face of the forceful popular demand for fictions in which "true" amour functions as a means of existential redemption rather than damnation.

Both of the novels in the present volume are effective in isolation, because rather than in spite of their insistent peculiarity, but when juxtaposed and placed in the context of the entire series of *romans de moeurs antiques*, they gain a further dimension of effect, which fully justifies their translation as elements of a compendium. In spite of their enormous variety, the ensemble of ten short novels and nine shorter stories included in the present set of volumes do contain an overarching narrative of their own. The narrative in question is murky, meandering and enigmatic, but Jane de La Vaudère was a Decadent Symbolist, typical of the French *fin-de-siècle* and its immediate aftermath, and imaginative groping in the dark was part of her stock-in-trade, to be construed as an artistic and exploratory device rather than a fault. The narrative is also incomplete here, and *Les Prêtresses de Mylitta*, the last long item in the sequence, also failed, inevitably, to provide a real conclusion; the shorter work published after it, Le Rêve de Mysès (tr. as "The Dream of Myses") similarly made no such attempt.

Most of the novels in the sequence, in fact, including the two in the present volume, illustrate the perennial problem that the author had in figuring out how to conclude her stories, even when she was writing pseudohistorical novels in which the climactic event was pre-programmed by an existing stock of knowledge or myth. In most cases, she took refuge in the fiction writer's ever-available last resort—death—and, one way or another, she eventually found her own way to the same essentially unsatisfactory narrative conclusion, as everyone must.

The translation of *La Sorcière d'Ecbatane* was made from a copy of the 2006 print-on-demand edition published by Elibron Classics, which includes a photographic reproduction of the Flammarion edition. The translation of *La Vierge d'Israel* was made from a copy of the Méricant edition.

—Brian Stableford

THE WITCH OF ECBATANA

PREFACE BY A SPIRIT

I was present at a meeting of adepts in the home of Dr. X***, the amiable scientist who invites to his soirées all the intelligence of the living and the dead.

The secret effluvia were already flowing from the walls, the furniture and the curtains; a mysterious presence was manifest by frictions, sighs and slight creakings in the woodwork. Motionless and silent, we were waiting for the revelations of the Afterlife, for there was no unbeliever among us.

Soon, raps resounded and a side-table was displaced by the action of an invisible force. An initiate having associated, for his amusement, the letters of the alphabet with the number of raps struck on the wood, a spiritual telegraph was established and the evoked spirit was able to converse with the audience.

A few illustrious souls were asked to respond to our appeal, and they all deigned to respond, but remained clad in an astral envelope invisible to our senses.

Our will being increasingly disengaged from matter, however, in order to command the fluids scattered in the air, strange forms belonging to no human being appeared to us; then, warm and soft hands touched our eyes, traversed the room and vanished. There were movements of heavy bodies, the sounds of vague music, as melancholy as the wind in reeds, and the somnolent murmur of waves.

Apparitions generally take place at the moment of death and also after death. At the sight of them dogs are seized by fear, cats leap up, their fur bristling, and horses stop dead, trembling in every limb.

Some of Dr. X***'s adepts had seen phantoms surge from the shadows, stand up in deserted rooms, or in the countryside, on the edge of a wood. Others had heard distant and menacing voices, and seen the impressions of fingers on blackened paper. In the room where the meetings were held we observed the apparitions of smiling or tragic faces, against a luminous background, rains of flowers that seemed to be made of a transparent paste, and a kind of frost that the heat gradually melted. Phosphorescent rays surrounded us; the medium, in particular, was clad in them, and lips posed on ours as if in a kiss.

Everything proved the persistence of life beyond the grave, for the doctrine of Spirits is transformed and further clarified by work and progress. Spiritualists, Theosophists and Kabbalists have affirmed the persistence of the conscious Self after death, and direct communications between the living and the dead via telepathy and second sight.

The soul, clad in a fluid envelope—the perispirit, or astral body; which the Egyptians called the double and the Persians the *fravashi*—abandons the body to decomposition in the tomb, and remains the external form of the spiritual personality.

Lost in a profound reverie, I was thinking about the marvelous lands of ancient civilizations, the grandiose ruins of old Asia and the land of the Pharaohs, the gigantic Pyramids guarded by the Sphinx with the eternal smile. More than a hundred thousand years before historic times, many centuries before Biblical traditions and the Golden Age of the poets, humans were already suffering and weeping, but their first whimpers remained enveloped in thick darkness, and it is only since the glorious times of Greece and Rome that the tangled skein of human existence has been unwound.

Thanks to the modern research of science, however, the Sphinx has babbled vague words, the necropolises, the obelisks and the labyrinths have revealed some of their secrets; magical capitals and gigantic palaces have surged from the profound entrails of the earth. We know that superb empires flourished on the banks of the Nile and in the plains of Chaldea; Assyrian bas-reliefs illustrate by their sculptures texts written on stone; through them we evoke those immense Asian empires, the magic splendor of which Hebrew writings allow us to divine.

✳

Suddenly, a singular shudder ran through my being, and the fiction became precise; a great phantom surged from the shadow, and a grave voice was heard in the sympathetic meditation of the initiates.

"I am the magus Sariasys," said the specter, "who was celebrated in the reign of Darius I, successor of Cyrus and Cambyses.[1] My power extended throughout anterior Asia to the limits of Egypt. I was the master of all the hearths of civilization that enlightened the world and I almost substituted myself for the sovereigns of Assyria, Babylonia and Persia.

"I have already lived several existences and I shall reincarnate myself again in order to expiate my errors and the sins of others. Justice is not of this world; it is only accomplished by a sequence of terrestrial proofs, for every human must eventually bring to the Great All the same sum of pains and joys. The difference of the sexes is only temporary; in their return to life beings are alternately men and women, and suffer reciprocally in order to expiate previous injustices until the moment when they become androgynes, their perfect incarnation.

"Krishna, Zoroaster, Hermes, Moses, Pythagoras, Plato and Jesus have thrown to all the winds the seeds that fecundate intelligence, but most of that marvelous grain has been lost. The average human is not capable of perceiving the elevated conceptions of the soul. Krishna addressed his disciples thus: 'You and

---

1 The reign of Darius I extended from about 522 B.C. to 486 B.C.

I have had several births. Mine are only known to me, but you do not even know yours. Although I am no longer subject to birth or death, by nature, every time that virtue declines in the world and vice or injustice prevail, I render myself visible, and thus I show myself from age to age, for the salvation of the just, the punishment of the wicked and the reestablishment of virtue. I have revealed great secrets to you. Only tell them to those who can understand them. You are my elect, you embrace space; the crowd only sees a part of the road.'

"He also said in his sublime language full of symbols and images: 'The elite man must fall under the blows of the unworthy, but, like the sandalwood tree, he perfumes the ax that strikes him.'"

⁕

The specter of the Magus had paused momentarily, and rose petals descended on my forehead; an intoxicating perfume of myrrh and cinnamon caressed my nostrils.

I looked around. All of Dr. X***'s guests seemed to be plunged in a sort of ecstasy; the greatest silence reigned in the room.

Sariasys continued in these terms:

"The singular gods with the heads of bulls, cats, snakes, jackals and vultures were symbols of life in its multiple manifestations; the sphinx, with its feminine face, its eagle's wings and its lion's claws, represented the eternal mystery that presides over the destinies of terrestrial beings. All ancient peoples believed in the interventions of Spirits in human affairs, and there is a kind of great mystical current that unfurls in the meanders of history, to reach us after ardent fluctuations. But our globe is a very small thing compared with other worlds, gigantic celestial flowers that illuminate the divine garden. The suns, followed by their corteges of planets, are as many corollas variously blossoming; the clusters of florets and grains tumbling in the azure abysms, the scintillating waves of the Milky Way roll in space an innumerable multitude of living calices, admirable nuclei of heat, light and electricity.

"The Earth, compared with the giant vegetation of Heaven, is merely planetary dust, an atom, an embryo of seeds floating in Infinity. However, this humble globule shows us the action of a precise will, an occult, formidable and secret power. Humans only see the corner of the world that they inhabit during their ephemeral existence; they cannot understand the eternal order of their destiny. They only have aspirations toward a different state, a nostalgic desire for progress and justice; but the unlimited needs of the soul summon and prove a better life.

"Death and the reincarnation that follows, after a variable time, are dolorous proofs that ought to raise us toward perfection. Clad in our carnal envelopes, we will lose once again the memory of past existences, and the struggle of Good against Evil will be long . . ."

The phantom appeared to recoil into the shadow. Again an odor of incense and aromatics floated, more penetrating; a distant music, come from who knows where, traversed the walls. Faint, harmonious, troubling sounds brought the murmur of a cantilena to our ears, and I listened with an infinite delight to the mysterious song, cast into space by some celestial musician.

Then, suddenly, the melody seemed to come toward me, swiftly, like a songbird in a sunbeam. I was overwhelmed by a burning wind full of the feverish breath of myrtle, lavender and tuberoses; I was left shivering, intoxicated by strange sensations, as if I had heard perfumes and respired music.

The specter of the Magus approached me.

"Truly," he said, "you do not have respect for your dead. You pile them up at random in corners of your towns, as far as possible from the living. They are so tightly packed together that their astral bodies struggle for a long time before being able to free themselves. When nothing any longer remains in the sinister fields but a sort of cadaverous clay, you dig them up with blows of a pick-ax in order to draw out the scattered bones pell-mell: the arms, legs and skulls of males and females, which you bury in some hole, in order to replace the ancient dead with new cadavers in the freshly shifted earth.

"We had reverence for the defunct. Thanks to our magical formulae they had the assurance of conquering a blissful immortality. The priests recited the chapters of the *Book of the Dead* during the funeral ceremony; and the family often came together to evoke the members it had lost. The dead, ever-present in their doubles, inspired human actions, and watched over the security and wellbeing of the survivors.

"But there were also evil influences that paralyzed the efforts of some humans and pursued them throughout their existence. The disciples of Hermes, Zoroaster and Solomon suffered greatly from those otherworldly hatreds. The Magi were accused of the criminal and blasphemous practices accomplished at the Sabbats of sorcerers and witches. All the murders of stryges[1] and vampires, rapes, evil spells, poisonings and sacrileges were imputed to the charge of superior initiates. The bloody orgies and monstrous priapisms of black magic were confounded with the marvels of the true Science, a gigantic and splendid synthesis that translates the august thoughts of divine genius.

"You have sung the praises of the titanic civilizations of the primitive world, the great intellectual cycles of Thebes, Babylon and Nineveh; it is necessary for you, at present, to divine their tenebrous errors. This is the adventure of a nocturnal visitor of souls, an impure vestal of desert places, who mingled with the

---

1 The term *strix*, of why *stryges* is the plural, is sometimes used in modern parlance to mean "witch," having occasionally been adapted for that purpose during the seventeenth-century witch-panic, but in Graeco-Roman mythology a strix was a supernatural creature produced by post-mortem metamorphosis, with the form of a bird (the word is now applied to a genus of owls), which fed on human blood.

impure sap of henbane and hemlock extracts of aconite and mandrake, as well as frightful and mysterious venoms . . .

"Everyone knows the legend poeticized by Homer, which shows the companions of Ulysses changed into pigs and capering under the wand of Circe. All of them, having drunk the beverage, were subjected to metamorphosis. That is the symbol of human weakness submissive to evil passions. Medea too owes the sad privilege of her illustriousness to poets. She poisoned her relatives, murdered and burned her children, and gave free rein to her instincts of sanguinary depravity until the day when the people in revolt forced her to flee under a rain of stones.

"Those stories are known, but no one has yet recounted the reincarnation of Zaroccha, the sorceress of Media, who emerged from the tomb to espouse her murderer and drag him after her into the eternal night.

"Yes, the abominations that people narrate on the subject of empusas, stryges, lamias and vampires were realized by the sorceresses of the ancient world, but the Magi, in their limitless power, were inviolably enthroned and sacred, like the sovereigns of a better world, the divine initiates of Justice and Verity."

Having spoken thus, Sariasys disappeared in blue smoke, and, continuing my somnambulistic dream, I saw the tumultuous scenes of the drama unfold that I am transcribing faithfully.

PART ONE

Chapter 1

> There were angels that allowed themselves
> to fall from Heaven in order to love the
> daughters of the earth.
> (*The Book of Enoch*.)

Zaroccha, the witch, was reputed to know the secret of the future. She had sacrificed to Astarte, Baal and Moloch, all the gods of lust and blood of the Chaldeans and Babylonians. She was one of the hallucinated prophetesses who always have a profound influence on the souls of the weak, and all brides, virgins and courtesans came to consult her.

The priests and the poets of the red idols drew their inspiration from her, and their works bore the imprint of the fear that she inspired in them with her incantations and grim practices.

Zaroccha lived in Ecbatana in Media, in a house at the northern extremity of the city. She lived modestly with a girl named Nysista, an adorable child of fifteen with eyes full of dreams and sadness. The old woman, wrinkled, stooped and desiccated, resembled a mummy penetrated with bitumen and natrum. Her angular features were petrified in a bizarre, terrifying form; only the eyes shone strangely behind the brown eyelids withered by age. Those yellow eyes, as mobile as a flame, illuminated the entire face, and glowed in the dark.

Nysista obeyed the old woman tremulously, fetching water, dates, olives and herbs picked at the foot of Mount Zagros.

That evening, the child seemed sad, preoccupied with some secret trouble, and Zaroccha stimulated her zeal in vain.

The calm of the night descended over the fateful house, and the breeze, charged with the scents of box, myrtle and tuberoses, caressed the girl's forehead.

"Come here," said the old woman, "and separate these plants that you've brought."

Nysista approached. She was wearing a narrow blue skirt retained by braces over her delicate shoulders. Her small pert breasts were palpitating beneath a necklace of cornelian beads, and her harmonious arms were adorned by numerous circles of glass and metal. Her eyelids, fringed with long lashes, partly veiled the soft, dark, voluptuous, languid eyes. The thin nose with pure ridges emphasized an imperceptibly African profile, which corrected the tender, infantile mouth, opening like a flower. Nysista's thick hair covered her like a blue-tinted cloak, for she wore it cut squarely and inflated in the Egyptian fashion.

"You're not mistaken, at least?" added the old woman, examining the herbs, already wilted.

"Here's the mandrake, collected under a crucified body. I was very frightened, and I won't go back to the field of executions!"

"Stupid girl!" said the old woman, disdainfully. "You're not worthy to know the secrets of Zoroaster. High science is reserved solely for those who can govern their minds, and are strong enough to possess the occult powers of nature."

Nysista bent vervain stems between her fingers. "Magic," she said, "is the worship of death. This flower is lovely; why do you make it serve for frightful practices? Why so many needless murders?"

Zaroccha snatched the plants from the young woman's fingers.

"Vervains are agreeable to the gods, and their perfumes charm the spirits of water and fire. The great floating divinities without definite form that surround us demand our homage. To forget them is a grave fault. I offer them oil or soma to ward off the lightning, I appease the vengeful soul of rivers, mountains and forests."

"It isn't Ahura-Mazda, the god of virtue and justice that you serve, but the dark genius, the evil spirit that torments humans. It's Ahriman that you admire, the cruel demon Ahriman, who unleashes storms, gives birth to frightful maladies and deformities, moral ugliness and crimes."

"The universe is a battlefield, my girl, and life emerges from the tomb. Everything renews itself by good and evil alike. As well as the spirits of light there are the monsters of caverns, ghosts, ghouls and vampires, which it is necessary to appease and charm. I try my incantations and exorcisms on them. In exchange, they give me divination, and it is to please them that I'm assembling, this evening, these sprigs of tamarisk, these reeds and these willow wands."

Nysista breathed in the acrid scents of the plants that she had collected, and a kind of intoxication rose in her brain. For the first time since she had been living with the charmer of ghosts she dared to rebel.

"I hate your false gods!" she said.

"Beware!" said Zaroccha. "Their anger is terrible."

"They can strike me, if that is their desire. I offer my existence to them gladly."

The old woman did not deign to respond, fully occupied as she was in shifting something in a dark hiding place.

"Oh," Nysista went on, "I've seen you making odious sacrifices. I no longer want to live under your roof. You've created oracles with the heads of infants that you've allowed to dry out, after placing a sheet of gold inscribed with unknown characters under their tongues. You've placed them in a hollow in the wall under the magical plants that I bring every evening."

"Yes," said the old woman. "I offer them incense, and I consult them for the benefit of the living. They've often responded to me."

"I've also seen you digging a ditch that you fill with warm blood, and I ran away in order not to witness your incantations."

"You were wrong, child, for if you had stayed you would have seen livid shadows crawling, climbing, descending, flocking from the entrails of the earth, lamenting . . ."

"And it's to boil the blood of victims that you light those fires of laurel, alder and cypress. It's to pray to your dark gods that you weave crowns of asphodel and vervain. Yes, yes, I've seen the phantoms wandering around the house and I've heard the dogs howling mortally."

"The principle of enchantments is to dare everything."

"Well," said the child, "I desire to return to Egypt, to my own people, for I'm not of your race and you have no rights over me . . ."

"No one knows you any longer. What would become of you in such abandonment? Here, you lack nothing; I've served as your mother . . ."

"Oh, don't profane that name. You stole me as I was playing with other children on the road. I know full well what people say about you."

Zaroccha shrugged her shoulders.

"Sleep," she said. "Sleep will calm your nerves, and tomorrow you'll thank me for having opened your intelligence to the great verities of good and evil."

Chapter II

> I await you in darkness and the
> sandstorms enter my dwelling
> with the plaint of the wind.
> (Zoroaster.)

Nysista withdrew to the redoubt that she occupied in the company of Safou, a black cat with eyes like embers. Safou adored the young woman and rubbed his undulating back against her skirt affectionately. He stretched himself, purring, retracted his claws into his velvet paws, and demanded a caress with multiple tender provocations.

The young woman, however, had been listening for several moments to a dull rumor, as profound as that of the sea, which covered all the sounds of the night, as it grew.

A concert of metallic instruments accompanied the distant rumble of war chariots and the rhythmic steps of foot-soldiers following their leader, Ariaramnes, to join the King of the Persians.

Since Cyrus had abandoned the ingrate soil of his fatherland in order to shrug off the yoke of fertile Media and conquer its opulent valleys, everything had smiled on the conqueror. He had marched against Ecbatana, the capital of the northern land, had taken possession of it by force of arms, and had put Persia in the foremost rank of the powers disputing the heart of Asia.

The conquest of Lydia and Babylon affirmed the greatness of Cyrus, who dominated Asia Minor and all the ancient hearts of civilization, of which the world had been proud for so many centuries. His son Cambyses, on succeeding him, had continued his work, and Egypt had been added to the immense and redoubtable Persian Empire.

After the death of Cambyses and the usurpation of the magus Smerdis,[1] who had passed himself off as Cyrus' younger son, the throne was occupied by Darius I. Darius continued the gigantic work of his predecessors, penetrating into India and taking possession of a part of the Punjab, of which he made a new satrapy. A little later he added Macedonia to the Empire, and that marched the apogee of the astonishing Persian domination.

It is at the moment that saw the birth of the drama of the Median wars that this true story commences. Since Darius, son

---

1 Smerdis is usually regarded as an alternative name for Cyrus' younger son Bardiya, who probably succeeded him, although Darius, in the Behistun Inscription, the text of which he allegedly provided, claimed that the person who occupied the throne after Cambyses was really an impostor named Gaumata—but Darius, who murdered the person in question, could have made that up in order to justify his homicidal usurpation.

of Vistapa, governor of Hyrkania, had surprised and assassinated Gaumata in his palace, in order to mount the throne in his place, his reign had been nothing but a sequence of victories. On that mild and calm evening, his Satrap Ariaramnes was assembling his troops for new battles, and the soldiers, avoiding the heat of the day, were going to join their leader.

There were entire populations that the kings of Persia sometimes drew in their wake in times of war. Carts accompanied the troops containing abundant provisions of wheat, and ships followed the coast, heavily laden with everything that might be useful to such a formidable army.

Women sometimes took part in those distant expeditions, and Nysista said to herself that it would be pleasant to fight next to a beloved man and die with him.

Passing in the distance, she saw the shiny-crested helmets of the Assyrians and their padded linen breastplates. She recognized the pointed bonnets of Scythians, the white tunics of Indians, the gleaming scimitars of Caspians with fur mantles, the striped hides of Ethiopians, the loose garments of Arabs, the russet fox-fur bonnets of Thracians and the painted wooden helmets of the inhabitants of Colchis.

The Persians, not very numerous, enrolled in their armies all the nations that they had conquered successively. They ensured the possession of fertile fields and the vast pastures necessary to their livestock; their yoke was not cruel.

Nysista listened to the distant fanfares, and her heart leapt with emotion. A kind of pale brown mist, like that raised by the desert wind, invaded the sky in the direction from which the men were advancing, and the tumult increased in the darkness. Drums, tambourines, trumpets and sistra marked the rhythm of rapid strides.

Women were now arriving from all directions, scarcely dressed, dragging weeping children. Zaroccha too appeared on the threshold of her dwelling, and, her fleshless arm extended in the direction of the tumult, she uttered a strident burst of laughter.

Nysista shivered with anguish and impatience. She had promised to go to the spring of Cayoka, where Arynes, the son of the Satrap, was waiting for her, and time went past in uncertainty, for the old woman could not make up her mind to go out, as she habitually did every night at that hour.

Finally, she picked up her white staff and drew away, after having carefully locked the door—but Nysista knew the secret of the catch, and as soon as Zaroccha's footsteps had died away in the distance, she ran in pursuit of her amour.

She went rapidly, following a path shaded by mimosas, which snaked around the city. Holding her breath, scarcely putting down her delicate feet, she seemed to be flying, so great was her impatience. An ardent passion impelled her; she did not feel fatigue, and her pace accelerated.

The hoof-beats of horses, the thunder of wheels and the metallic friction had ceased. A great calm reigned in the remote spot where the young people had been meeting for some time.

Arynes, the Satrap's son, loved Nysista, or, at least, was occupied with her in the hope of making use of her in his ambitious projects. Perhaps, in the certainty of her possession, he had not interrogated his own heart very seriously; but he nevertheless found a great charm in their encounters every evening on the edge of the spring of Cayoka in the gardens of Ecbatana.

"How late you are!" he exclaimed, on perceiving the young woman.

"I couldn't come any sooner, alas, because Zaroccha couldn't make up her mind to leave. One might have thought that she suspected something."

"I've come to say goodbye, Nysita. I have to join my father."

"Oh," she sighed. "I won't be able to live without you . . ."

"You'll doubtless see me again, unless . . ."

She put her small hand over his lips. "Don't finish, Arynes. In any case, I'll protect your life; I won't leave you."

"That's impossible."

"My decision is made."

"How do you expect me to take care of a woman in the midst of the hazards of war?"

"No one will know my sex. I'll put on garments like yours."

"No," he repeated. "I can't grant you what you're asking of me."

"I beg you! If you knew how unhappy I am!"

Arynes frowned. "Well," he said, with an effort, "perhaps I can take you with me. But it's necessary that I interrogate the old witch first."

"You want to question Zaroccha?"

"Yes."

"What can she do for you?"

"Everything."

"You believe in her power, then?"

"She has the spirit of darkness in her favor."

"And you want to deliver yourself to the accursed Ahriman?"

"It's necessary." He went on, in a lower voice: "Listen. I need to make a fortune, for I've lost mine gambling."

"Isn't your father rich, since he possesses a Satrapy?"

"My father has other sons; he doesn't want to do anything in my favor. So I thought that Zaroccha might inform me of a means of winning infallibly."

"And you'd sell your soul to the powers of Evil?"

"My soul is shielded from spells. I played dice yesterday and lost everything I own. I want to know the magic formula that has already enriched two lords of Ecbatana."

Nysista considered the young man sadly. He was standing before her; his light steel bonnet had a dull gleam, and on its front the emblem of winged wheels accompanied the profile of King Darius. A crimson mantle enveloped him, all the way to the gilded leather of his shoes. His features were handsome and bold, his dark eyes widely spaced; thick coarse hair fell over his neck like the black mane of a lion.

The young woman looked at him with an adoration mingled with dread. She felt herself shivering all the way to the heart, and it was in a breathless voice that she went on: "What need do we have of redoubtable gold?"

"I want to adorn you like a princess of legend. I want you to be the most beautiful among beauties."

The young woman sighed. "My love isn't sufficient for you any longer! You need the satisfactions of pride."

"Yes," he said. "I like luxury, finery and pleasures. And you'll be more seductive for me in the precious stones with which I'll decorate your fragile grace."

"Don't you have to fight soon? Let me go with you and serve you as a slave. You can resume your ambitious projects afterwards."

He was not listening.

"Zaroccha is very old; she might die keeping her secret. I want to be as rich as Cyrise and Mazuda, whom she heaped with wealth by teaching them the magic formula."

"Chance, simply."

"No. Cyrise and Mazuda had lost everything; they were about to kill themselves when the idea came to them of consulting the witch."

"She didn't tell them anything . . ."

"She sold them her marvelous secret."

"But she's poor. If really knew a means of enrichment, she'd employ it for herself."

"Zaroccha is doubtless only poor because she wants to be. We can't comprehend the mystery of her life."

"Your fravashi will abandon you or turn against you. It's necessary not to tempt the Evil Demon. Renounce your project, I beg you, my beloved."

Arynes took the young woman in his arms and kissed her lips gently. He knew that she could not resist his caress, that all doubts would fall before his ardent and grim desire.

"Oh!" she said, in anguish. "I give in, my beloved. I'll speak to the witch. I'll take you to her."

"Tomorrow?"

"Yes, tomorrow."

"Well, I'll be at your door at the same hour."

"And you'll take me away, you'll keep me with you?"

"I promise."

Chapter III

> Amestris, the wife of Xerxes, having
> reached a very advanced age, had
> forty children of the most illustrious families
> of Persia buried, in order to give thanks
> to the god who dwells under the earth.
> (Herodotus.)

While the young woman was running to her amour, Zaroccha, skimming the walls, headed for the Towers of Silence, which are particularly venerated by the fire-worshipers, the followers of Zoroaster, whose sacred book, the Zend-Avesta, also contains magical formulae.

It was in those towers that it was customary to expose the dead, in order to deliver them to the voracity of vultures, for fire, earth and water must not be touched by any impure contact.

The funereal birds circled around the sorceress, doubtless demanding a prey that they sensed would soon belong to them. The approaches to the sinister monument seemed particularly desolate. A special atmosphere, heavy and painful, reigned there; one respired an odor of aromatic plants and corruption, mingled with the bestial reek of the birds of death.

The lamentations of mourners and muffled cries arrived at intervals, gleaned by the breeze, and the bodies destined for the vultures were brought on stretchers. The bodies were placed on a circular platform a few feet from the summit of the towers. A first circle, against the wall, received the men, a second, slightly narrower, contained the women, and the last, confining the central shaft, was reserved for children. The shelves of those supports were disposed in a steep slope leading toward the gulf.

The terrible work of destruction was accomplished quickly. The executors of the funereal labor, enormous and always famished, waited in the trees or flew with a great clatter of their heavy wings. They tore the cadavers apart in less than an hour, leaving the skeleton, which the sun and the wind finished drying out. The bones were then cast into the gulf, anonymous and fraternal, mingled for eternity.

The four elements being sacred for the Persians, Fire seemed to them too august to devour corrupt flesh; blood could only pollute Water by mingling with it; and bodies ought not to infect Air or Earth. A corpse ought therefore not to be made to disappear by inhumation or incineration, and the sacred breath of the winds ought not to caress deliquescent flesh. Only living beings could engulf redoubtable remains, and birds of prey took charge of that duty. They began with the eyes, lovely and delicate morsels, dead gems with reflections of opal and nacre; then they cleaved the breast and extracted the heart, which they turned in their claws like a red and flavorsome fruit.

Mourners brought perfumes of cinnamon and myrrh to combat the frightful exhalations of the somnolent and sated vultures; then their lamentations rose slowly into the night.

Only monarchs escaped the terrifying law. Sumptuous tombs were erected for them, for a terminal means existed that permitted them to be buried without committing sacrilege. August bodies were coated in wax and thus were not mixed with the earth. It is also alleged that, in order to honor the elements, and particularly the redoubtable god dwelling in the bowels of the earth, the Persians buried young virgins alive, chosen from among the most beautiful and accomplished.

Without a Magus, however, no sacrifice was possible; astrology, incantations and divinations were also mingled with all the practices of the ancient Zoroastrian religion.

The Persians did not build temples and did not sculpt idols. They erected altars devoid of ornaments on the summits of hills, on which they maintained the sacred fire while singing and praying to the benevolent deities. After their triumph, however, the Magi established sacrifices, sorceries and singular and cruel rites everywhere.

Zaroccha had reached the place where the soldiers were passing. She advanced into the forest of pikes, between which sharp blades sprang up like steel reeds splashed with green and red gold.

The men drew apart fearfully when they perceived her. "The witch!" they said; and the most resolute laughed scornfully at the bizarre emotion of their companions.

Without looking back, Zaroccha continued her route. She arrived in the garden surrounding the Towers of Silence. The nearby trees were clad in polished and rutilant bark; delicate plants starred with red and yellow corollas were suspended from the branches, letting their ardent florescence dangle.

The witch broke off a few branches, which she selected carefully. Some bled at the break or were crowned with a little milky sap. Other revealed a black and venomous juice that seemed to rise from a secret fungus.

The earth was cold and damp under the carpet of somber moss and grass. Zaroccha pushed a large stone, and a gigantic sticky toad emerged from beneath it, darting its yellow eyes into the darkness like phosphorescent gems.

The witch whistled softly, and other reptiles emerged from the ground, lifting up stones and leaves with their pustulent backs, swarming all around her in flaccid waves; and through the interstices of the disentangled branches, the moon showed its golden face.

For an hour the woman circled the huge garden, followed by the viscously slithering toads, and a crystalline plaint, a soft and monotonous note, responded to her incantations. Then she sat down on a kind of granite altar, and it was as if her gaze turned inward, for she no longer saw the trees with red flowers, the birds of death or the torpid reptiles in the black grass.

Chapter IV

> Nature has given me the body of a woman,
> but my actions have made me the equal
> of the most valiant of men.
> (Epitaph of Semiramis.)

Soon Zaroccha, shaking off her torpor, descended into the well by means of a secret passage, in order to search for bones, which she disposed on the altar in the midst of the fateful plants.

On the Towers, the birds of prey, ardent in their sinister labor, were sinking their beaks and claws into the quivering flesh of three new cadavers, fighting over the morsels of flesh.

Zaroccha raised above her head a figure of wax in which a wick was burning, and crimson lines danced over the trees. Like a terrible prediction of murder, a bloody gleam colored a skull that she had placed close by.

The sorceress shivered.

"The moment is near!" she murmured. "Let my destiny be accomplished!"

She had brought hemlock, aconite, mandrake and cantharides. Shadows rose up around her; reptiles undulated in the grass; white bodies lacerated by the vultures seemed to lean over the walls, and hoarse cries mingled with the clink of rings, bracelets and anklets, which fell with a metallic sound. The breasts of the dead rose up like the palpitating wings of a strangled bird, and contracted faces showed the black holes of their orbits. At times, arms and legs dangled in the void, illuminated by the moon; human remains had just fallen on to the altar, among the flowers and the bones.

On the other side of the wall, the grave chant of the mourners resounded, reciting the list of the dead. Zaroccha quit her sinister work in order to make sure that she was quite alone. She walked as far as the garden gate and, hidden in the bushes, looked out on to the road.

Heavily made-up women with thick waists and blackened eyelids were waiting there for the desperate, those vanquished by life, in order to offer them their facile caresses. In sordid houses, through openings carved into the walls, the candles of merchants of aromatics and wax could be seen shining. Everything in the city that was strange or impure came to vegetate in the shadow of death.

Reassured, Zaroccha returned to the altar, her feet, bare on the slippery earth, and her long garment marked with lunar rings made her resemble a specter beneath the tremulous mass of the foliage.

Now the fires of the torch rose higher, and the witch pronounced fateful words before a stove. Her voice rose and fell over the final two syllables of strophes; then, with her arm raised in a grim gesture, she circled the altar seven times, repeating a bizarre hymn. She had selected and mixed plants, and had thrown them into a receptacle placed on the stove.

Raising the bundle of sacred stems again, she invoked the spirits of darkness, and shadows emerged from the bushes, sliding softly around her. The entire garden was populated by silent phantoms, which vanished and were reborn in the pale light of the wax figure with which the altar was adorned.

Suddenly, Zaroccha seized a small golden cup that she carried between her breasts; then she dipped it into the black receptacle, letting green and yellow droplets fall around her, which sparkled like fireflies. Finally, tipping her head back, she drank, slowly.

Soon, a kind of intoxication set her veins ablaze; her eyes shone like the mysterious liquor, and her body swayed in an accelerating movement.

Now her entire being was trembling, and it was in a hoarse, torn voice, like a storm wind, that she pronounced further incantations. A little foam emerged from her mouth; her features convulsed; her limbs became as rigid as stone.

Her rounded eyes no longer quit the altar, in the expectation of a diabolical manifestation, which doubtless would not be long delayed in appearing. She drank the liquid flame again, while the shadows tightened their sinister circle around her. A swarm of stryges, ghouls and vampires covered the swarm of interlaced reptiles; a sabbat of incubi surrounded her, awaiting the miracle that was about to burst forth in the long quivering of nature in revolt.

Finally, over the stove, an image sprang forth in a cloud of red smoke. It was the face of an old woman with wrinkled eyelids, black and hairy nostrils, and lips retracted in a grim rictus. Gradually, the torso was disengaged from the flame, punctured by holes, with sagging breasts and extinct nipples; then the thighs appeared, like desiccated vine-branches, knotty knees, limbs with carded tendons, and feet like two roots.

Zaroccha uttered a burst of strident laughter, for that figure resembled her in every detail. It really was her, or her fravashi: her terrible, sinister and menacing double.

Prostrate before the altar, however, she prayed more ardently, and her shrill, quavering, high-pitched voice rose into the night. Gradually, the sound swelled, and became a cry of tumultuous passion, which curbed the branches around her. Before her eyes, in the acrid smoke of the stove, the figure seemed to grow prodigiously, sometimes yellow and sometimes red, the colors of flesh, gold and blood. Her heart was swollen by desires, and the dementia of her crimes whirled in her head. The clamor of the birds of prey magnified her voice; it was the roar of the tempest, the formidable appeal of the wind over breaking waves, the reckless unleashing of all the elements for the fall of a world.

Finally, a great silence reigned, and Zaroccha got to her feet, shivering.

Over the altar, a marvelous image now appeared, as radiant as a glorious hearth.

Eyelids fringed with long lashes framed moist pupils, lustrous in the caress of life. The slender and delicate nose, with pure ridges, had transparent nostrils more delicate than flowers, and the mouth, with voluptuously parted lips, was smiling sweetly over the enamel of the teeth. The shoulders presented an exquisite model, the breasts stood up proudly in the triumph of youth. And yet, in that adorable figure, Zaroccha found all the indications of her own resemblance. The movement of the forehead, the line of the nose, the curve of the mouth, the separation of the breasts and the hue of the eyes were identical.

"As I have been," she said, "so I shall be."

She sank again into profound ecstasy, while the flame was slowly extinguished, and the sated vultures went to sleep over their sinister feast.

Chapter V

I was raised to the heavens, I saw Ormuzd
face to face, and all the secrets
of life were revealed to me.
(Zend-Avesta.)

Meanwhile Arynes had arrived at the old woman's dwelling.

"No," said Nysista, "you can't come in."

The young man, peering into the mysterious hovel through a skylight, made no reply.

"She'll do you harm," the young woman went on. "Her conduct is strange, her designs cruel and tenebrous."

The officer straightened up slowly.

"I'm ruined," he said, "and that woman can help me, since she has already saved Zofyre and Hertes."[1]

"How do we know that?"

"They won a fortune at dice after having seen the witch."

"That was only chance, my beloved. Let's flee instead; the road is open, the future is smiling on us, for we're young and we love one another."

But Arynes pushed Nysista away impatiently.

"You promised to let me in to the old woman's house. Why are you refusing today what you granted me yesterday?"

"I've reflected . . . I'm afraid."

"Zaroccha can do nothing against me."

"She knows the secret of the gods!"

"In that case," said the young man, laughing, "let her tell it to me too. That's all I desire."

Again he had put his eye to the skylight.

The terrible old woman was sitting in a corner of the room. Her eyes were shining singularly in the light of a small horn lamp suspended from the ceiling. Thus placed, she resembled a maleficent genius, one of the monsters of bronze, basalt or granite that the Chaldeans made. She was like those terrible idols of punishment, with the faces of apes, ibises, jackals, cows and vultures, which take on bestial masks in order to frighten humans more. She was sniggering hideously, like the demons that usurp libations, offerings and sacrifices to the Divinity.

Nysista leaned over in her turn.

"Do you see," she said, "how she's gazing into the darkness? She's summoning the souls of the dead against the living."

"Show me the way," ordered the officer,

"For the last time, I implore you, don't tempt destiny."

"Go ahead," he repeated, impatiently.

"All right, I'll obey, since you desire it. But I won't go in with you. You'll come and find me and we'll leave together, for good?"

---

1 The author appears to have forgotten that the two names she cited in this context in chapter II were Cyrise and Mazuda.

"Yes."

"I'll wait for you in the garden."

The house seemed dead, with its narrow openings and its coarse brown plaster, of a sinister ugliness. Down below, the alleyway plunged into blackness, and in front of the door there was a step to climb, which the gutter often overflowed.

Arynes followed the damp wall with his hand, for fear of making a false step in the dark. It seemed to him that he was descending into a cellar, with the sensation of sticky ground underfoot, always covered in mud.

"Bend down," whispered the girl, trembling. "The doorway is low. There, we've arrived. Don't be imprudent, for the old woman is malign. I'll wait for you outside."

She ran away, leaving him on the threshold of the room, dimly illuminated by the little ceiling lamp. An icy chill, similar to the sensation of a damp cloth, gripped his shoulders. The walls, from which a thin whitewash was flaking, were stained with leprosy and stitched with scars.

The old woman turned her gaze slowly toward the young man.

"Ah," she sighed, "the moment has come."

A few dogs were baying at the moon outside; an owl was uttering its monotonous cry, as soft and a child's whimper.

Arynes advanced slowly, and the old woman's eyes, round and shining, had such a singular expression that a shiver ran through his entire being.

The atmosphere around him was populated by invisible beings, whose malign and terrifying presence he sensed. By the faint light of the little horn lamp, he thought he perceived the hideous forms of crouching beasts. There were carnivores with human heads, winged reptiles, fleshless felines with powerful claws and eyes of fire. He would have liked to deflect the wrath of the monsters by means of the incantations, spells and magical formulae that his skepticism had disdained thus far.

Amulets, talismans, philters and fateful stones would doubtless have preserved him from evil fate, but he had nothing on him but his dagger.

The old woman, who was still contemplating him with her bloodshot eyes, certainly knew the secrets of the alchemists, astrologers and sorcerers. She cast spells and enchantments at her whim; the mysteries of life and death were known to her. The entire cortege of the somber terrors that haunt the human imagination had entered with Arynes, and he recalled the phrases full of dementia by means of which the Magi conjured spirits.

Zaroccha had not budged; her basilisk eyes, wide open, followed the officer's every movement; her lips seemed to be twisted in an equivocal rictus. Arynes felt something like a gust of madness pass through his brain.

"Zaroccha," he said, "I've come to beg you to help me, for my honor is at stake. I have no more hope except for your magic power. You extracted Zofyre and Hertes, who were about to kill themselves, from difficulty; will you treat me more cruelly?"

The sorceress continued gazing at him silently. Thinking that she had not heard, he repeated his plea; but the old woman conserved the same immobility.

"You can," he said, in a louder voice, "indicate to me the formula that enables one to win with certainty. Tell me those beneficent words, I beg you, and I will give you in exchange anything you ask of me."

Zaroccha opened her mouth, but no sound emerged from her lips.

"Speak, and have no fear. The secret will be more closely guarded by me than by yourself."

She seemed troubled, indecisive. Her face expressed a sort of passionate attention, but soon resumed its terrifying immobility.

"The words, the words! Tell me them, quickly, and take my life in exchange!"

Zaroccha remained silent. He went on: "Why don't you want to speak? You're old, and no one will profit from your science. Tomorrow, even if you want to reveal the mystery to me, it might be too late. In any case, I'm going away; you'll never see me again."

He stopped, quivering with impatience. The old woman's lips were obstinately sealed.

"Come on, one last time, I implore you; I'm humbling myself before your power." Arynes had fallen to his knees. "If your heart has ever known the sweet ecstasy of tenderness; if you have ever palpitated in the arms of a lover or a husband; by everything in existence that is consoling, I beg you to respond."

It seemed to him that a more human sentiment had awoken in the soul of the prophetess, and, burning with the desire to triumph, at all costs, he had the dream of a magical power, a favorable divinity that would arrest destiny for him, change the course of things and gratify him with its benefits. Reality had revealed itself odious; an immense need for illusion and deception was born within him. Certainly, the power of seers and magi must render youth to the old, resuscitate the dead and discover all the treasures buried in the earth . . .

Zaroccha, however, was at the limit of age, her decrepitude and weakness appeared to be extreme—but he no longer perceived that, in his increasing error. In any case, if the witch remained thus, it was doubtless because she wanted it thus, with a hidden design that he could not fathom. A source of hope sprang forth in his soul, flowing in a prodigious flood of magical light, divine and supernatural images. It was like a tide of resurrection that lifted up his entire being, extending it toward the expected prodigy.

Safou, the house cat, went by, arching his back and mewling in a sinister fashion. Bats that had flown in through the skylight were fluttering around the expiring lamp. The pale gleam seemed to the crazed young man to be a living nucleus of hope and illusion. It was the revolt and triumph of the impossible over inexorable matter.

He had taken hold of the cold hand of the sorceress, but the contact of that viscous flesh filled him with fear and disgust. He stood up, supporting the shining gaze of the old woman, which seemed once again to be tinted with irony.

"Oh, odious creature!" he cried. "I'll soon be able to extract your secret from you!"

She uttered a high-pitched snigger, which exasperated Arynes' nerves to the point of crime. He threw himself upon her, while she extended her arms as if to push him away. He had seized his dagger, and the blade disappeared entirely into Zaroccha's breast.

"What have I done?" he murmured.

Again he knelt down, inundated by the blood that emerged from the wound, seething.

"Come back!" he implored. "I didn't want to strike you! You exasperated me with your silence. Have pity, Zaroccha, look at me; I recognize my wrongdoing, you see, I deplore it, I shall expiate it, I shall serve you forever and everywhere, whatever you decide . . . !"

The old woman slid to the ground, and Arynes perceived that she was dead.

Chapter VI

> We shall see one another again by night,
> and it is then that I shall kiss you.
> (The Oracle of Belus)[1]

"Oh! Beloved, we're doomed!"

Nysista was weeping on her lover's bosom.

He was gazing at the pink moonlit peaks of the mountains that protected the city. They were like the half-vanished appari-

---

1 Belus was a mythical King of Egypt mentioned by numerous Classical writers; but the similarity of names led to confusion with the Babylonian god Bel-Marduk and the Semitic god Ba'al. The oracle of Belus mentioned in accounts of Alexander the Great's campaigns was in Babylon.

tions of visionaries. Both of them were steeped, as if haunted, in the mystery of beings and things, no longer seeing the city asleep beneath the distant summits, flown away into the white light with the lightness of a dream.

The girl was still weeping, with great sobs, and her frail shoulders were heaving convulsively.

"I'm afraid, my beloved! Even dead, the witch will avenge herself."

"Child," he said, disdainfully, "that woman was a miserably obscure creature like any other. I was mistaken regarding her power."

"No, no—you'll see!"

"I won't see anything. If Zaroccha were a witch, she'd already be on her feet in order to pursue us."

With a scornful gesture, he pointed through the open door at the bloody corpse of the old woman. "Look," he said. "She isn't moving. She'll never frighten the weak and the credulous with her spells again."

But the girl clung to Arynes more tightly. "No, no, I don't want to look at her."

And, in spite of everything, pity overcame her for the person who, until then, had been the unique companion of her life. With her, for as far back as she could remember, she had lived her melancholy dream, in the youthful and naïve error of childhood. When the old woman did not beat her, she told her prodigious stories to make her tremble with fear and joy. She planted a long nail in the ground at random, and charming images appeared in a little puff of smoke, diaphanous figurines that ran and frolicked among the flowers. Sometimes, those exquisite creatures flew up lightly to a great height, and then fluttered all the way to the ground, on which they posed on tiptoe like ballerinas, ready to take off again. At sunset, there were bloody combats, constructions and besieged fortresses, the frightful blows of clubs that felled thousands of warriors, and everything vanished into red dust. Nysista was very fearful; she had never been seen at night passing close to the Towers of Silence, where the black vultures were tearing cadavers apart.

Everything around her seemed populated by mystery. Old walls sang in the darkness, beasts with seven horns leapt up in the ditches. She knew that certain accursed men entered into the skin of dogs and howled mortally on moonless evenings. She believed in the resurrection of the fravashi, the double that everyone bears within them, in reincarnation, and in all the powers of good and evil.

Certainly, Zaroccha was not dead; she would reappear on earth in order to punish her murderer, and nothing could appease her wrath.

"It's necessary to take her to the vultures," said Arynes.

"No, for she's not of the Persian religion."

"Of what religion is she, then?"

"No one knows. Perhaps she had none; but she has chosen her tomb, and it's there that she'll be placed, in balms and aromatics. I want to render her the last duties."

"What's the point?"

"Perhaps she'll be appeased by my submission."

"Stupid girl!" said Arynes. "Better to abandon her to the birds of prey."

"Listen," murmured the girl, "there's a kind of murmur in the night."

"It's the last troops joining the camp. I have to leave too."

"Oh, don't abandon me," she moaned.

"Come with me."

"Can I leave her like this?"

"Certainly. Her old carcass isn't worthy of your respect. Let's go, Nysista. Anyway, isn't that what you want?"

"Yesterday," she said. "But today . . ."

"All days are alike. Only our imagination gives birth to specters and dramas. Everything in life is a lie; it's necessary to live for oneself, and not for others."

But Nysista was obstinate in her determination.

"I want to put her in the tomb. Afterwards, I'll be tranquil. The stone of a sepulcher is heavy to lift. Then, too, those who remain ought to grant the wishes of the dying. Who can tell whether the evil spirits didn't desire that death, in order to prove their omnipotence? Threats are traversing the air and striking me with fear in the sobs of the wind. An icy breath, coming from the invisible, passed over my face; a frisson is running through you, in spite of your incredulity."

Arynes, his eyes vague, did not reply.

"Oh," she went on, "your hands are red. It seems to me that the blood that had spurted over you is suddenly catching fire and enveloping you with a scarlet veil. I want to beg the beneficent spirits to be favorable to you. I'll beg them with all my strength, until I no longer know who or where I am, I'll speak to them as to beings of power and light, I'll pray to them, as one loves and as one dies, in order for them, to grant you the grace of avoiding evil. And the violence of my adoration might perhaps combat evil fate."

"I'm leaving," said Arynes, "for it's necessary that I efface the traces of the murder."

"Go, then," she said, in a sigh. "I'll join you soon, whatever happens."

He kissed her on the lips and disappeared into the night.

Chapter VII

> I summon the spirits and souls of who are just
> and those possessed by the sacred fire.
> (The Text of the Yaçna)[1]

Nysista had washed the old woman's body and, her soul filled with fear, she remained with her. In the garden of fluttering birds, the great tumult of day had replaced the murmurs of the night. The sun was weighing on the distant mountainsides in a slow golden dust, and a great fiery breath was passing over things.

---

1 The Yaçna is one of the sacred texts of ancient Persian Zoroastrianism.

Through the open skylight, an acacia was agitating its light foliage; mimosas and fig-trees were pouring a living cascade over the walls, the ruddy ocher hue of which they were enlivening.

At the ends of the deserted streets, above marble terraces, the summits of pylons were outlined, and columns surmounted by winged bulls, unicorns and lions. Women with gilded complexions and large brown eyes were passing by with jars full of fresh water. They wore skirts tightened at the hip and pointed bonnets of stiff cloth, and the compact curls of their hair descended over cheeks in the radiance of golden rings suspended from their ears. They were alert and smiling, but their gaze became grave when they interrogated the interior of the house.

"Is Zaroccha dead, then?" they asked, with surprise.

"Yes," Nysista replied. "She died suddenly."

"What are you going to do now that she's no longer there to send you into the mountains to search for sacred herbs?"

"Oh," said a young woman with a dainty, almost infantile face, "she'll be a witch like the old woman."

"No," cried a tall black girl with hard eyes, "she wouldn't want to evoke the spirits of evil—she's too simple and naïve."

They all stopped and stood on tiptoe in order to see. Narrow robes with colored stripes molded the contours of their bodies; crude and heavy jewelry decorated their arms and shoulders. They sometimes laughed disdainfully, and it was as if the fibers of Nysista's being were being twisted, as if her heart were being gripped by iron fingers.

The girl found herself alone again, as weak and lost as a child. She wept quietly, feeling too miserable and too abandoned to reflect. Unconsciously, however, she wanted the help of a supernatural support, and a divine power that was thinking about her, wished her well and was bathing her in its clemency. It was Arynes, her lover, who had killed the witch! She had opened the door and he had gone in tranquilly to accomplish his detestable crime. So, his passionate words, his embraces and his caresses had not been inspired by love. Ambition alone and the desire to obtain a treasure had driven the Satrap's son. She, Nysista, had submitted blindly to the will of a murderer; what could she do to redeem her sins?

But everything clouded over in the head of the young woman, who fell into the annihilation of great sadness.

Then neighbors came in, embalmers and mourners who offered their services, curious to contemplate the face of the sorceress. They circled the dead woman, moaning, cracking their knuckles and clapping the palms of their brown hands. And they repeated the words of the Magi: "Come, then, with your enchantments and your terrible secrets, to change the face of destiny. Come to confound the auguries of life and death. Do you not have the clairvoyance, the wisdom and the power?"

But the old woman retained her closed mask, her hollow lips and her vague pupils raised behind her eyelids. And the women, who no longer feared her, were cheerful by virtue of her impotence. The amazing events now left them full of incredulity; they recounted those imaginations of dementia with scornful laughter, forgetting the environment of visionary fever in which they had lived.

Nysista was still weeping; her reason was struggling, like a poor creature thrown into water, caught by the slow waves and choking. Then, after minutes of annihilation, she revolted, telling herself that, after all, she had a right to her share of happiness and that evil spells should not take it away from her. Zaroccha would avoid the torment of remaining without a sepulcher, wandering between earth and heaven, a restless shade. Her vengeance could not, therefore, pursue the forgetful or sacrilegious lovers. Her irritated spirit would not become a malevolent demon intent on their doom.

"I want her to be swathed in bandages," she said to the embalmers, "and coated in bitumen, and the objects she loved during her life must be placed in her tomb, as well as the aliments necessary to her life as a phantom."

"Was she of Chaldean origin, then?" asked the women, disdainfully. "Here, *madjous* belong to the vultures."[1]

---

1 The term *madjou*, which appears in a number of 19th-century texts relating

"No," said Nysista, "I want her to be buried. In any case, the worshipers of fire would refuse her body, as you know very well. Zaroccha had no religion, and her practices were culpable."

"Yes, yes," said a tall woman with dark eyes, who reeked of earth and aromatics, "her soul will vegetate in eternal darkness; she'll nourish herself on dust and weep for the daylight."

"One night, a night of fear and horror," murmured a mourner whose fingernails were stained with blood, "a specter will fly over the city; it will enter the houses that are not marked in red, and the little children will die in horrible convulsions."

"Do your job," said Nytista, "and I'll pay you well."

"With what?" said the tall woman with hard eyes. "You don't possess anything but your gilded lies."

"You're clad in rags like beggar-women."

"Yes," the mourner said. "Your cornelian necklaces and glass bead bracelets have no value."

"Your striped skirt is coarse cloth."

"Do your job," Nysista repeated.

Then, having lifted the lid of a long wooden box, she showed them an accumulation of precious stones with dazzling gleams.

Then, zealously, the women lifted up the old woman and set about their lugubrious work.

Chapter VIII

Gambling is like a beautiful woman who
smiles and offers herself incessantly to
men, but whose smile is only a lie.
(Rig Veda)

Zaroccha had been buried the day before, and the Satrap's son was waiting for Nysista.

He was thinking more about the losses he had suffered than the joy of seeing the young woman again. His last hope had

---

to ancient Persia, appears to be a corruption of "magus."

flown away with the death of the witch, and he would never be able to regain the fortune he had risked.

The passion for gambling was as keen among the Persians as their brothers, the Aryans of India. They wagered enormous sums, and sometimes staked their wives, children and themselves. The beautiful hymn of the Rig Veda, which relates the follies and sorrows of that terrible passion, could have been written on the Iranian plateau.

Arynes played dice, and other games involving ivory and wooden figurines. There were also colored tablets, not unlike our card games, although the symbols were much more varied. People paid one another in darics—coins struck with an effigy of Darius—or coins of various forms bearing the seals of petty individual sovereigns, the right to strike money having been respected by the King of Kings. In the beginning, gambling had been favorable to Arynes, and his luck, which astonished all his friends, did not impress him at all, so much did he imagine himself able to enchain his fortune by his marvelous will-power. A few officers sometimes asked him to interest himself in their wagers, or, at least, to place himself beside them when they played games of chance, in order to ward off the evil genius that pursued them by his presence.

The Satrap's son consented, laughing, to protect the unfortunates that a deadly fate never ceased to overwhelm. His constant success made him the topic of all conversations, and mysterious legends circulated regarding his intimate life and his commerce with spirits. In his dreams he heard the clink of gold and saw more precious stones sparkling than the sovereign Master and the nineteen Satraps of the realm possessed.

He placed the ivory figurines almost blindly; he did not choose the signs on which he placed his gold; it was not him who guided his play, it was destiny, or the mysterious influence that combines with chance to direct its strange effects.

There are two kinds of fanatics. Some find an enveloping and intelligent charm in the reasoned manipulation of figures, the multiplicity of combinations that unfold, are entangled and succeed one another with rapidity. The occult and supernatural power of a kind of invisible guide is manifest, and the communion of the soul with its double operates invincibly. That is precisely what excites the mind to tempt fortune; one might think that it wants to try to penetrate the domain of the unexplored, to pierce the redoubtable secret of the future, of life and death.

Gamblers of that kind have a certain grandeur, and only ask of gambling the competition of reasoned effort and the surprises of the known.

But there are others, who only hope to win, and consider gambling as a facile means of enrichment without effort. It was to that class that Arynes belonged, for he was avid for luxury and pleasures, and nothing deterred him from satisfying his expensive passions. His foolish and unruly life had already effaced all the amiable qualities that had once attracted the amity of his comrades to him. His taste for the art and sciences of war had been extinguished; he thought of nothing but acquiring greater wealth for the satisfaction of his desires. In his handsome face, hollowed out by fever, his eyes were animated by a supernatural flame; he no longer knew anything but the lust of lucre.

But the luck that had smiled upon him at first soon turned against him. In a short time he not only lost all that he had won, but even his personal wealth. His father, Ariaramnes, the Satrap of Cappadocia, refused him further subsidies, and his disdainful comrades turned away from him.

It was then that, passing through Ecbatana in order to join Darius' army, he heard mention of Zaroccha and her marvelous powers. Thanks to the witch's advice, two lords, Hertes and Zofyre, had triumphed over the demons of gambling; a word from her could change the face of destiny.

Loitering near the dwelling of the Magi, Arynes encountered Nysista, who was going to collect herbs on Mount Zagros. The girl was sad, like him; he had consoled her, and the honey of his words had slid into that young heart like a voluptuous wave.

While he remained preoccupied, chilled by the great frisson of his odious calculation, she had abandoned herself to the sweetness of that first amour, and gradually, he had obtained from her what he desired.

Now, he was waiting for her, in the midst of his soldiers, for women were allowed to penetrate into the camp. The yellow leather armor and scarlet cloaks were flamboyant in the last rays of sunlight. The camels, arranged in long lines, charged with baggage and provisions, were kneeling gravely in the warm sand, stretching their melancholy heads toward the cool watercourses, and the men were finishing setting up the tents. There was a quiver of harness and weapons everywhere; horses and mules were pawing the ground; it seemed curious to see those warriors with curly black hair and torsos the color of brick, clad in simple blue shorts, coming and going in the ruddy crepuscular light. The mountains, with their faded hues, closed the horizon, serving as a backcloth for the gigantic constructions of Phraortes, Astyages and Cyrus. The pylons with banked corners and the tapering cornices of temples were already blurred in the distance, and only the camp was still ablaze, with the bright colors of its tents erected on the yellow sand like monstrous flowers grown in a single day.

But the time went by and Nysista did not come. Slaves brought torches of wax mixed with pine resin, but the officer, plunged in his dream, paid no heed to them. Outside, the shadow was now extending over the region; the stars were beginning to make their long golden lashes quiver in the profound azure. Vultures, gorged on human flesh, were hovering over the Towers of Silence, and owls were uttering funereal cries in the desolation of the roads.

Arynes found himself in one of those melancholy moments when the anguished soul doubts everything, and suddenly revolts. He got up slowly and went out into the camp. The night was admirable, calm, quiet and clear, embalmed by the odor of the mountains. A great buzz rose up, breaths of wind passed that gave the sensation of thousands of creatures lying on the ground in heaps around litters.

Suddenly, in the distance, a brilliant flame zigzagged, like the thunderbolts that are seen to fall from the black sky during rainstorms. But the luminous trace did not disappear; the light advanced with a slow and stately glide, seeming to dance over the tents like a golden bird.

Arynes followed it with his eyes, slightly anxious, unable to explain the vagabond flight of the shooting star emerged from the black depths of the unknown. Then a voice rose up, so distant and so faint that it seemed to be nothing more than the small rustle of a moving gust of wind.

Everything in the camp remained vague; the human silhouettes were outlined in unequal shadows, and nothing moved except for the fantastic light strayed from the blue sky.

Prey to an extraordinary malaise, Arynes lay down in his bed, hoping that sleep would chase away the sinister visions.

Chapter IX

> Come to me, beloved, in the sadness
> of darkness . . . and your kisses will
> warm me to the heart.
> (Old Persian Hymn)

When the officer woke up, it was still dark, and yet it seemed to him that he had slept for long hours.

At that moment, someone lifted the thick curtain that veiled the entrance to the tent, as if to look inside, but the flap immediately fell shut again.

"Is that you, Nysista?" the young man asked. "Come in without fear; I'm expecting you."

A long murmur replied to him, but he did not understand the vague words that struck his ear, doubtless pronounced in a foreign language.

Then, after a few moments, a fleshless hand lifted the curtain that served as a door again, and a long phantom slid toward the bed.

"Is that you, Nysista?" Arybnes asked again, fearfully.

The specter leaned toward him, and he recognized Zaroccha.

"What are you doing here?" he said, angrily. "Get back to your tomb, and don't trouble the sleep of the living."

The old woman leaned over again, and put an icy finger on the young man's forehead.

"I am here by the will of the spirits of the shadow, who have ordered me to grant your desire. I can indicate to you the magic formula that will make you rich and master of the world."

Joyfully, Arynes sat up on his bed.

"Speak! Speak quickly!"

"But whatever happens, you'll obey me?"

"Yes," he said, "since you're assuring me happiness and fortune."

"My will shall be yours?"

"I swear it."

"You will even love me, if I desire it?"

With a smile, Arynes contemplated the fleshless mask of the specter, in which the round staring eyes were glowing strangely.

"It would be necessary for that for you to be a creature of flesh and blood. I can't cherish a phantom . . . in any case, are you not dead?"

"I am, in fact dead," she said, with a terrible smile, "but the dead sometimes return."

"Well, return with the features of a young and beautiful woman, and I'll love you, word of an officer!"

"Now," she said, "you will surely win. It will be sufficient for you to pronounce my name three times, when you tempt your fortune."

The specter of Zaroccha glided slowly toward the entrance, and disappeared without the slightest sound.

The officer remained motionless for some time, thinking that he had been the victim of a hallucination. Then he went out of the tent and interrogated the night again. Soldiers were sleeping heavily next to tethered horses and mules, but a mysterious light was dancing over the camp. It seemed that a star had poured down something like a dust of sunlight, that an atom of the Milky Way had fallen from on high, an ungraspable moth trying to regain the heavens.

Chapter X

> A reasonable man never tries to
> tempt the spirits of evil.
> (*The Book of Enoch.*)

The next day, Arynes wanted to try out his marvelous power, and luck was, indeed, favorable to him. He won, again and again, as the phantom had predicted.

A breath had passed, changing the course of things, and the officer's soul palpitated with an inextinguishable desire, an infinite hope.

A dream had sufficed to illuminate his thoughts; he took refuge in the mystery, forgetting reality in order to plunge back into the phantasmagoria of the unknown, for the miracle that one cannot certify is necessary bread for human desperation. Already he accepted the prodigy, finding it quite natural and well deserved.

For three days he won, without luck deserting him for a single instant.

On the evening of the fourth day, Nysista came to join him, and he told her joyfully about the change that had occurred in his life.

"Ah!" she said, sadly. "You've won?"

"Yes, I've won, and I'll win again; an unknown power is protecting me, directing my play."

"That strange favor frightens me, my beloved! Don't play any more, I beg you. In any case, since fortune has already rewarded you lavishly, that ought to be sufficient for your ambition. Conserve your winnings, and don't tempt the future any longer."

"Oh," he said, disdainfully, "one is never rich enough, and I shan't stop half-way."

She sighed. "Nothing separates us any longer; we could be so happy!"

"I don't understand happiness in the same way as you."

"Happiness," she said, "is in the union of two beings, the communion of those who love one another."

He did not reply, an ironic crease in his lips.

Again, she shivered. "Oh, if only you could love me as I love you."

Tears filled her eyes; she wept for herself and for all the poor feeble creatures who need an illusion of joy, a support, a devotion, in order to escape the sorrows of the world. Confusedly, she heard the rumor of the waking camp: the crowd of twenty thousand men from which a spray of flourishing hope also rose up, exhaled like an incense under the sun. They too, perhaps, would be disappointed in their desires for glory, nothing being worth as much as the quiet of a hearth, profound peace in the company of those one cherishes.

"What about Zaroccha?" asked the officer, tormented by an obsession.

"We've put her in the tomb."

"And you haven't been visited by her unquiet soul?"

"No," she said, calmly, "I've prayed so much for her repose that she must be delivered from evil spirits. We put her in the Black Valley, in the depths of a granite hypogeum, for she had gold and precious stones."

The officer started. "She had gold, and you didn't say anything!"

"The gold wasn't mine, so what was the point of saying anything to you about it?"

44

Arynes remained silent, but his eyes flashed.

"In her tomb," Nysista went to, "I hid what remained of her riches: a necklace of pearls, carbuncles, rare coins, statuettes of enameled plaster, blue and green, of marvelous workmanship, unknown idols in gold and silver. She's sleeping like a queen in the midst of her treasure. And she was certainly content, for I saw her smile when the mask was placed on her face, in the Egyptian fashion."

"She was really dead?"

"Yes," said Nysista, "she was quite dead, since she had undergone all the operations of embalming."

"But her double, her fravashi, might still escape?" Arynes trembled again, and the young woman looked at him compassionately.

"Have no fear; I've appeased her by means of my prayers."

"And you didn't keep the smallest jewel?"

"No, Beloved, I've already told you."

"But what's in the basket that you're hiding so carefully . . . ?"

"This is Safou, the domestic cat."

"What—you've brought a cat?"

"With me gone, who would have taken care of him? Anyway, he's meek and faithful; he won't importune you."

Liberated, Safou arched his back, and his phosphorescent eyes gleamed mysteriously.

Arynes thought that the souls of the dead sometimes take refuge in the bodies of animals.

"Don't you think that the cat's gaze is singular?"

She smiled. "Safou consoled me and caressed me during my hours of sorrow. Before knowing you I told him my troubles; he seemed to understand me, always submissive and tender as you see him now. Could I abandon such a sympathetic friend?"

The cat, leaping on to the young woman's shoulder, rubbed his muzzle against her cheek affectionately. He was blacker than the night, but his fur, long and fine, shone like silk.

"Where will we put him?" asked Arynes.

"Oh, he won't take up much room," said Nysista. "The end of this carpet will be sufficient for him to sleep on."

The officer thought about Zaroccha and the sinister visit he had received. The pale glimmer of the moon illuminated his tent, and Safou's ardent eyes also sparkled like little living stars.

"And you sealed the entrance to the cavern well?" he said.

"We put heavy stones over the slab, which blocked any issue hermetically. No one will be able to move that heavy door again, for sure. Only the fire of the mountain might be able to annihilate Zaroccha's body, for in her tomb it's as if she's in the opening of a furnace. We placed over her the seal surmounted by the globe with outspread wings, with the clay jackal lying on its belly, and the symbolic serpent the color of the sky."

Arynes uttered a sigh of satisfaction. "Yes," he said, "nothing in the world will be able to resuscitate her, and you were right, Nysista, to put her wealth next to her. That way, her double won't seek to do us any harm."

Reassured, he hugged the young woman to his heart, and in a long kiss, poured into her the forgetfulness of everything that was not his love.

Chapter XI

When you are near me, the birds sing,
the sun shines, the flowers embalm;
but when you are far away from me,
everything remains in desolation.
(Persian poem)

However, Arynes was not at peace. After the first caresses, the long embraces, the confidences whispered lip to lip, he was seized by dread again in the secrecy of his heart. Had he not made a pact with the witch? Did he not belong to her by virtue of the mysterious influence that she exercised over him and the promises that she had extracted from him?

While Nysista, exhausted by so many ordeals, was asleep next to him, he started trembling and interrogating all the corners of the tent with a troubled gaze.

Safou, the black cat, was wandering around the bed, and his phosphorescent eyes made two luminous dots in the shadows. The feline sometimes uttered a plaintive mewl, arched his supple back and raised himself up on his paws as if about to pounce on an invisible enemy.

Mentally, Arynes made a supreme appeal to the benevolent spirits that watch over human destinies. Involuntarily, he called them to his aid to combat the accursed influence. Then, hugging Nysista's charming body, he tried to lose himself in a voluptuous dream, and solicited her kiss tenderly.

The young woman woke up, naming him in a low voice: "Arynes, my dear lover!"

"Oh," he murmured, "tell me that you love me and that I'll find in you protection and affection. This darkness frightens me. Doesn't it seem to you that you can hear footsteps?"

"No, my Adored, I can only hear the beating of my heart. I'm happy next to you; I'd like to die like this. After the terrible proofs of recent days, I believe that I've been reborn, to plunge into a blissful wave, sweeter than milk and honey. Red and gold flowers are opening around me. Everything is perfume, everything is melody. Oh, let's recommence the divine ecstasy of our amour!"

He applied his lips to hers and clutched her to his bosom. "Protect me!"

"Protect you? But why?" she asked, a little surprised. "What danger is threatening you?"

"The shadows are hostile. Birds of death are weeping in the night."

"Imagination, my Beloved! I only hear the noises of the camp. In any case, your soldiers are on watch, and will be able to keep you safe from any surprise."

"It isn't the invasion of the enemy that I fear. Human attacks are not as terrifying as the touch of the invisible beings that surround us."

Nysista had wound her delicate arms around her lover's neck; she tried to put his fears to sleep by means of exquisite and passionate caresses.

"Nothing exists but my love; sleep on my heart and don't think about anything else. The witch is vanquished, she can't harm us any more."

With vague words, from which thought was perhaps absent, she reassured him, consoled him and lulled him to sleep.

Next to her he felt strong and courageous; a sensual intoxication replaced the somber preoccupations, her eyes closed under the lips that brushed them. Gradually, slumber numbed his soul.

A raucous mewl from the cat extracted Arynes from his torpor. Everything around him was plunged in darkness. He raised himself up with difficulty, lending an ear to a kind of whisper coming from outside. It seemed to him that someone nearby exhaled a profound sigh.

"I'm here," said a faint voice.

And the specter of Zaroccha emerged from the shadow, as it had before.

The officer felt an icy finger pose on his forehead again.

"Why have you disobeyed me?"

Troubled, he put out his hand to repel the frightful vision; but the specter did not move.

"I am not a body of flesh and bone; I am the astral double of the charmer, and you can do nothing against me."

"Go away!" he said, angrily.

"No, for you cannot do without my help. I'll give you all the gold you want if you keep your promise."

"I haven't promised anything."

"Oh, the ingrate heart!" sniggered the old woman. "Have you forgotten, then, that you gave me your amour?"

"My amour goes to things of the earth, not specters from unknown worlds."

"It's for Nysista that you're betraying me?"

"I love Nysista; she will be my wife."

A cold hand was placed once again on the lips of the young man, who shivered.

"You believe yourself to be invulnerable because you won at gambling, and you want to ignore my benefits. So be it; I abandon you to the malevolent spirits of Air and Fire. I withdraw from you, but my prediction will be accomplished even so, for your murder links us. You were my assassin, Arynes, my blood reddened your fingers, and you retain in your mind the unforgettable vision of my death throes. Whatever you do, this haunting will trouble your days and your nights. You will return to me, as the murderer always returns to his victim. You will love me and hate me equally, in spite of all your revolts."

"Go away!" repeated the young man.

"You will have orgies of memory!" sniggered the specter. "Your soul will burn, fully and broadly, with a sinister and growing flame. You will insult my shadow and you will summon me desperately in the savage energy and devouring ardor of your passion!"

"No," he said, "I was mad, and Nysista's presence will sustain me against malevolent temptations."

He picked up a weapon that was gleaming nearby.

"Be careful," murmured the phantom. "You might hurt yourself, for I am invincible henceforth. But your life belongs to me, since you have given it to me. I have you in my guard, and I shall employ my power in a punishment more complete than death, which destroys and does not repair. I know the terrible secret of human destinies."

Arynes struggled against the terror that was gradually paralyzing him. It seemed to him that the blood in his veins was leaking away, drop by drop, and that Zaroccha, like a vampire, was feeding gluttonously on his life.

He made a supreme effort, and sat up on his bed with a cry of anguish; but the specter had disappeared.

Chapter XII

The king declared: while I was in Persia
and Media the people of Babylon
rebelled against me for the second time.
(Story of Darius.)[1]

Arynes did not tell his mistress about the terrible dream he had had. Joyful and confident, she recovered the sweetness of belief, and he remained attentive and tender beside her. The demon of gambling appeared to have abandoned him. His unique concern was to adorn Nysista, to buy her jewels and precious garments in all the colors of the rainbow. He had never found her so sumptuous, although she resembled a Babylonian idol.

"Thus," he said, "you remind me of the goddess of amour that we saw in a temple in the perverse city. She was named Mylitta, the queen of victories and voluptuousness."[2]

"Mylitta, the lascivious goddess of the women of Babylon? Zaroccha had an amulet that represented her."

"I saw her standing on a bull, coiffed with a tiara streaming with stars like a sky inundated with moonlight. She was equipped with a bow and a quiver, in order to wound hearts, but even so, she was the beneficent mother of the generation and reproduction of beings."

"On the fetish that I put in the witch's tomb with the other jewels, she was naked and pressing her hands over her breasts in a modest manner."

Arynes' expression darkened. "Why did you bury all those valuables in that woman's sepulcher?" he said. Involuntarily, he expressed the regret of so much lost wealth.

---

1 Like most of the headquotes to the chapters, this one is invented; the original has "Babirus" rather than Babylon, but that makes no sense, so I have made the substitution.

2 Mylitta was the name given by Herodotus to an Assyrian goddess whom he considered to be the equivalent of Aphrodite, presumably the goddess known in various parts of the region as Ishtar, Inanna and Mullissu.

"Because those riches didn't belong to me," said the young woman. "Then again, that is how the dead are buried in Egypt. I've already told you that."

"We're not in Egypt . . . and you've told me that there was a veritable treasure in Zaroccha's hiding place."

"Yes, a marvelous treasure; my eyes couldn't support the glare of it. I saw rubies and diamonds so large that no similar ones surely exist."

The officer remained pensive in the desire for all those splendors lost forever. A harsh crease striped his forehead, and Nysista was troubled by his meditation.

A crimson tint colored the internal partitions of the tent, painted in bright hues and florid with gold palm-leaves. Arynes and his mistress were reposing on a low bed ornamented by four jackals' heads. Around them the ground disappeared under furs, caskets and precious carpets, distributed randomly.

Nysista scanned those things with an indolent gaze; she was divinely beautiful, satisfied amour having magnified the graces of her young body. Ardent reflections now colored the mat complexion of her face, in which her long onyx eyes shone, emphasized by a line of antimony. Her heavy painted eyelids fluttered voluptuously over the fulgurant flash of her gaze, and her dainty mouth was still smiling in the ecstasy of a dream.

As Arynes was no longer speaking, she got up slowly and proceeded with her scrupulous toilette in a corner of the tent. A polished bronze mirror with an ivory foot sent back her image, and she drew the powders, pastes and unguents that she loved to employ from jars of jade, amber and agate.

A delicately-wrought perfume spatula lay next to multiple cassolettes with subtle effluences.

"Adorn yourself," said Arynes, "for we're expecting Darius, the King of Kings."

"Darius is coming!" she said, joyfully. "And he'll come in here?"

"Yes; you'll offer him palm wine in the golden cup from Babylon. It will remind him of his conquests, and he'll be sensible to that flattering attention.

"Darius, the King of Kings! How imposing and proud he must be!"

With even greater care she assembled her thick and heavy blue-tinted hair to either side of her cheeks, retained by golden disks. A network of enamels and cornelian beads imprisoned her charming cleavage, transparent under the mesh of stones, and a silky fabric garnished with embroidered strips, tiny bells and fringes was draped over her slender hips, maintained by a girdle of gold and lapis lazuli.

"Do I look good like this?" she asked the thoughtful officer.

"You're no longer Mylitta the Babylonian goddess but Mitra, the Persian idol a hundred times more exquisite."[1]

"Am I worthy to serve the King of Kings?"

"No slave more beautiful than you will ever have poured the welcoming wine.

"Then I desire nothing more," she said. "I am happy if you are happy."

At that moment there was a great rumor in the camp. It was a dull noise, as profound as that of an approaching wave; then the strident sound of bronze instruments was detached from the rumble of chariots and the rhythmic tread of assembled troops, and a cloud of blond dust invaded the tent.

"It's the conqueror!" said Arynes. "It's the master of the world!"

Two soldiers came to notify him, respectfully, of the arrival of Darius. The tumult increased; the swirls of sand rose higher and officers of an inferior rank were already arranging themselves in a hedge in the drill-field in order to clear a passage for the conquering sovereign.

---

1 The Mitra mentioned in a handful of Persian texts is usually considered to be a masculine deity, the equivalent of the deity of the same name featured in the Rig Veda and the Zoroastrian Mithra, known in ancient Rome as Mithras.

The drums, trumpets, sistra and short bronze clarions played a glorious fanfare, and the royal advance guard had already reached the center of the camp when Nysista's lover went to his post.

The drummers were arranged in a semicircle, the drumskins struck with sycamore wands resounded in their cases; the trumpets clamored the universal joy and the supreme hope of the victorious army more loudly.

Behind the musicians, prisoners were lined up, in the bestial masks of cynocephali, with frizzy hair. Necklaces of knucklebones rattled on their chests; scarlet loincloths circled their hips. Those howling and grimacing captives had their wrists held in blocks of wood, and they were roped together so tightly that they could not take a step without pulling the rope and bruising their ankles. Guards maintained them with whiplashes, also striking the women with long dangling hair and thin limbs, exhausted by hard labor. A few, however, had large enamel eyes and a bouncing rump, which excited the covetousness of the guards and obtained a more humane treatment.

The beautiful women with glass bead necklaces and slender and harmonious limbs were destined for the officers who would save them from death and maintain them in servitude. They seemed calm and resigned, counting on the prestige of their charms to live at the expense of the conquering male.

Behind them, the standard-bearers raised their sacred emblems, representing cartouches with the name of the King, and banners seized from enemy populations and gloriously covered in bloodstains.

A herald proclaimed the latest victories, the sum of the booty and the number of prisoners and war chariots conquered by Darius, who was also bringing back lions, panthers, tigers, elephants, giraffes and carts full of gold ingots.

The soldiers uttered joyful clamors, and then cries of enthusiasm, when Darius, the King of Kings, appeared on his great white horse with golden harness.

In the space that had been reserved for him, he pulled on the reins of his horse, which stopped abruptly, as if it had been transformed into a marble charger. In a firm voice, he spoke to his men.

Arynes, to Darius' right, had bowed profoundly, after having raised the royal mantle to his lips. "Welcome, Monarch of the World! Live forever among your submissive subjects! May eternal glory surround your name!"

"Greetings, son of Ariaramnes, my faithful Satrap," said the King, tenderly. "May the glorious conduct of your father serve as your example! He has been commandant of the fortress and the treasure of Ecbatana; he witnessed the funeral of the prophet Daniel, and has rendered me good services."[1]

Again Arynes applied his lips to the hem of the crimson mantle, and struck his forehead three times as a sign of submission.

"I shall be worthy of the name I bear; I shall sacrifice my existence to the glory of the King of Kings, my Master and my God!"

Darius had leapt lightly to the ground. He was tall, powerful, with coarse black curly hair. His dark eyes had a sort of voluptuous flame; his thick lips parted over dazzling teeth in an enigmatic smile.

"What you do, Arynes, will be well done, I am certain," he said, nobly. "Thanks to Ariaramnes and my faithful Satraps I have vanquished the Babylonian rebels; you will serve me zealously in order to facilitate further conquests for me."

"I am your servant," said the officer, humbly. "Would you care to rest for a moment and drink the wine of amity?"

Although it was broad daylight, torches of wax mixed with pine resin were illuminating Arynes' tent, and Nysista, like a celestial apparition, stood beneath the pale flames, with a smile

---

1 Josephus alleged that the prophet Daniel, who supposedly served several Persian kings (although he probably never existed), was buried in Ecbatana, but other sources offer different accounts and six modern cities in Iraq, Iran and Uzbekistan claim custody of his tomb.

on her lips and a golden cup in her hand. When Darius came in, she knelt before him, and her long tresses undulated over the ground like blue-tinted serpents.

The King, surprised, contemplated her for a few moments; a gleam passed through his eyes.

"This woman is yours?" he asked.

"She is only my cherished companion as yet, and I wanted to ask you for the authorization to marry her."

"What is her family?"

"I don't know."

"Ah!" said the King. "You know that your rank does not permit you to marry a daughter of obscure birth?"

"I know that, but I thought that you might permit me to unite myself with a woman who loves me, and whom I love."

"Where does she come from?" Darius asked, again, with a singular curiosity.

"She lived in Ecbatana in the dwelling of Zaroccha the charmer . . ."

"A witch?"

"Oh, Nysista is not of the accursed clan; she sought flowers in the mountains for the beverages of life and death, but she does not know the magic formulae."

"And how did you meet her?"

"When I was passing over Mount Zagros with my soldiers I encountered her there, and as I was weary, she gave me a delightful balm, which comforted me. Since then, we have seen one another often, and we love one another."

Nysista had risen to her feet, but remained tremulous under the King's ardent gaze. The golden cup had slipped from her hand, and she dared not pick it up, so great was her emotion.

"Give me something to drink," said Darius, softly. "I am fatigued, as Arynes was when he encountered you on Mount Zagros."

He had sat down on the bed with the jackals' heads, and the young woman, finding another goblet of precious metal, filled it with thick perfumed Shiraz wine.

Darius drank it avidly; his eyes were shining more strangely in his somber visage.

"Do you know how to sing and dance like your peers?" he asked.

"Yes," said Nysista in a low voice. "Zaroccha initiated me into the métier of the charmer. I've danced before people in order to earn a little money."

"Sing," he said, "to lull me gently, for I'm weary with lassitude."

"My songs are not worthy of you."

"Sing," he repeated, authoritatively. "I want to hear your voice, which must be similar to the murmur of waves and the plaint of the wind in the reeds . . ."

Nysista interrogated her lover with an anxious glance.

"You must do as the Master orders," said Arynes, with a hint of harshness. "Although your knowledge is not great, perhaps it will have the gift of soothing the preoccupations of our august leader momentarily."

Accompanying herself on a kind of viol with a long shaft, fitted with three strings, the young woman started to intone a languorous chant with a soft and monotonous rhythm. Her voice was pure; it threaded the crystalline notes of an old amorous ballad that Zaroccha had taught her.

Nysista's song acted on Darius' nerves like an excessively penetrating perfume. It seemed to him that the strings of the light instrument that she was causing to vibrate were the very strings of his heart, and he had never experienced such a sharp emotion.

"Oh," he said, "the gods have revealed to you the passionate secret of amour and the caress. It must be sweet to be loved by you!"

Confused, Nysista had stopped, and her saddened gaze filtered through the lines of antimony on her long eyelids.

"I am only the humble pupil of an old seeress," she said, "who died a few days ago."

"You're still mourning her, then?"

"No, for Zaroccha had no affection for me and was not my mother. I know nothing of my birth, which was doubtless obscure, since no one has ever reclaimed me."

"Dance," said Darius. "After your song, I want to know the rhythm of your feet and the science of your lascivious poses."

Again the young woman consulted her lover with a desperate glance. She was confused, and felt herself shivering under the royal covetousness. It seemed to her that the Master's desire was undressing her and violating her in spite of her protestations.

"Dance," said Arynes, forcefully. "Dance; I wish it."

With her foot, Nysista pushed back the furs covering the ground; then, light and supple, she executed the voluptuous dance of the Daughters of the Sun. Large golden disks struck her cheeks and, her skirt, opening momentarily, allowed the sight of her slender legs, which were agitating in an increasingly rapid movement. Her upper body inclined and straightened again gracefully; she moved her hips beneath the girdle of precious stones, flexing her hamstrings and cracking her knuckles in order to beat time.

Suddenly, the fabric that draped her flanks came undone, and she appeared to the King's eyes with the simple network of cornelian that surrounded her breasts.

Darius got up as if to embrace her, but already she was far away, shivering and confused.

Arynes threw her the long silken sheet that he had let fall, and she enveloped herself in it in haste, with an awkward charm. A tear rolled over her nose like a drop of the water of a sacred pool over a lotus petal. She stood motionless, not daring to raise her eyes to look at the monarch, whom she thought she had discontented.

Darius left the tent, inviting Arynes to accompany him.

"That woman pleases me," he said. "Give her to me, and in exchange, you can choose among my slaves the one you like the best."

"I love Nysista," sighed the officer, "and it would be painful for me to be separated from her."

"You love her?"

"O King of Kings, live forever in the glory and pride of your people! Be the greatest and most venerated of monarchs! I would give my blood to serve you, but don't oblige me to quit that young woman!"

"All right," sighed Darius. "I'll leave her to you, since you attach such a value to her possession. I could demand her, but I don't want to impose that humiliation on you. Anyone but you would be punished for his audacity and put on a cross on the highest tower in Ecbatana. The son of Ariaramnes will escape such a punishment. Return to that girl and be happy, if that is your destiny."

Arynes prostrated himself, touching the ground with his forehead, while the sound of the short bronze clarions and the strident appeal of the trumpets burst forth again.

Darius had thrown back his scarlet cloak, displaying his golden breastplate and the broad collar composed of even rows of enameled beads and precious gems, which sparkled in the sunlight. He marched rapidly, heading toward the uncovered area where the chariots of the vanquished chiefs had been lined up. Behind them, twenty thousand men were waiting, ready to obey the slightest signal of the King of Kings.

The stamping hooves of horses, maintained with great difficulty, the distant thunder of bronze-rimmed wheels and the bright quiver of weapons reanimated the monarch, dispelling the burning thoughts that had intoxicated him momentarily like an excessively generous wine. He became once again the redoubtable warrior that his people were acclaiming.

His soldiers truly had a fine appearance beneath the gleaming helmets, the corselets studded with scales and the bronze bucklers. Swords, spears, axes and slings accompanied their bellicose accoutrement, as well as the stolen enemy banners. The allied troops were recognizable by the form of their helmets and their redoubtable weapons, carved like saws. The keepers retained the ferocious animals that were scratching the ground with their impatient claws; slaves were carrying booty on buckling stretchers, and a gold ingot occasionally rolled heavily under the hooves of the horses.

Chapter XIII

Thou, O King, art a King of Kings, for the King
of Heaven hath given thee a Kingdom,
power and strength and glory.
(*The Book of Daniel*.)[1]

Arynes had rejoined Nysista, who was weeping silently.

"Forgive me," she said. "I have attracted the anger of Darius to you, and perhaps he will punish you for disobeying him."

"Yes," said the officer, somberly, "it's my future that I've gambled. I ought not to have shown you to the sovereign, who has a rapid imagination and a feeble heart."

"I can kill myself," said the young woman. "That way, Darius won't desire me any more and you won't have to fear his vengeance."

"No, the harm is done; but forgetfulness will come, for it's only, in sum, a fleeting whim . . ."

"Oh," she sighed, "why did you command me to adorn myself and make myself seductive? Did I need to excite the covetousness of others, since I only desire your tenderness? Does the King not have all the women he covets?"

"Certainly, and the slaves of his gyneceum present the most varied specimens of feminine flora. He has only to raise his scepter to designate the chosen flower, and the one that he has nonchalantly plucked, in one nostalgic night, is glorious forever."

1 *Daniel* 2: 37.

"Why did he notice me, who am only a forest floret devoid of grace and beauty?"

"You're beautiful, Nysista, more beautiful than the superb roses of the royal flower-beds, and that's why the King desires your smiles and your caresses."

"If I'm beautiful, it's only because your kisses have enabled me to blossom; I owe you life, since you have given me amour."

The young woman took refuge in the officer's arms, imploring the supreme consolation of lovers.

He pressed her against him, kissing her long feverish eyelids, her delicate cheeks and her quivering lips; and he seemed to be tasting the delicious fruits of the Rig Veda, the fruits of amour and science, the fruits of glory and happiness reserved for the elect.

It was charming, that amour of two young and beautiful beings, two beings made to unite themselves in the eternal poetry of nature. When he quit her, however, she went in quest of her happiness shivering, along the roads of ambushes and sin.

Did Arynes truly love Nysista? Certainly, but not in the ideal sense that excites the ardent hope and the unique desire to dissolve heart and soul in a single tenderness. Self-absorbed and somewhat disdainful, the young chief was not capable of experiencing such a vivid emotion. Only his flesh was subservient to the warm suppleness of another flesh; his nerves quivered gloriously when the woman, a creature of beauty and amour, humiliated herself before him.

Perhaps he believed that he loved the young woman, and doubtless he offered all that he had that was good and tender in his nature. From warm lips he drank the wine of forgetfulness, intoxicating himself with kisses, falling asleep in the affectionate arms of the exquisite lover.

Is not vanity the essence and the condition of masculine happiness? Nysista was desired; a glorious monarch coveted his florid youth. Was that not enough to give the lover the pride of that conquest and the determination to keep her against all opposition?

Darius had shivered at the sight of Nysista, and by virtue of that royal desire, Nysista was adorned with an invincible attraction.

Witnesses to his passionate ardor, his companions in arms talked among themselves about demonic influences, bewitchment and black magic. A kind of hostility grew around the young woman, who paid no heed to it, entirely devoted to her dream. She imagined, candidly, that the philter she employed to make herself cherished came from her immense tenderness, and firmly believed that such an amorous expenditure ought to be worth a durable felicity.

Arynes, like all Persians, had the religion of death and that of nature. He sprinkled oil and soma on the primitive altar of old legends. His ancestors, having settled in the fertile valleys of Bactria, had established their pastoral and agrarian mores there, of which he still conserved the benevolent influence. Outside of the ravages accomplished by his deadly passion, he sometimes showed a credulous and enthusiastic soul, feared the power of the Wind and the Wave and Fire, and begged the elements to be favorable to him.

He believed that he had sufficient self-mastery to arrive, without any cerebral lesion, at the threshold of the great mystery of life and death. He rendered an exact account of the road traveled, and, having reached the rim of the abyss, measured its frightful depth. But the obsession of gambling had to triumph sooner or later over his firm resolutions and deliver him to all the demons of the earth. The antagonism of Good and Evil was sometimes affirmed with so much evidence that the entire universe seemed subject to the mysterious power of those two forces, and he trembled that he might not have the strength to follow the more beautiful into the victorious field of eternal light.

In that duel with the infinite he abandoned the golden sword that was the only thing that could have assured him victory. That sword was the amour that he sometimes allowed to fall into the dust in order to follow his culpable fantasy. Nysista suffered from that cruelly, for she had hoped to find in the man she cherished, above all, the recompense or her tenderness and abnegation. What irony of fate, then, had delivered that mystic flower of profound sentiment and idealism to the man least able to understand the poetry of long liaisons?

Arynes, a starveling of sensations, could not resist the vertigo of the kiss. He belonged to all those who loomed up in his path with the prestige of youth and seduction. The habits of gallantry and libertinage, contracted in the course of a life, delivered to all the disorder of camps, could not be dissipated in the breath of a pure affection. Fidelity was contrary to the instincts of his nature; it seemed to him to be an infraction of the law by virtue of which beings come together and quit one another for the renewal of desire and the embrace.

It was only when fortune ceased to smile upon him that he resumed a sort of superstitious and jealous tenderness.

"Protect me! Save me!" he said to his mistress then, "for I'm weak against temptations."

"Is my love not sufficient to give you the courage to struggle?"

"Your love imparts its exquisite tenderness to me, but it's necessary that it isn't always tender and submissive. Try, my Beloved, to make me forget evil passions—and for that, be as harsh and cruel as reason itself."

"I can't, alas."

"You see, at this moment, I'm drunk on your caresses, your kisses, I'm your lover and your slave, but an evil genius will soon awaken in my soul, and I shall listen to it in spite of myself, and follow it along the tenebrous path that leads to the gulf!"

"Are you so feeble against evil, then?" Nysista wept and hugged her beloved passionately to her bosom. "Alas," she said, "I'm only able to cherish you."

"But at least you'll always remain as tender and compassionate to me as you are at this moment, in spite of the temptations, the sorrows, the felonies and the treasons?"

"I will always be yours."

"Even if the King of Kings offered to make you his wife?"

She smiled confidently through her tears. "Even if the King of Kings offered me the empire of the world. Nothing exists for me but my amour."

"Oh, repeat that again, to give me the strength to remain on the narrow path."

"Nothing counts in my life except for your presence, I swear to you, my dear lover," she repeated, meekly.

But a frightful anguish gripped her heart.

PART TWO

Chapter I

Human passions are stronger than religions.
(Zoroaster.)

Like the Egyptians, the Aryans believed in the perpetual struggle of Virtue against Evil, of the Light against the Darkness and all the antagonistic spirits of Air, Fire and Water. Ahura-Mazda, their god, the Master and Creator of the universe, maintained the life of all beings, rendered the earth fertile and inspired in human beings their good resolutions. Everything that was noble, beautiful and generous came from him and returned to him in an eternal glory. He did not resemble Yahveh, the somber idol avid for agonies, tears and blood whom the Israelites worshiped, but the powerful and just God of the prophets.

"The God of the heavens," Cyrus declared, "has given me all the kingdoms of the earth, and has ordered me personally to build him a house in Jerusalem, which is in Judea."

Arynes believed in Ahura-Mazda, the God of the Persians, and that belief retained him on the rim of the gulf in the same way as his tenderness for Nysista.

For as long as the sums won gambling lasted he was an attentive and submissive lover, having no other care than his companion's happiness and the passionate worship of her beauty. Then, as the money gradually diminished, Ahura-Mazda, the Master of all light and all justice, was vanquished by Agra-Mainyu, the redoubtable Ahriman, who, in the Persian religion, represents the infernal god of darkness.

The officer's soul was no longer anything but a battlefield in which a terrible combat was being fought. Each of the powerful chiefs had innumerable equally active spirits of good and evil under his orders, and his fravashi, his living double, struggled in vain to restore equilibrium.

When he had spent his last daric, Arynes sold his mistress' jewels and returned to gambling. He tempted fortune with a new fever, risking himself nevertheless with a certain prudence, in the dread of losing his last resources too rapidly. Luck no longer smiled on him, the favorable spirit had withdrawn, and he thought that Zaroccha's double was taking a cruel vengeance for his disdain. Were all the crimes for which sorcerers and magicians were reproached real, then? But those who allowed themselves to be drawn into the accursed path were condemned to perish violently, to become the prey of vultures whose beaks would empty their eyelids eternally!

He would have liked, in his sacrilegious curiosity, to open the tombs of the ancient world, to make the dead speak, to see the monuments of the past again in all their splendor, to comprehend the enigmas of all sphinxes and penetrate into all sanctuaries.

Since he had received the visit of Zaroccha's specter, he had not dared to implore her influence again, but he thought that by employing the magic formula, luck would perhaps become favorable to him again.

Having rejoined his companions in pleasure, he mingled in their games, repeating the name of the witch three times, as she had advised him to do

"Zaroccha, Zaroccha, Zaroccha," he said, in a low voice, "guide me, assist me. Let my hand, conducted by you, bring forth the fateful point that will ensure my fortune."

Tremulously, he threw the dice—but a somber cloud passed before his eyes, and it seemed to him that ironic laughter responded to his appeal.

That day, Arynes lost his mistress' jewels, and all night, irritated and feverish, he refused her kisses.

"What have I done?" she moaned, putting her arms around him. "Why are you rejecting me when I'm offering you the habitual caress?"

"Leave me alone," he said, harshly.

"Ah!" she said, despairingly. "You've been gambling. You've lost."

"Yes, I lost."

"Does nothing remain, then?"

"I took some of your jewels. I daren't tell you . . ."

"Oh, take them all; they belong to you. What I have comes from you, and I regret not having more to offer you."

She opened a casket that she kept in a corner known only to her. "These are the most precious things I possess: my necklaces, my enamel and cornelian collars, my lapis-lazuli girdles, the rings of my arms and ankles, my clasps, my rings, my pins. Take it all, my Beloved."

"You're despoiling yourself for me!"

"Oh, I have no need of these vain adornments, if you find me beautiful with my beauty alone."

Joyfully, the officer pressed his mistress' lips beneath his own.

"For me, you will always be the most exquisite and the most precious!"

"Listen," she said, "these jewels are very valuable; can we not live on the product of their sale? I beg you, don't return to gambling. It's that accursed passion that will doom us."

Arynes promised everything she wished, in the intoxication of her kisses and caresses, but the next day he went to gamble her collars and clasps, entirely repossessed by the demon of lucre.

And he lost; he lost again, in spite of his rage and determination. His resources exhausted, he staked his wealth to come, all the darics and gold ingots that he might receive.

In the midst of noisy orgies, at the gaming table and in the arms of courtesans, he suddenly sensed the influence of an evil spirit.

A shadow palpitated around him, intoxicating him with its cold breath, insinuating its redoubtable frisson into his veins, and he fainted with superstitious dread. Although breathing, acting and suffering, he scarcely belonged to the earth. When he tried to speak to Nysista, a leaden seal nailed his lips shut and an icy hand placed itself on his heart. He remained devoid of strength under the indulgent and tender smile of his mistress.

Arynes always lost; the sum that he owed would have made a powerful monarch turn pale, and he feared never being able to acquit himself.

Every day he allowed himself to be drawn by his invincible passion, and while he gambled, the beating of his heart accelerated, a bloody veil descended over his eyes, and a bewildered rage contracted his lips.

Chapter II

The tree of knowledge gives death when
one absorbs its fruit, but those fruits
are the adornment of the world;
those golden apples are the stars of the earth.
(*The Kabbalistic Book of the Magi.*)[1]

Astrology, incantations, exorcisms and divination were beginning to mingle with the simple practices of the ancient Zoroastrian religion, and the desperate officer wanted to vanquish the evil influence that he attributed to Zaroccha. He went to find the most renowned Magus in Media, in order to ask him for his

---

1 *Livre Kabbalistque des Mages* [The Kabbalistic Book of the Magi] is a translation of a handbook of ceremonial magic compiled in 1801 by Francis Barrett, *The Magus; or, Celestial Intelligencer.* Much of it is derived from apocryphal supplements to *De Occulta Philosophia* (1531-33) by Cornelius Agrippa; Barrett's book became an important source for the French occultist Éliphas Lévi (Alphonse Louis Constant), one of the leading figures of the French Occult Revival.

assistance in his enterprises, and for his protection against spells and bewitchments.

The Magus, whose name was Sariasys, predicted the future in accordance with the disposition of tamarisk sprigs bound in a bundle, reeds or willow wands; he retained a sage moderation in everything, and consulted the stars for the greater good of mortal beings.

The celebrated seer, clad in a long white robe, maintained the sacred fire on a granite altar, and made libations with the juice of the haoma, which is nothing other than the soma of the Vedic Aryans.[1]

Behind him, the colossal figure of Assur loomed up in the center of a winged disk.

"What do you want of me, my son?" he asked, majestically.

"I'm possessed by malign spirits, and I've come to beg you to help in my deliverance."

"What have you done to attract the vengeance of perverse powers?"

"I listened to Zaroccha, the witch, after having murdered her. Her specter is influencing me; I've seen her in a terrifying hallucination."

"It's necessary to combat the fluid phantoms and their mysteries."

"That's why I'm here, and I beg you to assist me with your omnipotence."

"I'll try, my son, but the pact to which you've consented binds you beyond this world and human interventions."

"What!" cried the officer. "Am I, then, doomed to eternal malediction?"

---

1 Haoma, which features as an aphrodisiac later in the present story and as a brainwashing hallucinogen in *Le Vierge d'Israel*, is a sacred plant named repeatedly in Zoroastrian texts. It is nowadays identified, but not uncontroversialy, with a plant of the genus *Ephedra*, although that does not grow in India and cannot be the source of the Sanskrit soma; nor does it produce any hallucinogenic substance in significant quantity.

"I don't know; that will depend on you. I can see from the lines of your face that you're weak and passionate. Hallucinations and fits of vertigo still trouble your thoughts."

"Have I truly seen the phantom of the witch? Can the dead return, then?"

"Certainly," said Sariasys, "and these are the oracles of Zoroaster: Nature informs us by induction that incorporeal demons exist; but there are mysteries therein that it is necessary to bury in the most impenetrable coverts of thought . . . Fire always agitates and, bounding into the atmosphere, can take on a configuration similar to that of bodies. Fire is full of images and echoes; it radiates, it speaks, it unfurls; it is a fulgurant charger passing by, when the stars have ceased shining and the lamp of the moon is veiled. The earth trembles, and everything is surrounded by lightning; terrestrial dogs emerge from the limbo where matter ends, and show ever-deceptive appearances to mortal gaze . . . But when, after all the phantoms, you see the incorporeal fire shining, the sacred fire whose arrows traverse all the depths of the world simultaneously, listen to what it says to you."

"Alas," sighed Arynes, "those oracles are beautiful, but I shall not see that celestial light."

"Why not?"

"Because I have killed, and my soul is full of darkness."

"When your will is disengaged from the senses and affirmed by a series of proofs, you will know the magical initiation. There is no solid body that cannot be pulverized immediately, vanish into smoke and become invisible if the equilibrium of its molecules suddenly ceases. There is no fluid substance that cannot acquire the hardness of diamond in the equilibrium of its constituent molecules. Your fravashi, your double, is a magnet that attracts or repels hallucinations under the pressure of some emotion. The chimeras of your mind take on substance and seem to acquire a soul; they appear radiant or terrible to you, in accordance with the form of your desires or your fears."

"So I was dreaming?"

"Perhaps. Fluidic maladies have their fatal crises, and all abnormal tensions of nerves end in contrary phenomena, following the laws of equilibrium. Exaggerated amour changes into hatred, and exalted aversion into tenderness. That reaction happens suddenly with the violence of lightning in a stormy sky."

"My soul isn't free, then?"

"Not from the moment it abandons itself to the vertigo of passion."

"I'm doomed forever, then?"

"Perhaps," said the Magus again, pensively. "But other passions exist than hatred and amour. The passion for gambling is equally tyrannical, and can make those who possess it fall into the gulfs of debauchery and crime."

"Indicate the means of recovering what I've lost, and I won't gamble again!"

"You'll gamble anyway, for gambling alone exalts your imagination and procures you the sensations you desire. Amour can occupy you momentarily, but it will never fill the void of your thought completely."

"I only gamble to recover my losses."

"You believe that, but in reality, it's the intoxication of the doubt that charms you; it's the alternation of fear and hope; it's the pride of triumph by unpunished murder. You've heard the fatal bell, you've entered into the macabre round, and you'll follow the whirl until the end. The oracle tells me that I would try in vain to initiate you into the science of good."

Arynes prostrated himself before the Magus.

"Enable me to regain what I've lost," he implored again. "I'm at your feet, as you see, plunged in the dust. I'm begging and weeping!"

"I don't want to struggle against the malevolent powers to which you're submissive; I'd be defeated. Listen to this story and profit from it. The scene is set in Bactria; it's a sumptuous wedding followed by maidens crowned with flowers carrying the nuptial cake and singing the praises of the advent of amour. Nynos, the bride, is very young, with innocent eyes, pure lips charmingly designed, and long perfumed hair. She is marrying Cetias, the disciple of a famous Magus who is still venerated.

"However, the Master has promised to come to his pupil's wedding, and Nynos is troubled every time his name is pronounced. Instantly, she begs Cetias to depart, to flee with her to some solitude where no one will come to disturb her happiness. The groom resists, not wanting to go away without having seen his illustrious friend and received his affectionate good wishes.

"The day goes by, and the announced Magus has not yet come to the dwelling of the newlyweds. Nynos is breathing more easily and Cetias is desolate. But the moment of the nuptial bed has arrived; the young woman, full of fear, runs away screaming . . .

"Before the calm and smiling Magus, who finally appears, the bewitchments and spells collapse; the veritable science of good and evil triumphs over the spirit of darkness. There is a profound silence, so redoubtable is the moment. Nynos is found, but nothing can any longer be seen but a sordid old woman, the witch Creops, an excavator of cadavers and eater of little children. The disabused Cetias thanks his master; he is saved."

"Your story is interesting," said Arynes, chagrined, "but I don't understand."

"You'll understand later, my son. Go now, for I repeat, I can't change your destiny. In any case, you've killed and you must be punished, since your eyes are closed to the celestial light. You will, therefore, have difficulty in following the laws of this world."

Chapter III

Forces that are produced without being
balanced perish in the void. Thus have
perished the kings of the ancient world,
and the princes of the giants. They fell
like rootless trees, and their place
can no longer be found.
(*The Book of Zohar.*)[1]

Mortally sad, Arynes returned to Nysista, who was praying outside the Magus' dwelling.

"Go," he said, "no longer think about the one who has only been able to make you suffer. You have paid him generously for the love he has given you and you have a right to a better future . . ."

"I shall never leave you. Where would you find a companion as faithful, as devoted, as loving? I want to watch over your existence, share your chagrins."

"It has required your touching blindness to dress me in all the qualities that I am lacking. I am a strange, anomalous, proud and wicked being. On looking closely, hatred would doubtless be found at the bottom of all my actions—hatred and scorn for those who remain on the right path . . ."

Nysista smiled indulgently.

"I love you thus; what does the rest matter."

"Go find the King of Kings, the man who possesses the metropolises of Assyria, Babylonia and Nineveh, the worthy successor of the ever glorious Cyrus. With him you will see rising in the night the colossi of granite fallen from their pedestals, for he wants to rebuild the temple of the gods, with its winged bulls and its golden lions with glittering eyes. The lamps of the idols

---

1 The Zohar is the foundation-text of the Kabbalah, which originated in the thirteenth century (although it claims, naturally, to be much older).

will be lit for you; you will know all the caresses of Mylitta, the goddess of amour, and you will penetrate into the dwelling of the monarch, the god of the earth . . .

"Go, Nysista, the priests protect the palace, and the servants of Darius will welcome you as a queen. They will prostrate themselves before you, ready to strike death into anyone who dares to raise his eyes to your splendor. May the shadows of Belus and Semiramis be kind to you! You will be fêted as the daughter of the gods, the princess of the earth and the heavens."

"Arynes," the young woman repeated, "I want to stay with you."

She was walking beside the officer, brushing him with her elbow, sometimes seeking to hang on to his arm, but he did not seem to be paying any attention to her; his somber gaze reflected the trouble of his soul.

For two days he isolated himself in the country, and Nysista, who had sacrificed her jewels, her perfumes and her precious fabrics to her lover's grim passion, waited in vain for his return.

Sariasys, who was passing with other Magi to go to Mount Zagros, took pity on her.

"I know," he said, "that you love Arynes, the son of the Satrap of Cappadocia, the illustrious Ariaramanes, who precipitated the fall of Gaumata."

"Yes, I'm devoted to him body and soul."

"But your lover has abandoned you and you're languishing miserably."

"Alas."

"Ariaramnes has palaces, paradises of flowers, a court, bodyguards and harems. He divides taxes as he pleases, administers justice and possesses the right of life and death. Why is he doing nothing for his son?"

"Because his son has offended him gravely. In any case, Arynes has just lost one fortune. Nothing would be able to satisfy him."

"He requires a new mission. His inaction is weighing upon him, and is harmful."

"I don't want him to go away!"

"Listen, child, for his salvation as well as yours, it's necessary that your friend employ himself in the noble profession of arms. I know that Darius is going to launch an attack on the coast of Heptahendu.[1] A fleet constructed at Peuleka is to descend the Indus to its mouth in order to subdue in passing the tribes on both banks. While Darius is still among you, ask him for a command for Arynes. You can accompany your lover, if that is your desire, and he'll forget his fatal passion."

"Oh," she said, gratefully, "you've saved me, Sariasys! I'll follow your advice."

"Go, then, and find the King of Kings today. He will be sensible to your beauty, your youth and your amour."

The Magus touched Nysista's forehead with his willow wand, and then drew away along the dusty road.

Chapter IV

> You will be prey to the fire you light, you
> will be devoured by the lions you unleash.
> (*The Book of the Magi.*)

Darius was resting in his tent on a kind of throne sustained by chimerical animals. Slaves were pouring essences of penetrating perfumes over his hair, massaging him with aromatic oils and fanning him gently with ostrich-plume flabella.

Around him there were very young women, almost naked, whose loins were surrounded by thin metal circles. Some were holding onyx cups filled with Shiraz wine; others were presenting the monarch with sorbets of snowy fruits, or floral pastes on

---

1 Heptahendu was a Persian name for part of the Punjab.

jade, amber and alabaster plates. Others were holding amphorae of clay, glass or metal, filled with date, palm or grape liqueurs, rosé wines from Phoenicia and Greece, and white wine from Lake Mareotis with a bouquet of vanilla and heliotrope.

Behind the glittering fabrics falling to the floor of the immense tent, musiciennes were plucking the strings of harps and lyres artfully, while others were blowing into double reed flutes.

Darius was nonchalantly inhaling the perfume of grains of nard and cinnamon, which servants were throwing on to the embers of amschirs. His thoughts were elsewhere, pursuing a dream of war or amour, fluttering lightly over people and things without deigning to alight.

The King of Kings gazed distractedly at the charming creatures kneeling before him, begging for a word or a smile. All his slaves would have martyrized themselves for one voluptuous night, and they all possessed the charm that awakens desire.

Darius, a lover of luxury and laxity between his warrior conquests, had made magical science one of his prostitutes. The great men of the kingdom sent their daughters to him, and he was able to choose his august spouses from among the most beautiful. But for three legitimate wives he kept a thousand slaves of amour who attempted incessantly to satisfy his fantasies.

He remained indifferent to the songs and dances, however, and the lascivious poses of the superb creatures who were agitating for him. It was in vain that the networks of pearls quivered over round throats, that gauze scarves parted over agile legs like crystalline waves over the lustrous bodies of naiads. He did not see all those exquisite forms; he did not hear the golden rings and scintillating necklaces.

Little girls crouched before him struck the onager-skin of tambours, or clicked bronze castanets with the heads of lions, striking timbals while uttering shrill cries of a sort in order to beat time.

But there was a movement of recoil among the dancers. A woman more beautiful than all of those agitating around the

King had just entered and was fraying a passage toward the throne.

At the sight of her, Darius shivered and his eyes gleamed.

"Ah!" he said. "I was expecting you."

She prostrated herself before him, picking up a little dust, which she spread over her forehead.

"I am your slave, O powerful Master, King of Kings!"

"Has Arynes sent you?"

"No," she said, "I've come of my own accord."

Darius' expression darkened. "Why have you come?"

"To ask you for a favor."

"Oh," he sighed. "I thought you were finally rendering to my wishes."

She stood there, confused, and then prostrated herself again.

"I love Arynes."

"So it's on his behalf that you've come to solicit me?"

"Alas," she groaned. "You can save him from a great peril."

Darius could hardly contain his anger. "I've done too much already for that officer, who doesn't merit my indulgence."

"Permit him to redeem his errors, to distinguish himself by means of a splendid action. Give him a command in your new expedition of war. Already, O King of Kings, you have gained Media, Persia and Babylonia; you are thinking of new victories, and you need leaders to attack Heptahendu. Do you not have the desire to conquer extensive territories in order to form other Satrapies there? Arynes, the son of the favorite warrior, is entirely indicated for that choice mission . . ."

"You want him to go away?"

"Yes," said Nysista, lowering her gaze. "It's necessary that he doesn't remain inactive." She added forcefully, however: "But I shall go with him; I shall be his companion and his slave. Chiefs can take their wives with them."

"He's a gambler—do you fear that he'll commit some culpable action if he remains in camp?"

Trembling, the young woman made no reply.

"Listen," said Darius. "Your trouble touches me, and I'd like to do something for you, but I can't confide the command of my troops to an officer as inexperienced as Arynes. The conquest of Lydia, the submission of its cities and the Greek islands has given me subjects dangerously fashioned for war. The Greek chiefs are curious, bold, avid for gain, and hardened to the fatigues of voyages, and I know that they're plotting against me. I need devoted friends to resist them and protect me, if necessary."

"But Arynes is a faithful subject."

Darius smiled, a trifle sadly.

"Oh, my reign has been strewn with reefs, and I've often had to avenge myself cruelly, in spite of my horror of carnage. At the slightest disobedience it's necessary for me to be severe. I prefer not to give the son of Ariaramnes an opportunity to infringe my orders. Then again, has he not refused me your possession? He knew that I coveted you; why has he resisted the will of his Master?"

Sensing that her cause was lost, Nysista knelt down one last time in order to take her leave, but the King, descending from his throne, took her hand passionately.

"That which Arynes refuses me, you can grant me," he said, fixing his glittering gaze on the young woman.

"Oh," she sighed, "I'm not worthy to take a place among your slaves; the humblest of them is more beautiful than me."

"No, it's you that I desire. Stay here, Nysista, and I'll grant Arynes the command you're soliciting for him."

He pressed her against his vast bosom, and she felt the coarse ringlets of his beard against her forehead.

Women had approached, presenting golden cups full of haoma, the intoxicating liquor that delivered the grimmest of virgins to the King's desires. Darius offered the divine beverage to the young woman's lips, and tilting her head back gently, he obliged her to drink in spite of her resistance.

She saw him before her, proud and powerful in his scarlet robe. He had placed his scepter surmounted with the royal globe on the steps of the throne, and he exhorted her by means of confused and passionate words to obey him.

A few priestesses had drunk the haoma, and already, their veins were ablaze, their faint voices united in a voluptuous hymn to Mitra, the goddess of amour.

Their flexible bodies swayed in cadence; their arms opened to grasp the chimeras of dreams; their lips were quivering with intoxication, and their large eyes were veiled by feverish eyelids. The priestesses were now arching their backs and lowering their heads, flexing like willow branches, almost touching the crimson carpet with the napes of their necks. A few were pursuing one another with daggers, sometimes inflicting broad wounds from which blood escaped in tumultuous waves.

Darius, who had drunk the sacred haoma, like the women of his harem, attempted to tip his victim over, but she struggled desperately, in a residue of reason, a revolt of all her quivering flesh.

Three favorite priestesses, Sinyse, Raya and Nonoche, drew nearer in order to hold Nysista, who, no longer uttering anything but a feeble groan, closed her eyes in an agony of her entire being.

"Be mine, Nysista," said Darius. "I'll give you lattices of lapis-lazuli and pearls, fabrics embroidered with precious stones, and as many golden rings as your arms and ankles can support! I'll give you a palace, servants and slaves; you'll be the foremost woman in my harem, and the most cherished. You'll command my people, and myself, and you'll never regret having realized your King's desire!"

But Nysista, with a panic-stricken effort, succeeded in freeing herself, and breaking through the women who surrounded Darius, she ran to her lover's tent.

Chapter V

It is necessary to tame the fantastic dogs that bark
in dreams; it is necessary to hear the light sing.
(Zoroaster)

Since Tomyris, the Queen of the Massagetes, had plunged the
head of Cyrus—the first conqueror—into a bowl of human
blood, all the Persian sovereigns had died tragically. Cambyses,
the eldest son of Cyrus, murdered his brother Bardiya and
succumbed more covered with murder than glory. Herodotus
recounts that the prince in question, wanting to humiliate the
vanquished, sacrificed the ox Apis and tortured the high priests
of Memphis. Penetrating thereafter into the temple of Ptah, he
violated the ancient tombs there in order to profane the mum-
mies. He killed his own sister, whom he had married clandes-
tinely, and buried twelve of the principal Persian leaders alive.
Shortly thereafter he ordered the execution of Croesus, and was
afflicted by madness as a punishment for his sacrileges. He was
found dead, pierced by a dagger thrust, in the very place where
he had struck the ox Apis.[1]

Gaumata, his successor, who passed himself off as Cambyses'
brother, reigned for six months without anyone discovering the
imposture or seeing in him anything but the legitimate heir to the
throne; but the women of Gaumata's harem, who had belonged
to his predecessor, recounted that he had cropped ears, and it
was concluded that the legitimate heir to the throne would not

---

1 The death of Cambyses remains mysterious. According to Herodotus, who
greatly embroidered the account given in the Behistun inscription by Darius,
who was present when Cambyses died, the latter died in Ecbatana after acci-
dentally stabbing himself in the thigh while mounting a horse. Skeptics, not
unnaturally, wondered whether Darius might have murdered him, as well
as making up the story about the impostor Gaumata in order to excuse his
murder of Bardiya, with which he then charged Cambyses. The story about
Cyrus being killed by Tomyris is, however, entirely due to Herodotus, and
extremely dubious.

have been subjected to that mutilation. It was then that Darius, son of Vistapa, the Satrap of Hyrkania, who belonged to the royal house and could claim the succession of Cambyses, came to an understanding with six resolute chiefs of Persia and killed Gaumata in his palace in Media.

When the crime was accomplished, the seven administrators of justice decided to choose as sovereign the one among them whose horse whinnied first after sunrise. Either by subterfuge or fortunate chance, it was Darius' stallion that first made itself heard, procuring supreme power for its master.

Darius was, in any case, the man best endowed to unite and maintain the gigantic estates conquered by Cyrus and Cambyses. He made war like his predecessors hoping, after Egypt, to subjugate India and take possession of the Punjab. He also thought of undertaking the Median wars that were to be so fatal for his son Xerxes.

Asia was already growing old, for the domination of the Persians had followed the bad habits of the ancient kings of Babylon and Nineveh. The conquerors forgot themselves in all the pleasures and refinements of a decadent civilization. Darius' court resembled that of the proud and sensual tyrants he had vanquished, although that monarch was a remarkable organizer; with him the submissive peoples conserved their customs, their mores and their laws, but gave their conquerors their defects and their voluptuous laxity.

From the Indus to the Nile and from the Black Sea to the Persian Gulf, a hundred various peoples were established, speaking twenty different languages. Darius divided them into nineteen Satrapies and remained the sole leader of those numerous States, which earned him the title of King of Kings, or the Great King.

Numerous tributes in kind were added to the regular taxes, and the immense revenues of the Persian sovereign were paid in ingots and darics. Media sent horses, mules and sheep, Egypt the produce of the fishing in Lake Moeris, Babylon slaves and particularly esteemed young eunuchs. The Persians offered their monarch weapons, precious fabrics, chargers, fruits, grain, expensive furniture, works of art and jewels.

In his distant expeditions, Darius took the most beautiful women of his harem with him, and was followed by a numerous court, in order that he did not regret the delights of Susa and Persepolis.

At any rate, Darius was a shrewd leader and a redoubtable warrior. Marching from victory to victory since his accession, he had lifted the siege of Babylon, launched an army into Armenia and another into Media, put down rebels and punished conspirators. Thirty thousand Babylonians had been impaled, the walls were razed to ground level, and the city had been repopulated by foreign colonists. The noses, tongues and ears of the rebels were cut off, their eyes put out and they were chained up at the doors of palaces. Then, when the people had been sufficiently sated by the specter of their frightful agony, they had been impaled in long funereal lines, and the vultures had completed the work of destruction.

Darius was then at the apogee of his glory; all the surrounding countries were submissive, and he was thinking of ensuring the possession of distant lands, marvelous valleys and forests of which mysterious envoys had given him a description.

But if he was thinking about war, he was also thinking about amour, and he did not admit that a coveted prey might be stolen from him. Not wanting to punish the son of Ariaramnes, his faithful Satrap, he therefore headed for the camp for a second time, in order to offer Arynes the command of the troops that he intended to send into the Punjab.

But Arynes and Nysista had disappeared. Only Safou, the black cat, crouching in a corner of the tent, stood up at the approach of the King, his phosphorescent fur bristling, mewling hoarsely.

Chapter VI

It is in tombs that you will find
the secret of the gods.
(Occultism of the *Zohar.*)

Zaroccha had been buried in the middle of the desolate southern steppes, in a place consecrated to the accursed sepulchers from which the Persians turned away in fear, for it was not permitted to them to conserve their dead. There was the bitter sadness of a land of silence, where only birds of prey opened their sober wings. Herbs the color of ash and rust grew between the ruins of tumulary stones, and everywhere, the foot stirred the bones of the executed in the greasy dust.

After a depression in the terrain, similar to a large natural amphitheater, the walls of a deserted temple loomed up in a sinister fashion, and within that enclosure, a spring had emerged whose waters flowed slowly in trickles of crystal purity. It was the sole smile of that desolate location.

However, a traveler was advancing carefully between the sepulchers, sometimes bending down to scan the mysterious inscriptions. Terror made him shiver, a poignant sensation of the immense shadow that surrounded him. A hot wind lifted the dust of the tombs and groaned faintly against the old stones. The visitor, who was none other than Arynes, the son of the Satrap, tottered then, and stopped, indecisively. It seemed to him that a band of specters was running, sniggering, from the blackest part of the solitude. White forms passed through the ruins; a heavy mist rose from the ground; the stones were strewn with golden spangles.

Arynes shook off his fear, though, and set off again at an ill-assured pace. Beads of sweat were forming on his brow, for he was thinking about the culpable action that he was about to commit, and preparing to struggle against the spirits of the dark. They were there, coming and going, dancing before him, calling to him in shrill voices, quickly extinguished in bursts of laughter.

The rocks seemed immeasurably large; a few dead trees, having served for ancient tortures, raised the skeletal arms, which creaked. Green lights, like fantastic fireflies, rose up on all sides, and there was now a noise of bones and chains in the distance. The round of swirling fire-follets rose higher, voices wept more loudly, and the ghouls of the accursed sands, damned souls with fiery hair, the hostesses of profound caverns, were doubtless about to defend their domain.

Now the rocks were becoming animated, the evil spirits changing into stones in order to crush the imprudent under their heavy mass. But the officer continued on his way in spite of the grimacing faces that drew nearer and the terrible wind that made him stagger.

Suddenly, a stone reared up under his feet and he fell into a ditch, while laughter burst out around him more ironically. The capricious little lights agitated hectically; everywhere, enormous birds of prey flapped their wings heavily. The sky seemed to descend with them; it was a black and tumultuous vault that was about to stifle the cries, the sobs and the last gasp of the profaner.

Zaroccha reposed in a sort of sepulchral chamber in the Egyptian fashion. Her mummified body seemed to be guarding the magical casket that Nysista had piously placed beside her. It was the one that, in the witch's wretched hut, had excited the covetousness of the neighbors: the humble box filled with precious gems and rare jewels. Rubies and emeralds slipped through the ill-closed lid; a necklace hung over the black wood like a fiery serpent . . .

That was the first thing the officer saw when he had succeeded in violating the triple subterranean door of the hypogeum. With a trembling hand he raised a torch above those riches, from which his eyes nevertheless turned away, in fear of a terrifying and maleficent intervention.

It seemed to him that the mummy, swathed in its bandages, was about to emerge from its sarcophagus in order to oppose his criminal larceny. The lid did, in fact, move slowly aside, and the coffin appeared, covered with gilt and hieroglyphic characters. Drawn by an invincible force, Arynes could no longer take his eyes off the wrappings, exactly molded to the body of the dead woman.

Zaroccha, therefore, really was in her tomb, and was doubtless about to defend jealously the treasure sleeping beside her. Beneath the gilded mask, the features of the witch seemed to grimace; a rictus twisted her painted lips.

Indecisively, Arynes remained standing next to the riches that lay on the ground, of which it would have been so easy for him to take possession.

Who, then, would perceive his larceny? Those jewels, useless to the dead woman would give him back the wealth that he had lost. He would surround Nysista with luxury and tenderness; nothing would be too beautiful to adorn her adorable grace, and nothing henceforth would any longer trouble the reconquered felicity!

The officer also promised himself not to gamble again, to conserve his treasure jealously for a future of tranquil joy and security.

While the young woman was interceding on his behalf with Darius, he had been fleeing toward the southern solitudes in order to rob Zaroccha's tomb. For a long time, already, he had been thinking about the riches sleeping in that mortuary place, their presence unknown to anyone except his lover. These stones and jewels belonged to him, in a way, since he had taken Nysista in, and had now decided to keep her with him forever.

However, new terrors paralyzed him next to the magical box. Fever caused his hands to tremble; he insulted the phantoms that he could not vanquish, the spectral guardians of a futile gold that had become animated for him, and had taken on a warm and luminous life, a beneficent and pleasant life.

The mocking spirits swarmed and stirred in the darkness, in spite of Arynes' sighs, as he murmured ancient and sovereign magical formulae with his eyes closed.

He sensed the baleful influence like a dog that barks at the moon; he recalled the chilling legends that had made him shiver in his childhood when his nurse spoke in a low voice and the nocturnal wind whistled through the reeds.

And then, had not Zaroccha come to visit him in order to solicit his amour . . . ?

But no, Zaroccha was dead, and the dead did not return. He had doubtless been dreaming, and his excited imagination had conserved the terrifying imprint of the dream.

Certainly, he was wrong to be frightened; only his nerves and his heart, subject to the black superstitions of his race, were culpable of fear and deception. How many times, over the years, had his ancestors shivered like this without reason at the telling of infantile legends of gnomes and vampires?

He opened his eyes again, and fixed a fearful gaze on the tragic mask of the sorceress.

It seemed to him that the cardboard lips had parted, and that a cold breath was emerging therefrom that made the pale flame of the torch vacillate.

A profound horror paralyzed the officer, who dared not bend down to pick up the casket and flee with his treasure without looking back. The nightmare hovered over his weakening intelligence; he trembled with impotent rage.

Perhaps, he said to himself, *Zaroccha was buried alive. Am I certain that I stabbed her? Was that not another error of my morbid imagination? People buried prematurely can be conserved for a long time in a state of somnambulism. Their doubles are still chained to the earth by an invisible bond, and they must, if they are avid or criminal, suck the quintessence of the blood of those who invoke them. Is not Zaroccha, a grim vampire, impeding my movements, paralyzing me frightfully, in order to transmit my life into her rigid body?*

He recalled what was said about the exhumation of ghouls who sweated blood, bearing in their breast a robust and vivacious heart, in the fashion of vegetables.

He had already drawn his sword in order to strike the monster, but an occult force had paralyzed his arm and the weapon had fallen on to the magical coffer with a resounding noise.

The wind outside was moaning more sadly; it was a large and profound lamentation, punctuated by the shrill laughter of gnomes and goblins.

Arynes, however, had put his cloak over the mummy's head, in order not to see the grimacing mask any longer, and not to feel the icy breath emerging from the painted lips. Kneeling beside the treasure, he got ready to pick up the casket, in spite of the furious beating of his heart, which he could hear distinctly above the sobbing of the wind and the laughter of the spirits. He had already tipped back the lid in order to contemplate the rare jewels, more scintillating than the radiance of the sun: an entire furnace of stones with multicolored flames.

Ecstatic, he drew a new strength from that sight, a hope of immediate deliverance, of salvation. All the vain fears and remorse were forgotten; a triumphant life was about to commence for him.

Arynes tried to lift the heavy box, but a cold hand emerged from Zaroccha's coffin and placed itself on the sacred deposit like a monstrous and terrible black spider.

Arynes uttered a scream, dropped the torch, which went out, and ran out of the tomb.

Chapter VII

The golden sword of Mithra must
immolate the sacred bull
(Zoroaster.)

All night long the officer wandered among the ruins, under the ironic laughter of malign spirits. Then, finally, he went to sleep, exhausted and worn out by terror and fatigue.

He dreamed that a great shadow weighed upon him, like the web of a spider upon an imprudent fly. The mesh tightened incessantly, imprisoning him more narrowly, more cruelly . . .

It was like a furry shroud that stifled the heartbeat in his breast, closed his eyelids, formed a gag in his mouth, entered into his ears and nostrils. And the breath of a filthy, viscous creature passed through the mesh, an iron hand clutched his heart, with increasing force, bruising his flesh invincibly.

A soft female voice extracted him from the frightful nightmare, and he saw Nysista sitting nearby on a fragment of rock, looking at him sadly.

"I've been searching for you all night," she said. "What have you come to do here?"

He no longer knew; he interrogated his memories, his head heavy and his thoughts incoherent.

Insistently, she went on: "I've found you next to Zaroccha's tomb. Oh, what mortal solitude . . . !"

There was a glimmer of light in the officer's mind; he remembered that he had come to this sinister place in order to steal the witch's treasure, and he tried to win Nysista over, to associate her with his project.

"Yes," he said. "I've come to recover the casket."

She stood up, shivering.

"Oh! You wouldn't dare."

He seized her wrist forcefully.

"Who would know? I need that treasure, for we no longer have anything."

"But those jewels don't belong to us."

"They don't belong to anyone, and you have the right to take possession of them."

"No, no," she moaned.

"Perhaps you're the daughter of the woman who lies here?"

"You know very well that I'm not."

"I don't know anything, and I don't want to know. Do as I order you. Go fetch Zaroccha's gems; the doors of her tomb are open."

The young woman threw herself at her lover's feet. "Don't ask that culpable action of me! In any case, I wouldn't have the necessary energy; I'd die before being able to obey you. My only Master, my beloved Spouse, don't be crueler than your worst enemies, don't order me to do what is beyond my strength!"

She hugged his knees, looking up at him, her eyes streaming with tears—and he felt his heart softening before that dolor. For a moment, love chased away the culpable thoughts and the bitter folly of lucre. He let his sadness wander through the fluttering world of tender memories; he no longer saw anything but the flavorsome lips of his mistress, no longer scented anything but the subtle perfume of her warm hair. Her breasts swelled softly beneath his feverish fingers; her beauty was revealed, pervading the world, in that desolate landscape, which she endowed with her passionate and affectionate soul. Her eyes were as radiant as stars in a somber sky, and everything was miraculously illuminated by them.

He rediscovered the sensual joy, the invincible voluptuousness, of first kisses. The cup of divine pleasures filled again, and he yearned to put his lips to it.

He drew the young woman to his heart, while the birds of prey circled more narrowly above their heads. But he no longer saw them, and he no longer heard their savage clamors in the fervent delirium of his entire being.

Nysista abandoned herself in his arms, offering her moist eyes, her ardent lips, and all the intoxicating flowers of her triumphant youth.

They were embracing one another on a tomb, in the dust of the dead, but what did the funereal memory of human tortures, crimes and despairs matter to them? They only existed for their tenderness and the divine work of resurrection.

Chapter VIII

> The astral light is emanated by the sun;
> the earth is its nurse.
> (*The Emerald Tablet.*)[1]

"Let's go," said Nysista, returning to herself after the adorable intoxication of her amour. "Perhaps Darius will have given you the command for which you're ambitious. I begged him for it so ardently!"

"Ah!" said Arynes, joyfully. "That would, indeed, be salvation."

"Our great King is good and just. He would like to save you, for others and yourself . . . Let's flee, flee to the verdant forests across the radiant plains, to the fresh and beneficent waters!"

She was animated by a pious ardor, wanting to remove him from the perverse influences that had already stolen him from her heart.

---

1 *La Table d'émeraude* [The Emerald Tablet] is a brief Arabic document translated into Latin in the twelfth century, whose original probably dates from the eighth century but which claims to be the work of Hermes Trismegistus. It was known to most Medieval alchemists. French translations dating from the seventeenth century were inherited by the scholars of the Occult Revival.

"Your grace is resplendent, Nysista," he said, admiring her as in the early days. "Your soul, too, is a little light that guides and warms me. I am better for it, and the specters of evil are going back into darkness. But I would have liked to reopen Zaroccha's coffin, for I believe that she's only in lethargy."

"Madness!" said Nysista, trembling involuntarily. "I adorned her for the sojourn from which no one returns."

"Are you certain of that? It would have been better to burn her body or give it to the birds of prey, in accordance with our custom."

The anxious young woman remained silent.

"Do you remember the story of the Magus who was left in foreign ground? When he was found again, twenty years after his death, the heart remained intact in his breast, full of fresh red blood, still beating for the holy verity; and that heart remained thus for long years in the desiccated cadaver."

"Let's not think about such things; they're too mysterious for us and they frighten us; let's live for our kisses, for the odorant woods and the flowers that snow overhead. I'll dangle pink and white clusters from my wrists, my bare arms will make you a necklace of amour that will protect you against enchantments!"

"Yes," he said, "let's go back. This place is sinister."

"Let's go back among humans, for this is the abode of the dead. Come and savor the sorcery of caresses, the ecstasy of the voluptuous secrets that you have taught me, and be the prisoner of my embrace forever!"

He enjoyed the images stimulated by the ardent speech of his mistress; he saw the splendid apotheosis rising, the triumph of amour. He held Nysista, tenderly embraced, in the burning sands, in the ashes of the dead, which seemed softer to him than the pollen of a flower. He had forgotten the fatigues, the long irritations of the struggle, the defeats and the miseries . . .

Imprudently, however, she recalled him to reality.

"Darius," she said, "will be helpful to us."

Arynes resumed his chagrined expression. "No," he sighed, "Darius will do nothing for me, because he desires you and I refused you."

"Let's still hope—hope is so sweet, my Beloved!"

For a long time they walked along the dusty roads; then, by night, they reached the camp again and slipped into their tent, in the midst of soldiers slumbering heavily.

Nothing had changed in that warm shelter, padded with silky fabrics and furs.

Safou, arching his back, came to greet them with a hoarse and affectionate purr. Then, leaping on to the young woman's shoulder with a single bound, he rubbed his black muzzle against the cool and satiny cheek. The feline closed his green eyes, retracted his claws, and magical sparks crackled over his somber pelt.

The night was generous to the lovers, who forgot everything that was not the adorable poem of faith and confidence. Then, when the hour of habitual labors arrived, Arynes thought about his vain terrors, his failed expedition, and his precarious life in the midst of the envied luxury of his chiefs. Why had he hesitated to take Zaroccha's jewels?

His troubled imagination had made him believe that he saw the dead woman's gesture in defense of her property, but in reality, only the mysterious power of his fear had acted. Was he not strong enough to combat the chimeras of dream, and even the real enemies of his happiness?

A morbid intoxication persisted in him. His intelligence, as debilitated as his will, collapsed with lassitude; and again, he told himself that the phantoms surged forth in the nightmares of feverish night exist and live in human being, incessantly present although almost always invisible. If they are magnified and transformed, when our refined senses permit us to distinguish them, it is because our fear envelops them, involuntarily, repels them and flees them. But the specters return more menacing than before, for they attack, above all, those who fear them, or those of whom they are afraid themselves.

Ghosts have an aerial substance formed by the vapor of the human body. They seek spilled blood and nourish themselves on the smoke of sacrifices. They are the phantoms of impure nightmares known as incubi and succubi; but, the cohesion of their fantastic bodies being very weak, they fear air, fire and water. Those ghosts, attracted to vital warmth, rapidly exhaust those they persecute. Vampires only release their prey when they have dried up the very wellsprings of thought and life.

Was it not, therefore, an emanation of his own anguish that the officer had seen in Zaroccha's hypogeum, or simply a lie of his morbid imagination, overexcited by shadows and mystery?

No, he said to himself, *witches exist, and everyone knows that they practice horrible elaborations, devote themselves to abominable rites. Jealous of amour and of life, they return by night to devour with frightful caresses the victim they have chosen. They steal children and sacrifice virgins, whose bodies they keep innocent. They are the lamias, the stryges and the empusas that poison existence. They are the perverse women who degrade their lovers; they are the grim poisoners who make use of nature herself in their crimes. They are all those whose souls are weakened by lust and who only know how to inspire shameful passions. When one is possessed by the monsters of madness and vice it is necessary to subjugate them, to vanquish them by dread and scorn.*

After his fine virtuous resolutions, however, Arynes suddenly felt drawn toward the abyss of redoubtable passions. He appealed to Zaroccha, who would doubtless give him wealth and glory. For a little gold he was ready to sell himself to the evil genius, to deliver himself body and soul to monstrous caresses.

"What are you thinking about?" Nysista asked.

And he revolted against her tyrannical affection.

"I'm thinking," he replied, "that I'd like to live all lives in one alone, in spells and bewitchments. What does the enemy matter to the man who is intoxicated and forgets? Famous among all was the tyrant of Babylon who awaited death in the midst of his wives and slaves, in the splendor of the most sublime orgy. The clamors of drunkenness mingled with the noise of instruments, in the smoke of perfumes, and domesticated lions roared meekly under illuminated terraces. Then there was an immense and sinister light, such as the nights of Babylon had never seen: an invincible flame that seemed to repel and enlarge the somber vaults of the heavens; a noise similar to that of thunder bursting simultaneously from all points of the horizon, overturning the city from top to bottom beneath a rain of ash, lava and fire!

"Finally, the shadow descended over the beings that had lived, on the riches buried forever; Sardanapalus no longer existed, and the next day, the conquerors searched in vain for traces of his magic palace . . .[1]

"Oh, to die in that apotheosis! What a divine bliss!"

Chapter IX

The Persians had a passion for gambling.
Sometimes they gambled their wives
and daughters.
(Herodotus.)

Arynes was sleeping next to Nysista when an icy breath passed over his face.

---

1 Sardanapalus was named by the Greek writer Clesias as the last king of Assyria, in the seventh century B.C. No such king existed, and the name might be a corruption of Ashurbanipal, an earlier king of the empire, but Diodorus Siculus embroidered the account of his reign with the anecdote cited here, and the imaginary Sardanapalus thus became a personification of ultimate decadence. His death is depicted in a famous painting by the Romantic artist Eugène Delacroix, based on a play by Lord Byron.

He opened his eyes, his soul suddenly filled with anguish. Was the nightmare about to recommence, then, morbid, cruel, tenacious and invincible? Was the phantom about to take his strength, drink from the very source of his life, accomplish its accursed work with the perversity of all spirits consecrated to evil? An implacable sorceress, was the spectral form about to lavish upon him, with the feline dilettantism of a succubus, the magnetisms that burn and devour, to leave him forever neurotic, devoid of energy, his marrow and his brain melted like lead in an alchemist's crucible?

The phantom, the double, the fravashi had entered as it had done before, without raising the heavy flap of the tent, and it was standing beside the lovers' bed, illuminated by a mysterious light.

"You! You again!" murmured Arynes.

"Me, whom you wanted to strike even beyond death! But the predictions of the spirits will be accomplished even so, whatever you do."

"What predictions?"

"You will be mine, Arynes, since you have given yourself freely."

"Ah," he said, "one does not give oneself to something that has only a vague human appearance. If I wanted to embrace you, my arms would close upon the void, since you are only an impalpable form."

"I will reincarnate myself for your amour, when the moment comes!"

Arynes strove to laugh, in spite of the icy frisson that ran through his limbs.

"Why do you want me to keep my promises, when you haven't kept yours?"

"Speak," said the specter.

"Were you not to enrich me by means of your magic formulae? Were you not to give me the superhuman power that triumphs over all obstacles? I've gambled, and I've lost . . ."

"I know."

"Nysista has given back all her jewels, I have pledged my wealth to come, I no longer possess anything."

"You can still win."

"Ah!" said the officer, in an irrational impulse. "If you gave me that supreme joy, I'd be yours, body and soul."

"You have already sworn to belong to me, and you are lying next to another."

"This is my slave, my lover; you would be my wife."

In his reckless desire for wealth, Arynes no longer knew what he was saying.

"I don't tolerate sharing," the phantom murmured, disdainfully.

"I'll do whatever you wish, Zaroccha, but teach me the means of winning again . . ."

"Listen Arynes. Tomorrow you will gamble, and you will go to sleep happy."

"Oh," he said, ecstatically, his eyes shining with covetousness. Then he said, sadly: "What will my stake be, since I'm ruined?"

"You will gamble your mistress!"

But he uttered a cry of revolt. "No, never! Surrender Nysista, whom I adore! The cherished woman who has sustained me and consoled me in my troubles, whose smile is softer than a moonbeam! Don't demand that, Zaroccha, for I won't be able to obey you."

He extended his arms toward the specter, which gradually recoiled and faded away into the darkness. But these words still passed as if in a breath of wind:

"You will gamble your mistress."

Chapter X

Do not sing verses if you have no lyre.
(*The Gilded Verses of Pythagoras.*)[1]

Everything was calm now in the officer's tent. A little lamp in a jade receptacle launched its last glimmers, and Safou, who had leapt on to the bed, was curled up on Nysista's bosom.

Moving the familiar cat away, gently, Arynes contemplated his lover.

She was profoundly asleep, one arm folded under her delicate head, paled by the emotions of recent days. A passionate kiss did not wake her; a feeble respiration scarcely parted her lips. The officer thought about his sumptuous childhood in the home of the powerful Satrap. He had had weapons, horses, devoted servants, and all the toys that his young pride could desire. Why had he not been able to conserve those rare benefits of existence? Why, on a day of stupid revolt, had he stood up against and insulted his father? Doubtless the evil seed was within him, its poisoned shoots sprouting in spite of healthy cultivation and a sage education. Then, expelled from the paternal roof, delivered to himself, he had lost his possessions and, in order to recover them, had slid into all the abysses of vice.

How little it requires, he said to himself, *to overturn a human conscience! A few imprudent words and a few unhealthy orgies can lead to crime by mysterious paths strewn with ambushes. Nothing down here, therefore, is indifferent, since the most minimal circumstances sometimes determine an entire life. A voyage, an imprudent enterprise, even less, an unthinking word, engage the future of human beings, and all their efforts cannot untie what a banal event has knotted forever. That little girl who is collecting plants in the mountains, whom no traveler has noticed, will soon be the element*

---

1 "Les Vers dorées de Pythagore" [The Golden Verses of Pythagoras] were "explained and translated" (or, more probably, invented) by the occultist Antoine Fabre d'Olivet in 1813.

necessary to a man's existence; his eyes, scarcely having turned to-
ward her, will moisten with the tears of the most ardent passion; his
mouth, which has remained mute, will stick to hers with cries and
sobs. Yesterday, they were nothing to one another; tomorrow that will
no longer be able to comprehend how they cannot always have been
together; yesterday, a world separated them; tomorrow they will only
be one and the same being of amour and harmony.

Arynes remained motionless, buried in the tortures of the
dream. His heart was dolorous, as if a hand had squeezed it
within his breast. His unquiet thought palpitated like a wounded bird with an impotent, agonized wing. Was the vampire still
there, then, although invisible, menacing him in the shadows?
It seemed to him that dense vapors were enveloping him, and
he shuddered at the slightest sound. The only things that could
be heard, however, were the sputtering of the little lamp and the
confused rumor of the camp, beginning to wake up.

Suddenly, Nysista uttered a long sigh and propped herself up
on her elbow.

"Arynes," she said, gazing at her lover fearfully, "don't leave
me, don't listen to the voices of dementia that speak in sleep.
You know full well that they lie and can only suggest culpable
thoughts."

The officer was troubled.

"What do you mean, my Beloved? I haven't quit your bed, I
haven't seen anything or heard anything."

"Perhaps you're sincere," she said shivering, "but I've had a
horrible dream."

"What dream?"

"I dreamed that specters drew you into their macabre round,
and that you swore to sell your soul to them for a little gold.
They sniggered as they obliged you to sign the shameful pact."

"My Beloved," said Arynes, hugging his mistress, "it's necessary to chase away those funereal visions. You know that I only
exist henceforth for your amour, and that I would gladly give my
life to calm your dread."

"Alas," she sighed, "nothing will render me confidence and calm as long as we stay here. Darius promised me a distant mission for you, which might cover you in glory and assure your future. We'll depart, my Adored, and we'll seek elsewhere a felicity that nothing can render us in this accursed land. I'll put on masculine dress, I'll fight by your side; then, in the evening, in the isolation of our amorous retreat, I'll become your maidservant again."

Ayrnes remained thoughtful.

"Yes," he said, after a protracted silence, "that would doubtless be salvation, but Darius won't give me the command of his troops."

"Why not?"

"Because he loves you, and he still hopes to possess you, in spite of my refusals."

"Darius is just and good."

"Thwarted passion can neutralize any justice and benevolence."

Nysista bowed her head, because she understood that her lover was right, and that all happiness might be lost for her.

The young woman was superb thus, with the somber gleam of her eyes and the bruising of her eyelids with the long curved lashes. Her eyebrows combined their thin lines grimly at the root of her aquiline nose, the nostrils of which were quivering, and the twin cups of her breasts stiffened in revolt.

Arynes thought, sadly, that it would be necessary for him to abandon the adorable creature in order to obey the occult influence of the witch, if such was the will of the evil spirits, and he strove to drive away the somber presentiments that had been clouding his life for a long time.

Nysista inclined her forehead over her master's breast, like a flower overloaded with perfumes and dew. Her long warm hair imprisoned the young man, who respired its voluptuous aromas with delight, and she offered her eyes veiled by tears and her mouth swollen by sobs to the consoling and soothing caress.

Their hands clutched one another feverishly; their lips caught and abandoned one another alternately, with lascivious and dolorous sighs.

"Don't go away from the camp today, my Beloved," she said. "I'll be more tranquil if you remain in the midst of your companions, close to me."

"I won't go away," he said. "Anyway, where would I go? You know that I don't have the wherewithal to adorn myself or do myself honor. I've wagered or sold my weapons, your jewels, and even my black charger, of which I was so proud."

She became affectionate, passing her arm around the young man's neck.

"If you wanted," she said, "I could dance for the chiefs and reveal the future to them in accordance with the lines of their hand. Zaroccha initiated me into that facile science. That can still bring us something."

But he refused, haughtily.

"The woman who belongs to me won't make a spectacle of herself for a derisory salary. You're too pure and too proud to amuse those coarse individuals . . ."

"What will we do, then, if Darius doesn't come to our aid?"

He made a wild gesture, the meaning of which she thought she divined.

"Oh, my Beloved!" she cried. "How I understand you, and how glad I am to see you so resolved. Yes, with you, death would be a blessing, and nothing would be worth as much as the sensuality of your supreme embrace!"

Chapter XI

The spirit dresses in order to descend,
and strips in order to rise.
(Kabbalist axiom.)

By means of conjurations and maleficia, Arynes would have liked to put himself in direct communication with demons and gods, driven by an anarchic instinct of revolt. He was suffering, above all, from the inability to expel the occult influence that weighed upon him, sensing himself so weak before the mysterious will that was directing him, in spite of his resistance, and dictating its laws to him.

He was intoxicated by dizziness, and no longer feared falling into the abyss of dementia, since he was nothing but a visionary and a victim of hallucination.

None of the phenomena that had once caused his reason to revolt now seemed impossible to him. He admitted the existence of the most diabolical miracles and the presence of an invincible force that paralyzed his own. But he dreaded the future utterly, for he knew that the evil spirits are avid for blood and only grant their protection at the price of treason and murder.

The officer had quit Nysista in order to rejoin his chiefs. He marched slowly in the midst of his soldiers, who followed him with a curious gaze, sometimes hazarding a smile, for they judged him slightly insane and possessed by evil spirits.

A band of snake-charmers was occupying the attention of about fifty men arranged in a circle around a dirty carpet. A few musicians accompanied the performance, blowing into long reeds in the form of flutes, pierced at both ends. They were drawing sad and harmonious sounds from the hollow stems, which they prolonged until their breath was extinct.

Jugglers were whirling frenetically around three baskets covered in the skin of jackals, and the reptiles soon lifted up the furs. They were snakes spotted with green and orange, of the dangerous species that can inflate their heads by parting the scales that cover them, and whose bite is a mortal burn.

After having crawled for some time, the reptiles reared up on their tails and swayed gently, following the measure of the reed flutes. Then, their jaws agape, darting their bodies toward the charmers, they tried to catch their naked legs. They dilated their scales hideously, giving voice to an angry hiss.

One of the dancers stopped suddenly, and the serpents coiled around his arms and legs. Immediately, the man was covered by them, but, having pronounced a magical invocation, he collected the long, supple bodies without difficulty, which swayed in his hands like living stems, henceforth submissive and inoffensive.

Arynes had stopped to contemplate the snake-charmer.

"Your reptiles have lost their fangs," he said, disdainfully, "and you no longer fear their venom."

A soldier had offered his arm, laughing.

"Take care!" cried one of the flute-players, who had seen the movement. But already, cruelly bitten, the man had withdrawn his arm, moaning. He writhed convulsively for a minute, tottered and fell dead, while his flesh, immediately decomposing, took on a blue tint.

"You see," said the snake-charmer to Arynes, "my serpents can give death, and it's only by virtue of my incantations that I avoid danger."

Arynes thought that he had only to offer his fingertips to the dangerous reptiles in order to be delivered from the torture of life, and involuntarily, he had already moved into the front rank of the spectators when a familiar voice called to him. He turned round, ill-humoredly.

"Oh, it, you, Mirjam!"

Mirjam, an officer in the royal guard, seemed to have acquired an affection for the Satrap's son for some time. In reality, he was obeying the orders of Darius, who hoped to obtain by cunning what had been refused to him willingly.

"Is the spectacle offered to you by these tricksters very attractive to you, then?" Mirjam asked, approaching curiously. But he made a grimace of disgust on perceiving the blackened body of the soldier.

"It's not our fault," the charmers explained. "The man got himself bitten in spite of us."

"Seize these impostors," said the officer, "and punish them as they deserve, for the murder of one of your own."

Then, drawing Arynes away, he led him to the extremity of the camp.

"Where are we going?"

"Wherever you wish, provided that we escape the spectacle of the flaying and impalement of those scoundrels."

"They weren't guilty . . ."

"Bah! If they really had a mysterious power, they'd be able to escape the torture. I'm giving them an opportunity to prove their science."

"Perhaps," said Arynes, thoughtfully.

They were marching in a fiery atmosphere; the air was dry and painful to breathe: the horses of riders passing by were respiring noisily, numbed by a morbid somnolence.

A scream cut through the air, however; Arynes understood that the torment of the snake-charmers had commenced, and that Darius' soldiers were amusing themselves in their fashion. Already, in their path, lamentable individuals buried to the neck were imploring a drop of fresh water; others were finishing dying in ox-hides exposed to the sun, frightful shrouds that stifled their victims as they shrank. Three men near a tent had introduced a marauder into a wooden sheath, only leaving the head exposed, which they were using as a target. Twenty arrows, protruded from the face of the unfortunate, whose punctured eyes were bleeding abundantly. Further away, two soldiers, very attentive to their work, were plunging long thorns under the fingernails of a woman accused of theft; a third torturer was clutching her breasts in pincers, preparing to cut them into little pieces, for she had been unable to indicate to him the place where she had hidden the fruits of her larceny.

Habituated to such executions, Arynes and Mirjam drew away indifferently. Now they reached the limit of the tents; large flocks of vultures announced the proximity of impalement stakes ornamented with their human prey, in the midst of lamentable circles of crucified men. The bloody avenue extended into the distance, poisoning the air, in spite of the voracity of the birds of prey.

"Where are we going?" Arynes asked again, irritatedly.

"Don't you want to flee this sickening spectacle to find a few joyful companions of pleasure?"

The officer stopped.

"Gambling," he said. "You want to make me gamble again? But you know I no longer have anything?"

"Bah! I'll lend you as many darics as you wish."

"No, don't insist; temptation is dangerous for me."

"It's necessary never to resist a desire, for satisfaction offered in vain is lost for us."

"After pleasure comes remorse."

"Not always. You might win, Arynes."

"No, no, don't give me that culpable hope. I'm afraid, I tell you . . ."

Mirjam laughed scornfully. "Afraid of what? What danger threatens you?"

"I'm afraid of the invisible, afraid of mysterious enemies who surround me and are pushing me toward the abyss."

"So it's because you've run off with the daughter of the witch Zaroccha that you're trembling like this?"

"What, you know?"

"We all know," said Mirjam, ironically, "that the old woman made oracles with the heads of those who died under torture, by putting a sheet of gold covered with magical characters under their tongue. Perhaps you've kept some of those bloody trophies as well as the girl?"

"No," said Arynes, "but I've promised my mistress not to gamble again."

"If that's all it is, you'll easily obtain pardon by taking the beauty the jewels and adornments she loves. I sense that the spirits of air and fire are protecting you; a strange presentiment tells me that everything will be successful for you today. I'm so certain of what I say that I wouldn't risk anything against you."

"Truly?" said Arynes, indecisively.

And he allowed himself to be drawn toward the sumptuous and cool tent where the gamblers were gathered.

Chapter XII

> Dolor is the dog of the unknown shepherd
> who leads the human flock.
> (X***.)[1]

It was with an indescribable emotion that the officer approached the gaming table. The redoubtable moment was about to decide his fate. Everything thus far had been in league against him, but the smallest event, the slice of luck of which one does not take sufficient account, might save him or lead him to the most terrible catastrophe.

He staked the gold coins that Mirjam had lent him, and lost, time and time again. In spite of his friend's predictions, chance was decidedly not favorable to him. With every daric risked, he seemed to hear a sardonic snigger, and a kind of blue mist passed before his eyes.

The physiognomy of the players had a sly and cruel expression, which troubled Arynes even more than the persistent adversity. However, the fire of the passion set his veins ablaze; already, he could no longer resist its magic waves, and Mirjam drove him into the furnace by means of his advice and the generosity of his gifts.

The game of figurines succeeded the dice; but the number of points scored by the officer was always inferior to that of his

---

1 This quotation actually comes from *Histoire de la magie* (1860) by Éliphas Lévi, although Lévi claims that it a translation from an unnamed German poet.

adversaries. A bloody mist was now drowning out people and things for him. He saw pale and debilitated shadows crawling, rising and descending, which mocked him; all the voices of the earth were whispering sarcasms and anathemas around him.

Trembling with rage, he drew his sword and traced the circle of conjuration in the air, in order to drive the phantoms away. He struggled against the fatality, cursing his dementia, begging the good spirits to come to his aid. But every baleful memory brought its reflection, every evil desire created an image, and very remorse engendered a nightmare.

Until nightfall, Mirjam handed him darics and gold ingots; the sum that he owed was formidable; his hair stood on end at the idea that he could never acquit himself, and that human reprobation would weigh upon him until his death.

"I'm stifling," he said. "Let me go back to my lodgings. I'll come back tomorrow and might be more fortunate. Tomorrow, I'll have regained possession of my reason; I'll no longer wager at hazard, like today. I'll be able to acquit myself, I'm certain of it."

His companions, however, who were certain of winning, thanks to Mirjam's cares, refused to allow themselves to be persuaded.

"You owe us too large a sum," they said, "for us to consent to your leaving. What guarantee can you give us, and what assurance can we have of your sincerity?"

Arynes quivered at the insult, but he had lost the right to avenge himself, and his lips stammered vague protestations

It is not beyond the tomb but in life itself that it is necessary to seek the mystery of death, said the prophet Daniel. Salvation or reprobation commences in this world, and if the golden key, the instrument of good and evil, sometimes seems to be the share of the wicked, it only opens for them the door of the tomb or the inferno.

Arynes, however, would have given his soul to possess the magic talisman; his eyes, striped by bloody fibrils, and his dry lips, convulsively taut, declared his desire clearly enough.

Mirjam, judging him ripe for the crime, put a hand on his shoulder.

"Listen," he said. "I can offer you a means of acquitting yourself, if you want to be reasonable."

"What means?" The officer's gaze sparkled with desire.

"I'll wager everything you owe me against Nysista."

"Against Nysista?"

It seemed that he no longer understood, having forgotten the existence of his mistress in his furious passion.

"Do you consent?"

"I don't know. I haven't reflected . . ."

He thought, now, about Zaroccha's prediction, and new frissons ran through his flesh. He had disturbed the sanctuary of the tomb; the irritated manes of the witch were taking a cruel revenge. The stryges presiding over enchantments were already intoning the hymn of victory.

"Do you consent?" demanded Darius' envoy, again.

"It's necessary," signed Arynes, shaking the dice in a tremulous hand.

This time, chance was favorable to him; he fled with a clamor of joy and terror.[1]

Chapter XIII

It is the hour of Dreams, Sabbats and Metamorphoses . . .
Why do you fear the mysteries of the dark?
(*The Book of the Magi.*)

Arynes had been gambling all day. A profound darkness now drowned the sleeping camp. He heard the rustle of mysterious beings that were crowding around him beneath the sinister flight of vultures.

---

1 It is unclear exactly what has happened here; logically, if Arynes has won the throw of the dice, his debt has been wiped out and he has not lost his own stake—i.e. Nysista—but that does not seem, subsequently, to be what has happened.

In order to have everything, he said to himself, trying to recover his courage, *it's necessary to dare everything*. His brain, phosphorescent with magical light, was full of reflections and innumerable figures. When he closed his eyelids, a vision that was sometimes enchanting and sometimes somber and terrifying, was designed in the dementia of his thoughts . . .

He was running now, in order to embrace the sacrificed companion one last time, the sad lover that he would never see again; and still the reek of corruption and poisons floated in the air, among the ironic specters, lemurs, goblins and gnomes.

Nysista, sitting in the sand, was waiting for him impatiently.

She was almost naked; her body was a white patch in the dark.

"Oh," she said, "it's you. I thought that you weren't coming back. I begged you so much not to go away."

Already she was pressing against him, offering him her lips.

He held her against his heart, feverishly. "Forgive me," he groaned.

"Forgive you?"

She could not see his gaze in the darkness, but she sensed his immense sadness.

"You've been gambling again?"

"Yes, I've been gambling."

"And you lost?"

"I lost," he sighed, so quietly that she divined it rather than heard it.

By virtue of a charming generosity, she did not want to increase his pain, and talked about what she had done while waiting for him. An envoy of the King of Kings had come with perfumes and presents; he had been full of solicitude, asking about her slightest desires. She had not consented to receive him in the tent, and their conversation had taken place in view of everyone, for she had nothing to hide.

"And the presents?" asked the officer.

"As you can well imagine, I refused them all."

"Ah!" he said. "But wasn't the messenger charged with a mission for me?"

"Alas, no, Darius hasn't kept his promise."

"Darius desires you, Nysista, and in spite of all human strength, you'll be his."

"No, Beloved, I will only be yours."

"When you've lived in the splendor of palaces, in the midst of adorations and homages, you'll forget everything, as the priestess who had eaten the sacred nepenthe forgets. Your past life will seem go you to be an obscure dream, your anterior affections will evaporate like incense on the stove of evocations. The woman loved by a King no longer remembers men."

"Why are you saying this to me, Beloved?"

"Because I know women."

"The others are not like me."

"You can't speak about what you don't know, my Adored. When you have drawn upon the treasures of the omnipotent Master, and gold runs through your fingers like a fulgurant wave, you won't think any longer about the poor officer. The priests, the army, the people and all the sublime possessions of the King of Kings will belong to you, and perhaps he'll repudiate his other wives in order to make you greater."

"You're delirious," she said, smiling.

"No, I have all my reason. The future is designed before me in characters of flame."

"Let's talk about our love."

"If you wish," he sighed. "Love me well while there's still time."

But she was no longer listening to him. She had stretched herself out on the bed, feebly lit by the little lamp, and her lips were already seeking those of her lover, in the desire to forget everything, to plunge into the invincible intoxication of the senses.

Once more, they drained the chalice of amour in an incessantly renascent fever. They embraced one another in an intense fury of possession. Oh, how she would have sought divine fecundation in the irritating felicity of those kisses! To make life, to unite for the adorable mystery of the supreme Law; that was now her dream.

The same passionate tenderness still consumed her, and she would have liked to be able to give herself more, to exasperate herself with holy lust to the point of the intoxication of suffering and death.

But Arynes, while responding to her caresses, forgot himself in morbid dreams, and she felt sorry for him, calming him with tender words, like a troubled child whom it is necessary to send to sleep.

She had heard his terrified plaints and somber predictions too often to lend any serious attention to them. Gambling alone, she thought, had caused all the harm, and as poverty did not weigh upon her disinterest, she was not anxious for the future.

Chapter XIV

You will soon appear on a chariot of light,
victorious spirit and king of matter!
(*The Gilded Verses of Pythagoras*)

Nysista was reposing in the exquisite sweetness of sated pleasure, and her lover was listening to the voices of darkness. A kind of diaphanous blue-tinted cloud surrounded him; he had the apprehension that a mysterious presence was about to become manifest, as on other nights. But would not that execrable phantom become a creature of flesh and muscle in order to poison his life and solicit odious caresses?

In any case, he thought, *Zaroccha certainly exists. Death is a phantom of ignorance; everything in nature is alive, for everything moves and incessantly changes form. The body is a vestment of the spirit, which falls in old age, and which the spirit abandons in order to clothe itself differently. However, it can reintegrate in any envelope, either by its own effort or with the assistance of a will greater and more active than its own. That resurrection is only accomplished by the strongest chains of attraction, and phenomena of that order are explained by assimilating them to cases of lethargy of variable duration. Either by resurrection or the cessation of lethargy, the vampire of the witch can still appear to me; I shall infallibly become her prey.*

Safou, the black cat, darted his gleaming eyes at the officer. The torch of the beyond seemed to be burning therein, and letting its fateful sparks fall. A bizarre melody, which participated in the plaint of the wind and the murmur of the waves, came from who knows where; the visionary was oppressed by a sensation of exquisite and troubling perfumes. Around him grew an entire vegetal world in which flowers and fruits were mingled in their most adorably strange forms. Tall trees with emerald foliage and luminous herbs came together over his head; he was imprisoned in the florid toils of lianas and orchids, like an amorous insect.

Soon, words of prayer and gratitude struck his ear; they were ardent words that bit the senses and flew away in order to make way for other more vibrant and more passionate sounds. He seemed to be able to hear, in that path of light, the sobs of the wind, the rumble of thunder and the monotonous plaint of waves. It rose up everywhere, and yet, nothing changed in the placid and radiant décor. He experienced paroxysms of joy, desire unknown until that moment. He was outside the real world, in a state of perfect somnambulism, and his brain was only giving birth to enchanted images.

The phantom of the witch did not manifest itself; what would it be doing in that apotheosis? The hideous guests of the tomb, ghosts, ghouls and stryges, only haunt sinister places and flee solar radiance.

Even so, the officer made futile efforts to shake off his torpor and regain possession of himself. Everything had darkened in a dazzle of aromas, radiance and color. He heard the swinging of golden censers; the magical friction of bewitching plants intoxicated him more and more. His heart was beating heavily, the warm breezes that bathed his brow were charged with magnetic effluvia, while immaterial lips abandoned themselves to his.

Burning thoughts were haunting him now, and the voluptuous temptations of caresses: a fervent delirium of unknown ecstasies.

The raucous mewling of Safou extracted Arynes from his dream. The exquisite vision had vanished, but the bed was strewn with red roses of a marvelous brilliance and perfume.

Chapter XV

He who forges the image, he who enchants
the maleficent face, the maleficent eye, the
maleficent lips—spirits of the earth,
pursue him!
(Engraved terracotta cylinder found at Nineveh)

Nysista, who was dressing slowly, came to huddle against the officer.

"Protect me!" she said.

"What's the matter?"

"Someone has pronounced my name and is coming to fetch me. Oh, my presentiments haven't deceived me: you've sold me to the King!"

"No," he murmured, feebly, for he did not remember the bargain to which he had consented.

"You've sold me!" the young woman went on, indignantly.

And she drew away from the pillaged bed, which the red roses covered with their bloody splendor.

A great rumor was coming from outside, and suddenly, the curtain that veiled the entrance to the tent was drawn back violently.

"What is it?" demanded Arynes, standing up feverishly.

112

In the midst of a numerous cortege, Mirjam was waiting outside.

"I've come to take what you promised me," he said.

"Have I promised you something?"

In truth, the young man had forgotten everything in the delirium of the dream. He rubbed his eyes, seeking painfully to recall his memories.

"I've come," said Mirjam, laughing, "to claim what you've lost. Don't you recall that you staked Nysista?"

Completely sobered up, Arynes uttered a cry: "Nysista!"

"Yes, and I paid well for her. All the royal slaves put together would not have fetched such a price."

"You're mistaken, Mirjam. I couldn't have consented to such a bargain."

"Oh, my companions will tell you that you owe me that woman . . . and I've come to fetch her."

Lying on the ground, the young woman was weeping copiously.

"Take her away," said Mirjam.

Soldiers approached in spite of the resistance of Arynes, who had placed himself in front of his lover. In a matter of moments, Nysista, wrapped up in her garments, with a gag over her lips, was dragged out of the tent and placed in a chariot at Mirjam's feet. He picked up the reins and uttered a sort of guttural appeal. Immediately, the horses departed at a gallop, and the sound of wheels resounded like dull thunder in the midst of the other noises of the camp.

The officer had clung on to the edge of the chariot, attempting vague supplications, threats and plaints.

It seemed to him that his poor happiness was fleeing on the wings of the wind, and that the spirits of darkness were attaching themselves to him in order to precipitate him into the abyss. He heard their burst of laughter, and felt their cold breath passing over his face, and clung on harder to his enemy's chariot.

The mounted guards who were following Mirjam had seized their spears, and their bronze breastplates resonated in the rapidity of the course. The crests of their helmets glinted in the sun; as they passed by they raised an acrid odor of earth stirred up in a brown dust.

In the distance now, an imposing cavalier appeared guiding a black charger harnessed with gold. He wore a grand tiara of white cloth and the royal kidaris; a long crimson cloak was ablaze behind him, like a veil of flames.

At the limit of his strength and courage, Arynes closed his eyes and allowed himself to roll on the ground.

The guards passed over him like an avalanche, and everything disappeared in a fantastic whirlwind.

PART THREE

Chapter I

She bewitches the absent, she makes wax
simulacra, and plunges slender needles
into the liver of the unfortunate.
(Ovid, *The Heroines*.)

The hours succeeded one another; already the sun had disappeared behind Mount Zagros, and Arynes, lying by the side of the road, had not recovered consciousness. Alongside him stood the cross of a crucified man, beneath the circling of vultures. A few agonizing plaints troubled the silence of the funereal place, a great shadow drowned everything, while the stars were beginning to extend their golden network in the azure.

The Persians did not carry out on prisoners of war the frightful chastisements of the Assyrian domination, but rebellion was punished severely. After the revolt and the long resistance of Babylon, Darius had three thousand Chaldeans crucified. Mutilation was a very successful means of repression, so it was not rare to see troops of prisoners circulating in camps with bloody eye-sockets, their hands, ears and noses cut off. The submission of the Persians with regard to their sovereign remained complete, and Prexaspes, seeing Cambyses' arrow in his son's heart, said humbly: "I do not believe that even a god could have shot as accurately."[1]

Arynes, however, came round. Gradually, light dawned in his agonized mind. He understood that it was not for his own ac-

---

1 Another anecdote from Herodotus.

count that Mirjam had taken Nysista, but on behalf of the King, who destined her for his harem. Darius only had one legitimate wife but the concubines spent one night in his apartment, and the most beautiful was raised to the rank of favorite. Doubtless Nysista would be the Master's favorite, for she had made a profound impression on him.

Arynes raised his eyes; a ray of moonlight illuminated the dolorous face of the crucified man, whose gaze seemed to be fixed on him.

"Oh," groaned the officer, "is that not another deadly presage? Is it not enough for me to suffer the hatred of the living? Is it necessary for the dead to persecute me as well."

The man shuddered on his cross.

"My soul has not yet quit my body. I remain attached to the tangible matter that is already decomposing."

"Ah!" said Arynes. "Can nothing recall you to life?"

"Nothing."

"Then what do you want of me?"

"My fluidic body is being purified and ennobled before abandoning matter definitively. Soon it will fly away in order to float in space until its reincarnation."

"Its reincarnation?"

"Yes. Go home, for the reincarnate soul of a wicked spirit is waiting for you and desires you."

"What are you saying?"

"By a crime you have attracted the vengeance of stryges and vampires. You will be their prey until your death. Go, and let your destiny be accomplished."

"But I don't want to! I'm not guilty!"

"You have killed, remember."

"I've killed? Truly, I no longer remember that."

"You have killed," the implacable voice repeated; "for a miserable reward you have profaned a tomb and sold your companion."

"Oh," said Arynes, "that happened in spite of my will . . ."

"Everything happens in spite of our will, but we must arrive at the good via suffering. It is in conformity with the demands of that law that we achieve the supreme calm, that we free ourselves from the shackles of form and the attractions of desire . . ."

"But if I'm unconscious, I'm not culpable," said the officer. "I have within me the passion of gold and, in consequence, that of gambling. Why was I born thus? Is that my fault?"

"No," said the tortured man. "All the forms of good and evil are linked together following the law of evolution and metamorphosis. Death is only an illusion, one of the agents of existence, which necessitates an incessant renewal. The invisible world dominates us and envelops us; good and evil spirits serve as guides for humankind and never cease to communicate with it. But when our garment of flesh has fallen, the light will penetrate you and you will finally understand your actions, your will and your passions. Your terrestrial career will reveal its faults, its weaknesses and its miseries to you. You will contemplate yourself fearfully through vanished times and lives."

The face of the tortured man immobilized in the supreme repose. A vulture circling above him pecked out his eye and carried the bloody orb away.

Painfully, Arynes returned to the camp.

The landscape around him was less lugubrious, for he had taken a path that isolated him from the place of tortures. The delicate leaves of acacias were detached by the slightest gust of wind, spun in the air momentarily like light moths drunk on perfumes, and fell soundlessly. Others had already fallen in great numbers, for the cold season was approaching, and the officer's feet, treading on that leaf-litter, made a soft and monotonous sound.

But the vegetal realm, like the human body, seemed to be suffering a mysterious exhaustion of the nourishing juices of sap. Arynes was struggling in vain against something implacable, stronger than him. The burden that weighed upon him all the more as he stiffened himself in order to shrug it off, was the reprobation of beings and plants, the scorn of everything that surrounded him.

His energy, in revolt, tried to defend him against that inconceivable paralysis; a tremor agitated his hands; his breath became hoarse; he felt that a black wing was fluttering over his head, hiding the stars from him.

He interrogated the mystery of the night; he listened to the murmurs that were now rising in the depths of the woods, the confused tones rustling in the foliage, emerging from everywhere at the same time. It was the grave and profound song that makes the immensity vibrate, and of which only the phantoms wandering over the earth understand the melancholy meaning.

Chapter II

> Base and wicked souls remain chained
> to the earth by multiple rebirths.
> (Hermes Trismegistus.)

Arynes went through the sleeping camp. He was unhappy beyond all expression. His doubts and apprehensions had become realities, for he sensed that nothing protected him henceforth from evil influences. He uttered inarticulate lamentations that resembled an infant's plaints, and which expressed better than any words the infinity of human sadness.

He looked round, full of stupor and fear, imagining that he heard the voices of the occult powers of darkness, the voice of the strange world that the living cannot comprehend.

When he recovered possession of himself after a few seconds, he saw a white form in front of him gliding in a moonbeam, seemingly guiding his steps. Sometimes it turned toward him, but he could not penetrate the mystery of its veil, and it fled lightly, scarcely touching the ground with its graceful and rapid stride.

He went into his tent, surprised to find that Nysista was no longer there, for a vague hope had remained to him, and, in spite of the evidence, he thought that a miracle might perhaps have returned her to him. Safou, the familiar cat, had also disappeared; everything was dark and desolate in the narrow redoubt pillaged by Mirjam's soldiers.

Arynes threw himself down on his bed and fell asleep: an agitated slumber shot through with muffled groans, abrupt starts of the body, and nervous contractions of the face, attesting that the enemy haunting his dreams was continuing its slow and implacable work of possession.

Then his lips moved and he extended his arms, as if he wanted to seize and retain the vision born of the fever that filled his eyes with an ardent ecstasy. After stammering vaguely, he fell asleep again, his face illuminated by a superhuman joy.

An amorous frenzy suddenly took possession of him, a contagion of spontaneous and terrible desire that threw him into the delirium of the dream.

Now a muted sound was audible, similar to that made by waves crashing into one another. It was the camp waking up, and the noise gave the impression of a blind, irresistible force suddenly put in motion.

The sound of trumpets punctuated that confused rumble; an impalpable dust raised by multitudinous feet, floated into the tent, misting the first light of day.

Arynes, who had sat up on his bed, uttered a cry.

Among the shredded roses, a woman was sitting, staring at him.

Her eyelids, fringed with long lashes, framed moist onyx irises, lustrous with the caresses of life. Her slender and delicate nose with pure ridges, had transparent nostrils more delicate than flowers, and her mouth, with voluptuously modeled lips, was smiling softly over the enamel of her teeth.

Amazed, the officer contemplated the harmonious shoulders of the unknown woman, and her proud breasts, which stood up in the triumph of youth. And in that charming face he rediscovered the indications of a redoubtable resemblance. The movement of the forehead, the line of the nose, the curve of the mouth and the hue of the eyes had already struck him before . . .

Silent and immobile, he interrogated his memories, and a terrible light suddenly dawned in him.

"Zaroccha!" he said.

She uttered crystalline laughter, opened her arms, and her voluptuous mouth put on the officer's lips the poison of delirium and subjugation.

Chapter III

Men only know the things of his world of
which the end combines with infinity.
(The Great Initiates: Pythagoras.)[1]

"I shall be able to devour your consciousness and slake my slow desires on your submissive being. You will be intoxicated by my intoxication and you will obey me in my strangest fantasies. In exchange, I shall give you wealth, for I have brought my adornments, my bracelets, my massive chains, and my clusters of monstrous gems, which launch forth stellar radiance. For you, I shall be more sumptuous than the queens of magical tales, and you will find me incessantly clad in gold and precious stones. Finally, I shall have the marvelous beauty of legendary princesses and you will remain at my knees with cries of admiration and prayer."

"If you are not Zaroccha resuscitated, who are you, then?"

---

1 The quotation is actually taken from *Après la mort* (1905) by the spiritist Léon Denis, although it is credited there, apocryphally, to Pythagoras. La Vaudère must have encountered Denis, if only as a member of the audience at one of his many lectures.

"Give me any name you wish: the one that will sing most sweetly in your ears and will be like flowing honey on your lips. Come to rejoice on my erect breasts, come to repose on my clement heart. By virtue of your past struggles, by virtue of the effort of good and evil that you have sustained, you merit my amour, and, if you believe my prophecies, you have already vanquished. After the long cycle of my tenebrous existences, I have finally emerged from the dolorous circle of accursed generations to rediscover joy and confidence."

"Who are you, then?" asked Arynes again.

"What does it matter? Listen to the truths that it is necessary to keep silent from the crowd and which constitute the strength of invisible beings. Spirits are innumerable and various, for the existence of the soul is eternal and infinite. But you have entered into the bosom of mysteries, and human chances will be propitious for you."

The unknown woman was marvelously beautiful. She appeared to the officer as a sorceress of Babylonian legend, a creature of dream and chimera. Already, he had forgotten Nysista and was intoxicated by this new amour, more burning than the sands of the desert, more luminous than the purest dawns. And everything succeeded for him without him even having to express a desire.

In the company of that new lover, the days passed rapidly. Then Arynes, reconciled with his father, fought on the coasts of Thrace and Macedonia,

Ariaramnes, the Satrap of Cappadocia, brought back prisoners that furnished the Persian generals with the information they needed. Enriched by gambling, which, since Nysista's departure, was favorable to him, Arynes had a considerable retinue and led a sumptuous existence

For his part, Darius crossed the Bosphorus with eight hundred thousand men, subjugated the eastern coast of Thrace and crossed the Danube over a bridge of boats constructed by the Greeks. For two months he traveled the steppes from the Ister to the Tanais, and then penetrated into the very heart of Russia, burned the villages and carried off all the booty he could find. The monarch stood up audaciously against the enemy, no matter what; he sustained a prodigious struggle against the combined powers, and his reign was illuminated by an epic glory. Every day was marked by some victory: a town captured, a capitulation, an enemy retreat, or a battle won. His invasion, like a river in flood, inundated, drowned and carried away everything.

Chapter IV

> While I was in Babylon the provinces deserted me.
> (Darius, The Behistun Inscription.)

Nysista, cloistered in an apartment of the royal harem, knew nothing of what was happening outside. She began to believe again, in her solitude, that everything was not finished for her. A great frisson passed through the cities where new armies were toiling. There was a muffled sound of legions on the march, coming from the north, the south and the west; the ring of bronze and clamors of victory passed into the clash of weapons, and the young woman hoped that her lover might come to liberate her, for Darius had tired of her. The Great King did not keep his favorites for long and the young woman had wearied him rapidly with her tears and sorrowful face.

Oh, she thought, *Arynes cannot have forgotten me. He must scorn the intrigues, the sterile struggles, even glory. His exhausted body would fall asleep in my arms delightedly; how sweet it would be to believe and to live!*

Images and forms continued to surge forth spontaneously in the field of her thought, without her doing anything to evoke them, for her entire being was struck by a singular torpor. She allowed herself to be captured, however, by those visions of blue sky and sunlight. She crossed mountains and plains in the wake of her dream, floating with it in the light.

Then, very weary, she lay back, with the slack movement of a flower with a broken stem, put her hand to her breast, and fainted.

One day, one of her slaves informed her.

"The Great King is making sure of his conquests, but the Satrap Ariaramnes is among us."

Nysista uttered a cry of joy.

"The Satrap of Cappadocia! What do you know about his son?"

"His son Arynes has traversed the city in the midst of a superb escort. It's said that he was covered in precious stones and that his golden helmet shone like a sun. A woman was beside him."

"A woman!"

"Yes, a singular creature mounted on a black horse . . ."

"A woman!" Nysista repeated, shivering. "What did she look like? Did you see her features?"

"No," said the slave, "I'm only repeating what I was told, and I don't know any more."

From that moment on, Nysista had only one desire: that of deceiving the vigilance of her guardians and quitting the royal harem.

The city, in any case, had been turned upside down by the story of Darius' marvelous victories; triumphal arches were being erected everywhere, with florid pylons, obelisks captured from the enemy and masts ornamented with garlands and banners. The high brick walls of the palace did not permit the sight of all those festival preparations, but their echo reached the favorite's ears vaguely, and the surveillance around her relaxed.

One night, enveloped in a thick veil, she was able to leave the chamber where she lived and flee through numerous halls, almost all deserted.

On the walls, bas-reliefs represented hunting scenes, furious lions devouring bulls, monarchs pursuing wild beasts and deformed demons borrowed from Assyrian art. Then came the magnificent hypostyle halls, constructed on a model borrowed from Egypt, the vastest of which was the hall with a hundred columns. The walls, pierced by eight doors, allowed the sight through their principal entrances of columns supporting a portico flanked by two immense androcephalous bulls.

In that room was the golden throne on which the sovereign sat, above a pavement of porphyry and dappled marble, as described in the Book of Esther.[1]

In the interior galleries, a ray of moonlight illuminated the admirable colored enamels of Mesopotamia. But the fugitive lost her way and returned to the sumptuous apartments decorated with the ivory and jewels of Egypt, the glittering fabrics of India, the vases and statues of Asia Minor, artfully grouped around profound divans and precious bowls. Servants sometimes crossed her path, and let her pass, believing her to be employed like them in the vulgar work of the palace.

She went down a broad marble staircase terminated by tall columns with palmate capitals, traversed a courtyard between two vast ponds bordered by a pink marble margin over which perseas with metallic foliage were dangling.

The moon illuminated the trees in the center and the pylons of the portico, the large bay of which framed an entire corner of blue sky.

Gliding through the shadow of high walls, Nysista succeeded in getting out of the palace without attracting the attention of the guards. A kind of occult power impelled her; a mysterious protection extended over her.

---

1 The palace described briefly in chapter 1 of the Book of Esther is attributed in the Authorized Version to "Ahasuerus" and in the Septuagint to "Artaxerxes," generally thought to be Darius' successor, Xerxes I.

Chapter V

Listen to the verities that it is necessary to
keep from the crowd and which are
the strength of sanctuaries. The solemn
hour has come in which I shall enable
you to penetrate the sources of life.
(Orphic Hymns.)

In the streets, still asleep, the columns and entablatures of temples
were outlined bizarrely above the terraces, with capitals in the
form of rams, winged bulls and lions, seemingly sustaining the
celestial vault. In the center of the royal square stood the statue
of Ahura-Mazda: a figure standing on a winged disk, facing the
statue of Darius in front of the palace gate. The King, leaning on
his bow and making a gesture of command, was placing his foot
on the breast of a prisoner, who was raising his arms to implore
mercy.

Nysista drew away rapidly, going past imposing portals ornamented with gigantic bulls, the marble staircases that ten cavaliers could climb abreast, porticos garnished with lotus leaves,
the aerial colonnades and propyleas with monumental doors.
Daylight was now beginning to appear, and passers-by were
becoming more numerous. Merchants were lining up baskets
of fruits, bunches of flowers and drinking cups along the walls.
Slaves enveloped in blue or green striped cloth were circulating hastily, pushing away semi-naked beggar-women who were
carrying their infants suspended from their shoulders in esparto
baskets.

The preparations for the fête were continuing everywhere, and
houses were being decked with flags for the royal procession.

Nysista sat down on the edge of a basin and waited for the
parade of honor, for she knew that her lover would be part of it,
along with all the victorious leaders of the recent conquests.

She was filled by a dolorous emotion; a thousand singular thoughts were agitating in her head. Palpitating and indecisive, troubled in the utmost depths of her being, she abandoned herself to the course of events, feeling cowardly before cruel destiny. She watched the passers-by vaguely, with the melancholy gaze of a woman in love who is suffering: a gaze moistened by regret and desolation.

The head of the procession had already appeared, while the sound of short bronze clarions and the strident appeal of trumpets burst forth. The hoof-beats of horses retained with great difficulty, the thunder of bronze-rimmed wheels and the rattle of weapons accompanied the martial fanfares.

Now came the palace guards with their glittering helmets, their corselets covered with scales and their bronze shields. The light cavalry, which fell upon the enemy like lightning, pranced behind the guard of honor. They were indomitable soldiers who leapt from their horses at the gallop and returned to the saddle without interrupting their course. They unleashed rows or javelins and rarely missed their target. The heavy cavalry, covered with metal plates and coats of mail, preceded the infantry, the horses' hooves raising a thick cloud of dust. The equipment of the infantry consisted of felt tiaras, tunics, neck-pieces and leg-guards of imbricated plates; the men carried wicker shields, bows, arrows, daggers suspended from the belt, and short javelins.

Visible in the cortege were the helmets with glittering crests of the Assyrians, the pointed bonnets of the Scythians, the loose tunics of the Indians, the heavy robes of the Arabs, the scimitars of the Caspians, the fox-fur headdresses of the Thracians, the leopard-skins of the Ethiopians and the black wooden helmets of the inhabitants of Colchis. The soldiers seemed genuinely bellicose, with the swords, lances, axes and slings that accompanied their accoutrement.

The animal-tamers retained ferocious animals that roared, yapped and mewled as they tugged at their tethers. Slaves carried booty on stretchers covered with precious fabrics garnished with foliage. In the middle of the file came the statues of the gods, and finally, the King in person, followed by his Satraps and victorious chiefs.

The cornices of the palace were sketched in the distance, where the mystic globe deployed its broad wings, alongside monstrous bulls that seemed to want to pounce upon the mobbing procession.

The tumult increased, the swirls of dust rose higher, and Nysista thought that she might faint in her feverish anticipation. She sensed that she was about to experience the greatest emotion of her life, and feared such a shock in the morbid weakness of her being.

Crowned with the great tiara of white cloth circles with gold and enormous stones, Darius was holding the royal scepter. A crimson cloak fell over the rump of his horse and trailed behind it like a pool of blood. The lance-bearers of the Guard, with their rutilant armor and their beards trimmed in equal curls came next, surrounded by the great chiefs.

Nysista raised herself up with a cry and extended her arms toward Arynes, whom she had recognized in their midst.

The young man was advancing proudly on a large white horse. A scarlet cloak, like the king's but shorter, covered his shoulders, allowing the sight of a breastplate encrusted with gold. He passed very close to his lover without recognizing her, but she uttered a strident cry and tried to launch herself toward him. A blow from a spear thrust her back into the crowd, and coarse laughter made her blush with shame.

Next to Arynes she had seen a strange rider mounted on a charger blacker than the night. That glorious bosom, that slender waist and those finely modeled legs could only belong to a woman

The unknown woman wore a necklace with seven rows of enamel and cornelian beads. Her flanks were enveloped by a linen drape with multiple pleats, held at the hips by a girdle imbricated with turquoises and amethysts. Hooked sandals embroidered with pearls shod her slender feet.

Arynes' companion had pure and harmonious features imprinted with a mortal pallor, staring eyes, immense and cruel, and a childlike mouth with lips sealed in a kind of disdainful sadness.

Again, Nysista made an effort to precipitate herself toward the bizarre couple, but the guards pushed her back brutally, while the cold gaze of the unknown woman descended slowly upon her.

Where had she seen those redoubtable eyes before, and the fixed expression of that enigmatic face?

Suddenly, she remembered.

"Zaroccha!" she said, terrified.

The earth resonated and trembled dully under the innumerable wheels of the chariots of war; the cortege was still filing past, and Nysista was still shivering at the memory of the metallic gaze fixed upon her, and the expression of that face, as motionless as the mask of a mummy.

Chapter VI

Souls come toward us and return;
others return and come again.
(The Philosophy of the Vedas.)

Nysista, who had been walking all day, reached the desolate steppes from which the Persians turned away in fear.

She rediscovered the savage sadness of that silent land where she had already wept and trembled beside her lover. It was in that vegetation the color of ash and rust, between two tumulary stones and beneath torture-stakes that she had found Arynes. The officer, she remembered, had wanted to take the witch's jewels. He had disturbed the stones that forbade entry to the sepulchral chamber in order to steal the magic coffer, but a mysterious fear had paralyzed his soul.

She knew full well, however, that the Persians never came into this solitude, for the Mazdan religion did not include either temples or tombs. Only the desire to raise funerary monuments to the glory of heroes had been able to bend the religious law, but it was not this redoubtable place that public worship had chosen to hollow out royal speos in the rock.

The young woman had shivered as she went past the Towers of Silence, where the vultures were tearing carcasses apart, but she had not experienced the sentiment of terror and horror that the solitude of this accursed ground caused her.

It also seemed to her that sniggers emerged from the stones, and that hideous forms were dancing before her. The air was full of monstrous figures; the sky reflected mountains, forests and waves agitated in a sinister fashion. A heavy and feverish wind surrounded her with a veil of fire. Mirages succeeded one another with an ever-increasing rapidity. Twisted, convulsed beings, gnomes of madness and nightmare, passed through the ruins, staring at her with their empty eyes, laughing atrociously or howling their superhuman terror.

And everywhere there was a chaos of enormous rocks that emerged from the ground, gray, bare, rounded or pointed, imprisoning the body of some stranger forgotten by the living. Everything around that reproved earth was hollowed out in nostalgic valleys, enclosed by other mountains, broadening a horizon of peaks and summits.

Nysista advanced painfully, sometimes stopping in front of the entrance to a tunnel, for she could no longer find her way over the ground, uplifted like a sea with monstrous immobile waves.

Finally, she arrived at the ruined temple that sheltered Zaroccha's tomb. The walls were still standing in the middle of the desolate landscape. At their feet the sun had burned and eaten the sand, and corroded the soil; but there was also in that place the profound fire that burns the entrails of the world, and sometimes emerges into the light of day by tearing the earth's crust. A sulfurous glow bathed the witch's hypogeum. Pustules covered the ground all around it, seeming a strange malady of nature; warm mud leaked from their crevices, like mysterious pus. Gases launched forth, noisily, from those burst abscesses, and Nysista, seized in the throat, recoiled, tottering.

She was more and more terrified by the changes that had been produced in that hypogeum. The prodigious phenomena were undoubtedly very recent, and the fantastic florescence of sulfur had not been able to reach the interior of the cavern. She ventured over the warm ash, while further sniggers slapped her as she passed. A round hole vomited fire, smoke and sulfur, with the muffled sound of a boiler. She descended slowly, breathless, panting, suffocated by the morbid breath, obstinate in her desire to search the tomb in order to convince herself that Zaroccha was still there, that it was not her that she had seen at Arynes' side.

The mummified body ought still to have the magic casket that the young woman had piously buried. It was the one that had excited the covetousness of the mourners in the witch's wretched hut; it was the treasure that the officer had wanted to steal from the dead woman, in his criminal desire for wealth.

Arynes had violated the triple subterranean barrier of the hypogeum. Nysista penetrated without difficulty to where the sarcophagus lay. With a tremulous hand she palpated the sides, and uttered a terrible cry.

The body of the witch had disappeared.

At that moment, the sulfur boiled more violently at the threshold of the cavern, fulgurant acids decorated the red lips of the hearth; a formidable shock caused the earth to quake, and the light of the sky was suddenly extinguished.

Nysista ran toward the entrance, but fell back with a scream of agony. By means of the pressure of the flame and vapor that the soil had expelled, the door of the hypogeum had closed upon its living prey.

THE VIRGIN OF ISRAEL

PART ONE

I

> I have had six enclosures constructed in accordance
> with the rules of art. I have done that myself!
> (Nabu-Kudur-Usur.)[1]

Priestesses were dancing backwards before the image of
Mylitta and throwing her tuberoses taken from golden baskets.
Courtesans and women, already drunk, their hair sparse and
their breasts bare, were drinking palm wine from precious vases
stolen from the gods.

In the distance, the walls of Babylon extended, which, by
virtue of their prodigious height and thickness, counted among
the seven wonders of the world.

Profound ditches were hollowed out at their foot, interrupted
at intervals by gigantic towers placed to either side of a hundred
bronze gates.

At their summit the walls could support several chariots trav-
eling abreast, and defied catapults, battering-rams and all the attacks of assailants. An entire army maneuvered there in times of
war, surveying the surrounding area on all sides simultaneously.

The only danger to the immense capital was its river, the open
breach of which, often enlarged by floods, offered the enemy a
chance of invasion. The Oracle had predicted for Babylon, as

---

1 This version of the name rendered elsewhere in the text as Nabuchodonosor, and rendered in many versions of the Bible as Nebuchadnezzar, is
recorded in several nineteenth-century accounts of Babylonian inscriptions;
this one is reproduced in *Les Arts méconnus* (1881) by Émile Soldi, where La
Vaudère probably found it.

for Nineveh, that the city would never be taken by assault, but would perish via its river. The Prophets had added that children would be crushed before the eyes of their parents, the houses pillaged, the women raped, and that Babel, the ornament of the empire, the precious stone of Chaldean vanity, would be annihilated, like Sodom and Gomorrah, by the fire of Heaven.

"It shall never be inhabited, neither shall it be dwelt in from generation to generation; neither shall the Arabian pitch tent there; neither shall the shepherds make their fold there. But wild beasts of the deserts shall lie there; and their houses shall be full of doleful creatures; and owls shall dwell there, and satyrs shall dance there. And the wild beasts of the islands shall cry in their desolate houses and dragons in their pleasant palaces."[1]

In spite of those sinister presages, Belsharuzur,[2] son of Nabunaid, was amusing himself in the midst of his courtesans, flowers of beauty collected from all the points of the globe for one night of amour. The women of his harem appeared with stone masks, long red and yellow robes of precious fabrics and angular headdresses terminated by a floating veil. Behind their masks shone the flame of their long eyes charged with ennui.

Syrian, Tyrian and Arab dancers were agitating gently, rattling the jewels on their upraised breasts and undulating flanks. They had narrow corselets and jackets studded with silver coins. Their hair, woven with turquoises and coral beads, beat their rumps with coarse strips. Idumeans and Phoenicians

---

1 *Isaiah* 13: 20-22.

2 This version of the name rendered in the Bible as Belshazzar is unusual, but by no means unknown in nineteenth-century sources, and is the natural Anglicization of La Vaudére's Belsharouzour; she appears to have been appropriated from Gaston Maspero's *Histoire ancienne des peuples de l'Orient classique* (1885), it being otherwise rare. I have also Anglicized her Nabounaid, which is commonplace in nineteenth-century French documents, although Belshazzar's father—the actual King of Babylon when it fell, although his son did serve as his regent while his father was absent—is nowadays more usually known as Nabonidus. She also renders the latter name with different spellings; I have preserved the inconsistency.

with slimmer limbs, voluptuous physiognomies and large green-speckled eyes were draped in stiff fabrics woven with gold and silver, which, as they parted, allowed glimpses of their agile legs and tattooed flanks.

Belsharuzur, on an ivory throne, sometimes held out the end of his scepter for the most beautiful to kiss, and that was a great favor, which left them dazed and vainglorious.

The prince had a low brow, a strong face, a hooked nose and yellow eyes with an animal beauty,[1] a woven, rolled and curled beard, ruddy black in color, fleshy lips and a slightly receding chin, more sensual than willful. A long crimson cloak, heavy with silver and gold embroideries, swept the throne behind him; a high tiara ablaze with rubies and topazes allowed his braided hair to pass either side of his temples in cordlets terminated by a black pearl. A silk robe woven with gold and embroidered with precious stones designed his harmonious torso, and the sleeves hung down, weighed by pearly fringes. His shoes, edged and embroidered, were sparkling with sapphires, sardonyxes and opals, and were fastened at the instep by a single jewel made from a prestigious diamond. He was leaning on the shoulder of a frail adolescent more adorned than a woman, whose gaze was somnolent, shadowed by long silky lashes

Nigabael might have been sixteen or eighteen years old. He belonged to an enemy race, and nothing was known about him except that Nabunaid had taken him prisoner during a recent war and that he had escaped the habitual massacre by some miracle, along with his brother Phédyne.[2] Prince Belsharuzur

---

1 The word used constantly to describe Belsharuzur's eyes is *fauve*, which means "yellow" or "tawny" when applied adjectivally to a color, but when used as a noun refers to a "wild beast" (a predatory carnivore such as a lion or leopard), and that untranslatable double meaning is crucial to the description of the king's gaze.

2 Although the name Nigabael is entirely idiosyncratic, Phédyne is not, appearing in Pierre Davity's *Les Etats, empires et principautez du monde* (1616), and other texts derived therefrom, as the name of a concubine of the Persian king Cambyses.

had taken the young man in affection and scarcely quit him. He loved his supple limbs, polished with pumice stone, and his delicately modeled flesh, which retained thee unctuousness of baths of oil with rare and penetrating essences. The adolescent's rings and bracelets scintillated, as did the loose tunic that covered his breast and shoulders with multicolored coruscations. He remained charming and fragile beside the powerful and masculine prince, forming a strange contrast with him. As for Phédyne, he was never seen in the palace and his existence was hidden and mysterious.

Belsharuzur passed his fingers through the curly hair of his favorite.

"You seem sad, Nigabael. What do you lack?"

"Nothing, Master. It's sufficient for me to rest my head on your knees and to plunge my gaze into yours to be perfectly happy."

"Is that really true?"

"What more could I want? Have you not saved my life? Have you not heaped me with presents and affection?"

"Yes, you would indeed be very ingrate not to remember that. But the human heart is fickle. Perhaps you regret your homeland and your relatives?"

Nigabael's face darkened, and a flash passed through his blue eyes. "I no longer have any relatives."

"What about that brother . . . whom you have hidden away since your liberation and his?"

Nigabael made no response.

"Yes, you have a brother," the prince insisted. "Why do you never mention him to me?"

"My brother is ill," said the young man, "and hardly ever goes out."

"Am I causing you chagrin by interrogating you?"

"Yes, for I see him getting worse every day, and I fear a fatal outcome."

Belsharuzur did not persist.

136

The dances had ceased around the ivory throne draped with scarlet tapestries fringed with gold, which descended over the steps of the platform amid the skins of leopards and lions. A crimson awning pinned with golden eagles and bordered by spearheads extended over the prince's head. Behind him loomed the immense palace, blistered by glittering domes, glanced by apses and transepts, like a stone god with multiple faces and arms. It was an accumulation of edifices, temples, houses, arches and porticos, traversed by shiny waters of a turquoise blue as dead as the sky.

The palace was divided into three distinct groups of edifices: the seraglio, including the monarch's apartments and the banqueting halls; the harem, or habitation of women; and the khan, which contained the rooms of the officers of the royal guard, the dependencies, the storehouses and the immense stables.

The Assyrians rarely employed anything in their constructions except wood and brick, which did not make them very solid. The form of the column, with its capital, was frequently used as an ornament, but it had no utility, being applied against the wall to produce an optical illusion and only sustaining, more often than not, an allegorical animal.

The façade of the royal dwelling was to the south-west, and the monumental entrance was guarded by a squadron of winged bulls, in accordance with ritual. A courtyard extended behind that door, and then came armories and the main courtyard, which occupied the center of the palace.

When he was in his apartments, the Master expedited business matters under the protection of eunuchs, in the company of ministers and scribes. Afterwards, he went into the ostentatious halls where the host of courtiers assembled.

A discreet daylight fell from above through narrow windows accommodated in the thickness of the vaults. Long strips of bas-reliefs in gray gypsum, painted in bright colors, dressed the walls to a height of three meters above the ground, reproducing the episodes of the royal day: pompous receptions, lion hunts, wars and tortures. A few curt legends accompanied the images and explained them in chronological order.

The gods reigned outside, on the terraces dominated by the ziggurat. The latter was composed of seven stages consecrated to the divinities of the seven planets and painted in their colors, the first in white, the second in black, the third in crimson, the fourth in blue, the fifth in vermilion; as for the last, they were silvered and gilded. The platform bore a chapel spangled with gold, where the religion of Assur and Ishtar was celebrated.

The harem, the Bit-ridouti,[1] was relegated to the southern corner of the enclosure, overshadowed by the Ziggurat. There were three queens and fifteen hundred secondary wives, who were only seen veiled. The queens sometimes attended parades sitting opposite the king, when the latter deigned to send them an invitation to his pleasures, but they had no influence on affairs of State. Very young and utterly charming, their names were Sahuradha, Ussary and Amat-Sula.

The population flocked to the hanging gardens, the magical imagination of verdure that was not the work of Semiramis but that of a Syrian king sufficiently amorous to carry out the grandiose and demented will of his mistress. Those extraordinary gardens extended to either side of the acropolis, for some four plethra,[2] and represented, in a rising slope interrupted by ravines and precipices, a succession of fantastic edifices that seemed to be scaling the clouds for the apotheosis of some titanic fête.

---

1 This term, and much of the descriptive passage in which it features, is borrowed from the previously-cited text by Gaston Maspero.

2 A plethron was a Greek unit of measurement equal to a hundred Greek podes [feet]. The measurement is taken from the widely-quoted account of the hanging gardens given by Dioduros Siculus, a prolific inventor of details embellishing the many legends he recycled. There is no historical evidence for the existence of the gardens in question, although some modern commentators suggest that there might have been actual gardens of some sort in Nineveh. The legend appears to have been invented by a Babylonian priest name Berossus, writing circa 290 B.C., who credited Nebuchadnezzar II with building them for his wife Amytas. (Semiramis is also mythical.)

Those Babylonian monuments, by virtue of their strange boldness, had defied the outrages of time and the attacks of men. The monstrous city, like a sated beast, had become torpid in the inaccessible enclosure of its walls. Drunk on wine and blood, the satraps went to sleep in the arms of courtesans and the priests proclaimed their fears in vain.

From the height of the hanging gardens, sacrificial fires could be seen night and day. According to the hour, they were lit on the thresholds of the temples of Bit-Narris, Nebo, Sin, Samas and Adar-Sandam. Long files of prisoners traversed the low quarters, somber streets bordered with houses of fired bricks and asphalt, violently daubed with yellow and red. Terraces loomed up bordered with viburnum and aristolochia; women leaned over the wooden balustrades insulting or calling out to the vanquished soldiers who were going to the torture.

II

I have put the enemy to flight, I have expelled the inhabitants from their land, I have broken their pride. Me! (Inscription in the temple of Nebo.)[1]

Now filing in front of Belsharuzur's throne were the doriphores[2] and the eunuchs, clad in scarlet robes embroidered with gold and armed with darts, the horses of chiefs led by hand, and then the Persian, Median, Armenian, Caducean and Sacian cavaliers escorting the war chariots. Finally came the prisoners, who were to be immolated to conclude the fête, in accordance with a very ancient custom.

---

1 There is a famous inscription credited to Nebuchadnezzar in a temple excavated at Borsippa, apparently of a temple of Nebo (more commonly known as Nabu), but this passage does not appear therein, and seems to be invented.

2 Doriphores are defined in some seventeenth and eighteenth-century documents as guards appointed to carry a king's cloak.

After the carnage of battles came the slow and pitiless carnage of vengeance. The vanquished enemies were skinned alive, sawn in two, impaled or crucified. The privileged had their heads cut off in the presence of the impassive monarch, while a scribe recorded on a papyrus the number of heads that rolled in the dust. Soon, the golden throne seemed to be borne by red waves, like a glittering and terrible ship of death. To his right, severed hands were piled up, like strange stranded jellyfish; to his left, fearful faces grimaced, monstrous flowers of murder and nightmare.

In order to distract himself, the king sometimes nonchalantly gouged out the eyes of a captive brought to him with a ring passed through his lips.

These scenes were retraced in Assyrian bas-reliefs with a naïve brutality. Here, there were artists cutting out long strips of flesh, removing the skin from palpitating bodies, of which they made sinister trophies. Elsewhere there were scattered limbs, elongated or twisted like reptiles, and artfully-flayed trunks. Planted on stakes, long frightful files of black specters bordered the roads, while lugubrious flocks of birds of prey passed overhead.

Egypt possessed the sentiment of mildness, grace and beauty; Syria and Chaldea, on the contrary, showed themselves in their warrior valor, but also in their pitiless cruelty and their excessive lasciviousness, and never among any people did the delicate chisel of the sculptor take pleasure in displaying more monstrous scenes of orgy and murder.

Belsharuzur perhaps surpassed his predecessors in lust and strange fantasies. Lying in the midst of his concubines, he loved flowers, jewels and perfumes. He made up his eyes and tinted his beard, which naturally had none of the reflections of gold and copper that made its blaze like a sun. He loved all intoxications, and, like Diodorus Siculus' Sardanapalus, abandoned himself not only to the pleasures that food and drink could procure but the enjoyment of the amour of both sexes, abusing both without modesty. Like the hero of legend, he would have been able to compose this epitaph for his tomb:

Passer-by, sure that you are mortal, open your soul to pleasure; there is no more enjoyment for the man who is dead. I, who was once king of great Nineveh, am no longer anything but ash, but I possess all that I have eaten and all that has diverted me as well as the pleasures that amour has procured for me. Only my power and wealth are no more.[1]

Babylon, the cruel, refined and savant city, like its monarch, equaled in bloody and ambitious follies its rival to the north. It prospered and was annihilated by reasons analogous to those that had sown the splendor and then the decline of Nineveh. The shifting sand of destroyed empires has spoken as the Egyptian sphinxes have spoken; great peoples veiled in shadow have emerged from their tombs in order to heap us with admiration, dread and horror.

Nigabael, the sad child, placed his forehead on the king's knees.

"I ask for mercy for them!" he moaned.

Belsharuzur contemplated him with astonishment. "Why?"

"Are you not weary of carnage and crime? How can you repose without seeing the specters of your victims agitating near your bed?"

With a slow gesture, the prince caressed his favorite's hair. "It's war," he said. "Those who die on the battlefield are no more fortunate."

"Yes, but at least they don't have the anguish of torture. They can hope until they're in the arms of death."

"The enemies one kills don't return against you. Destruction ensures the triumph."

"Oh," said Nigabael, "how hard it is to be a king."

But Belsharuzur laughed, cruelly. "Shut up! You talk like a child. Remember that, without my pity, you would have been tortured like these men . . . you, and your brother too."

---

1 The French version of this epitaph, cited verbatim by La Vaudère, first recorded by the ever-inventive Diodorus Siculus, is reproduced in numerous nineteenth-century texts.

The prince had plunged his curious gaze into Nigabael.

"Oh, my brother . . ."

"Yes, your brother, whom you hide from me—I don't know why."

Obstinately, the prince returned his gaze to the child, whom he had granted mercy because of his pretty face, his soft and delicate limbs and his long gazelle-like eyes. He had wanted to unite the two adolescents in the same affection, associate them with his secret pleasures, but Phédyne, the more accomplished of his prisoners, had suddenly disappeared, lost in the miry quarters of the Babylon that he had never been able to subjugate completely.

Already, the severed heads were rolling in the blood like open watermelons, and red jets were flooding with sinister gurgles; rapidly, the executioners brought new victims, who knelt down, without even struggling, knowing that any resistance would be futile.

The brown faces of the spectators, drunk on murder, leaned over the field of carnage. Their eyes no longer reflected anything but a cruel lassitude; only a few women's mouths were still panting, crowding more tightly behind the carriers of clubs and bows, the wielders of thongs, swords and whips, and the satraps costumed in leather, iron, silver and gold.

The decapitations, the severing of limbs and the butchering of entrails continued. Executioners plunged their knives between ribs expertly; others punctured eyelids; several cut pieces of flesh from faces, sculpting frightful masks of dolor and hatred.

Nigabael had closed his eyes and plugged his ears, while the prince, beside him, laughed disdainfully.

"Take him away," he said to Sil-Assur, the palace eunuch. "He's weaker than a woman, and I can feel him trembling like a reed agitated by the breeze."

The young man got to his feet swiftly and went down the steps of the throne behind the nonchalant eunuch.

He belonged, however, to a race that, in the earliest times, had worshipped the frightful Moloch, god of fire, the monster who devoured living children, launched the lightning, set fire to crops and sterilized plains. The first divinities of Israel had been Iahve, Baal and Ashera.[1] Iahve, particularly ferocious, demanded monstrous sacrifices. In order to satisfy him, Solomon had had the throats of so many bulls and sheep cut in a single day that, the bronze altar on which they were immolated being too small, the king went on to the great parvis, from which a river of blood ran for a week, spreading into the countryside. Iahve also liked human blood, since Jephthah sacrificed his own daughter and Abraham nearly killed his son. But the grim Iahve of the Sinai, the terrible idol of David and Solomon, had already become the Elohim of the patriarchs; a great leap had been made toward monotheism, peace and wisdom. Nigabael, the pale and suffering child of an exhausted race, sensed his nerves twisting at bloody effusions; his tender and reflective soul dreaded manifestations of brutal force. With the eunuch he went back into the great hall of the palace, plunged in a melancholy semi-darkness.

Walls covered in panels of enameled faience supported, on pendentives, a round dominant silvered vault, with cabochons of shiny stones, beneath which naves originated and extended like the tentacles of a giant octopus. Metal monsters with human heads and extended wings watched over each entrance. Along the corridors there were representations in bas-relief of Assyrian gods, individuals that were half-bull and half-lion; inscriptions recounted the wars, ambitions, endeavors, hatreds and amours of ancient conquerors. All of them had indulged in debauchery and murder, in bloody orgies depicted on the wall as admirable titles of glory. The cruelty of monarchs was slaked at the slightest pretext. Periodic uprisings, pillages, massacres and frightful executions were the events found on almost every page in the history of the four empires.

---

1 Iahve is much more common in German sources than French ones as a rendering of Jehovah/Yahveh, as is Ashera as the name of the goddess (more usually rendered as Asherah) whom the Jews apparently worshiped along with Jehovah and Baal in their pre-exilic polytheistic epoch. The original of the present text occasionally substitutes Jehovah.

Sadly, Nigabael contemplated the barbaric bas-reliefs and the inscriptions under the paneling of the palace, cataloguing the massacres and registering the tortures as enviable trophies. Terrible maledictions unfurled alongside criminal images, threatening with the anger of the gods anyone who destroyed those proofs of Babylonian grandeur.

As he plunged into a dark gallery, a hand was placed on his arm, and a voice murmured in his ear: "This evening, behind the temple of Nebo."

"Yes," he replied, "when I've seen Phédyne, who is waiting for me."

"All right, but hurry."

The person who had spoken to Nigabael was the satrap Smarnis. He moved out of the shadow, took a few paces, as if to follow the young man, and then disappeared through a secret door.

He had gone to assemble his friends, revolutionaries and conspirators like him, who had sworn to bring down the tyrant.

III

> O Babylonians, I declare to you a misfortune
> that neither my father Belus nor Queen Baltis
> have the power to persuade the goddesses of
> destiny to turn away.
> (The Book of Daniel.)[1]

As soon as Nigabael had reached his apartments he sent the eunuch away and swiftly threw off the sumptuous garments with which he was covered. His slender torso appeared, and his thin neck, adorned with glaucous radiance by a triple collar of gold and aquamarines. That jewel, a present from the prince, sup-

---

1 The quotation is not taken directly from the Biblical book of Daniel, but paraphrases Eusebius, citing Megasthenes, who credits the statement to Nebuchadnezzar.

144

ported figurines of gods, monsters and bulls, accompanied by a delicately engraved prayer.

Nigabael unfastened the bauble, put on a linen tunic bordered by blue designs, put on top of it a fleecy kaunakes mantle that did not stand out against his dark brown skin, and then went out of the palace by means of a hidden door.

Night was falling gradually over the accumulated crowds, which, gorged with wine and massacre, were returning to the poor quarters. The outlying districts were resuming their laborious life; lamps were being lit in the sordid hovels. A few women's voices trailed along the terraces, calling to passers-by, and the fixed statues of terrible gods made white and black patches, depending on whether they were marble or bronze, on the thresholds of temples.

Nigabael isolated himself as much as possible, fleeing the brown prostitutes with thick lips whose hair, in heavy strips, whipped him in passing. Almost all of them had hooked noses, abrupt chins and long nostalgic eyes with an animal gaze. They emitted a strong odor of sweat and coarse essences of herbs and make-up. A few, clad in blue and yellow, were very dark-skinned, almost black, but without presenting any similarity to the negro type; they were more reminiscent of the Ethiopian race; their speech was unctuous and soft.

Nigabael went down a narrow street bordered by a section of the walls. Rickety and makeshift houses with pink and gray terraces seemed to be jostling one another like the restless populace flowing toward the river. Following the movement involuntarily, the young man arrived at the water gate, near a boat ornamented by a monster with clawed feet and the bearded face of a ferocious god. It was moored to the bank, but the rower, asleep under a blanket, stood up at the first appeal.

"Go to the place you know," said Nigabael, "and hurry."

He lay down in the bottom of the boat and remained pensive, while the man struck the troubled water rhythmically, which splashed in soapy droplets, hollowing out a black wake behind it all the way to the shore.

Meanwhile another boat had quit the bank and was quietly following the travelers in the shadow of the wall that extended to the right. To the left, cupolas rose up and terraces fled, edged with climbing plants, like as many miniature hanging gardens.

After having surpassed the height of the quay that limited it, the Euphrates would have reached the houses of the city if it had not had caverns and lakes to collect it; those earthworks, like almost all those in Babylon, were made of fired bricks and bitumen.

Diodorus attributes the construction of a marvelous bridge to Semiramis:

"At the narrowest part of the river she had a bridge five stadia wide constructed, artfully supported, on the river bed, by pillars distanced from one another by twelve feet. The superimposed stones were attached by iron crampons and the joints filled in with molten lead. On the side where the pillars had to contain the current she had angles constructed that presented an inclined plane over almost the entire width of the pillar, in order that the abutment of the pillar would cut the current of the river and that the inclined planes, yielding to that fury would soothe its violence. The bridge was covered with cedar and cypress beams, over which the enormous trunks of palm trees were laid; it was thirty feet wide and did not appear to cede in magnificence to any of the other works."

The Tunnel was in the royal sector, while the Bridge was in the middle of the city, a little to the south of Hillah.

In its double enclosure, Babylon contained agglomerations of ruins and temples that had originally constituted distinct towns. First there was the ancient part, the center of civilization, the heart of the city, which, under the last monarchs, became the royal city with its palaces protected by immense walls, isolated from the new city. To the north was the town of Cutha, comprising the Treasury and the temple of Nirgal, and to the south, the town of Borsippa, with its acropolis and its famous tower of

Bit-Zida. Outside those great centers, however, everything that was not occupied by low houses, intersections and sordid streets remained neglected.

Nigabael saw the ruins of Babil go by, formidable and desolate, then the Kasr, still crowned by a majestic platform. Those residences overlooked the entire city, seeming to cover it with their melancholy shadow.

Lost in his dreams, the young man paid no heed to the maneuvers of the second boat that was gliding slowly behind him, and appeared to be following all the detours of his mysterious excursion. For months, already, he had gone almost every evening into a lost corner of the ancient city, where Phédyne was hidden. Those sorties had always been effected without difficulty and without danger. Why should he have been more anxious than usual after so many fortunate expeditions?

But the constructions were filing past more slowly; the oarsman's arms were beginning to tire. They had reached the temple of El Kalaieh, guarded by winged bulls with human faces—the temple of Bel of which Herodotus speaks, and which was respected by Xerxes. Then came the sanctuaries of the goddess Nana,[1] constructed on the very ramparts of Babylon. Finally, the temple of sacrifices, situated at the extremity of the city, designed its sinister façade.

Having reached the goal of his voyage, Nigabael had his boat moored. Adjusting the dark folds of his mantle, he plunged into a narrow street bordered by houses and small neglected gardens full of brambles and rubbish.

---

1 The name Nana is derived from Herodotus, and therefore common in nineteenth-century French sources, although modern English sources usually give the name of the goddess in question as Inanna.

IV

To the goddess Nana, the sovereign Urkham, the
powerful male, constructed the palace of his desire.
(Inscription on a brick in Sinkereb.)[1]

"Finally it's you! I was dying of impatience! It seemed to me that
an occult danger was threatening you, that I would never have
the gentle pressure of your arms around my shoulders again."

"Today is the feast of the month of Abu. Belsharuzur has
risen at the command of Babylon, via the divine will of Marduk,
and has immolated the prisoners of war. How could I come any
sooner?"

"More murders! Blood, always blood."

"Alas."

"And you watched that killing impassively?"

"No, I veiled my eyes and plugged my ears in order not to see
the red stream flowing and in order not to hear the screams of
terror and torture."

Meanwhile, Phédyne contemplated the ephebe.

"You're handsome, Nigabael. Your hands are delicate and
cared-for; they retain the unctuousness of oils with rare essences;
your hair also gives off troubling odors. Your garments are simple,
but you must have taken off the precious fabrics that would have
betrayed you."

"Yes," the young man murmured. "The prince loves me and
heaps me with presents. However, his generosities chill me and
his affection horrifies me. I think of my relatives who were immolated by his caprice and his cruelty, and my heart quivers with
hatred."

---

1 The citation is a modified version of an inscription of a tablet in the British
Museum, translated into French in Joachim Menant's *Babylon et la Chaldée*
(1875). Nigabael's enigmatic reference to the prediction of Marduk and the
month of Samma (of which nothing further is heard) comes from Menant's
text.

"Oh, Nigabael, let's try to flee his accursed city. Let's return to our homeland!"

"Yes," said the young man, with a somber expression. "I've already had that thought; but the time is not yet ripe."

"What do you want to do?"

Nigabael put a finger over his lips. "Three months hence, on the twentieth day of the month of Samma, during which Marduk's prediction will be accomplished, you'll know the secret of the gods."

Nigabael clasped Phédyne against his heart. The latter was a frail and gentle adolescent with a pure face, long tawny hair, fine and shiny, which flowed over the shoulders. Large glaucous eyes seemed to contain the mystery of sacred pools; the mouth, grave and sad for the moment, had a charming curve full of juvenile seduction.

"I'm afraid, my dear brother."

"We've escaped the greatest dangers; let's have confidence."

"Does life, in these conditions, really have much charm?"

"You don't know what the future holds. At our age, it's still permitted to hope. Revolt is already rumbling; the aristocrats and the people are murmuring against the prodigalities of Nabunahid and his son Belsharuzur. The party of the impatient and that of the interested are showing particular hostility this unworthy reign. Has not Sedicias brought to Babylon a Prophetic scroll in which the predictions are recorded of what the city must suffer?"

Phédyne sighed and clung to him more tightly. "Jerusalem has succumbed. Its king is in the hands of the Chaldeans.

"Yes, the war is without quarter. After the victory, the prisoners are put to the sword, and trophies from the destroyed cities are raised aloft with their bloody heads. Cadavers, eaten away by birds of prey, put the horror of their whitened bones into the furrows. Today, again, Belsharuzur put out the eyes of the vanquished and butchered their limbs."

"You see," said Phédyne. "These massacres will never end. I can't live among these executioners."

Nigabael caressed the child's long blonde hair.

"The Chaldeans have taken the treasures from the temple of Solomon. The punishment will follow the crime, whatever happens. Let us have confidence."

"Your friends are working for liberation?"

"Yes, I have to meet them again this evening."

But Phédyne began to tremble. "Don't abandon me!"

"It's necessary."

"It seems to me that a danger is threatening me. I've never felt a similar emotion."

"What can you fear?" murmured Nigabael, tranquilly. "No one among our enemies knows your retreat, and your brothers in exile won't betray you."

Phédyne raised eyes full of fear upon the young man. "Can't you hear footsteps in the road?"

"Some night prowler He won't attack our poverty."

"They've stopped. Listen—someone's stumbled over our doorstep."

Nigabael opened the rickety door of the hovel and looked outside. Everything seemed calm; a distant song trailed over the river.

"You're mistaken," he said, returning to the child huddled in the shadow. "No one is spying on us. Only a big dog ran away on seeing me. It was gnawing a bone outside our house . . . that's what you heard."

"Perhaps," Phédyne murmured, wearily.

"Can you imagine," Nigabael went on, "that the prince has summoned the satraps, the magistrates, the judges, the army officers, the stewards and all those who hold the principal responsibilities of the realm to witness the edification of his statue. The colossal statue is solid gold, like that of the former tyrant. But the Prophet has said: 'You shall be expelled from the company of men and you shall live with the wild animals.'[1] The man who has stolen the gold and silver vessels from the temple of Jerusalem must perish by the hand of God. The man who adores idols of bronze, iron, wood and stone will be eternally cursed. The prince will perish like his unworthy ancestor."

"A terrible prediction."

"It will be realized completely," said Nigabael. "I am profoundly convinced of it."

The young man had risen to his feet.

"You're going to meet the companions, then?"

"The satrap Smarnis has summoned me for tonight. I can't miss the rendezvous, for the peril is grave. We have to unite all our affections and all our strength."

"Go," said Phédyne, sadly. "My prayers will accompany you, and I associate my desire with yours."

The two children embraced for a long time, and then Nigabael, having thrown his mantle over his shoulders, disappeared into the night.

V

> The women also with cords about them, sitting
> in the ways, burn bran for perfume.
> (The Book of Baruch 6:43.)

Phédyne had sent one last kiss after her brother. In spite of her efforts, fear remained in her soul, and the darkness seemed to her to be full of phantoms. No sound, however, troubled the dormant surroundings; the distant song had ceased; the moment was filled with calm and sadness.

---

1 The prediction in question, allegedly made by Daniel, actually applied to Nebuchadnezzar, and had supposedly already been fulfilled before the time when the present story is set.

Slowly, Phédyne prepared her bed, put oil in the lamp and unfastened her clothing. A round shoulder appeared, and then a delightfully modeled breast with a pure bloom. Phédyne was, in fact, a woman, a still-indecisive and candid flower, but ready to blossom at the first ray of sunlight.

The young woman remained motionless, seized by a new fear more legitimate than the others, for someone had just knocked on the door. Frightened now, she interrogated every corner of the room with an anxious gaze, seeking a refuge against the attack that she feared, the quarter being populated by dangerous vagabonds.

"Who's there?" she demanded. "And what do you want?"

A voice that was deliberately softened replied: "I'm a stranger and I've lost my way. Have no fear, and deign to help me."

Even though her brother had enjoined her not to speak to anyone, she opened the door in order to inform the lost traveler.

A man of tall stature with a ruddy beard and long yellow eyes appeared on the threshold.

Phédyne trembled more forcefully under the flash of his gaze, and recoiled instinctively into the shadows of the room.

"Oh," he went on, quietly, veiling the gleam of his eyes under somber eyelids, "I've come a long way, and repose would be salutary for me."

"I'm poor and I have nothing to offer you."

"Only a little water to refresh my lips. That can't be refused."

She gave the man what he desired, strangely moved by his insistence and the brutal beauty of his visage.

"You aren't typical of the women of this land. Are you a foreigner too?"

"Yes," she said, faintly.

"And you regret your homeland?"

She did not reply, not daring to reveal herself to the unknown visitor.

"Speak without fear," he said. "Like you I'm of a race subjugated by arms. My people have been murdered and my entire being is extended toward deliverance."

152

"Is that true?"

A strange smile twisted the unknown man's lips, and a brief flame passed through his eyes. "I am of the people expelled from everywhere and always combated, who only venerate one God and refuse the crude practices of idolaters."

Phédyne put her hands together. "Oh!" she murmured "You'll support us in the revolt? You share our beliefs?"

"Yes, I'm one of yours. With your friends I'll struggle against the invasive wave of polytheism. While people curb their heads, accept or submit to the principles of tyranny, we protest from the depths of our obscurity; we summon vengeance upon our conquerors."

"Oh," she sighed, "I no longer doubt. You have a noble heart."

"Yes, yes, we are bringing a new religion," the man continued, with an ungraspable hint of irony. "Bel will be broken and Marduk crushed. But the god who will triumph might not be the one whose advent the Jews await."

"Why?" she asked, anxiously.

The stranger was troubled. After a silence, he said: "The time has not yet come, but it is imminent."

He had sat down next to the young woman, and his bright gaze did not quit her. "Will you permit me to come back and speak to you about your cherished homeland and those you love?"

She remained hesitant. "I'll introduce you to my brother . . . but for you, as for others, I'll only be a faithful companion, a boy . . . for," she added bushing, "I've quit the costume of my sex."

"Ah! That is, in fact, more prudent." The same equivocal smile floated over the stranger's lips. But Phédyne, in the generous candor of her youth, did not notice it.

"It's late," she said, after a moment of silence. "Let me rest . . ."

"Yes, I'll leave . . ."

He had reached the door; before going out, he said, in an imploring voice: "Let me return soon . . . tomorrow?"

"Oh! No . . ."

"I don't know anyone in this city; your pity would be such a help! You won't refuse?"

"At least consent to see my brother . . ."

"Certainly, later . . . when you know me better. First, it's necessary that I tell you who I am."

Your name . . . will you tell me your name?"

"Warka."[1]

"Warka . . . I'll remember it."

"Adieu. Tomorrow, I'll tell you about my life. Tomorrow, at the same hour."

"Yes," she said, in a whisper, as if hypnotized by the animal gaze that weighed upon her. "Tomorrow . . ."

Phédyne remained in a strange disturbance. Then, gradually, the balm of silence and solitude descended within her like dew into the heart of a flower. Her temples ceased to throb, her thoughts became torpid, and she fell asleep on her virginal bed. Dream extended its golden wing over her.

VI

It is not the god of the Jews but Ormuzd, the god
of Zoroaster, who will vanquish Babylon.
(Zend-Avesta.)[2]

The Israelites were Semites, which is to say that they belonged to the same race as the Assyrians and the Arabs. The sojourn of the ancestors of the people of Israel in Mesopotamia is proven by their traditions, which have Abraham originating from the city

---

1 Warka was one of the names given to a series of mounds some distance to the south-east of the site of Babylon; some nineteenth-century archaeologists linked it to the "Ur of the Chaldees" from which Abraham was said to have originated.

2 Not a traceable quote.

of Ur in Chaldea, and by their cosmogony, entirely borrowed from Babylon.

But the kings of Juda incurred the hatred of Nabuchodonosor by taking up the cause of the Pharaoh of Egyptians. The powerful monarch of Babylon marched on Jerusalem, overthrew the temple, destroyed the city and took the Jews into captivity. After that, the petty people had only struggled for further falls, and had been attacked in all its refuges. However, the rebels still came together to conspire against the conqueror, sustained by the predictions and the vengeful dreams of their Prophets. The interpretation of their sacred works gave them ardent illusions; they wanted to vanquish, and awaited with confidence the hour of chastisement that would soon sound for the accursed city.

As in many of the peoples living under the patriarchal regime, the members of each tribe among the Israelites formed a unified family, all of whose members sustained one another valiantly.

"If there be among you a poor man of one of our brethren," says the book of Deuteronomy, "within any of your gates in thy land . . . thou shalt not harden thine heart, nor shut thine hand from thy poor brother. But thou shalt open thy hand wide unto him, and shalt surely lend him sufficient for his need, in that which he wanteth."[1]

The Jews therefore united against their executioner, seeking the surest means to deliver him to enemy nations similarly in league against his power.

In a low quarter, miserable and poorly watched, the conspirators met on fixed dates and conferred at length while Belsharuzur, confident in the strength of his militias, forgot himself in feasting.

The outlaws thought about everything that had been stolen from them; the ivory thrones of Solomon, the golden shields and precious vases that had ornamented the temples.

---

1 *Deuteronomy* 15: 7-8.

"For the king had at sea a navy of Tharshidh with the navy of Hiram; once in three years came the navy of Tharshish, bringing gold, and silver, ivory, and apes, and peacocks."[1]

In those days, science, wisdom and opulence made the glory of Israel. The divine people had built fortresses and pierced roads through the mountains; they had had the illusion of strength, power and eternity. However, an audacious monarch had pillaged the temple and drawn the people into slavery. To ornament his table, the tyrant had stolen the gold and silver vessels of the sacred altars. He had no fear of drinking from the precious cups with courtesans and satraps, insulting the glory of the sole God.

But that crime, like others, would have its punishment.

"That night," says the Prophet, "a great cry will go up in Babylon, a sound of ruins and debris will resound through the land of the Chaldeans. For the Lord will ruin Babylon and he will make the voices of its great people cease. It is thus that Babylon will fall, and it will not rise again. It will be destroyed forever."[2]

After having quit his sister Phédyne, Nigabael had headed for the temple of Nebo. The shops decorated with plaques of faience and frescoes had been closed for some time; an almost complete obscurity reigned in the narrow streets. The low houses of red and yellow bricks could no longer be seen, and if a woman with rouged lips and eyes magnified by antimony brushed him in passing, he could only divine her age by the timbre of her voice.

Men enveloped in somber fabrics passed invisibly. Like Nigabael, they were going toward the temple of Nebo in order to hear the prophetic word and submit to its high wisdom. It was not that they understood its deep import very well, but the very simple form pleased their primitive souls. According to them, the religion of Elohim was the religion of Good combating Evil; the poor, the humble and the weak had to range themselves under

1 1 *Kings* 10:22.
2 Not a direct quotation, although it paraphrases part of *Jeremiah* 51.

the standard of the unique God, who would later curb the rich, the proud and the strong. Good, which was also wisdom and life, was symbolized in the venerated image of a master whose adoration brought joy and illusion to the spirit.

The Israelites obeyed the suggestion of the holy word against Babylon and its detested sovereign. They were ready to deliver the city to the king of the Persians, and were only waiting for a favorable opportunity. The moment was therefore approaching when the city of blood would bleed in its turn. It had been the scourge of God; it had continued the work of death that destroyed Jerusalem, razed the temple of Solomon and stolen Juda into captivity. It would be sacked and burned, and the old royalties, which it had humiliated under its yoke, would astonish the world by the vigor of their rebirth.

In a low, smoky room only illuminated by a few papyrus wicks dipped in rancid oil, men of all ages and conditions were assembled. One of them was speaking without raising his voice, but the silence was such that the words vibrated distinctly.

Nigabael had slipped into the first rank of the audience, and everyone had drawn aside to let him pass. He was well known, and precious information was expected from him, which his presence in the palace permitted him to pick up. He was a traitor for the good cause, and nothing would soften the hatred that was gnawing his heart.

Smarnis who was next to him, interrogated him when the orator had stopped speaking.

"Why are you late?"

"Phédyne retained me longer than usual."

"A danger?"

"No, a causeless anxiety that I strove to calm."

"No one suspects her in that distant quarter?"

"She hasn't quit masculine garments, and she doesn't see anyone."

"See to it that she goes out as little as possible, Nigabael. The place seems more dangerous to me than you believe."

"Oh, she only goes out for the provisions, which are very modest."

"Your sister is pretty . . . very pretty," said the satrap, with a tremor in his voice, "and her fragile beauty would please the masters as well as the servants of this accursed city."

Anxiously, Nigabael drew closer to Smarnis. "Your words are singular. Do you have some suspicion?"

"What suspicion could I have? I've noticed, however, that the tyrant often interrogates you about your pretended brother, and that his bestial gaze has disquieting glimmers."

"Yes, you're right; it's not sufficient for him to have consummated my shame and to hold me in slavery, Phédyne's charms and grace must have awakened his covetousness too."

"He'll doom her as he's doomed you."

"Oh, Smarnis, how painful my destiny is! Better death than that frightful suggestion!"

"Have you no relative who could take charge of the child?"

"All of mine were killed in the last massacre. But no one suspects you, Smarnis, and perhaps you could give shelter to my sister?"

The satrap reflected, and it was in a confused voice that he replied, after a momentary silence. "Yes, I've already thought of that. Unfortunately, Phédyne would be noticed in my house, as elsewhere. She'd be denounced, and everything would be discovered. The best thing is to be patient still. The revolt is rumbling and our sect is working for us. The people of Juda will be avenged; believe in the predictions of our Prophets!"

A man was standing immobile at the podium. Conversations ceased and the orator began.

"The enemy is advancing on Babylon. They are not disorderly bands of kings and haphazard warriors, temporarily united by the ascendancy of a single man but divided by hatreds and reciprocal mistrust. The Egyptians, the Libyans and the Greeks are in the hands of an experienced leader who is making progress irresistibly with his invincible troops. The mass of combatants is similar to the waves of the Nile, which rise, inundate the ground, drowning the cities and fields; nothing can resist its attack, for no barrier can stop the surge of nature and the will of God. We have been vanquished, humiliated and destroyed by the stronger, but the petty people, in their turn, will be able to vanquish by means of cunning, intelligence and patience; the future belongs to them!"

Enthusiastic cries departed from all the corners of the low room. Then the orator, who was old and sad, in spite of the warmth of his words, gave all the reasons that he had for believing in the certain and definitive triumph.

"Peoples are still colliding, coming to grips with one another and tearing one another apart. That is good; the cooking-pot, of which the Prophets have had the vision, is boiling, sometimes overflowing into neighboring nations and sometimes falling back upon itself in sterile agitations. The industrious valleys of the Euphrates were still rich, in spite of the losses that tyrants made them suffer, and the submissive cities have continued to prosper under the authority of satraps. Babylon, the impure capital, soiled with all vices and all crimes, nevertheless offers an inviolable refuge to rebels, who can act from there upon their distant brothers. A devoted man, a man without fear and without reproach, can take them the holy word . . ."

The Prophet Daniel, who attended these meetings like a god surrounded by the veneration of all, stood up in his turn.

Daniel was of the tribe of Juda and the royal race. Nabuchodonosor had brought him to Babylon as a child in the third year of the reign of Joachim, in order to have him brought up in the court and educated at the king's expense. Later, he became skillful in the interpretation of dreams, and the favor that he enjoyed awoke the jealousy of the mages, who had him thrown into the lions' ditch. But the Prophet, triumphant over those attacks, rose up in all his power to overthrow the masters of Babylon. As he had condemned Nabuchodonosor he condemned Belsharuzur, and his great voice already dominated the noises of the crowd.

With a gesture, he indicated Smarnis. "This is the man whom the Eternal has chosen."

The satrap prostrated himself. "I will obey, since it is the will of the One who has taken Israel under his holy protection."

"Israel is the blessed people, the one that will enjoy the abode of Canaan and remain without sin."

Daniel commanded as a master, and no one ever raised a voice against him. The Prophets were no longer veritable Statesmen, but they still plunged into the politics of their time and modified it by persuasion or violence. They addressed themselves to religious men in order to show them their corruption and to frighten them with sinister presages. Their speeches were collected and written down for the edification of impartial posterity.

Juda trembled with fear at the thought of the tortures that awaited the incredulous and the indifferent: ferocious peoples were to traverse the expanses of the earth in order to conquer the wealth accumulated by the sons of Israel. "Their horses also are swifter than leopards, more fierce than the evening wolves . . . and their horsemen shall come from afar; they shall fly as the eagle that hasteth to eat. They shall come all for violence; their faces shall sup up as the east wind, and they shall gather the captivity as the sand. And they shall scoff at the kings . . . they shall scorn every stronghold."[1]

"Do you want to accomplish what the Eternal desires?" the Prophet asked the satrap then.

"I want that."

"And you will be the savior of our race?"

"Yes," said Sarnis, who dominated the audience by virtue of his tall stature.

"You will brave all dangers?"

"What is it necessary to do?"

"You will know when the time comes."

---

1 *Habbakuk* 1:8-10 (The version employed in the original is, as usual, slightly modified.)

"So be it," said the satrap, calmly. "I shall wait. The wise God, who has made everything, has put into our bodies and ardent souls that which will be able to combat and triumph. I will obey the Prophets and I will listen to the great voice of the ancestors, who still speak to us from the depths of tombs!"

VII

All go unto one place; all are of the dust,
and all turn to dust again.
(*Ecclesiastes* 3:20.)

Nigabael and Smarnis were now walking between flattened houses, silos, cisterns and stairways carved in the rock, calcareous blocks and the ruins of temples, mysterious sanctuaries of maleficent idols dear to the Babylonians. Figures of goddesses and gods standing on their sacred animals, lions or bulls, still received the offerings of their faithful.

Nigabael turned away with disgust, hastening his steps in order to flee the baleful images.

He regained the palaces by way of long detours, in order to evade the suspicions of anyone who might have followed him. The banks of the Euphrates did not present themselves, like those of the Nile, under the aspect of grandiose constructions that announced to the world the activity of a powerful and laborious people. Stone was very rare in Babylon; architects scarcely employed it except for lintels, uprights and friezes sculpted on the exterior walls of monuments. Bricks, fired or enameled, and beds of dried reeds formed the principal elements of houses and temples, which deteriorated rapidly, dissolving in every storm. Then the streets filled with a gray mire; the plan of edifices was effaced and buckled, as if drowned in mud.

Smarnis, who was walking alongside Nigabael, told him how facile the victory seemed to him. The grim warriors went to sleep in perpetual orgies; they would be struck as they had struck, unrelentingly and without mercy. The enemy would take possession of the pikes and clubs that had served in the recent massacres of their brethren. Under furious blows, brains would spring forth in red floods. The enormous irradiation of captured weapons would envelop the tyrants brutalized by pleasures and debauchery. Surrounded and arrested, they would be pierced with spear-thrusts, beaten down by clubs, decapitated by axes, and their flesh, torn to pieces, would nourish stray dogs.

Habituated to continual slaughter, those spectacles of death would no longer revolt the inhabitants of Babylon.

"So you want to sacrifice yourself to the good cause, and defend our brethren?" Nigabael asked.

"Yes," said the satrap. "By virtue of my position, I'm less suspect than anyone else, and I'll be able to act more cleverly. I don't know yet what's expected of me, but whatever the desire of our people is, I'll submit to it."

"Thank you," murmured the young man, shaking his friend's hand. "In my turn, if I can be useful in any way whatever, count on me. My influence over Belsharuzur is considerable at the moment; do you want me to speak to him about you?"

"No."

"Why? Tomorrow I might be in disgrace; it's necessary to take advantage of the favor I have."

"I don't have any ambition . . . and in any case, it's wiser not to attract the prince's attention."

"You don't wish for anything, then?" sighed Nigabael. "I'd be happy to prove my gratitude."

"You could fulfill my prayers."

"Really? Tell me, what is it necessary for me to do?"

"It's necessary," stammered Smarnis, "for you to speak about me to Phédyne and tell her that I love her."

"You love her!"

"Since the first time I saw her."

"But when have you seen her, then?"

The satrap was troubled. "I saw her when she was with you among the captives. No one else divined her sex, but the impression she produced on me revealed the truth. I've spied on you in your sorties and I've seen you go into the little house on the water's edge. Phédyne, half naked, sometimes showed herself at her window, with no fear of being seen in that deserted quarter, and I, hidden in the shadows, was intoxicated in her presence. For her, I wanted to know your God and I've defended your cause."

"It was for Phédyne . . ."

"For her, whom I cherish at this moment more than anything in the world."

"Oh, what joy!"

"That pleases you?"

"Yes, because I can prove my gratitude a little by giving her to you."

"I can marry her," said the satrap, gravely, "since her belief has become mine . . ."

"I'll take you to her tomorrow."

"Will she want to listen to me?"

"Can you doubt it, my friend? She will love you, as I love you, and will surely put her hand in yours."

"May you be telling the truth!"

"What reason could I have for doubting her sentiments? Phédyne only has me on earth; her existence is spent in meditation and solitude. She has even lost the taste for adornment, since she has renounced the silky clothes and jewels that adorn her peers. I've often found her in tears in the dreary hovel where she lives, and I've understood the desolation of her soul only too well. Oh, how she'll thank me for having thought of her, and how she'll repay you in caresses and kisses for the amour you're bringing her!"

"I want to believe you, Nigabael. I need that assurance to accomplish loyally what is expected of me."

"You'll accomplish it, Smarnis, and you'll need courage to vanquish this grim people which, in the words of the Prophet 'march through the breath of the land, to possess the dwelling-paces that are not theirs. They are terrible and dreadful, their judgment and dignity proceed of themselves. Their horses also are swifter than leopards, more fierce than the evening wolves ... and their horsemen come from afar; they shall fly as the eagle that hasteth to eat. They come all for violence; their faces sup up as the east wind, and they gather the captivity as the sand. And they shall scoff at the kings ... they shall scorn every stronghold, for they heap dust and take it ... They fall like the hurricane; they pass at the gallop, charged with crimes, and their strength is their god.'[1] Remember the grim prediction!"

"No," said Smarnis, shaking the young man's hands, "amour is the only force in the world!"

"Until tomorrow ..."

"Until tomorrow."

When Nigabael reached his apartment the first light of day was extending a veil of crimson and gold over Babylon.

VIII

> My beloved put in his hand by the hole in the door,
> and my bowels were moved for him.
> (The Shulamite.)[2]

On her burning couchette, Phédyne was thinking about Warka; she could not find sleep, and the image of the stranger still presented itself to her. She saw him again, tall and strong, with his caressant and terrible eyes, brighter than enchanted stones.

---

1 The last sentence of this supposed quotation is not in *Habbakuk*, from which the rest is taken, most of which has been cited previously. It appears to be improvised rather than translated from elsewhere in the Old Testament, although it is somewhat reminiscent of the early verses of *Joel* 2.
2 *Song of Solomon* 5:4.

Where had she seen him before? It seemed to her that his face was not unknown to her, and that it had leaned over her in a terrible circumstance of her life. Where? When? How? Then she reflected on the improbability of that encounter and told herself that a singular vision was doubtless obsessing her.

How insinuating his voice was at certain moments! How one sensed in him the will and the ability to please, purely by the power of his gaze and his speech! He came from Juda, like her; he believed in the same God, and his intervention would be beneficial in the milieu of her own people.

She closed her eyes, and remained bewildered by everything that was happening within her that was disquieting and new. That visit had come to surprise her like a thunderbolt in the midst of the melancholy existence that she led in her reclusion, separated from Nigabael. Her being was suddenly transformed; her former anguish had disappeared to give way to a sentiment in which she could neither rejoice or be chagrined. It seemed to her that a burning wave was running through her veins, and that a mysterious hand was gripping her heart, which was beating irregularly, struggling like a captive bird.

Certainly, she had seen the unknown man before when she was walking in the arid countryside, treading the golden sand with long burning plaints. Here and there, formless blocks, like aeroliths fallen on a mass of molten flint, arrested her march; the river passed slyly behind the immense rushes, and, at a great height, thanks to the silence, she could hear the sound of wings and the cries of birds There were black flocks of crows, eagles with brown-striped undersides, vultures patched with black and bright gray, which circled around the highest bluffs.

Phédyne sometimes spent a part of the day sitting in the harmonious rushes. She listened to the sad plaint of the wind, playing in the tightly-packed stems with sharp, broad leaves. She was inebriated by the bitter perfumes of the water and the vegetation, until a tribal chief, followed by a brilliant escort, interrupted her reverie. Sometimes the man was young, handsome, elegant and dressed with the sumptuous expertise of Chaldean satraps. Often, too, a thin old man, almost naked, with leather bags suspended over his chest like half a dozen flutes, addressed prophetic words to her that she did not understand.

A few thin trails of vapor floated over the horizon like tresses of golden hair. Toward evening, the luminous wisps scattered in a light sheet in the midst of the unwrinkled azure, drifting slowly like the rounded sails of a ship seen from a distance shrinking and subsiding at the entrance to a harbor.

Phédyne thought that she must have seen the stranger during one of her long walks in the melancholy countryside.

She lay down on her couch and closed her eyes in order to recover the beloved image in her sleep. In spite of her efforts, though, she could not sleep, wishing for and dreading the presence of her brother. However, she had decided to say nothing to him yet, obedient, in spite of herself, to the order she had received.

At dawn, she got up, in order to go fetch water, as she did every day, and to prepare her modest meal. With more care she disposed around her face the braided wisps of her hair, steeped in perfumed oil, and she neglected to put on her masculine garments. A white sheet bordered with blue espoused the harmonious and fine contours of her body more faithfully, a silky scarf gripped her slender waist. When she had arranged the few objects that served her life, she let herself drop once again on to the bed and resumed the interrupted dream . . .

What disturbance was she going to bring into her brother's projects? Where would the hazard that had revealed the secret of her heart lead? It was impossible for her to keep quiet and enclose the sentiment permanently within her being. But how would she tell him, and what would become of her after having spoken? Her head was laboring in an unhealthy tension while she remained inert, prey to a kind of torpor that she had never felt before. The hours passed in long and troubled meditations, which increased her disturbance and her weakness.

Nigabael came, as usual, and was astonished to find her so different from the way that she normally seemed.

"Are you ill?"

"Yes," she murmured, confused and blushing. "I think the fever hasn't quit me since yesterday."

The young man was anxious. "You don't go out enough, and I ought to do more to distract you. Unfortunately, I'm not free; the tyrant I serve has been particularly eccentric and demanding of late."

"Oh!" she said, indifferently.

"He's asked me a lot of singular questions about you."

"About me? But he doesn't know me."

"He's only seen you once, when my brethren were tortured. You were wearing masculine clothes."

"The mercy he granted us astonishes me."

A singular smile creased the young man's lips. Oh, it was not out of pity that Belsharuzur had acted, he knew that full well, and was indignant about the suggestion to which he had submitted. But Phédyne, the pure virgin, must not know anything about that.

"Soon," he said, "we'll be free, and you'll be a beautiful bride."

"Me!" she thought she would fall over, so great was the violence of the shock.

"Yes," he said, "it's marriage that you need, for a woman only really lives in amour."

The young woman lowered her eyes. Certainly, the idea of marriage made her smile, and if the stranger of the previous evening wanted her, there would soon have been two happy people on earth.

"I'll do anything that you desire," she said, "provided that you leave the choice of the husband to me."

"But of course," he said, joyfully. And he thought that Phédyne did not see any men, and that the young, handsome and sedative Smarnis was bound to please her, he would have pleased any other woman.

"It's necessary to sleep," said Nigabael, caressing the young woman's cheek. "Your eyes have a flame of fatigue and fever. Rest, little sister, in order to rediscover your visions of tenderness and joy. Happiness, for us, only still shines in your dreams!"

He kissed her gently, and went back to the place where he had left his oarsmen, behind the water gate. As on the previous evening, a boat was waiting a short distance from his own, but he paid no heed to it, entirely intent on his plans for the future and the hope of success.

In the moonlight, the water had blue and hyaline reflections; the banks were languidly dressed in soft shadows, and everything was silent in the deserted quarter. Nigabael drew away, his soul tranquil, cradled by a new hope. As they drew closer to the city, the brick edifices were clothed in enamel and golden grooves in the midst of the verdure of hanging gardens. Distant rectangular flower-beds ornamented the squares, and between the houses, terraces covered by awnings were staged, edged by flowers with vehement scents.

Temples launched toward the sky and the conquest of the stars. The angular profiles of Ziggurats displayed unequal prisms, piled one atop another in retreat and crowned with a light edicule in which a god was lodged. The stages were as many full blocks of raw clay, and the terminal chapel only contained a single chamber equipped with an altar facing the door. Ornaments of enameled plaques, of a flat turquoise blue, decorated the exterior walls, while precious wood of cedar or cypress paneled the sanctuary. Thin leaves of gold laminated the woodwork in places, and mosaic panels composed of thin pieces of alabaster, onyx and agate, alternated with them. The statue of Nana stood up in stiff and heavy icons; the idol watched over the tumultuous people, whose rumor rose as high as her.

Scornfully, Nigabael thought about the terrible gods who persecuted the city, those disquieting monsters armed with knives and spears, who menaced humans. Some floated in the air and presided over unhealthy winds. The south-west wind, the most maleficent, lay in ambush in the deserted quarters; the spirits of fever and folly insinuated themselves slyly and perfidiously into dwellings in order to sow desolation and death there; ghouls awaited travelers, and fleshless specters quit their tombs in order to drink the blood of the living.

Those monsters had birds' feet and the scales of fish, the tail of a bull and vast outspread wings. Some displayed the head of a lion, a vulture, a hyena or a wolf. They balanced the body of a dog on legs terminating in eagles' claws, and their appearance was always terrifying.

But Nigabael did not believe in those evil spirits, and a smile parted his lips before the glorious temples to those chimerical gods.

The magnificence of the constructions increased as one approached the center of Babylon. There was no more waste ground with suspect vegetation, as in the poor quarters, paths full of grass, mallow and thistles, through which reptiles slithered; everything appeared majestically splendid, to fête the fortunate of the earth, and the young man thought about the words of the Prophet: "Fortunes change, and the humble of today will be the powerful of tomorrow."

Imprudent for the first time, he forgot to go ashore in the poor district, and the insouciant oarsmen pushed the frail boat all the way to the terraces of the royal palace. But the sky, that evening, was so full of stars that the god of the Jews could not wish death to his children!

The eunuch Sil-Assur, however, was watching in the shadows. He had a cruel smile on seeing the young man enter slowly, his head held high, ignorant or disdainful of danger. He knew that favorites passed in the master's ephemeral caprice, but he, the spy, sexless and ageless, remained standing on the threshold of the temple, like the monsters of stone that guarded its entrance.

IX

By night on my bed I sought him whom my soul loveth:
I sought him but I found him not . . . I charge you,
O daughters of Jerusalem, if ye find my beloved,
that ye tell him that I am sick of love.
(The Song of Songs.)[1]

Fearfully, Phédyne interrogated the night. Would he come, the man who was already for her the earth and the sky, the vision of sweetness, amour and forgiveness, the one who consoles life and gives the strength of consented death?

It seemed to her that the celestial vault had never shown so many golden nails, pinning the veil of eternal mystery over the heads of humans.

And she hummed a song of Juda, the one that the virgins of Israel say very quietly in appealing to the husband.

The forest is full of roses,
Like the garden of my heart
Enter my lord, O my master,
Here are the roses of my heart!

May Yahve, Baal and Ashera
Direct the beautiful god Tammuz
Toward the garden of my amour.
Enter, my lord and my master,
Here are the roses of my heart!

But a shadow approached, and a tall silhouette loomed up before her.

"Enter, my lord and my master, here are the roses of my heart."

---

1 The first part of the quotation is 3:1 and the second part 5:8.

In truth, the sage Phédyne no longer knew what she was saying, in the emotion of the first sentiment that a sad life of solitude and regret rendered more intense.

"You were waiting for me, Phédyne?"

Blushing, the virgin lowered her eyes, confused and nonplussed.

"You were waiting for me? Oh, nothing in my existence has been worth such a felicity to me!"

"My brother," she said, "has talked to me about you."

The stranger shivered. "Your brother?"

"Yes, he told me that you desire to be my husband."

"Your husband?"

The stranger's astonishment became fear.

Phédyne drew closer, smiling. "Oh," she said, naively, "he didn't name anyone; but as I've never seen anyone but you since I've been living here, there can't be any question of anyone else."

"Indeed," said the man who had named himself as Warka, "you've never received anyone but me? And what did your brother say?"

"He said that a friend would soon ask for my hand. I divined that it was you. Am I mistaken? Oh, answer quickly, it would be so painful for me no longer to believe in your affection."

"Your brother told the truth. I am the one who loves you and who wants you for a wife."

With a joyful cry, the young woman nestled in Warka's arms. Confidently, she lifted her large tender eyes toward him, and did not refuse his kiss.

She pressed herself against that broad chest joyfully, the tumultuous heartbeat of which she could feel, and the consciousness of her own fragility augmented the pride of is protection. The great yellow eyes poured out their mysterious effluvia, the sharp white teeth shone in the lascivious laughter of the thick lips. Warka was handsome, with a beauty unknown to her race. He had power and will. She sensed that he was habituated to triumphs, and that exuberance of life and strength augmented the submission of the fearful virgin.

"I'll marry you," he said, "but later, when our brethren are happy."

"Yes, I know that you have a mission to fulfill."

"A holy mission, which already absorbs a great deal of my time. However, I'll see you every evening; you'll be the sweetness of my life, and henceforth, I shall only obtain joy through you."

He respired the amber of Phédyne's hair, and let his lips wander in the voluptuous fleece. The entire slender body of the young woman was emphasized beneath the thin fabric that covered her, and the breasts were pointed like buds full of sap on the tree of desire. She had within her all the promising freshness of spring; she was as supple and as smooth as a rush, and her complexion presented the luminous softness of flowers gorged on sunlight.

Phédyne was as charming as Nigabael, the fragile adolescent, but she had, in addition, the candor of her ignorance.

"I could carry you away like my own thing," Warka said, "and intoxicate myself constantly on your presence; but I prefer to wait for better days. It would be dangerous to forget the enemy oppression, and your kisses would have too much power."

It pleased Warka to play this entirely new game; and, although he was able to take Phédyne, he nevertheless respected her, not wanting to spoil his pleasure by too rapid a possession.

"So," he said, after a long caress, "your brother is conspiring?"

Her gaze was astonished. "But you know that as well as I do, since you're one of ours."

"That's true. Oh, your kisses are strangely intoxicating, since they take away from me even the consciousness of peril."

"Warka," she said, "I love you more than anything in the world, but I also think about the promise you've made to our friends. You have been chosen among all to defend our rights in the great struggle that is in preparation, and only you can escape the terrible surveillance of the Master."

Warka smiled. "Yes, yes, my beloved Phédyne; I'm ready to depart, since I know that it is up to me, uniquely to me . . . Never hide anything of your life from me. It is infinitely sweet for me to hear you repeat the words of justice and duty. In passing through your mouth, the holy words acquire a greater power. They are not only the expression of a thought of vengeance, but also that of a mission of love. Everything that you tell me will render me better and more active. I need that encouragement, that support, in order to be able to obey, for the separation will be very painful for me."

He had taken her against his breast again, and, forgetting himself in an exquisite caress, he drank at the fresh source of all felicity.

She closed her eyes, abandoning herself to a singular frisson that she had never felt before.

The sadness of her existence, the long solitary days spent in the abandoned building, had slowly prepared her for this blossoming of joy. Ignorant of the danger, she was devoid of weapons with which to fight. Warka had been the first person to talk to her about amour, the first to seek her virgin lips, and he was the husband that her brother destined for her—so she believed, at least. Why would she hesitate to welcome it, since her heart counseled her, invincible, by tenderness? How, in her innocence, would she have been able to suspect that the man was only an impostor desirous of her doom?

"Oh, Warka," she murmured, "I shall have no secrets for you. In any case, you know the dolorous events that have darkened my youth. You know that all of my people have been killed by the infamous tyrant of Babylon . . ."

"Yes," he said, softly. But he held her against him so tightly that she thought she was going to faint.

"That man, you see, I hate as much as I love you, and if I had him before me, I would not hesitate to strike him. But I don't want to think about that infamous monster. I love you, Warka, and nothing, henceforth, can any longer trouble our amour. Give me your lips, warm with kisses, hold me against your bosom, and swear to me to belong to me as I belong to you!"

"I swear it," said Warka, with a mysterious smile. "Until tomorrow, my beloved. You see, I respect you; I adore you immensely, and I want to keep your immaculate image in my heart until you are my wife . . . Until tomorrow!"

Warka was already disappearing into the night.

"Until tomorrow!" she shouted, from the threshold of her dwelling.

Intoxicated by joy and hope, she did not hear the light laughter that was carried on the breeze.

X

> All things come alike to all; there is one event
> to the righteous, and to the wicked; to the good
> and to the clean, and to the unclean; to him that
> sacrificeth and to him that sacrificeth not; as is
> the good, so is the sinner; and he that sweareth,
> as he that feareth an oath.
> (*Ecclesiastes* 9:2.)

Nigabael, his eyes lowered, stood before the Master, who was examining him curiously.

"What were you doing yesterday, and why did I not find you at the usual hour?"

"I fell asleep waiting for your return, and time fled . . ."

"Truly?"

"Yes," said the young man, with assurance, "I was in my room and I was reposing. You can ask the eunuchs of the guard."

Belsharuzur did not insist, but a darker fire shone in his yellow eyes.

"Come," he said, "come and lean your forehead on my knees, while I occupy myself with the good of my land. Order reigns

174

everywhere, is it not so? No conspiracy is to be feared for the moment? Reply, Nigabael, and give me your opinion on these important matters."

The young man was troubled. "I have not seen anything or heard anything. I do not know anything, Master."

"Yes, you're faithful to me. You love me, Nigabel, and you would defend me, if necessary—if my life were in danger?"

"You cannot doubt it, lord of my days."

Belsharuzur caressed his favorite's silky hair with his ring-laden fingers, for that delicate face, which was extended toward him, presented a perfect resemblance to the beauty of Phédyne: the same gaze with glaucous gleams streaked with gold, the same slightly morbid delicacy of the features, and the same velvety suppleness of the skin. Nigabael's linen tunic was parted over the breast, retained by an emerald clasp. Like a woman, he wore pendants of green stones that fell to either side of his forehead, and ear-rings. One might, at first, have hesitated over his sex, so languid was his pose, so soft was his voice. Submissively, he lent himself to his Master's caprices, and one sensed an immense sadness in him.

Belsharuzur was wearing a miter on his head with cabochons of precious stones, and his left hand was playing nonchalantly with an ivory staff ornamented with a lion's head. His long and bristling beard formed symmetrical curls. His hair was staged over the nape in brilliant waves, tinted with russet flames. He was handsome, with a somber and brutal beauty, disquieting in its cruel expansion. Next to him, the frail adolescent seemed even more refined, haloed with a touching grace.

Around the throne pressed the crowd of courtiers with sumptuous jewelry, gold bands, and long robes embroidered with silky designs and fringed with multicolored pearls. Their thick, curled hair was adorned with pointed or angular bonnets, depending on the importance of their rank. The soldiers wore yellow footwear, which came up to their knees, and tunics garnished with embroideries and tassels. All of them had bracelets, thick circlets at the top of the arms, necklaces of lapis lazuli and cornelian, amulets of gold or fine stones, and enamel plaques framed in gold.

The mores of the voluptuous Babylonians were in accord with these effeminate decorations, for all the enjoyments of the mind and the flesh were familiar to them.

Belsharuzur interrogated the satraps regarding the latest feats of arms.

"We have," said Ourouka, the Assyrian chief, "recruited the best of the material and mental forces of the realm. We have sacked Sais, Mendes and Tanis, in order to give an example of our power."

"And what have you done with the prisoners?"

"We killed them by crucifying them, as they crucified our vanquished warriors. Their chiefs were attached to trees in order to be eaten by the vultures."

"Yes," said another satrap, "but I brought back five enemy heads suspended from the neck of my horse. I nailed them on my door as a sign of my triumph. Oh, our country is no longer anything but an armed chaos in which only armed conquest can restore order."

"But you know, Master," Ourouka affirmed, "with your profound skill, how to subdue all these rebels, some by means of others, seducing some by means of caresses, selling others in order to extract a profit. You leave to the former their leaders and their laws, in order better to impose your supreme will on others."

Pensively, while the fearful Nigabael lowered his eyes, Belsharuzur asked: "Have you discovered any new conspiracies?"

"No," said Ourouka. "Babylon seems calm."

"That calm might be deceptive. Watch night and day, and at the slightest alert, come and warn me. Like Nabuchodonosor, I shall be a soldier, a mariner, a pioneer and an architect. I shall create fortresses and ships, I shall redirect rivers, if necessary, in order to conquer the world!"

Belsharuzur, however, forgot his bellicose resolutions in his celebrations. He was not a man capable of forestalling the stormy times that were announced. Without any real right to the crown, he had brought into play, in order to succeed, all the powers of intrigue and cunning, but he did not have in his ideas the intelligence of consequences that is indispensable to any man of action. Already, he was letting his army deteriorate, and his officers, like him, were delivering themselves to monstrous debauches. Drunk, their hair woven with flowers, they were seen running all over the city in sumptuous attire, between crowds of slaves, begging for a gaze or a smile. Their eyebrows painted, their faces rouged, they danced around chariots to the shrill sounds of the Babylonian asor and the Asiatic sistrum. A host of people, peasants and staggering soldiers, filled the avenues, frightening the chained leopards and lions that followed the king's chariot.

With an indolent gaze, Belsharuzur observed the movements of the lascivious dancers, seeking a mistress among the troop of beautiful women always offered to his desire. But those excessively facile conquests were quickly discarded; with a weary gesture he sent away the lovers of one night, seeking the impossible possession of a lasting joy.

The three queens, Sahuradha, Ussary and Amat-Sula languished at the court, similarly neglected by their royal husband. They even avoided walking in the gardens in order not to encounter the courtesans who charmed the Master's whim. At the most, Sahuradha was sometimes seen reposing in the midst of her women at the end of the day. She installed herself on the terrace of the gynaeceum between the bronze palm trees, the emblem of fecundity and grace, and a few nostalgic songs soothed her ennui.

The monotonous existence of the queens and princesses went by in the prison of the bit-ridouti, in the midst of the cares of their futile beauty. They embroidered, danced and played various musical instruments, received a few visits from titled women, and were sometimes mortally jealous when one of them had given birth to a male child. The sons remained in the bit-ridouti until their first adolescence; then they were taken away from the mother in order to enable their education as princes and soldiers.

They participated in fêtes, surrounded by the sacred eunuchs, and saw all the actors of royal rejoicing file past. There were men and women, lasciviously adorned, mages dressed in long white robes, semi-naked courtesans dancing to the sighs of lyres and the crystalline sounds of double red flutes. Then, after the beautiful young women with voluptuous gestures and long caressing eyes, came the sacrificers, agitating chaplets of severed hands, trailing bloody disheveled heads in the dust.

The priests of the temples of Bit-Narris, Nebo, Sin, Samas, Bel, Nana and Anu glorified those crimes, which they declared to be agreeable to Baal, the multiple god of hatred and vengeance. Babylon, the inflexible warrior, had to subjugate the world to his conquering glory . . .

But within its walls, a petty people was struggling against the invading flood of polytheism, and protesting, from the depths of their exile, against the indignity of the victors. Daniel was already meditating the fateful words that were to burst forth in letters of flame on the tyrant's walls.

Belsharuzur, unconscious, enjoyed life, and his thoughts only evoked images of murder or lust. Even in the midst of the satraps, great chiefs and powerful men of the realm, he kept his dancers and his musiciennes close by, who relieved him of the ennuis of power. Small boys clashed bronze cymbals and beat drums with their slender fingers; in the intervals of the council there was a burst of castanets, sistra and tambourines, accentuating the variations of horn and iron flutes, nebels, lyres and asors. All rhythms and all fantasies took flight from strange instruments and relaxed the nerves with their complicated harmonies. Young men of equivocal appearance alternated with women with brown bodies, offering themselves and slipping away by turns, in an expressive mime.

Thus, in the gravest hours of his life, the monarch lulled himself in the sonorous waves of psalterions and light flutes, seeking, everywhere and always, voluptuous sensation, forgetfulness of responsibilities, and perhaps ignorance of himself.

XI

I will give thee the treasures of darkness and hidden riches of secret places, that thou mayest know that I, the Lord . . . am the God of Israel!
(*Isaiah* 45:3.)

Meanwhile, the Babylonians themselves were becoming estranged from their king, and almost all of them were ready to welcome the foreigner who would rid them of a shameful suggestion. Nigabael sensed the revolt rumbling around him, and foresaw that it would not have a great deal to do in order to win over the people.

The king, in his moments of dread, confided himself to the priests. He had withdrawn the venerated statues of the gods from Uruk, Larsan and Eridu and enclosed them in the capital, in the shelter of the triple enclosure. Human sacrifices and bloody ceremonies celebrated the redoubtable power of monstrous divinities on a daily basis, but their anger was not appeased. A clamor rose up in the temples, and public consciousness "cast its eyes over all the surrounding regions, searching them with its gaze for a prince who was righteous in heart and mind, in order to summon him by name to universal royalty."[1]

---

1 The exact source of this quotation is unidentifiable, but it bears a strong resemblance to several passages in various nineteenth-century French history books in which the person to be summoned by name to replace a corrupt monarchy is the exiled emperor Napoléon.

That evening, Nigabael, before going to the temple of Nebo, where his friends were gathering, wanted to see his sister, in order to talk to her about Smarnis and engage her to receive him.

He found the young woman smiling and adorned as if for a betrothal banquet. Her hair was crowned by light clusters, a linen robe heightened by blue embroideries enveloped her flexible torso.

"How beautiful you are!" he said.

"That's because I'm happy."

"Happy? Why?"

"I've seen the man who loves me, and I've given him my heart, in accordance with your desire."

"You've seen the satrap?"

"Yes, and he has charmed me."

Nigabael recalled that Smarnis often wandered in the quarter where the young woman lived. He had confessed those frequent excursions himself, and his vigils before the closed door. Smarnis had doubtless spoken eloquently of his amour and his hope of an imminent union. A sincere tenderness pleases women and is able to conquer the proudest. There was nothing more to do now, then, except to fix the date of the marriage.

Nigabael had no suspicion of Phédyne's error. For him, the man she had seen could only be the satrap.

The young woman seemed to read her brother's eyes. Gently, she took his hand and squeezed it affectionately.

"You approve of me having welcomed the stranger well?" she asked.

"I approve, since it's me who mentioned that union to you."

"Oh, that was a revelation. Since you've sent me that friend, everything seemed resplendent with a new light. Only now am I alive, and happy."

"I can see that he has spoken better than I would have been able to do."

Phédyne lowered her eyes in confusion. "You haven't forbidden me to hear him . . ."

"No, certainly not, for I believe him to be worthy of your tenderness, in heart and mind . . . only . . ."

"Only . . . ?" she demanded, in anguish.

"He'll have to quit you for some time, for the satrap is doubtless going away very shortly. Our friends have given him a confidential mission."

"Ah!" The tremulous young woman plunged her ardent gaze into Nigabael's.

"Yes," the young man went on, "for the prisoners of Babylon, as for the exiled Jews, a man has appeared, like a liberator elected by the gods; that man is Cyrus, and his imminent advent is awaited with joyful impatience. It's him who will subjugate the tyrant and return our liberty to us. But it's necessary to inform him as to the weaknesses of Babylon and facilitate his entry into the citadel. The satrap, whom no one suspects, will have to traverse the enemy lines and reach the monarch . . ."

"And that expedition doesn't offer any danger . . . ?" she asked, trembling for her dear amour.

"No, since the satrap seems to be serving the tyrant. He will be a traitor for our good and that of the nation."

"He is going to leave, then?"

"Yes."

"Imminently?"

"Perhaps tomorrow."

"I won't see him any more!" exclaimed the young woman, desolately

"Ought you not to accept that proof, for the triumph of our cause? The separation, I assure you, will not last long, and afterwards, you'll be united forever."

"Forever!" The ecstatic Phédyne smiled at her dream.

"Will you promise me," Nigabael went on, "not to turn your fiancé away from his duty?"

"I promise you that."

"Be strong, dear sister. It's one last proof, which will render the moment of return sweeter, and make you appreciate the future happiness all the more."

"Go," she said. "I'll be brave."

However, as Nigabael drew away, she sensed sobs choking in her throat, and she leaned out of the window in order to implore the God of Israel, who never ceased to strike her in her heart and in her flesh.

The moonlight fell upon the deserted street. Violet shadow spread all the way to the zenith, drowning the area between the Euphrates and the gigantic walls of the city. But the young woman, in a sort of hallucination, saw enemy troops passing in a distant twilight, and heard the cries of the dying under ferociously brandished pikes and swords.

All the horrors of previous massacres returned to her memory. She recalled her captivity, the torture of her people and the hectic march along the bloody roads, strewn with cadavers. Smoke floated, like black veils, over the river and over the distant constructions, enveloping the summits of the temples, the tips of columns and obelisks with its dense clouds. The specters of warriors in scaly armor and silver helmets, were astride the clouds; a hideous host, dragging the wounded, was now running from all directions, and Warka, exhausted and dying, fell in front of her dwelling.

She uttered a great cry at that evocation, for Warka was indeed before her: a Warka placid and serene, as majestic and gentle as a beneficent god.

XII

Take the millstones and grind meal; uncover thy
locks, make bare the leg, uncover the thigh, pass
over the river. Thy nakedness shall be uncovered,
yea. Thy shame shall be seen . . . Sit thou silent
and get thee into darkness, O daughter of the
Chaldeans, for thou shalt no more be called the
lady of kingdoms.
(*Isaiah* 47: 2-3, 5.)

"Ah!" she said. "How happy I am!"

He took her in his arms. "You're weeping, Phédyne? What
has happened, then?"

"My brother has just left. He announced your departure to
me."

"My departure?" Warka's yellow eyes were sparkling, but
the young woman, swooning on his heart, could no longer see
them.

Prudently, the man interrogated her. "What did he say, then?"

"He told me that you're going to accomplish a sacred mission
for the deliverance of the land . . ."

Involuntarily, Phédyne stopped, surprised by the tumultuous
heartbeat in her lover's breast. A sort of occult presentiment suddenly sealed her lips.

"Speak," he said, in a curt voice. "It's necessary that I know
what has been confided to you."

She pulled away with a sudden terror. "Why? Can't you tell
me everything? What has been confided to me you know as well
as I do, since you're conspiring with my brother. Tell me what
you fear?"

"No. I've given my word, you understand? It's a redoubtable
secret, and I don't want to show myself to be more imprudent
than Nigabael."

"But I'm your fiancée."

"You're a woman, and certain revelations would be dangerous for you, as for me."

"So?" she asked, in a halting voice.

"So, tell me what you know, everything you know, in order that I don't show myself to be more imprudent than your brother."

The subtle glimmer that had traversed the young woman's consciousness disappeared; the omnipotent will of the man she loved created darkness in her soul. She pressed against his breast.

"I know," she said, "that you're going to depart to inform Cyrus and to enable him to enter the city."

He pushed her away brutally; his grim snigger made her tremble.

"Indeed. The tyrant, asleep in his pleasures, will allow himself to be dethroned without difficulty," he said, with a somber irony. An expression of cruel hatred creased his face, but the young woman paid no heed to it.

"Yes," she murmured. "For the Jewish people, Cyrus will be a generous friend, and his fortune will not betray him in this decisive moment of his career."

Warka was seething. "The plot is well woven, but the citadel is still intact, the walls, the ditches, the watercourses and the marshes might, however, stop the enemy."

"It's a people rather than an army that it's necessary to raise against Babylon, and the people are weary of Belsharuzur's cruelties and weaknesses," the young woman went on, blinded by her amour.

"The people are retained by the king's soldiers," said Warka, who had regained his self-possession and wanted to know everything about the plot.

"No, for the king has no suspicion, and the satraps are betraying him."

"Listen," said the man, after a long kiss as terrible as a bite, "for everyone else I shall depart, but for you I shall be the man who waits and watches."

She pulled away sadly. "What! You'll deceive the confidence of our brethren?"

"I have emissaries who will act for me. My secret presence among you is necessary, at least for some time yet. While I am believed to be in the conqueror's camp, I shall be close to you, my Phédyne, and we will work together to save the land. But keep my secret, even from your brother."

"I don't know the reasons that are making you act, and I tremble to do harm . . ."

"Have no fear; devoted friends will take my place, and everything will happen in accordance with our wishes."

Phédyne wanted to protest, but the man stifled the last hesitations of her conscience on her lips. A sort of languor invaded the virgin's entire being. It was a numbing intoxication, to which she yielded without suspicion.

But Warka felt the red hot-iron of desire, brushing his flesh with the warmth of that svelte and flexible body; his grip became more emphatic, more significant and more audacious. His ardent gaze searched the gaze that was dying beneath Phédyne's lowered eyelids. His avid mouth posed again on the tremulous parted lips, sucking in their virgin breath.

Suddenly, a slight sound extracted them from their ecstasy. Surprised, they separated, and Warka emerged from the house in order to examine the surroundings.

The moon was spreading all its wan light and the river, in the distance, behind the water gate, seemed to be groaning under a rolling of pebbles and a rustle of reeds. The two shores extended in a sinister fashion, dotted with indecisive constructions.

Warka, who had ventured on to the road, found himself face to face with a man of tall stature who blocked his path.

"Where are you coming from," demanded the unknown man, "and what are you doing here?"

"I don't recognize your right to interrogate me!"

"That dwelling," the man went on, in a low voice, "is that of my fiancée. I will defend her against everyone, and it's your life that I'll take first, for you're emerging from her house."

"Then let's move further away, for there's no need to put her in the confidence of our conversation," said Warka, laughing. Then, having glimpsed the face of the unknown man in a ray of moonlight, he uttered an exclamation of surprise: "Smarnis!"

"Yes, Smarnis . . . but you, who are you?"

Suddenly, the satrap shuddered. He had just recognized the man who had outraged him; already, though, two oarsmen had thrown themselves upon him, and they dragged him into the bottom of the boat that was still waiting near the water gate.

XIII

I wanted to see my fiancée and I only found her tomb. Iahveh disposes at his will of the life of his creatures.
(Ezekiel.)[1]

Now, this is what had happened.

Smarnis had quit his friends after the meeting at the temple of Nebo. Before departing on the secret mission that had been confided to him, he had wanted to see Phédyne, to tell her about his love and his gratitude, and, finally, to take away the first kiss of the young woman who would one day be his wife. She did not know him, but he told himself that she would be touched by that infinite tenderness.

He knew via Nigabael that his request had been favorably welcomed, and that he was expected, although he had always

---

1 The quotation as given in the original cannot be located in *Ezekiel*, nor anywhere else.

hesitated before a direct confession. Perhaps, in fact, the young woman had perceived him near her house and had encouraged him in the shadows, divining what his lips had not dared to murmur?

Yes, that must be it; Phédyne, informed by the tender and secret prescience of the heart, had summoned the amour that was offered in such a timid but conclusive fashion. She had been flattered by the delicate marks of adoration by which women are not deceived, and she had yielded to the desires of her brother, which were also her own.

Promising himself a great joy from that conversation, he had headed confidently toward the house of his very beloved. His brothers had just dictated his duty to him and, while walking through the deserted quarters he had remembered the words of the Prophets:

"Thus saith the Lord to the one appointed to loosen the belt of kings and break redoubtable scepters; I will go before them, and make the crooked places straight; I will break in pieces the gates of brass and cut in sunder the bars of iron. And I will give thee the treasures of darkness and hidden riches of secret places, that thou mayest know that I, the Lord, which call thee by thy name, am the God of Israel."[1]

Smarnis knew that everything would crumble before the man directed by the triumphant god. Bel would yield and Belsharuzur would be overturned from his throne, along with his sad idols.

The satrap, converted to his beloved's faith, desired to build a new house on the mountain of all joy and all sanctity. The temple of Solomon would be reborn from its ruins, more splendid and more majestic. The descendants of Zadok would have the rank of priests in the sacred place, because they had kept the divine light within them. The other Levites would kneel down in the dust on the threshold of temples, for they had participated in the errors of the nation and practiced idolatry like the children of Babylon, the unworthy and the prostituted.

---

1 This is a slightly modified version of *Isaiah* 45:1-3.

Smarnis had meditated the precepts of Ezekiel restated by his disciples: the imagination of the seer combined with the formalism of the sacrificer. He saw a marvelous source springing from the very threshold of the divine house and flowing toward the Dead Sea through an enchanted wood of flowers and fruits, the perfumes of which were intoxicating. The glorious remains of the twelve tribes of Israel would then divide the regenerated land, and found on the mountain of Sion the new Jerusalem of which the name is Iahveh!

Smarnis told himself that with his new friends, he would break the false Chaldean gods, and he was already trying to disentangle from the events of the day the precursory signs of deliverance.

"As a pregnant woman, when her term approaches, writhes and cries out in her dolor, thus we shall be before you, Iahveh!"

Meanwhile, he now perceived the frail buildings that surrounded Phédyne's house, among the brambles and the pale stunted trees. The moon was still sliding a scarf of radiance over the deserted road. The banks of the Euphrates were even sadder in their bed of reds and gray mud. The temple of Bel appeared distinctly now, as well as that of the goddess Nana, near the traces of sacrifices from which streams of blood were still flowing.

But the satrap wanted to ignore those images of death. He was entirely given to his happiness, to his dream of amour, finally realized.

Often, already, he had come to prowl in the vicinity of his beloved's humble house. His heart palpitating, he had seen Phédyne, motionless at her window, her eyes raised toward the stars. He had admired, secretly, her pure and gentle face, as well as the harmonious contours of her young body. Then, lost in the shadow, he had not dared to approach the luminous image, but today, he would be brave, he would tell the adored about his tenderness and his hope. He would cease to be the unknown; he felt full of love and pride, for she had divined him and encouraged him. Amour is like the luminosity of fireflies, which bursts forth in the night when the adorable hour of exchanges has sounded.

Smarnis was in front of the house, and he was approaching, his heart faint; but a murmur struck his ears: a sound of kisses mingled with the passionate sighs of two united mouths. The door opened and a man appeared on the threshold.

✳

The satrap, intoxicated by anger and despair, had recognized the mysterious visitor; a nameless horror paralyzed him; tears of impotent rage ran over his face, while he was disarmed and thrown into the bottom of a boat.

And while he was agonizing in futile fury, Warka had returned to the trembling young woman, and had said to her softly:

"Have no fear, my beloved; I've chastised the audacious individual who wanted to steal my property."

"That man, who is he?"

"I don't know. Some malefactor tempted by your beauty."

"What did he say, then?"

"He insulted me and threatened me, doubtless believing that he would intimidate me."

"Ah!" said the young woman, pensively. "You haven't done him any harm? What if he's an ally?"

"He's a bandit, I tell you, who had designs on your property or your youth. In any case, don't worry, I won't kill him."

Phédyne abandoned herself once again on Warka's breast, intoxicated by the magnetic breath that intoxicated her involuntarily.

The seducer was sure of his victory; he marched over rose petals, in the blood of hearts and sacrifices, without thinking that the flowery road might perhaps lead him to punishment.

But the population of Babylon remained humble, servile and silent before the powerful. Warka, who was none other than Belsharuzur, could still believe that the renown of his capital dazzled the world, and that the prestige in question came from his thought, his gaze and his will. The voices of courtiers proclaimed that he had commanded the elements; the waters of the Euphrates repeated it to the mountains of Armenia, whispered it to the Tigris asleep in its idle glory. The land saw itself, alive, joyful and radiant, in the person of its sovereign. That incarnation of an enervated people, that morbid unity in the form of a crown, that motionless and macabre sun, which, in the planetary system of power, attracted the other stars, was still able to create illusion.

The last kings of Babylon had grouped around themselves the wherewithal to strike peoples with astonishment and admiration: fêtes, barbaric rejoicing, frenetic orgies, the sumptuousness of a marvelous organization and a marvelous architecture. All the titanic forms of invincible and cruel power lent themselves to that apotheosis of sovereign grandeur, and nothing approached the renown of those deadly splendors.

PART TWO

I

Wherefore I praised the dead which are already
dead more than the living which are yet alive.
Yea, better is he than both they, which hath not
yet been, who hath not seen the evil work that is
done under the sun.
(*Ecclesiastes* 4:2.)

Belsharuzur had Smarnis imprisoned in a cell in the palace. He counted on tormenting him for a long time and making him perish in an exemplary torture.

In the meantime, he assembled his troops in order to confront any bellicose attempt on the part of the enemy. His army was composed of pikemen, archers, sling-wielders, and sappers, reinforced by squadrons of cavalry, which had changed the ancient methods of warfare. Those regiments supported the charioteers, surrounding them and protecting them in accordance with the requirements of their agile and multiple movements. They were made up of helmeted and armored soldiers clad in tightly-fitting loincloths instead of the floating skirts with long pleats that distinguished the old uniform. The cavaliers were equipped with swords, spears and bows shorter than those carried by the infantry. The horses had a bridle and a frontal harness but no saddle. They were ridden bareback, the upper body upright, balanced on the pelvis, the knees high, the thighs forcefully pressed to the flanks of the animal. Each combatant was seconded by a squire who rode beside him during the action and held his reins, in order to permit him to handle his weapons freely.

Belsharuzur was pleased with the progress of his new troops, who traveled in convoy with the chariots. He followed their movements, mounted himself on a horse admirable in its forms and its gait. He was beginning to force a way into cities as much by ingenious science as by tunneling or scaling. Although he knew nothing of terrible and complicated machines of war, he knew how to employ powerful engines to breach even the thickest walls.

He made use of mobile battering rams placed on four or six wheels, which adopted, at the whim of manufacturers, the most singular forms: sometimes a sow ready to plunge its snout into the enemy defenses, sometimes a roaring lion or a monstrous chimera. The besieged rained torches, flaming tinder and hot pitch down on the engine, and tried to capture the monster's head with hooks or crush it under slabs of rock.

Belsharuzur marched to the assault bravely, defeating barbarians of obscure races whose dwellings and possessions were strung out along the tributaries of the Tigris, and then the nomads and principalities of the West and North-West, which vaguely disquieted his power. The monarch set his hand to combating the most redoubtable enemies. Superb, in the midst of his men, he chose at his whim the chief that it would give him pleasure to vanquish, and, falling upon him unexpectedly, he overwhelmed him with his weight,

The neighbors dared not intervene; almost all of them, in fact, were happy to assist placidly in the crushing of a dangerous rival, without suspecting that their own fate was at stake, and that they were opening the way to a common enemy.

In order to test his strength, Belsharuzur ransomed the petty monarchs of the surrounding region, took possession of citadels, and lodged garrisons there that kept watch on the region. His treasury was swelled by multiple revenues; after his facile victories he could plunge himself into new fêtes and dazzle the country with the splendors of his magnificence.

He delivered himself ardently to voluptuous and bloody debaucheries, to orgies of torture, retraced on the walls of his palace like so many glorious trophies. Heaps of severed heads, like split watermelons, cluttered terraces under swarms of black flies gorged on blood; the skins of prisoners flayed alive covered the trees with a gray bark, and long files of impalements presented the spectacle of hideous agonies under the snoring cloud of birds of prey.

Babylon, the queen of the world, forced rivers to flow in accordance with her caprice. She raised powerful fortresses, pierced roads through gigantic rocks and laughed at attacks behind her triple wall. Around her, fierce battles were fought, and the cadavers of defeated enemies made her a bleak and heavy girdle.

Belsharuzur was proud of his crimes, which were inscribed every day on cylinders—or, rather, elongated prisms—of clay. They alone tell us today of the splendors and murders of the proud city, seeming to justify the words full of grim hatred by which the Jewish Prophets announced the accomplishment of the vengeance of Iahveh:

"The Lord will pronounce sentence on you, princes of Babylon. He will exterminate the statues and the idols of the house of your gods, which will be your sepulcher. Your hearts will dry up with fear and you will fall into scorn."[1]

In the meantime, Belsharuzur intoxicated himself on the incense of facile victories. More than ever, in that epoch, the court of Babylon was the abode of splendor and success. No veil of sadness floated as yet over the culpable city. Death, the bald vulture that follows the defeat of armies, and the public calamities and senility of empires, with a dismal and heavy flight, had not yet opened its wings over the city of blood and lust.

---

1 Not a direct quotation, but seemingly paraphrasing parts of *Jeremiah* 24.

"In the temple of the Eternal women can be seen
weeping for Tammuz, the god of amour."
(Ezekiel.)[1]

Phédyne was happy, for Warka, during his absences, sent a messenger to bring her his news, and Nigabael, confident in the skill of the satrap Smarnis, whom he believed to be still at liberty and fully occupied with the good of the tribe, was waiting patiently for the promised deliverance.

The brother and the sister, persisting in their common error, cradled one another mutually in their dreams.

For Phédyne, Warka was the lover, the fiancé that her brother and all the friends of his race destined for her. That passion created sentiments and ill-equilibrated impressions in the virgin, under the action of which she experienced stirrings of the flesh and aspirations of the soul whose violence disturbed her. She was like a traveler gone astray in a profound forest strewn with perils, and who was no longer able to recover the notion of a rational orientation.

The disorderly movements of her heart were independent of her thought. Involuntarily, she had shuddered under a gaze, the sound of a voice, the blossoming of a desire. She was in love, without having the consciousness of loving.

Neither the cloistered and nostalgic life that she led nor the legend of her beliefs had made her a creature of perfection. Her glaucous eyes had widened again, her mouth had opened in a more ardent breath in the oval of her face, which her fine hair surrounded lightly with a red-gold nimbus. Her neck and shoulders had developed a fine grace without becoming thinner, and her bosom had become rounder. She had retained a rather

---

1 I have translated the inaccurate original rather than substituting the actual text of *Ezekiel* 8:14, which refers to the women weeping for Tammuz.

tender beauty, an infinite charm that flourished in her innocent flesh and her enthusiastic soul.

Phédyne waited for Warka, and nothing else existed in her life any longer except that hope of amour . . .

Nigabael did not know Warka. He had put his confidence in Smarnis, the powerful satrap, who ought, by means of his cleverness and bold intelligence, to precipitate the fall of the accursed empire. Oh, if only he had understood the young woman's frightful error!

Both of them talked about the absentee without pronouncing his name, as a measure of prudence, but their gazes said a great deal about their tenderness and their gratitude.

Phédyne interrogated her heart, seeking there the wherewithal to be patient during long days of solitude. She took an interest in the men who were risking their lives to liberate their country. Without knowing them, she followed them with her good wishes in their heroic quest. But she was quietly anxious, anticipating mysterious complications. Warka possessed her. She felt that existence without him would no longer be possible. And Iahveh, the cruel god, was already capitulating before Tammuz, the god of amour whom women will adore eternally on earth. She was ready for sacrifice or sin, ignorant of her fault and the error of her soul.

Since her betrothal, everything in nature seemed to be in unison with her sentiments. The sand of the river banks gave her delicate feet the illusion of a caress. She walked slowly, sometimes surprising the walls of the city and venturing into the countryside. The earth there was almost as fertile as the mud of Egypt. Leaves of wheat and barley grew there as broad as four fingers; millet and sesame became veritable trees with cool and aromatic shade. Women went under the palm trees in order to shake the powerful flowers of the male trees on to those of the female trees. The gods themselves, according to legend, had taught that artifice to mortals, and they were often represented with a flowery sheaf in hand, with the gesture of a person fecundating a palm tree.

The honeyed odor of acacias mingled with the incense of cypresses and tamarisks, concentrating all the sunlight and the warmth of the sands. Galls flourished on the heaths with a penetrating charm that awoke a torpid brain. There was lavender, pink carnations, tuberoses with peppery breath and other plants with voluptuous aromas.

The songs and stridulations of insects rose up in the spirit of the flowers, in the ardent caress of the sun that set over the river. Further away, scattered groups of mimosas, intercut with threads of water scintillating like silver ribbons, surrounded wormwoods and wild mallows. But even further away the rushes rose up like gigantic thickets, concealing banks of black and putrid mud, the breath of which was mortal.

Phédyne did not go that far, frightened by the sinister aspect of those tall stems, swayed by the wind in a continual murmur. In that direction, a large somber tent closed the horizon. One found oneself buried in that moist shroud, which did not take away all light, but allowed waves of lead and plaster of an odious monotony to be discovered.

On the road, the young woman waited for the messenger who was to bring her word of Warka. He was a bright-eyed, brown-skinned cavalier who showed sharp teeth in a smile. He draped himself artfully in a long blue cloak with red designs, and spoke eloquently about the chief's efforts to bring the mission with which he had been charged to a successful conclusion. The seducer acted in accordance with his conscience in giving Phédyne the best of his thought.

She sometimes received a thin tablet on which the tender thoughts of the chief were engraved. He also sent her objects of iridescent glass, enameled faiences, gold combs, carved Babylonian stones, and jewelry in onyx, porphyry, cornelian and chalcedony.

The messenger was mounted on a large white horse, the rump and feet of which were tinted pink. With a fine proud gesture he threw his long garment over his shoulder, and departed at a gallop. The young woman watched the little cloud of dust that the mount made and the shadow of the cavalier against the bright sky. She contemplated the golden horizon, the fiery solitude and the cloudless sky; then her eyes, fatigued by light, turned toward the river bordered by immense rushes, the mysterious river, whose waves rolled gold and cadavers.

Sometimes, large yellow dogs scratched the earth, exhuming bones, a black head, reduced to the dryness of a stone, and a few formless shreds. Phédyne shivered, finding something menacing in the silence and in the air of that region populated by the dead, in that somber and mute nature, beneath the ferocious sun.

Flocks of crows and vultures flew over the ditches of the city as well as the charnel-houses, but doves pursued one another along the river banks, as if to affirm that, everywhere and always, death rubs shoulders with amour.

A few mud huts appeared near the city. They were low constructions, the mud of which, compressed, cut into slices and dried in the sun, was set in layers like bricks. All of that, gray in the morning, became pink at midday and orange in the evening. A few openings had whitewashed frames.

A woman leaning on the threshold sometimes watched the young woman pass by and smiled at her with gleaming teeth, astonished by her fragile prettiness. Little girls with black-rimmed eyes, squinting slightly under the dark waves of their curly hair, agitated fetishes of horn or carved wood on their meager chests. They carried their bodies forward, the breasts forcefully braced, and there was something simultaneously wild and simian about them.

It was a great joy for the young woman to receive a souvenir of the absentee. Faithful to her promise, she did not say anything to her brother about the testimony of amour that arrived regularly enough during his friend's absence. She obeyed the occult force that enveloped her, even at a distance, without reflection and without debate. She did not seek to penetrate the chief's secret thoughts; what was the point, since she loved him and believed in him? When she remained without news of him, a somber veil descended upon her.

For several days, a frightful tempest cloistered her in her house. The great howling of the wind penetrated her with terror, like a celestial threat, a warning of trouble and misfortune. She felt that she was in a whirlwind of foam and sand. The waters of the river, electrified by such a furious movement, had also taken on an animation and something like a fantastic soul. There were terrible apparitions of beasts with no eyes or ears, possessed of nothing but foaming maws.

Clouds of locusts arrived in the wake of the storm. First there was a sound like a distant crackling, and a streak of flame above the singing reeds. Soon, battalions of little winged bodies filled the atmosphere on every side, traversing it with a slow and uniform flight. Then the cloud suddenly settled, devouring everything like a conflagration.

The insects coupled and died after the devastation; only the memory remained of the plants, flowers and crops undulating with golden reflections.

III

> The daughter of Sun turned her thought to the house of darkness from which no one emerges. She took the road from which no one returns. She nourished herself henceforth on dust and ate clay.
> (*The Descent of Ishtar into Hell*. Chaldean legend.)

After that tempest, Phédyne, who was walking on the river bank, saw a boat arriving. It was gliding smoothly behind the reeds, appearing and disappearing between the spears of foliage like a fantastic vision. The rich fabrics of crimson and gold with which it was decked were trailing in the water; a precious tent, under arches of flowers, protected it from excessively violent radiance, and the monstrous image of Zou, the god of shipwrecks, loomed up at the prow. Zou, a terrible god, amassed the clouds and split them in downpours; he unleashed the winds and the lightning; nothing more remained where he had passed. Who, then, would dare to display such a terrible emblem?

On the other bank, a swarming crowd uttered acclamations whose meaning Phédyne did not know; the temple of Nana was illuminated from top to bottom, and a long file of victims was mounting the terrace of sacrifices.

The young woman often witnessed manifestations of that order, so she was not unduly surprised by those barbaric rejoicings. She thought, as always, about the man who was her life and who sometimes sent her news via elegant messengers. Perhaps that boat contained something to gladden her heart.

The young woman would have liked to devote herself to the object of her amour, to communicate to him everything she possessed of tenderness and abnegation, to spread over his wounds the reparative balm of her caresses. A radiant companion in joy, she would become, in dolor, the courageous and patient guide who reanimates. Her lips would have given, after sensuality, the soporific nectar in which a man forgets his pain; in her soul, the need would have been born for sacrifice, with divine pity.

The boat was still advancing, like a monstrous flower, over the gentle waves; it was undulating graciously, and songs rose from the other bank, songs of glory and sacred songs, alternating with the frenetic rhythms of instruments.

Women with somber faces were standing immobile on the banks of the river, watching triremes with short masts pass through the water gate, along with light boats in the form of a lyre or a rocket. Merchants of fish and fruits were hawking their merchandise.

Phédyne parted the dense rushes, leaned over, and uttered a cry of surprise. On the cushions of the sumptuous boat, Warka was lying, but a Warka she did not know, a Warka richly clad and mitered in gold like a monarch. A scarlet toga sewn with precious stones fell back behind him. His pectoral, embroidered with little pearls and garnished with emerald droplets, shone between the fetishes and clasps that overloaded his chest. His braided beard and hair, in multiple curls, were undulating slightly in the breeze.

She uttered a joyful appeal: "Warka! Warka!"

The man shivered, and launched a wild glance in the direction of the young woman.

"Warka! Warka! Can't you see me?"

Nonchalantly, he parted the fabrics and made a sign to the oarsmen, who drew nearer to the bank.

"What imprudence!" he said, in a tone of reproach. "Were you not to wait for me in the house?"

"I was too impatient. Remember that I've been without news for a fortnight . . ."

Already, he had joined her, put his arm around her waist and drawn her aside.

"Oh, I'm not my own master, you know that; my mission is delicate and I've been wrong to linger with you when my brothers believe me to be occupied with their salvation."

"Do you not have friends who replace you?"

"Yes, reliable friends."

"They'll act for you."

He had an almost menacing intonation as he asked: "You haven't talked, at least? Nigabael doesn't suspect anything?"

"Nothing."

"You've never pronounced my name?"

"Never. But why this mystery? Why doesn't my brother know your true name?"

"I'll explain later the reason for my silence. For the conspirators I have to remain Smarnis; for you alone I'm Warka, the friend, the lover, the fiancé. Isn't it preferable thus?"

Phédyne, dazzled and dominated by the omnipotent will of the man, was no longer reasoning. She was no more than a little fragile thing abandoned to the whim of the elements. Reflection and bitter experience were unknown to her. A novice in the surges of amour, she accepted their delicious awakening, the new intoxication. Warka, moreover, was able to adopt a tone of great sincerity in order to speak to her. He had touching supplications and ardent caresses that caused her to weaken and left her defenseless.

Nigabael would have been able to tell her that his confidence was candor and his generosity dupery, for, without being much older than her, he knew men and the suffering of life. But Nigabael believed that Smarnis was free and full of future. He thought that the satrap had spoken to the young woman before his departure for the sacred mission. How could he have learned that Phédyne was the victim of one of those perfidious comedies, one of those passionate lies, that intoxicate to the point of blindness, until death?

His conversations with his sister were full of tenderness, good intelligence and union. There was, on the part of the young people, a constant preoccupation to avoid anything that might displease the other, to seek out that which, on the contrary, would bring a tightening of affection and confidence into the fraternal relations.

Now, in Warka's arms, she was trembling and stammering.

"Why these expensive fabrics, these necklaces, these sumptuous garments?" she asked. "Don't you fear attracting the attention of our enemies?"

But he reassured her. "No one knows that I'm a traitor for the good cause. On the contrary, it's necessary that I show myself in the prestige of my situation. I'm rich, Phédyne, and provinces are submissive to me. Didn't you know that?"

"No," she said, "I thought you were poor, and I loved your poverty."

"You'll be happier in the midst of luxury, and nothing will equal your beauty under the splendor of gems and precious veils."

He drew her toward her dwelling, and she was slightly frightened by his violence. The almost cruel flame that she saw shining in her lover's eyes caused her a dolorous astonishment. That new expression of an indomitable amour chilled the tenderness and abandon on her lips. It seemed to him that Warka had undergone a kind of metamorphosis, that his gestures and attitudes were no longer the same. A soul was floating around her that was no longer his soul, and a burning breath passed over her like a storm wind.

The arteries of her temples swelled, beating precipitately in the fever that invaded her. A long shudder ran through her, and she let herself fall into her beloved's arms.

Immediately, she felt herself enveloped by a reckless embrace, and fainted.

IV

> The eagle said: Against my breast put your breast,
> on the whip of my wings put your two hands, and
> against my side repose your side. Thus we will
> dominate the earth.
> (Chaldean legend of Etana.)[1]

Warka sustained Phédyne, who slowly recovered consciousness. He gazed at her with the disturbance of his lust, and the mystery of his amorous appetites. He knew the caressing science of Hebrew women; some of them had revealed to him the secrets of life and death; he knew that he was the master of that virgin heart, and that he could dispose of it in accordance with his caprice.

---

1 This is not a quotation but is improvised from the fragments of "the story of the eagle" reproduced in George Smith's *The Chaldean Account of Genesis* (1876), on which several other passages in the text appear to be ultimately based.

Gripped himself by lovesickness, he had quit his royal vestments for that conquest; he had played the comedy of persecution and sacrifice. Now, alone with his victim, he hesitated nevertheless to accomplish his crime.

The breeze brought him the perfume of incense and aromatics burned in his honor on the banks of the Euphrates. In the temple of the goddess Nana, the priests were officiating and the dancers exciting hieratic steps before the idols, and on the altars, the throats of animals were being cut, to celebrate his recent conquests.

All the edifices were ablaze, from the base to the summit; tides of light were traversing them, putting reflections of the forge under their gaping porticos. Monstrous gods were oscillating on the shoulders of servants. There was Raman, with his head of a bird of prey and outspread wings; Zou, the terrible Zou, who unleashes the winds and thunderbolts; Siris, lady of the rain and the clouds; Matou, god of the squall; and Barkou, master of lightning flashes.

At each of the king's new expeditions, the people evoked those maleficent powers. They had the mission of hurling hurricanes against the rebel races and decimating them.

Phédyne ought to have been able to hear the cries of the delirious populace, and the name of Belsharuzur repeated with frenzy, but Phédyne could no longer even hear the ardent voice of her heart.

Before the young woman, however, Warka felt himself quivering in his entire being; the virgin that was about to belong to him refined his desire, and in the joy that was disengaged by his carnal ardor, he tasted a new and disquieting sensation.

The passionate subtleties that tempt and madden the blasé of life, the cruel perversities, and the dissolving joys that they research, create within them a sort of feverish atmosphere, which they want to enjoy as much as the material form of their covetousness. Warka therefore lingered in his pleasure, animated before that innocent by sentiments thus far unknown. She was full of charms, the woman who had jealously conserved the precious flower of her virginity. In her candid grace, she was a redoubtable tease, even for a monarch heaped with all terrestrial favors.

That changed the man of facile offers, reckless homages, unsated and insatiable by the sensation that dragged on its knees, imploring and tamed. All women, for him, were his victims, or mistresses of lust who passed in the monotonous practice of his desire like the ghouls of legend through the celestial pyre . . .

He had bitten all fruits, committed all murders and all lusts. His hands were red with blood and his soul black with darkness, so he listened with astonishment to the mysterious and seemingly distant song that rose up in his intimate self, rising to his throat, and cradling him with an infantile harmony. Under the rudeness of the wild bush, was there a nest, then, a secret refuge of pity and tenderness?

He would have liked to procure the woman he loved, at least for the moment, the divine pleasure of amour, not only to content his senses by the passionate manifestation to which he had given birth, but also because that manifestation would have satisfied his artistic taste. He wanted the virgin in order to contemplate in her the radiant and human figure, not just to steal from her, to the profit of his sensations alone, the whole sum of the coveted sensations.

"Phédyne," he murmured in her ear—and the breath of his exhalation raised her luminous hair—"I have said too much to be able to constrain myself further. You know that I love you in accordance with your religion and your god. But what you do not know is how profound that love is. Its excuse is in its violence, my beloved, and it would be futile to fight it. Like me, you must be adorably submissive to it . . ."

At the sound of that passionate voice, Phédyne trembled more forcefully. The blood was circulating ardently in her veins; her gaze was dying beneath her long dark eyelids.

"Let us not quit one another again," Warka continued, drawing her into the deserted street. "Let our destinies be united from

204

this day. This humble house, which has only hidden your tears until now, will hide our happiness henceforth. Receive, my beloved, the pledge of a bewildered tenderness. No woman, until now, has been able to win my heart, none has heard my oath of love. Let us love one another with an inexhaustible amour, and may our lives fade away, as if elapsed, in a delightful dream!"

Phédyne seemed to wake up, as if her entire existence had only been a long lethargy. She uttered a cry, and drew away from the man whose burning gaze weighed upon her. But he clasped her against his breast. "Have no fear, my beloved, have no fear! My kiss will be sweeter than honey, my hands lighter than the wings of a dove. When you know the mystery of amour you will only want to live henceforth for that, and any other desire will be abolished within you.

He had caused her to enter her house, and as she fainted again, he carried her to her bed.

Before that immaculate corolla on which he, the first, was about to let his gaze and his hand fall, whose petals he, the first, was about to crumple, he awoke from a bad dream. A singular emotion imposed itself on his ardor, enveloping his instinctive brutality with a sort of superstitious dread.

And then, would that violation not bring misfortune, when he had already sown mourning in the house of Israel? Would not so many prisoners tortured, so many victims offered to the sanguinary gods one day call down upon him the vengeance of Iahveh, the redoubtable spirit?

He took the young woman's hands, lifted them up, and linked his lips to them. Then he imprisoned the blonde head with the luminous hair, and he put his mouth on that dead mouth, which did not return his kisses.

However, the sexual appetite was exasperated within him; soon, there was the brutal, vertiginous possession, there was paradise or the inferno, the ecstasy in which everything is abolished in the carnal gulf . . .

The wild beast had killed the dove of dream.

V

The beast that you sawest was, and is not; and
shall ascend out of the bottomless pit, and go
into perdition.
(*Revelation* 17:8.)

Warka gazed at his victim. She was breathing painfully and her lips were murmuring vague words.

Then he took off his jewels, his amulets, his necklaces and the clap of his cloak. He put the precious gems on the young woman's breast and returned to the boat that had brought him.

The crowd, seeing him return, uttered a long clamor of delight, and the oarsmen resumed striking, rhythmically, the muddy water bordered by mimosas and tamarisks.

The cupolas of the city now rose gloriously on the banks swarming with people. The formidable ruins of Babil, and the Kasr, with its majestic platform, disappeared into the distance. The boat had surpassed the temple of Bel and that of El Kalaeih, guarded by bulls with human faces. The illuminated sanctuary of the goddess Nana no longer sent to Warka's ears anything but a confused hum of cicadas.

And the man advanced without a cortege, leaving on the bank the sacrificer priests, the enigmatic and cruel mages, and the host of courtesans and dancers drunk on songs and perfumes, before the bloody altars.

More somber, Warka reflected.

Now that he had sated his desire, the image of Phédyne was already blurred in his thought. She was similar to the others and no longer brought him the incomparable charm of mystery. What he had solicited from her was her kiss, and he had used his strength to obtain it. Only a pale memory remained of that flower, plucked for its perfume, the bird retained for its song.

He had deluded himself regarding the felicity of that possession, similar to others. The grace and delicacy of that new victim had become indifferent to him; he no longer perceived her as anything but a frail instrument of pleasure. Phédyne and Nigabael had wearied his desire of a whimsical tyrant. After being amused by that flavorsome game, having duped the sister and the brother, he became once again violent, brutal and demanding in the manifestations of his will.

He also perceived clearly all the danger of the conspiracies that were being woven around him. Although Smarnis, the guilty satrap, was in prison, other conspirators might take his place, and it was important to capture them all.

Confident in the prediction of their Prophets, the Jews were awaiting the hour of chastisement that was about to sound for Babylon. They were united against their enemy, seeking the surest means to deliver him to the enemy.

Warka knew that the meetings were held in a poor quarter of the city, but the secret was so well guarded that he had not been able to discover it. Only Phédyne could inform him, and it would be prudent not to abuse that faithful ally.

Undoubtedly, she would talk, confident in the thought of amour that fortified her penchants and gave free flow to the source of the tenderness always boiling in her heart. She would talk in order to undertake with her lover a long pilgrimage to the holy mountain, in order to savor there the glorious emotions of her race, in order to stop there and arrive at the only goal of the soul and body prepared for divine repose.

In any case, she loved him, and would be unable to stop herself.

Warka now perceived the immense palace with the scintillating golden cupolas, flanked by apses and transepts, the crouching monster whose multiple arms were raised toward the sky as if to implore or to curse.

The population was flowing toward the hanging gardens of the acropolis, where triumphal arches had been set up between the fantastic edifices, the ravines, the hills of extraordinary vegetation, the beds of rare flowers, and the precipices expertly contrived to give the illusion of a land of dreams.

A long file of prisoners was heading for the palace for the sacrifices that were to accompany the king's return, and the executioners were already preparing the instruments of death.

The scribes were scribing on papyrus the number of heads that would roll in the dust; flowers were ornamenting Belsharuzur's throne; in the royal gardens, coral and golden sand was felting the pathways.

Warka enveloped his head in his cloak in order not to be recognized, and dismissed the oarsmen. Alone, he took the road to the palace of dream and murder, cutting through the packed groups of citizens, slaves, and soldiers decked in iron and bronze.

Women whose long multicolored robes made moving patches invited him to enter their houses; men were striking drums covered in snakeskin while others blew into trumpets of shiny bronze.

Warka saw Nigabael, who was walking with his head bowed, somber and pensive, and he followed him all the way to the palace gates. Now, the memory of the latter returned to him, mingled with that of Phédyne, as if a rivalry of possession had just been created between the brother and the sister. And he could not distinguish, in the obscurity of his soul, the preferences that were dominant. Phédyne and Nigabael, for his blasé desire, were not so much prey of flesh and muscle as sentiments already distant . . . both were mingled in his troubled consciousness, united to form the strange androgyne of an ephemeral dream.

VI

After having dressed him in a scarlet robe, he
washed his face because of the great dust that
rose from the ground.
(Book of Daniel)[1]

The young woman, on her ravaged couch, awoke as if from a frightful dream. Was she the victim of a caprice of sadistic or criminal folly? A memory was evoked, killing all joy in her being, reviving extinct dread, dolor and anguish.

It was the end of her virginal power, the fragile serenity of her existence. A great destructive breath had passed over her, depriving her of the very essence of her strength, anemiating her energy, her youth and her beauty.

The future, henceforth, would no longer have anything for her but troubles, and her soul, fond of mysticism, instinctive and tender mysticism, would only any longer be able to adorn itself with the ardors of martyrdom.

The passionate movement of the senses, in the physical and intellectual exaltation that had borne her toward Warka, had brought her, momentarily, a very vivid joy, the joy of lovers that encloses within it the creative elements of all human visions, and which is the unique and supreme hope that women always retain. She had taken refuge in her dream, had allowed herself to be lulled by the soft words, the deceptive mirage of an impossible felicity

And now, one of those dolors which overturn everything until death had snatched away her chimera.

She had thrown herself into that adventure without reserving anything for the future; she had only known a part of her amour, ignorant of the trickery and the lie.

In this world, where a human being only loves for a few years, and is only happy for a few hours, if she learns to hide her tears

---

1 Not a direct quotation.

it is because her first cry of woe has fallen into the midst of an indifferent, egotistical or cruel crowd, and she has suffered as much from the abandonment of some as from the treason of others. She has, therefore, learned to hide her torture, in order to make an idol of it, hidden in the intimate sanctuary of her heart, into which no one penetrates. Everything within her can then sense that redoubtable presence, that grim union of the soul with a secret chagrin. The gaze is veiled by mystery, the voice muffled, like a musical instrument swathed in cloth.

What is harmful is trying the various paths of life, searching far and wide for what one has not found close at hand; it is not having said adieu to desire and the hope of a better future; it is wanting to continue struggling, no matter what the cost.

Phédyne wanted to be good and to forgive. She thought that her God had closed for her the book in which joys and memories are inscribed, that the last page had been written therein and that the others would remain blank until the day of the eternal departure.

Her dolorous being, the disorder of her garments and her solitude revealed to her that a crime had been committed on her person, of which she could only accuse the friend, the fiancé, the dear individual who had promised her tenderness and protection.

She tried to get up, and the bracelets and the necklaces that the man had deposited on her bosom slid to the ground like sumptuous reptiles. With disgust, she kicked them away, divining the price that had been paid for the sin committed. Thus, everything of which she had dreamed, everything for which she had wished in her ardent virginal heart of a fiancée had gone up in smoke, leaving her irremediably wounded and fallen

But she wanted to forgive . . . perhaps because she was still in love . . .

A light shone into the house; the moon appeared in the partly-closed window. Phédyne readjusted the pleats of her robe and leaned out, interrogating the road. Everything was silent; in the distance fires were burning under the porticos of temples; flames enclosed in lamps in leaves of horn or lanterns in linen cloth were illuminating the idols at the doors of the temples; but the sacrifices had ceased, the sand of the river banks was slowly drinking the blood of the victims.

Nigabael would come; what was she going to say to him? Was she going to weaken his courage and destroy his faith by the narration of the outrage she had suffered? In order to permit him to accomplish the difficult task that he had undertaken, it was necessary not to impede his will, which was barely sufficient for that great work.

She gazed at the road that he would take in order to return to her. She foresaw the blush that would cover her face, the disturbance that would paralyze her efforts, but, no matter what it cost, she would be brave and conceal her emotion.

The door finally opened and Nigabael came in.

"Why, Phédyne, are you still in the dark?" he asked, embracing the young woman, who was trembling. "But what's the matter? Your hands are burning and I can hear your heart beating."

"It's nothing, dear brother: a slight fever caused by the heat of the day."

"And then, you've heard the cries of the people, you've seen the temples ablaze on the other bank? The tyrant has returned, covered in homages; a long file of prisoners followed the carts of the conquerors in the dust of the roads. Several days will be consecrated to the tortures of our people."

"Oh!" she sighed. "When shall we be avenged?"

"Soon, soon . . . it's necessary to have confidence."

"I have confidence, but the wait seems very long to me."

"What troubles me," he said, "is that your fiancé, since his departure, has not given us any news."

Phédyne shuddered. "You'll doubtless see him soon . . ."

"It's necessary to hope so . . . In any case," the young man went on, after a moment's silence, "a great meeting is to be held in three days behind the temple of Nebo. We'll discuss the means of replacing the chief, who might have been taken prisoner. Don't you ever think of him?"

Phédyne's disturbance increased; an ardent blush invaded her face and it was with difficulty that she stammered: "That absence is certainly very strange."

"Strange and prejudicial to our cause. But we'll send Menilok to Cyrus."

"Menilok?"

"Yes, a friend, a devoted brother who will be able to pick up the satrap's trail and will serve us until death."

"Wait a little longer . . ."

"We can't wait. Our race is too weak to sustain a struggle of any duration. It's necessary to defeat the enemy by means of an audacious coup, to take him by surprise in his disarmed confidence."

"Yes, undoubtedly."

"It's necessary to take advantage of the popular agitation," Nigabael went on, becoming animated. "Even if the chiefs were killed, wounded or taken prisoner, we'd act. The most conservative and the most submissive class in the empire, that of the priests, is also weary of futile cruelties. Yesterday, still, it was crawling tremulously; today it is talking openly about reform and dissolution. The revolutionary movement is spreading to the aristocracy. The chiefs are tracing a line of violent demarcation between the two phases of Chaldean life. The recrudescence of energy and the development of revolutionary agitation are surpassing anything that could be desired. They recognize, like us, that an uprising of foreigners and the people is absolutely necessary, and that it's necessary to strike a direct, formidable blow at the autocracy."

But Phédyne was not listening. "You're going to meet again soon?" she asked.

"Yes, in three days, at the same hour, behind the temple of Nebo. I think I already told you that . . ."

"In fact, you did tell me, but I'm suffering, Nigabael, my ideas are confused, I need to rest."

"Adieu, then, dear sister. May your sleep be exempt from dread, and may the angel of dreams pour her golden powder upon you."

When Nigabael had gone, Phédyne threw herself on her bed and wept abundantly. Then she reflected, and searched in vain for the reason for Warka's conduct. Since he was in Babylon, why had he not informed his friends, or reassured them about the outcome of his journey? What did that singular attitude signify?

She assembled her ideas, anxious in the secrecy of her soul. No doubt came to her, however, regarding her lover's sincerity. She had heard the expression of his amour, he had held her, palpitating, in his arms. It was her property, her wealth, that he had taken away with him when he went, like a miser carrying away his gold.

The more she reflected, the more confused her thoughts became in her heavy head. The memories fled, became troubled, as landscapes reflected in suddenly agitated water become confused and disappear. She fell back into a bleak chagrin, and renounced any debate with herself.

Warka was no longer there to sustain her, and Warka remained, for her, intelligence and reason. Warka was the sole consolation of an existence in which there was no longer any hope or happiness. He had gone away, and Phédyne's lungs lacked air, her ears harmony and her gaze beauty. Her arms, devoid of strength, fell at her sides, her eyes remained fixed, her forehead tilted sadly, and fever burned her dry lips. She was in the desert and she begged Iahveh, the god of amour, or the angel of darkness, not to let her die in the arid sands.

VII

That day, the three queens of Babylon went to the temple of the goddess, surrounded by their women and their slaves.

Sahuradha was wearing a yellow robe embroidered with silver and a tall tiara of gems was oscillating slightly on her head.

Ussary, clad in gold brocade, had a turquoise capeline whose blue stones were trembling on her cheeks, and Amat-Sula, in a crimson sheath, was proudly sporting a pearly miter with a triple row of pendants.

Each of them held in the left hand a staff crowned with a rose, and in the right hand an ivory casket containing presents.

They were going toward Mylitta, the Babylonian Venus, who had fecundated Sahuradha's womb and who would doubtless grant the same favor to the other two queens, Ussary and Amat-Sula.

They were taking rare perfumes and jewels to the voluptuous goddess and her adorable son Tammuz, the god of amour.

The Babylonians venerated a large number of deities, beneficent or baleful, who all possessed a redoubtable power. Spirits, the Zi, similar to the Egyptian doubles, populated all the regions of the world like the superior powers which regulated them. They included, in addition to the material souls of the dead, all the good and evil forces of nature. They blew the wind, poured the rain, reached over the crops and gave life or death at their whim.

There were, by way of supreme forces: Zikia, the spirit of the earth; Enlil, the master of the demons in the depths of the abyss; and An, the governor of the sky. Ea, the great fish, or sublime fish, of the ocean, traveled his empire in a symbolic boat, for the conquest of Davkina, the earth, and spread over her, in order to fecundate her, to cover the valleys and the woods with fruits and flowers. From their embraces all the splendors of the world were born, and all the smiles of the heavens.

Enlil received humans, at the emergence of death, in the infernal empire. Transported beyond the eternal waves, culpable souls penetrated into the accursed country from which no one returns, the place where there is nothing but dust to appease hunger in the frightful darkness of damnation.

The Yatu, incubi, the Pairika, succubi, and the Drouges, ghouls of insomnia, also harassed humans in the cowardly heart. The Alal, destroyers of bodies, the Mas and the Lamas, sly combatants, and the Maskim, setters of ambushes, hid in the entrails of the earth, invincible and tenacious. They were neither male nor female, had no spouses and produced no children, but they crawled like reptiles, slithering into the bosom of dwellings in order to import trouble, shame and terror. Sometimes, introducing themselves into bodies, they fomented mortal maladies there and only emerged when expelled by sacrifices and invocations.

Incessantly subjected to the assault of phantoms, vampires, incubi and succubi, the human creature vegetated miserably in an atmosphere of nightmares and crimes.

No people was more borne to the cult of magic than the Babylonian people, and almost all the priests were sorcerers and diviners.

But the goddess Mylitta, queen of amour and war, mistress of the Moon and the planet Venus, who represented the feminine principle of nature, humid and fecund matter, reigned despotically over souls. While Marduk had risen to the rank of principal god and had been allied with Bel, and Nergal displayed the upper body and face of a man on his leonine body, Mylitta personified beauty, fecund grace and radiant, immortal glory.

In the temple that was devoted to her, she was seen standing on a bull, coiffed in a starry tiara and streaming with jewels. Her hair descended in curly coils over her shoulders, and she was holding a bow and a quiver.

When she represented the goddess of generation and the reproduction of mortal beings, she displayed herself naked, smiling and pressing, her hands covering her breasts in a modest gesture.

The three wives of Belsharuzur came to worship "the Lady of Life" who had favored one of them.

Sahuradha, quivering with joy and gratitude, wanted to thank the beneficent goddess before announcing the great news to the king.

She poured her perfumes at the feet of the statue, offered a marvelous necklace of emeralds, and then sank into a profound adoration.

Meanwhile, Amat-Sula and Ussary, slightly jealous, recited the hymn of grace with their companion:

> *Inspiration of the idea,*
> *Flame of lotus and orchid*
> *Flower of love, O Belita!*
> *You to whom Bel, lord of Chaldea,*
> *Gave birth in n a sweet infantile kiss,*
>   *O Mylitta!*
>
> *Deign to smile on our intoxication,*
> *And lend yourself to the caress*
> *Of this song that Tammuz dictated . . .*
> *Show yourself, divine Anata,*
> *To humans weaned of tenderness,*
>   *O Mylitta!*
>
> *In the mystery of pregnancy,*
> *We experience the holy ecstasy*
> *That your sensuality lends us!*
> *Like a ray of the fire of Ishtar*
> *Joy is painted in our gaze,*
>   *O Mylitta!*

It is an exquisite perfume of roses
That bathes beings and things
In this beautiful temple of Ecbata!
For Tammuz, of whom heaven sings
Has passed over our closed mouths,
* O Mylitta!*

Women were already crowding the temple. They were clad in linen tunics descending to the feet, and their long, loose hair escaped from tall pointed miters. A violent perfume surrounded their person, steeped in balms and rubbed with aromatics.

They came, as was customary, to offer themselves to the desire of a stranger, every wife having to sit down, at least once in her life, in the temple of the goddess, in order to deliver herself to prostitution.

Further away, nubile girls were being sold, one after another, to men who were jostling around them, laughing. A public crier put the charms of each amorous virgin up for auction, commencing with the most accomplished. The latter having been sold at an honest price, they passed on to the next, still very beautiful and desirable; and those sales were veritable unions, which were contracted by the will of both parties. The rich espousers bid enthusiastically, assessing the quality of the feminine livestock, praising the delicacy of the joints, the grain of the skin, the suppleness of the limbs, the charm of the voice and the softness of the voice.

The beautiful creatures of amour quickly found a collector and went gloriously to join their master. As for the ugly, their fate was less enviable, for the men who bought them only counted on making use of them for labor in the fields and in the house. But all the girls, the beautiful, the ugly and even the deformed, found a taker, and it was not permitted to the parents to marry them off as they chose.

When the three queens had entered the sanctuary of the goddess, the women had prostrated themselves respectfully, and then had gone into the aisles while the servants of Mylitta prepared the sacrificial altar.

An immense clamor of delight drowned out Sahuradha's voice when she announced to the High Priest that the goddess had fecundated her womb, and all the women present were already thinking of the fêtes that would celebrate the adorable event. Belsharuzur would doubtless be generous to his subjects, and for several days, the popular orgy would follow the royal orgy.

Sahuradha, smiling at the women who surrounded her, distributed amulets and precious stones. She displayed her slightly thickened waist proudly, and the bruising around her eyes.

The shrill voices of the virgins had taken up the hymn of amour; Ussary and Amat-Sula, the secondary queens, held Sahuradha's yellow veil to the right and the left, and the High Priest prayed fervently for the glory of Babylon and the felicity of the child who was going to be born.

VIII

> I await you in the darkness and burning whirlwinds
> of sand enter into my dwelling! But you are the cool
> and limpid wave that will calm my thirst.
> (Chaldean hymn to Tammuz, god of amour.)

Belsharuzur had clasped the beloved wife to his heart and had murmured to her with an unknown softness: "May the favor of the gods accompany you, Sahuradha."

"Live forever, O my Lord, my King, my venerated Lover!"

She had knelt down, and her crimson mantle, of delicate fabric from Srinagar, was spread out behind her. She was young and very beautiful; her tenderly submissive attitude summoned amour irresistibly, and her gaze was burning with a new fire. She had parted over her bosom the light veils that covered it, and a high golden tiara coiffed her admirable black hair, which, by a fortunate artifice, had blue-tinted reflections.

The king went on, amorously: "Fasten yourself in my arms, Star of intoxicating nights. Come into the warmth of darkness to mingle your breath with mine."

And she had replied: "I am your slave, your property, your thing; I am the one you can annihilate or elevate as you please."

"You are my wife, and the gods have blessed our union."

"Yes, for you have deigned to heap me with your favors, and my life would not be sufficient to repay that immense debt."

"The rejoicing of my people will prove their joy."

"My gaze, O my Master, will also prove my amour to you."

"You will appear on a throne by my side for the adoration of men. You will raise the royal cup to your lips and you will be honored among women."

"I will not have sufficient actions of grace to celebrate your praise."

She kissed his hands, devotedly, forgetful now of the humiliations that he had made her suffer; but a darker fire shone in her gaze, for she now believed in her right to the tenderness of her husband.

Belsharuzur was no longer thinking about Phédyne, who, in any case, had given him everything for which he was ambitious. At that moment, he truly loved the queen and was grateful to her for having shown him a fecundity that served his pride and his interests.

She forgot herself in the glorious dream and went on, in a caressant voice: "When you arrive, my beloved Lord, you are like the celestial dew that descends into the fields and the woods. Your left hand holds the sacred lily, and your head is crowned with roses of Sennar. All is clarity in my soul, since the spouse has returned and he will linger beside his humble slave."

"Yes," said the king, "I want to heap you with caresses as on the first day of our marriage. You appear to me today to be the most beautiful of women."

"I shall sing your praises until my last breath."

Sahuradha contemplated her Lord with ecstasy. She forgot herself in the admiration of his powerful, grim and handsome features. The king's gilded armor was partly hidden beneath an ample crimson garment. He wore a pointed helmet on his head, richly encrusted with gems, which was ornamented in front by an eagle with deployed wings, and his ceremonial costume added something savage to his grace.

He represented the brutal strength of the south, over which the burning breath of the desert had passed for generations during the war against Egypt. He was marked by the hot kisses of an implacable and superb sun.

"Are you satisfied, O my jealous Queen?"

Her only reply was a gaze of reckless adoration.

But as he got ready to leave, she said, softly: "Why leave me so quickly?"

"It's necessary that I speak to the people; I also need to announce the good news to my army, and that is why I'm dressed in this warrior costume."

"Yes," she murmured, smiling, "you must proclaim our happiness. May the gods accompany you! Live forever, O Master of the World!"

She prostrated herself in order to kiss his knees, but he lifted her up tenderly and clasped her to his heart again.

IX

As bracelets and ornaments are given to a courtesan
who loves to adorn herself, so ornaments are made
for deceptive idols.
(The Book of Baruch.)[1]

For two days Belsharuzur showed himself at the fêtes in the
company of the queen who had captured his favors once again.
In the beauty of Sahuradha, he forgot the sad and fragile grace
of Phédyne, her veiled gaze, her silky lashes, the delicate oval of
her face, her soft, penetrating voice with elongated syllables. At
that moment, Warka and Belsharuzur were only one, the mysterious lover and the grim tyrant united in a figure of pride and
indolence.

Sprawling under a florid awning alongside Sahuradha, he
bore choice dishes to his lips, and drank spiced wines from silver
bowls decorated with enamels, reserving the golden chalices that
Nabuchodonosor had taken from the temples of Jerusalem.

Women prostrated themselves to the brief impact of castanets and cymbals, and the soft caress of lyres and tambourines.
Then dancers, holding one another by the waist, their curly hair
fluffed up round the shoulders, processed around the throne.
They ran, taking very small steps, their number incessantly augmented, as if miraculously. They emerged from behind walls,
trees and bushes, giving the impression of a turbulent swarm of
voluptuous bees around an august hive.

After the women, cohorts were impelled into the immense
gardens, following musicians who blew into metallic horns and
long bronze trumpets with strident sounds. The men marched
in a radiance of helmets, pikes, javelins and round or rectangular
shields, their bodies tightened in leather coats with imbrications

---

1 Not a direct quote from the apocryphal book in question, although it echoes sentiments expressed in chapter 6, which supposedly quotes a letter sent
by Jeremiah to the Babylonian king.

of iron, in armor of tortoiseshell and wood. Behind them pranced the cavaliers, the Persians, the Medes, the Caduceans, the Saces and the satraps of the various provinces. Gods of marble and bronze were carried on litters, or on carts drawn by chained lions and tigers. The priests of the temples of Bit-Narris, Nebo, Sin, Samas and Adar-Sandam escorted monstrous idols, surrounded by twelve bulls that were to be sacrificed to them.

Already, the shadow was descending over the hanging gardens, drowning ancient Babylon, the royal city with its palaces defended by a triple ring of walls. It hid completely the annexed districts of Cuha, with its majestic temples, and Borsippa, with its acropolis and the famous tower of Bit-Zida.

The dances had resumed with a new frenzy. In the midst of the twirling women, dwarfs and mimes covered with hideous masks appeared. They pursued the dancers, attempting to catch them in ropes of flowers, to the sound of castanets, tympanons and sistra. Jugglers in Syrian robes with floating sleeves, with jewels on the arms and around the neck, alternated with athletes, gymnasts, runners and jumpers who turned somersaults on their hands and feet, falling back gracefully before the florid throne.

Poets recited a hymn to the omnipotent Master, the conqueror of the world, and the warm voices of women took up the strophes to the accompaniment of flutes and lyres, in a religious ensemble. The priests, burners of aromatics, incensed the sovereign, very handsome in his crimson robe, heavy with embroideries and gold fringes, with his pectorals of precious stones and the high tiara with pendants that surmounted his prestigiously curled tresses.

Silent and sad, Nigabael displayed a made-up face, painted eyes and hair powdered with gold, in accordance with the royal caprice. He was similarly mitered with gems and wore a white toga decorated with pearls. Belsharuzur, entirely given to his new amour for the queen, had forgotten his favorite—who did not seem, however, to be suffering from that disgrace.

The shadow thickening increasingly, torches were lit. There was a respite in the dances, and the golden cups stolen from the temple of Jerusalem were filled again.

At that moment, a mighty clap of thunder drowned out the sound of the tympanons, clarions, trumpets and sistra.

Some of those who were about to drink dropped the precious bowls and tried to flee through the gardens, without caring about continuing the festivities.

However, chariots arrived, harnessed to foaming horses, come from afar in order to process before the conqueror. Then, prisoners filed past for the habitual tortures, for every fête terminated in blood. Clarions and trumpets sounded more loudly, covering the noise of the storm.

Belsharuzur distributed presents to the chiefs of his armies while the executioners prepared the instruments of torture: scissors for cutting the skin into thin strips, tongs for extracting the eyeballs from the orbits, wedges, pincers, ropes, saws and hatchets.

After the periodic wars, frightful executions recur monotonously in the history of the four empires. Everything was scrupulously inscribed there: the victories, the massacres and the tortures, not to mention the terrible maledictions menacing those who might destroy those testimonies to the grandeur of the kings.

Ishtar, the goddess of love—the Babylonian Venus—presided over the tortures, while the choir of women recounted her descent to the abode of the dead in the entrails of the earth. Her golden statue dominated the host of prisoners in its serene glory, and the singers resumed more loudly:

"This is the dwelling that one enters, but from which no one emerges;

"The road that one travels but does not pass over again;

"The dwelling where he that enters finds darkness instead of light;

"The place where one bites the dust, where one eats the mud;

"Where one never sees the daylight, where the darkness dwells."

The executioners attached those who were about to die before the smiling idol, and the choir clamored in the tempest:

"Ishtar has descended under the earth and has not come up again!"

Huge clouds were arriving from all points of the horizon at a sinister gallop, and almost instantaneously, night fell upon Babylon.

Frightened, Belsharuzur had risen to his feet in the vertiginous blast of the tempest, which had swept away the remains of the feast and the golden cups from which he had drunk.

For the second time, he had dared to profane the sacred vessels of the temple, with his wives, his concubines, his favorites and the grandees of his court. He remembered then the words of Nabuchodonosor: "I prophecy to you, O Babylon, the misfortune that will fall upon you, which neither Belus, my author, nor Queen Baltis will have the power to persuade the goddess of destiny to turn away from me. A Persian mule will come, having your own gods for auxiliaries; he will impose servitude upon you. His accomplice will be a Mede, whom Assyria glorified. May it please the gods that he will have been able, before betraying his fellow citizens, to perish, swallowed up in a gulf or in the sea, or, turning toward other ways, wander in the deserts where there are neither cities nor paths trodden by the feet of men, where the wild beasts live freely, and where the birds of prey fly over the sterile rocks of ravines. As for me, may I attain a better end, before that thought enters my mind!"

A nameless terror paralyzed Belsharuzur, while the roll of thunder passed with the grim clouds, underlined by fulgurant lightning flashes. The darkness was so compact that the witnesses, panicking, knocked one another down in a vertiginous stampede, falling on top of one another, in the midst of cries and blasphemies. A great black tent had closed the horizon in all directions; everyone remained buried under a uniform shroud, pierced by the continuous howling of a great seething cauldron.

The palace trembled under the immense south-westerly wind, which brought a kind of deluge into the burning desert. A thousand bizarre, high-pitched, menacing, wayward voices proffered threats and then dissolved in the frightful and powerful clamor of unleashed elements.

The monarch tottered, feeling that he was inside a whirlwind. Everything that surrounded him was like a fantastic soul of murder and folly; there was a swarm of malevolent beasts consuming his arms and legs, apparitions of filthy beings, possessed of nothing but foaming mouths eager to devour . . .

When Belsharuzur finally found himself in safety in his palace, he thought about the sinister warning that he had just received, and promised himself to stop the conspirators in their secret work. Already, the satrap Smarnis was in his power, but that was not sufficient. It was necessary to capture the other leaders, to penetrate the heart of the outlying districts and separate the wheat from the chaff.

Doubtless Phédyne knew the sectarians' retreat. Phédyne would not refuse to talk to the lover whom she must still cherish in the depths of her heart . . .

And he told himself that he would return to Phédyne, since Phédyne alone could save Warka.

X

You have said: I no longer want to be a slave; but
upon every high hill and beneath every green tree
you have bowed down like a prostitute.

(Jeremiah.)[1]

The young woman had forgiven. Nothing turned her gaze away from the sky where the stars shone, from the horizon where the sun rose, or from the amour in which her entire suffering being took refuge.

What would she have done, in any case, in that great cruel city in which she knew no one except for brother and her lover? It was necessary for her to live for one and for the other, for her affection and her tenderness. But like those flowers from which one draws the sap in order to make them bloom too rapidly and which die while others are opening, her hasty passion developed at the expense of her life and consumed her slowly. She was no longer anything but a fragile lily whom the wind had inclined like the reeds of the river bank, and which a keener wind had carried away in a ray of light.

Fundamentally, Phredyne was waiting for a miracle, some manifestation of the invisible that would render her dear tenderness to her. Alongside her, she heard the flutter of wings and mysterious murmurs; she turned around suddenly and thought that a shadow was gliding behind her, a specter of grace and amour . . .

She waited, in the depths of her room, for the desired coming, but no footstep crossed the threshold; Nigabael, retained at the palace, could not come to her house, and Warka had disappeared, leaving her broken in heart and body.

For two days she had lived in a trance, seeing no one, and the nights, especially, were full of anguish.

---

1 Not a direct quotation, though clearly based on *Jeremiah* 2:20.

Then a storm such as she had never seen burst over Babylon. That was so singular in a country where it hardly ever rained that the young woman had thought it a divine warning, a manifestation of celestial wrath. The waters of the river splashed as far as the threshold of her house, the winds shook the walls with rage, making a long howl of distress heard.

Everything became confused in Phédyne's heavy head. Memories passed rapidly, with the indecision of landscapes reflected in troubled water. She had fallen back into the bleak dejection in which thought escapes.

Why had Warka not come back? His presence was for her, henceforth, intelligence and reason. Warka had forgotten her for cares and pleasures that remained unknown to her.

Air was lacking to Phédyne's lungs, harmony to her ears and water to her desiccated lips. Every hour that passed took away a little of her life. The torture recommenced, as after the fault. She mourned him, she desired him, with oaths to Iahveh, the almighty God, who had put him in her path.

And then, had Nigabael not said that a meeting was to be held the following evening behind the temple of Nebo? Warka would doubtless be there, since he was the soul of the conspiracy, and nothing could be done without his will.

The young woman resolved to go in secret to the temple and join the conspirators. She would put on her masculine garments again, which would enable her to pass for Nigabael's brother, if necessary.

On the evening of the second day, after the frightful storm that had fallen upon Babylon, she suddenly saw, looming up on the threshold of her dwelling, the majestic silhouette of Warka.

"Oh," she said. "You . . . you, finally!"

"Yes, me. Have you been thinking of me, then?"

"I thought myself abandoned forever."

He stroked her cheeks gently. "Dear Smile, I love you! How could I quit you?"

"Is that really true?"

"Certainly, since I've come back."

She shivered, not daring to believe in her good fortune. She had suffered so much for two days!

He went on, ardently: "Don't doubt any longer . . . I'm at your feet and I adore you!"

She had taken his hands in hers, assuring herself that he was not an errant vision of darkness.

"You love me! You love me!" she repeated, ecstatically. "I haven't offended Heaven, then?"

There was a bewilderment of joy, a minute of unhoped-for rapture in which she absorbed herself delectably. The pains of the day before and the obstacles of the morrow had disappeared, to give way to ecstatic confidence. In the very enchainment of her surprise, she could no longer find words to express her happiness, and remained as if paralyzed in an infinite sweetness.

"Oh, dear Beauty," he said, "I could no longer live without you, and I have come."

She smiled divinely. "I can die, since you love me! I'd like to go to sleep like this, on your shoulder, slowly . . . forever."

She started to reflect in the midst of the great felicity that had stunned her.

"You haven't forgotten that the decisive meeting is tomorrow?"

The man pricked up his ears. That was what he had me to learn.

"Yes, it's tomorrow."

"If you'd neglected me any longer, I would have gone to join you behind the temple of Nebo tomorrow, at the same hour."

Warka had a joyful frisson. Without asking anything, therefore, he had learned what he desired to know.

"Tomorrow, at the same hour, behind the temple of Nebo," he repeated, in a tremulous voice, as if to engrave the words in his memory.

Tomorrow . . . oh yes, certainly he would be there, but with a good escort and with forces sufficient to envelop the entire clan of conspirators. They would all be captured and thrown into cells to await the final torture. Finally, he would crush the muted revolt that was rumbling in the outlying districts of the city. He would exterminate all the inhabitants of the contaminated quarter if necessary.

Phédyne, ignorant of the harm she was causing, was not looking at her lover, in the reckless dream that was intoxicating her.

"Soon," she murmured, "we'll be together, when our bothers have triumphed over the tyrant and librated Babylon."

"Yes," he said, with a singular smile. "We'll soon triumph."

"And you'll be mine?"

"Forever, my Phédyne. I shall make you the queen of a marvelous realm; I'll take you away, tomorrow, lying on my bosom, and we'll go on forever, forever cradled and asleep in one another's arms . . ."

"And when day breaks, we'll continue in the sunlight, even further, until we arrive in the land where people are happy. That land is that of our brothers, and yours too. We'll know everyone there, we'll live there in great joy, only having the concern of cherishing one another more with each new day . . . oh, the beautiful land where the flowers resemble stars and where the fruits are as sweet as honey!" Her entire being was rapturous, in scattered breaths. It was all the legends of Israel that her imagination was evoking, as in her childhood, the mystic flight of which was born under the words of the Prophets. The darkness around her brightened, like a stream of stars.

Warka was so happy that he laughed with the young woman. Tomorrow . . . tomorrow he would be victorious, once again, and nothing would any longer obscure his glory.

He possessed her madly, with a frenzy of amour that astonished him, in his blasé habitude in regard to women. And she shuddered recklessly under that caress, which set her entire being ablaze. She fainted under the breath of ineffable joys, too infatuated to revolt, too feeble to resist. She was no longer anything but a little plant, carried away and tossed by the waves, submerged in a hurricane of desires and passion.

XI

Young man, rejoice before the silver cord breaks,
the golden lamp is broken, the pitcher is broken at
the well and the wheel is broken at the cistern,
before the dust returns to the earth from which it
was taken.
(*Ecclesiastes.*)[1]

It was a subterranean room, unknown, behind the immense temple flanked by lions with human heads, winged bulls and grim gods, half-beast and half-human. The entrance to that retreat expired on the threshold of a ruined house and was illuminated by a clay lamp elongated in the form of a gondola. Bronze candelabra with seven branches illuminated an altar of sorts before which Daniel, the Prophet, was standing, and other small lamps, which each contained a wick plunged into a mixture of palm oil and wax, sent a pale radiance into the depths of the hall.

The color of the walls was red, and that uniform hue became almost funereal under the low ceiling traversed by unequal beams.

Rays of moonlight bathed the courtyard of the temple, with its formidable statues, leaving the mysterious passage in shadow.

Men clad in long loose robes, their heads coiffed in conical bonnets, were filing along that narrow corridor, recognized by Nigabael, who interrogated them. Their number increased incessantly, and a song of voices arrived from the mysterious hall where the destiny of the city was about to be debated.

Everyone was astonished by the absence and the silence of Smarnis, who should have returned already. Menilok, in the

---

1 An inaccurate quotation improvised from fragments of *Ecclesiastes* 11:9 and 12:6-7

front row of the audience, offered to go to second him and bring him help if necessary. Menilok was liked, almost as much as Smarnis, and he had the confidence of the tribe.

His departure was decided, and the priests of Iahveh, clad in mantles of white linen, their waists girded with gold-spangled belts, gave him their instructions. Those Jewish priests, depositories of all power, interpreters of all law, judges and executioners, spied on the Babylonians via the eyes of their followers, hiding themselves in the ruins of old outlying districts, where the sun's rays scarcely penetrated.

Divided by the quarrels of the satraps and the rivalry of confederations, the country was no more than an armed chaos, to which only conquest could restore order. Above the abyss of the slavery and poverty of the people, a few privileged families shared the refinements of the court; but that very excess of civilization was to hasten the ruination of the first conquerors. Other masters were preparing to expel the unworthy sovereigns, in order to reign in their stead, if not with more dignity, at least with more skill.

Menilok had listened to the exhortations of the priests, who had asked: "Who shall we send, and who will speak for us?" Calmly, he had replied: "Here I am, dispose of me." And the Prophet had repeated the holy words of Iahveh:

"Hear ye indeed, but understand not; and see ye indeed, but perceive not. Make the heart of this people fat, and make their ears heavy, and shut their eyes; lest they see with their eyes, and hear with their ears, and understand with their heart, and convert and be healed."[1]

"Until when, O Prophet, depository of the sacred will?"

And Daniel said again with Iahveh:

"Until the cities be wasted without inhabitant, and the houses without man and the land be utterly desolate. And the Lord have removed men far away, and there be a great forsaking in the midst of the land. But yet in it shall be a tenth, and it shall

---

1 *Isaiah* 6:9-10.

return, and shall be eaten; as a tall tree, and as an oak, whose substance is in them, when they cast their leaves, so the holy seeds shall be the substance thereof."[1]

"Ah!" said Menilok. "We have appeased divine wrath by our repentance; let us render thanks to God for having sent the expiation and the hope of a new grandeur. We shall find ourselves again on the mountain of Sion, to glorify the Eternal, his justice and his invincible power!"

Standing before the altar, Daniel dominated the audience; his hair and his silky white beard were silvery under the light of the little lamps, and his long mantle enveloped him softly. He had the air of a divine apparition; everyone bowed down before him.

"A clamor," he said, "is rising over the heights of the empyrean, and the false gods are troubled in their temples. We have taken our gaze into the enemy regions in order to seek the savior of the world there. Later, we will convert our allies, who will become our brothers. For the moment, it is necessary to act, and I am speaking to you in accordance with the will of Iahveh, our Lord."

"Yes," said Menilok, supportively, "for the people of Babylon as for the exiles of Juda, Cyrus appears as a celestial envoy. He will deliver the oppressed, and what Smarnis has not been able to do, I shall attempt passionately for the relief of consciences and hearts. The immense citadel of Nabuchodonosor rises in the center of the powerful empire in anticipation of a Median attack, but the separated walls of his fortifications, behind the ditches and the moats, will be without efficacy before the genius of an adversary resolved to vanquish. We shall seek the means of evading the obstacle, and God will inspire us."

"Go, my son," said Daniel. "Our affection and our prayers will follow you everywhere. But explain your plan to me."

---

1 *Isaiah* 6: 11-13. The author modifies the final part considerably, but it is hard to believe that Daniel would have played fast and loose with holy writ, so I have stuck to the letter.

"My plan is that of Smarnis. We shall make a breach in the wall and, taking advantage of the dryness in the first days of Tammuz, we shall divert the low waters of the Diyala and the Tigris in order to be able to pass through them easily. Then we shall take the fortifications of the left bank. But it is necessary to act quickly during the month of the great ardors, for later, the waters, swollen by rains, will present an insurmountable obstacle to us."

The Prophet repeated in a sonorous voice: "Go, my son, for the good of Juda, for the grandeur and salvation of humanity."

Women intoned the Song of Songs, delightfully accompanied by the lyre. It was a celestial psalmody, a long amorous plaint, scarcely sighed by mouths avid for pure air, perfumes and kisses.

> *On my bed, during the night,*
> *I have sought the man whom my heart loves.*
> *I have sought him and have not found him;*
> *I implore you, daughters of Jerusalem,*
> *If you find my lover,*
> *Tell him that I am sick with love.*

Menilok resumed in a grave voice, lulled by the passionate sigh of the men: "Certainly, the tyrants will strive to impede the march of events by the futile plans of their perverse minds. But already the chastisement is rumbling over their heads. When Iahveh judges the punishment equal to the crime, he will be able to break the instruments of death. They have marched against Juda and imposed thereon the son of Tabeal, but their plan cannot be carried through to the end. If someone troubles the course of divine justice by stimulating a purely human action, it will be manifest above the versatile will of men. The Euphrates once quit its bed and passed over its banks in order to descend upon Juda, but in the same way, the river will annihilate the enemies of the sole God of the earth and the worlds. Nabuchodnosor cried; 'It is here, the Babylon that I have edified to be the seat of my sovereignty, for the virtue of my strength and for the eternal portion of my magnificence.' And while he was still speaking, the divine will metamorphosed him into a beast. 'He was excluded from among men, and he ate grass like the oxen, and his body was bathed in the morning dew, until his hair was as long as the plumes of the vulture and his fingernails like those of birds.' Jerusalem will be avenged, and our people will return to Juda in order to rebuild their city there and the temple of their God."

"Yes, yes," continued the High Priest, in a cruel excitement, "the children of the traitors will have their throats cut, children will be crushed before the eyes of their fathers, the houses pillaged, the women violated, and Babel, the ornament of the empire, the jewel of Chaldean pride, annihilated like Sodom and Gomorrah when Iahveh overthrew them. I tell you this, men of Juda, the time is nigh and everything that the Prophets have predicted will be accomplished. Pray! Pray, people of Israel, for the triumph of the true god and the annihilation of the accursed city!"

The priests and the levites prostrated themselves with fervor in the idea of that return to the homeland. They could already see themselves filing in a long caravan over the dusty roads, amid the ruins of the vanquished villages, and they were all thinking about the fallen temple of ancient belief, which their faith was going to reconstruct in its primitive glory. They would clear the sacred area in order to erect the altar of sacrifices there; they would form on the land of their forefathers a holy colony in the midst of pagan peoples. But the Philistines, the Idumeans, the Moabites and the Ammonites would be expelled in their turn from the kingdom of Israel, which would recover, along with its power, all of its ancient splendor.

A young woman had entered the tunnel, guided by Nigabael. Her face was veiled but her emotion could be divined by the quivering of her shoulders.

After being plunged in passionate prayer, she turned her head to the right and the left, seemingly searching for someone among the audience; then she leaned over to Nigabael's ear.

"Has the satrap not come, then?"

"No," said Nigabael, sadly.

"That's singular. And you're without news?"

"Without news since his departure."

"Perhaps he has his reasons for keeping quiet. And yet, I would so much like to know!"

A frightful doubt filled her soul. She was weeping now, kneeling in the shadow, overwhelmed by an immense desolation.

Menilok had disappeared through a secret door, and the passionate choir of women resumed the Song of Songs to a livelier rhythm:

> *I have put off my coat; how shall I put it on? I have washed my feet; how shall I defile them?*
> *My beloved has put in his hand by the hole in the door; and my bowels were moved for him.*
> *I rose up to open to my beloved; and my hands dropped with myrrh, and my fingers with sweet smelling myrrh, upon the handles of the lock.*[1]
> *Stay me with flagons, comfort me with apples: for I am sick of love.*
> *His left hand is under my head, and his right hand doth embrace me.*
> *Thou hast ravaged my heart, my sister, my spouse; thou hast ravaged my heart with one of thine eyes, with one chain of thy neck.*
> *How fair is thy love, my sister, my spouse! how much better is thy love than wine! and the smell of thine ointments than all spices!*
> *Thy lips, O my spouse, drop as the honeycomb: honey and milk are under thy tongue; and the smell of thy garments is like the smell of Lebanon.*

---

1 *Song of Solomon* 5:3-5; the song reproduced in the text then continues with 2:5-6, and then with 4: 9-11, all slightly modified, but I have substituted the A.V. text of the original lines.

Nigabael, prostrate before the altar, prayed ardently, asking the supreme God to purify him of his sins. His flesh horrified him; he would have liked to strip it off like a robe of infamy, in order to put on the immaterial tunic of the angels.

The little horn lamps of the subterranean space seemed to burn more brightly, elongating their flames like tongues of fire toward the vaults. At every moment, inclinations and invocations caused the long white robes of the priests to flap, and clouds of blue smoke emerged from the censers. The lyres had a softer sigh and the choir of women resumed on delicate notes, as light and airy as the flutes of archangels.

A very pure, crystalline voice, a very young voice, exquisite to hear, pronounced the Song of Songs alone now. It was the voice of Phédyne, who kneeling beside her bother, joined her voice with those of the tribe. And, while singing, she thought about her beloved who had not come, the Warka who already took up so much room in her life that she would have died at the idea of no longer seeing him.

> *Let my beloved come into his garden, and eat his pleasant fruits.*
> *I am come into my garden, my sister, my spouse. I have gathered my myrrh with my spice; I have eaten my honeycomb with my honey; I have drunk my wine with my milk.*[1]
> *Set me as a seal upon thine heart, as a seal upon thine arm; for love is strong as death.*

But there was a great noise in the cellar; armed soldiers fell upon the members of the audience, put them in chains, with ropes around their necks, and drove them with thrusts of pikes to the prisons of Babylon.

---

1 *Song of Solomon* 4:15 and 5:1; the text then continues with the first part of 8:6.

XII

As a pregnant woman, when her term approaches,
writhes and cries out in pain, so we are before
thee, Iahveh!
(Anonymous Prophet.)

Phédyne, protected by an occult power, remained alone in the subterrain. Men had bound her to the foot of the altar, in front of a candelabrum with the seven branches, and she had exhausted herself in vain efforts to rejoin Nigabael, who had been carried away with his head bloodied and his garments torn away.

The entire night passed thus in mortal anguish; then, in the morning, a visitor whom she recognized immediately approached her. Perhaps he thought that it was both a duty and a cruelty to bring her help, for his movements had an indecision that was singular in such circumstances. Doubtless he feared the heart-rending scenes that were about to succeed the state of prostration in which Phédyne remained.

Leaning over her, he interrogated her pale, contracted features avidly, on the lookout for the painful and yet desired moment in which he would see a gleam of anger or distress pass through her gaze.

He was mistaken in his anticipations, for he had only ever studied physical pain in the tortured, and mental pain remained unknown to him. The young woman raised her long eyelids, and then closed them again immediately. No tear flowed between her silky lashes, no sob inflated her lips. She remained icy, motionless and silent; if it had not been for the movement of the heart that he felt beneath his hand, the man would have been able to believe that she was already dead.

"Phédyne," he murmured, "it's me."

"You!" He divined rather than heard it, so faint was the voice.

"Yes, me, Warka, your lover, your fiancé."

She opened frightened eyes and contemplated him distraughtly.

"But why are you here?" she asked, after a long silence.

"To help you."

"Help me? When our brothers are in danger! First of all, you were not at the meeting that was to decide our fate. We were all waiting for you and we said prayers for you. What were you doing while our people we being massacred?"

Warka smiled. "You can't understand," he said, softly. "These things are mysterious for you. But soon, you'll know the secret of my life."

"The secret of your life? Oh, you're scaring me. Are you not, then, the man I believed you to be?"

"I am the man who loves you, and who will make you a royal fate. Allow yourself to be led, without interrogating the laws of destiny. Everything happens by the will of the gods."

"I only know one God, Iahveh Sabaoth." She gazed at him, her eyes dilated by fear, strangely disturbed by his new attitude. "Since you know where my brother Nigabael is, take me to him."

"No, I don't know anything," he said, effortfully. "I hid in order to remain free and act while the others were impotent."

"Oh, if you were telling the truth!"

"Why would I lie, dear Tenderness?"

Phédyne reflected. "But what about me? Why am I here?"

"Forgetfulness, no doubt."

She shook her head. "No, a formal order. I heard what the soldiers said."

"And what did they say?" asked Warka, lowering his yellow gaze upon the young woman.

"They said—oh, I can still hear them!—'This one isn't to be taken away, the Master is protecting her.'"

"Truly, they said that? Might you have touched the heart of the tyrant? Perhaps he desires you too?" And Warka laughed in a singular fashion.

Phédyne pushed her lover away and began to weep. Everything in and around her was dark. No miracle would be accomplished, then, to save her from the spirit of darkness? She gazed at the gray wall, thinking that she might see a luminous hand appear that would make her a sign to flee, or a flock of doves that might console her heart. None of the prodigies announced by the Prophets would have astonished her. If Warka was an enemy, why had no divine manifestation been produced?

But no, there was a great silence inside her. It was as if she were asleep between what she could no longer deny and what she could not yet believe.

"It's necessary to go home, Phédyne. Resume the road to your dwelling."

He helped her to get up and to repair the disorder of her garments. But she remained indecisive, standing near the altar.

"I no longer have a home."

"I can't show myself with you . . . but I'll see you often, as before. Go, hide your face under your veil and return to your house."

"No, no, I want to see Nigabael again. If he's doomed, I shall die with him."

"You'll see your brother again, but later. Do as I tell you; that will be your salvation, and it will also be his."

Phédyne took a few steps. Her heart had worked the miracle. With the grain of hope it built a mountain. If, at its final beat, it had been shown an atom of love, it would have started to beat again. The heart of a woman in love only stops forever when there is nothing more around it than the void, and even the shadow of what was dear to her has disappeared from the earth.

XIII

Thus, that light emanates from the sun: it receives its
form and its regular movement from the influence of
the moon; it has the atmosphere for its receptacle
and its prison.
(Hermes, *The Emerald Tablet*.)[1]

Phédyne had quit Warka, the only person she now knew in the
enemy city, the only one from whom she had the right to demand pity. She was Hagar departing for the desert.

She prayed again to the God who was afflicting her, because
that God was, for her, the one who could do the impossible,
the one next to whom hope recommenced when the hopes of
the world were extinct. Her profound and soft gaze arrested on
the sky, as if to search there for the mysterious sign of destiny.
Her mind was a book printed within and without, and when
her attention was exalted, the scriptures were confused. Dream
then triumphed over real life and plunged her reason into an
incurable slumber.

What had happened seemed so strange to the young woman
that she renounced understanding. In spite of everything, however, Warka could not be culpable, according to her heart. The
amorous woman still saw infinite perfections around the object
that intoxicated and fascinated her. She was drunk on the wine
of sensuality, unaware that the perfume of the wine of amour
is often, the day after the orgy, nothing more than a repugnant
reminiscence and a cause of disgust.

Alone in the obscure room where she had dreamed and wept,
her sadness was further augmented. She was like a reed bat-
tered by the tempest, and the hours passed slowly in a profound
desolation. Previously, she had wanted to live for her brother

1 This is not an accurate translation from the brief alchemical document
known as the Emerald Tablet, being somewhat embellished, presumably by
La Vaudère.

and her fiancé; there was in activity and hope a distant light that she wanted to attain, in spite of the difficulties of the road. Now, everything had crumbled at the same time and fallen into darkness.

She came back to sit by the door, interrogating the road, at the same place where she had awaited the coming of the beloved. Her bleak face was turned toward the exterior air, as if to ask the breeze that was coming from the river to bring her the echo of lost kisses, tender words and beautiful oaths; but her arms, extended by her sides, were dangling, devoid of strength, like idle or fatigued arms that have nothing more to do on this earth.

The joy of cares to give, the desire or an imminent liberation and the gratitude of affection, had all failed her successively, she no longer had anything but watching from afar, day and night, like a lamp burning under the vault of a temple.

But her strength was exhausted. In the midst of that dolor, returned to her point of departure—silence and immobility—after having tried in vain effort, courage and will, Phédyne was exhausted, like a delicate plant. She would have needed the sun of her homeland and a little happiness to give her the florescence of youth, and the radiance of the sun and the radiance of amour were both lacking.

Little girls went past her door, shaking their short-cropped hair, sometimes tinted red and forming a fleece. They laughed as they looked at her, and asked her for treats or trinkets. And as Phédyne did not reply, they drew away, furious, seemingly bristling like wildcats.

Some, showing their brown faces regretfully, surrounded by little brown mats woven in wool, sketched a dance-step in order to soften her. Their frail and supple bodies twisted and their arms, thrown forward, seemed to be repelling an invisible enemy.

Men also stopped in front of Phédyne, finding her beautiful, and smiled as they looked at her. It seemed to her that the deserted quarter had suddenly acquired a strange animation; but she persisted in her sadness and her mutism, too occupied with the obscure drama that was wringing her heart.

It was a long time before she perceived her decline, because she was not thinking about herself; then, one morning, she understood, and lay down at the back of the room in the warm shadow where she had believed that she might grasp her dream of happiness. Voices still brushed her; there was something like an appeal of the earth, an appeal of the water and the trees, and she thought that a miracle might perhaps be in preparation, for the realization of her desire.

Songs of victory reached her, with the plaint of the tortured, which sometimes dominated other sounds. And she shuddered with horror at the memory of the murders of that Belsharuzur, of whom the mere mention made her tremble.

It was in Babylon that iron and steel were forged into redoubtable blades for the most frightful tortures, and the entire city gorged itself on blood after every conquest. The king, here, was the center of everything, of the religion as well as the life of its people. He represented the god of good and evil, and could make heads fall at his whim. Even the famous mage descended from the first Chaldeans did not attempt to impede his power, and was only, at the most, summoned to give an explanation of his dreams or to pronounce auguries based on the condition of the constellations.

Babylon, the city of debauchery, pleasure and crime, really was "the hammer of the earth" of which Jeremiah spoke.

Phédyne evoked the bright legends of her religion: the walls of Jericho crumbling to the sound of trumpets; Joshua stopping the march of the sun; David, after Saul, charming the world with the sounds of his lyre and giving Jerusalem to the people of Israel. Oh, how she would have liked to see Jerusalem, the glorious and mystical city! Jerusalem, the divine city, always alive and luminous in spite of its fall!

Then it was Solomon and his marvelous temple, it was Palmyra and the voluptuous valley that occupied the young woman's demented thoughts. It was also the fall of Nineveh and the destruction of the holy city. She wept for the disgrace of the kings of Juda, overturned by Nebuchodonosor, the loss of the miraculous temple and the captivity of her tribe.

Only Cyrus would have been able to reestablish the ancient prestige of Israel, Cyrus, who had promised to protect the Hebrews; but would Warka act in accordance with his promise? Was Warka truly the friend of her race?

She no longer knew, and the torture of doubt recommenced, bloody and frightful.

She loved in desperation, struggled in the hopeless passion that was devouring her being. She would have liked to run toward her lover, to reconquer him by throwing herself into his arms; and the struggle of her amour against her reason recommenced. Sometimes, however, after extraordinary efforts, she believed that she was victorious; a great silence fell within her, like a calm of death, a complete insensibility, a sepulchral cold.

Then a flood of blood rose into her heart, seething madly, stunning her with desires. Her amorous ardor was reborn, more indomitable than before; she prepared for her flight, no longer thinking about anything but running straight ahead, hoping that a mysterious force would guide her to the dwelling of the Adored. Tragic hours went by in the midst of that uncertainty as to the decision to make, in the storm wind that incessantly threw her back from the frenzy of her passion to the horror of her sin.

That fever exhausted Phédyne; she had a wound in her side and was dying a little every day, indignant at not being able to attempt anything, even to save her brother, who was doubtless about to perish in torments more terrible than her own.

She formed the project, sometimes, of going to the palace, of throwing herself at the feet of the king in order to try to obtain his mercy. Then she told herself that Belsharuzur would not be moved to pity by her tears; he had never pardoned anyone, and the crime of treason must excite his hatred more than any other.

Only Warka, since he was free, could still save Nigabael. Why had Warka forgotten the road to her house? She wept for the lover, appealed to him, desired him with a revolt against Iahveh, the cruel god who had taken him.

Finally, at the end of her strength, she went to sleep in scorn for herself and disgust for the world. Oh, passion! the evil beast that she would have liked to crush in order to fall to the great calm of death! But something revolted within her, which she could not destroy or vanquish: a vague hope of tenderness and happiness, in spite of everything.

Like the Jewish people, she awaited her relief by a miracle. At the moment when the oppressed race was about to cease to be counted among the number of the nations, when the white bones of Israel were about to crumble to dust under the feet of its conquerors, she still hoped, driven by a great breath of youth and faith.

XIV

Dreams are the incarnations of light.
(Pythagoras.)

That night, Phédyne had not been able to sleep. She lay in the dark with dilated pupils, gripped by a sudden great terror, as if something grave were in preparation for her. Suddenly, her entire dwelling was full of light. Warka was before her, surrounded by armed men and sumptuously dressed people. Slaves held up torches, which projected fantastic gleams over the bare walls.

"Who are you?" she asked, trembling.

Smiling, Warka approached. "I'm the man you love. Don't you recognize me?"

She extended her arms, as if to draw the adorable vision to her. "Yes, I love you, and is that why you've come? You've taken pity on my weakness and my solitude?"

She passed her fingers over her eyelids with a mechanical gesture, and then looked at him ecstatically, as if in a dream;

and she believed that she was still asleep, for it often happened to her that she saw him thus in her sleep—which aggravated her malaise thereafter.

With her groping hands, however, she had taken his, in order to assure herself that he was not an errant specter of pleasant dreams.

There was a stupidity of joy, an initial moment of absolute happiness. The tortures of the previous day, the doubts and the anguish, had disappeared, in order to give way to the enchantment of the return.

"My brother?" she said, when her thoughts had become clearer. "Are you taking me to my brother?"

"You want to go with me?"

"Yes, take me away. I can no longer live like this; this suffering is beyond my strength."

A sudden energy had brought her to her feet. Will sustained her, rendered her valiant, and already, she was enveloping herself in her light veil, marching toward the door.

Warka laughed, and a bestial gleam passed through his eyes.

"Do you know where you're going?"

"What does it matter? Anywhere you take me, I'll be well. Anyway, are you not my lover, my fiancé, my friend?"

"Yes, yes, I'm everything to you, Phédyne."

He was still laughing, and those around him shared his hilarity.

Without being astonished by the liberty of those men, the young woman had thrown herself on to the breast of her Beloved, and her entire being was palpitating with joy.

"But it's a long road," he said. "You can't walk that far."

"Don't you have your boat?"

He made a sudden resolution. "It's also necessary that you learn the truth. Come, then, and let destiny be accomplished."

She followed him to the water gate, where the boat was waiting, displaying on its prow the image of Zou, the god of shipwrecks, and she recognized the crimson and fabrics and the jeweled tent that had already struck her sight; Warka was dressed himself in a scarlet toga sewn with pearls, and she found him handsome, with his woven beard and the multiple curls of his hair.

The men of the escort had taken their places in other boats almost as sumptuous as the first, and the oarsmen were striking the troubled and suspect water rhythmically.

Phédyne, leaning on Warka's shoulder, saw the fleeting ruins of Babil and the Kasr, which the shadow rendered even more fantastic, with stakes holding up their torture victims, enveloped by long processions of vultures. Now they passed alongside the temple of Bel, and then that of El Kalaeih, defended by monsters with human heads, androcephalous bulls, majestic and cruel, whose hindquarters bulged roundly while the body thinned and flattened against the walls, ornamenting the doors of the sacred edifices.

Those huge figures, imposing and proud, had widespread wings; they watched over the living and the dead, like the sphinxes of the Nile, in disdainful repose. But the inspiration was not the same on the banks of the Tigris, as on those of the Euphrates, always strewn with cadavers, always awash with blood. The noble actions of the Egyptian gods, leaning over the figures of the royal sons of the Sun, would not have been understood by the worshipers of black idols of vengeance and murder.

Here, the artist had not been inspired by any dream of the afterlife. The brutality of a warrior life left no room for the enchanted vision of poets, and everything was sacrificed to the barbaric pride of a Master.

The pale light of the stars animated the terrible phantoms, which displayed beards and eyes of gold, and fulgurant tiaras, weapons and shields against the backcloth of walls of enameled brick.

The sanctuary of the goddess Nana was still ablaze in the night; vague psalmodies emerged therefrom with the sighs of lyres and the clear stridulations of flutes. It was there that the mages and the sacrificer priests gathered after the ceremonies of the day.

Phédyne penetrated into all the sumptuousness of the imperial city, which she had not known before, because Nigabael had forbidden her to go in that direction.

The proud kings of Babylon, intent on surpassing the luxury of their Ninevite predecessors, had had the models that embellished the capital of the North hastily copied, and the temple of Bel, principally, presented ornaments and golden statues, of a rare magnificence. There were, in bas-relief, sovereigns on their chariots, impetuous hunts, and, always, long processions of prisoners awaiting the torture to which others had already been subjected, with details of monstrous exactitude. Everywhere, the victorious monarch was crushing his enemies, massacring lions, or witnessing frightful slaughter of which history presents no other example. It was a continuous nightmare of brutal force, insouciant ferocity and frightful triumph.

Phédyne closed her eyes, unable to understand that orgy of sanguinary images, which the moonlight rendered even more fantastic; and the heavy flight of the birds of prey followed the amorous boat like a sinister presage of vengeance and destruction.

Meanwhile, Warka had put his arm around the young woman's waist, and he pressed her against him feverishly. His lips fell upon hers. She could no longer see anything but his dear gaze under the stars, and could no longer hear anything but the tumultuous beating of her heart . . .

The rest of the journey was accomplished, for her, in an increasing intoxication; she had lost all sentiment of the world when her lover threw a thick veil over her face, begging her not to oppose his designs.

They landed at that moment, and men that she could not see carried her away into the night.

PART THREE

I

I have made mistakes and knew them not. I have
committed sins and knew them not. The God, in
the fury of his heart, has crushed me.
(Chaldean hymn.)

It was a high room surrounded by a plinth, colored in black,
bordered by bas-reliefs, crowned themselves by a layer of enameled bricks. The colors, in which pale blue, olive green, yellow
and white were dominant, melted into one another harmoni-
ously, represented blossoming flowers, svelte stems and gracious
clumps of rare plants. The furniture was ivory, and thick drapes
over the doors repeated in fine embroidery the principal scenes
of the bas-reliefs. The backs of the chairs, sustained by rows of
sculpted captives, presented a delicate workmanship, as did the
very low bed, borne by silver lions.

Phédyne, motionless, made up, her hair braided with pearls
and mingled with brilliant plaques, was listening to an amorous
chant. But her gaze remained sad beneath the blue-tinted ring
of her long eyelids; a slight tremor agitated her slender hands,
laden with rings.

In order to distract her, a slave was dancing before her. She was
a young brown woman with fleshy lips and large luminous eyes.
Her curled hair made her something like a rectangular woolen
mantle, slackly inflated. Her dance expressed an entire petty passionate drama full of amorous peripeties. She spun slowly, her
arms always agitated, as if to attract or repel caresses, her head
tilted over her shoulder and her eyelids half-closed. Then, as the

measure became livelier, she became animated, emboldened to the point of struggling with the invisible lover who was speaking to her through the voice of flutes. There were voluptuous surges, mingled with resistance, a provocative defense, a dying smile that summoned the kiss. Finally, after a long pantomime, she fainted, on a final amorously tremulous note like the plaint of a turtle-dove.

The dancer had an ardent beauty that retained the attention. Her long robe scintillated with gems, and when she extended her naked arms, ornamented with bracelets all the way to the elbow, a great languid charm emanated from her.

Other women, musciennes and mimes, succeeded her, until the arrival of Warka, who sat down beside Phédyne on the low couch.

"How late you are," the young woman said, in a reproachful voice. "Why do you no longer come every day, as before? I'm so unhappy far from you! Who are you? For what do you hope? What is your objective? I no longer want to know, for my mind goes astray trying to understand. Everything is mysterious in you and around you. I fear you and I love you as I love my grim God."

"Oh, your god is more covered with iniquities than ours. He's the brother of Moloch and Baal."

"Perhaps, I don't reason, but I adore him because he resembles you, even in his crimes. It appears to me that, with you, I am penetrating into the Holy of Holies, where the sacred Ark is. That Ark brings misfortune to everyone who touches it, and it's also by you that I shall perish, for your gaze has the hue of gold, like that of the accursed."

Warka clasped the young woman to his breast, attempting the habitual caresses, but she pushed him away.

"No, I'm afraid!"

"Am I not today what I was yesterday? You've been living in this palace for a long time, and you've always been submissive."

"Nigabael! Return Nigabael to me!" said the young woman, weeping. "Every day you promise to deliver my people to me, and every day you break your oath."

"Yes, later."

"Why later, if you're our friend? Ought you not to employ yourself for our salvation? How are you free in Babylon while my brother is weeping in a dungeon? Truly, everyone here deceives me, and when I interrogate the women who serve me, they're troubled and remain silent."

"Don't seek to know, Phédyne; retain your ignorance if you want to retain your happiness."

"What happiness do I still have, then?"

"That of loving. In the epoch of Ezekiel, Jews could still be seen in Juda, in the very temple of Jerusalem, with their faces turned to the Orient prostrating themselves before the sun. Imitate them, Phédyne, adore the star that shines, without looking elsewhere. Only the light is good."

"I listen to Iahveh, the God of truth."

"You would do better to adore Astarte, or the Babylonian Mylitta; she has already, by means of the voluptuous rites of her worship, won many of the daughters of Israel to her cause. Her altars stand on the hills above the burning plains. They are verdant and florid, for Tammuz, the god of love, reposes there incessantly . . ."

"Oh, what are you advising me? Mylitta is the goddess of prostitution!"

"She is not unaware of any voluptuous secrets. She teaches young women the adorable science of caresses."

"How can you speak to me about these monstrous customs? Do the women of Babylon not go to the temple of Mylitta in order to deliver themselves to the first comer? The richest are taken there in their sumptuous chariots and, breasts naked, their head circled by a cord, they summon the lover of an hour and ask him to remain beside them. Would you want me, then, to be similar to those wretches?"

Warka laughed, with slight disdain. "Every religion has its customs; nothing revolts me of that which concerns amour."

"And it is near that shameful temple that you would seek your fiancée?"

"My fiancée would seem more beautiful and more desirable to me if Tammuz had brushed her with his light wing. If it is very good to love, it is even better to know how to love."

"I no longer recognize you."

Phédyne wept, and Warka toyed distractedly with the pale curls of her long hair.

"Yes," he said, "you're too amorous to comprehend amour. And then, your tears are monotonous . . . After the sight of blood, what gives me joy is the gaiety of young woman. After the grimace of death, I want laughter and kisses!"

Phédyne had recoiled in fear.

"It isn't you that I'm hearing! No, no, you no longer resemble the man I cherished so much. Your voice, your gestures, and your gaze are no longer the same. Who are you, then?"

Warka, his eyebrows furrowed and his eyes somber, did not reply.

"Oh, this life is culpable!" she said. "Let me go; everything here penetrates me with dread."

Meanwhile, a loud noise became audible outside. But Phédyne's room was illuminated from above, in such a way that it was like being in a prison.

"What is that?" she asked.

"Condemned men being taken away."

She uttered a cry. "They're going into your house!"

"No, they're passing under the walls on their way to the torture."

"Oh! Perhaps my brother is among those unfortunates!"

Recklessly, she sobbed on Warka's shoulder; he remained still, his face somber, his brows furrowed. His desire was increasingly wearied. That frail lover, who only knew how to weep, had forgotten all the obedience and submission that a woman owes to a man. She was obsessed by her demands and her plaints. She was no longer the elect corolla of his flower-bed, but a bruised rose whose petals were strewing the ground.

However, Phédyne had straightened up, offering her lips, which Warka brushed with an indifferent kiss. Then he drew away from the voluptuous couch, without appearing to understand the mute supplication that his mistress addressed to him. Only a few icy phrases, a few inconsequential remarks, escaped his lips. From that moment on, she was dead to him, and he did not even try to give his face an expression of pity or tenderness.

Phédyne fixed her dying gaze upon him; a sudden fear took possession of that heart, which was beating tumultuously. She finally understood what she had not wanted to divine during her happiness: the uniquely carnal desires of her lover, the cruel egotism of his soul. It was an enemy that she had before her, not the protector of her tribe. Despair and terror were painted on her pale face. She no longer tried to implore, but she let herself fall at the man's feet, and said to him with an indescribable terror:

"You are neither Smarnis nor Warka! Who are you, then?"

II

The three companions, having struck Hiram, hid
the cadaver under a pile of rubble and planted an
acacia branch on that improvised tomb, and then
they took flight, like Cain after the murder of Abel.
(The Masonic legend of Hiram.)[1]

Like Smarnis, Nigabael had been imprisoned in the palace dungeons, and he was certain that he would be tortured with the other captives, accused like him of treason.

Belsharuzur had shown himself pitiless toward his former favorite. In any case, his caprices never lasted long, and the image of the sister had caused him temporarily to forget that of the brother.

---

1 The legend of Hiram, the architect of Solomon's temple, plays a key role in Masonic initiation, but it was also known to French writers by virtue of its adaptation in one of the subsidiary narratives in Gérard de Nerval's *Voyage en Orient* (1851), as a story within the story of Queen Balkis and "Soliman," which La Vaudère must surely have read.

While Nigabael and her fiancé were agonizing nearby, Phédyne, secluded in an isolated apartment, was able to believe that she was in the house of a powerful satrap. The noises from outside only reached her enfeebled by the high walls that surrounded her, which were devoid of any opening, and her sad illusion still persisted.

However, Smarnis, thanks to the interested benevolence of a jailer, had been able to communicate with Nigabael, whom he knew to be a prisoner like him. The noise of the preparations in the courtyards of the palace warned him that his final hour was soon to sound.

When he was able to join the king's favorite, he could not believe that it was him, so much had the young man changed. He no longer recognized his bright gaze, his tender grace and his soft smile. He was chained up next to his friend and he told him everything he knew about the Master's visits to the little house in the poor quarter.

"So," said Nigabael, "it's that unworthy girl who betrayed us? Are you quite certain, at least, that you recognized her?"

"She was accompanying her lover!"

"And her lover was the king! Oh, I no longer have a sister! I no longer have a family! I am alone in the world!!"

"You understand now our sterile struggles, our denounced projects, that entire odious defeat?"

The young man wept.

"Oh, the wretch! She has doomed us doubly!"

"Are all our brothers captive like us?"

"I don't know. Those who were present at the last meeting were captured . . ."

"All our chiefs: Gurshar, Sarady, Amath-Sula?"

"Yes, undoubtedly."

"And Menilok?"

Nigabael reflected. "If Menilok were free, perhaps nothing would be lost for us."

"He could stimulate the revolt in Babylon and summon the enemy forces."

But the young man sighed. "Our torture must be due imminently; no intervention can save us."

"Let's hope; God in strong . . ."

"No," said Nigabael, "I can no longer hope, and in any case, even granted mercy, I could no longer have any joy upon the earth. Phédyne has doubtless prostituted herself for a little gold: the person whom I believed so adorably pure, and whom I wanted to give to you, as the best pledge of my esteem and affection!"

"Doubtless she was obedient to an evil influence. Let's not accuse her so long as we remain ignorant of what led to her fall."

"You're defending her!"

The satrap bowed his head. "What do you expect? I still love her!"

"Oh!"

"Yes," Smarnis went on, confusedly. "I can't forget her charming grace, her dear smile and the veiled tenderness of her wide eyes. She remains in me like a joyful radiance in the midst of darkness; even the torture would be indifferent to me if it were given to me to see her again."

"But she's betrayed us! She's sold us!"

"How do we know that?" said the satrap, slowly.

"Doesn't everything accuse her?"

"Oh, your affection isn't as great as mine, since you don't seek to excuse her in spite of the evidence."

The satrap, who was in love for the first time, reviewed all the meanders of his past of conflict and joys. Still young, he had nevertheless lived centuries of glory. All the grandeur and all the enchantment of his victories illuminated his early memories. Then doubt had come, he had abdicated his former religion in order to worship Iahveh, the God of the Jews. From that moment on, the sun had set for him. The beautiful sky into which Babylonian triumph rose in gold and azure, in spite of the crimes and the sobs, had suddenly darkened, and would never recover its imposing serenity, either for the executioners or the victims.

Nabuchodonosor had scaled the clouds and Belsharuzur had fallen back covered in blood. But the warrior was still deluded in thinking that all that red was the crimson of conquerors.

The bellicose idols were doubtless weary; the Prophet Daniel, at the last royal banquet, had predicted that the Babylonian standard would fall into enemy hands: a signal of victory yesterday, today a rag of defeat. One day would suffice to annihilate so many admirable works, so many battles and so much wealth.

Smarnis, weakened by long days of captivity, spoke as if in a dream: "A human hand will write in sinister and mysterious characters on the walls of the palace. That hand I have seen in a dream, and I shivered in fear . . ."

Nigabael shrugged his shoulders. "It was only a dream, alas."

"Who knows? The predictions of the Prophets are formal: the trumpet of the Angel will resound in the sky, announcing the fall of the accursed empire. The stars, those luminous powers, will fall, one by one, like scythed flowers, and the earth will shiver recklessly."

"I no longer believe in anything," groaned Nigabael. "Everything is overwhelming me at once."

"It's necessary to believe, in order to bend Jehovah, who seems to have turned away from us. Doubtless we have offended the God of all justice. But he will come back to those who bow down with humility under his law."

"Let him deliver us instead," the young man murmured, bitterly. "In this prison we can't do anything for his glory."

The yellow light of a small lamp suspended from the ceiling illuminated Nigabael vaguely, and Smarnis was frightened by the cruel gleam that passed through his gaze. His delicate face was drawn, his eyes were widened by fever, and his lips were trembling with anger.

"Let's not surrender to hatred," said the satrap. "I don't believe that divine bounty has abandoned us."

256

"Oh, you don't know what I've suffered since my arrival in this accursed city! Anything would have been preferable to the favor in which I lived so shamefully and so sadly! Yes, I've deviated from the road that my beliefs traced for me, I've fallen into a gulf of misery from which nothing, henceforth, can extract me. I only had one thought: vengeance. I only had one consolation: fraternal tenderness. And it's necessary to renounce both. An immense black veil will hide the sky from me until my imminent death."

"No, the good that is in you will triumph over the sepulchral shadow; it's necessary to summon the light with all the forces of your being. I think that everything might yet change on earth, and I shall hope until my last breath. Let us pray, Nigabael!"

Smarnis had taken the young man's hand, and his lips quivered with an ardent invocation to the cruel God who subjugates humans.

III

Again I will build thee, and thou shalt be built, O
virgin of Israel . . . Thou shalt yet plant vines upon
the mountains of Samaria; the planters shall plant
and shall eat them as common things.
(*Jeremiah* 31: 4-5.)

That night, Phédyne had a dream. She saw herself in the midst of a long caravan that was returning toward Juda, and a flamboyant sun spread its caresses over people and things.

The horsemen were magnificently armed, and dressed as if for a fête. The priests were marching two by two, mitered in gold, clad in white, carrying crooked staffs, rope and precious vessels in which aromatics were burning. Women were following them in orange, green or blue robes, intoning canticles. Then there were the dignitaries and chiefs, in scarlet vestments, superbly mounted on large horses dressed in silk, their caparisons decorated with little golden bells that tinkled with the movements of the rump and the floating tail. The chargers were black, with blue reflections, or chestnut, the color of fine amber; others, beneath their trimmed white coats, were veined with human flesh tones and seemed pink. They were making the amulets on their breasts dance, while the gold braid of their bridles lit up.

The magnificently colored cavalcade surrounded an old man mounted on a gray mare with a dark tail, whose nostrils were palpitating ardently. It was Daniel, the Prophet, praying and watching over the tribe of Juda. His venerable face was turned toward the sky, and the breeze was agitating the wisps of his beard.

Behind the horsemen came the musicians clad in light tunics, some striking small frames tightening snakeskins, others shiny timbals. The flute players were extracting shrill sounds from their long reed-stems, alternating with choirs of virgins whose white veils were softly inflated.

The caravan traversed the Chaldean cities, still saturated with the civilization of Babylon. Palaces decorated with winged bulls, lions, steles and bas-reliefs sculpted in the marble of hills loomed up to the right and left. Monuments were ablaze and immense pyres smoking in a sinister fashion, still bearing calcined bones.

Then there were luminous landscapes, plains, roads bordered by surly mountains and steep slopes. Sometimes, the partly-dried bed of a steam cut across the road and the chariots were entangled in long grass. Sometimes, too, some splendid ziggurat loomed up, with seven stages recalling the seven planets and the colors that symbolized them. A little chapel covered with gold leaf sparkled like a mysterious star, the brother of the sun. Colossal statues stood at the extremities of the last platform, their heads lost in the azure.

Phédyne found herself at the rear of the cortege, in a granite litter carried by black slaves. She had Warka beside her, who seemed to be asleep, but the lover's nostrils were pinched and his lips were blue. She gazed at him with anguish, speaking to him softly in order to wake him, for he had been asleep since their departure, and an increasingly sinister expression had invaded his features.

"Can't you hear me, Beloved?" she repeated, passing her fingers over her friend's cold cheek. "Answer me, Beloved, I'm afraid!"

But no breath elevated Warka's bosom. He remained inert among the cushions, while the ecstatic canticle of the daughters of Juda rose around them:

> *Stay me with flagons, comfort me with apples; for I*
> *am sick of love.*
> *His left hand is under my head, and his right hand*
> *doth embrace me.*[1]
> *Thou hast ravaged my heart, my sister . . . with one of*
> *thine eyes, with one chain of thy neck.*
> *How fair is thy love! How much better is thy love than*
> *wine! And the smell of thine ointments than all*
> *spices!*
> *Thy lips . . . drop as honeycomb: honey and milk are*
> *under thy tongue; and the smell of thy garments is*
> *like the smell of Lebanon.*

Other litters were following Phédyne's; dromedaries were transporting the baggage of the nomad city. Young boys sitting on the rumps of animals uttered loud cries when the cortege became entangled; others were leading unruly rams by the horns as if they were dragging them to sacrifice; there were herds of heifers and flocks of sheep, and, finally, a howling, baying dog-pack, harassing the laggards in the floods of blond dust under the rays of a burning sun.

Phédyne pursued her dream, seeing the plains, hills and towns go past, which seemed at a distance to form an irregular gray and blue checkerboard. Distances shrank at the horizon

---

1 *Song of Solomon* 2: 5-56. The text continues with 4:9-11.

and the whole scene decomposed of its own accord; nothing more remained, when they approached the deserted cities, than poor towns sacked by the passage of conquerors, burned ruins, somber and lugubrious, which the solitude of death seemed to have invaded.

Now there was the desert: an immense, implacable desert, all yellow under the glare of the sun, the sands of profound solitudes, and the feverish breath of inflamed terrains. But the love of the desert was within her, and had passed into her veins, so she inhaled that fire with all her might, which entered into her nostrils and burned her all the way to the heart.

The soil was now bristling with tumulary stones, and Phédyne suddenly uttered a profound plaint, for Warka had slid from the litter and his body remained extended in the pale dust.

She wanted to get down in order to lift her lover up, but an invincible force paralyzed her efforts; a mysterious force held her enchained while the caravan drew away slowly with its priests, its horsemen, its musicians and its singers. She even followed the movement, lying in the great litter, while Warka's body diminished on the sand, and was soon no more than a dark patch that she could scarcely make out in the midst of the rocks and the tumulary stones.

Then the Prophet had turned round on his huge gray horse, and his voice had dominated all the other voices.

"Daughter of Sion," he had said, "do not look back if you want to follow us to the city of glory. The man that you cherished was unworthy of your love. It is necessary to abandon his cadaver to the birds of prey and forget his memory. It is necessary to curse your former aberrations and to devote yourself to the worship of the sole God, in order that he might pardon his culpable daughter. Choose, then, between good and evil, go toward the light or recoil toward the darkness!"

And Phédyne, finally disengaged from her invisible bonds, had thrown herself on the ground in order to rejoin her lover, and to die beside him!

She finally woke up from her terrible dream, wondering whether it might not have been a warning from Heaven, and whether the spirit of the Prophet might not have visited her in order to retain her on the edge of the gulf.

For long days she had waited for Warka, and her soul was overflowing with bitterness.

She no longer knew whether she still loved the man who was neglecting her, but she remembered ardently the tenderness experienced, and her entire being quivered again. Had she not done her duty toward Warka, the friend, the lover, the fiancé? His kisses had rendered light delectable; she would never forget them, in spite of the indifference, the ingratitude and the outrages.

She had given everything to the man she loved, and everything in her belonged to him without return. Why did he no longer come to find her, as before, when the case of the struggle oppressed him and he had need of solicitude and amour? Why did he no longer repose his fatigued brow on her knees when he came back from some dangerous expedition or when somber presentiments assailed him?

What had she done to incur that disgrace? And what could she do to bring the infidel back?

The days passed in their sad monotony and no one ever pronounced around her the cherished name. Warka had said nothing and had not left any indication that might guide her thoughts. Had he returned toward Cyrus? Had he died in some distant expedition? At that idea her heart screamed and quivered in pain. She sensed that she would always love him, invincibly, and that the deadly amour would possess her until death.

The King of Kings has endowed mortals for joy as
for dolor. Glory, glory to the All Wise!
(The oldest hymn of Zend.)

That morning, the slaves had quit Phédyne, after having combed
her hair, perfumed and adorned her, as was their custom. A great
agitation seemed to be reigning outside; confused cries arrived
as far as the young woman, and she had never felt her soul so
anguished.

She tried to open the door, which was usually locked, and the
heavy barrier yielded to the first push.

There was no guard behind the obstacle. The sumptuous
room that offered itself to her gaze of a recluse was empty. Then
the other rooms, in sequence, revealed their riches to her. She
traversed them in feverish haste, scarcely brushing the thick carpet laid over the polychromatic pavement.

As she advanced, the clamors grew. There were cries of murder
and death, mingled with glorious hymns that she thought she
recognized. But she got lost in the long corridors, the galleries
and the innumerable rooms. Everything frightened her in that
strange palace, which she was exploring for the first time.

A few motionless slaves watched her go by; women that she
had never seen were putting on robes glittering with jewels in
front of large metal mirrors.

Now she went down a staircase with slippery steps of red
marble, and a more violent blast of air lifted the folds of her veil.
The High Priest passed in front of her, clad in white and mitered
in gold, followed by fifty people belonging to the sacred order.
They were holding sacrificers' knives and their hands were red
with blood.

Where were they coming from? Where were they going, in
that pompous and redoubtable order? Phédyne followed them,
without exciting their attention, and reached the immense gardens with them.

An innumerable crowd extended before her, maintained by helmeted and armored guards. In the space between the palace walls and the people, a throne was set, and before that throne prisoners were filing, two by two.

Phédyne summoned her memories. Where had she seen that beautiful garden soiled with blood before, that palace, those priests and those barbaric preparations?

On the throne, two people had their backs turned to her: a man and a woman, royally clad.

The man was wearing a long starry crimson cloak; on his head, a radiant crown armed with spikes attracted the sun's rays, and he was holding a golden scepter terminated by the head of a lion, the ruby eyes of which were glittering.

The woman was wearing a diamond-studded tiara, and she was so covered in jewels that she seemed to be buckling under the weight of necklaces, fringes, amulets and clasps. A silver veil fell behind her.

Phédyne did not dare advance any further, and she made herself very small against the door of the palace.

But a troop of dancers emerged at that moment, dragging her away and jostling her. They surrounded the image of Mylitta, throwing petals of roses and tuberoses at it, kneeling down and getting up again, putting their arms around one another and quitting one another, laughing. Behind them came the women of the harem in long red and yellow robes. A floating gauze terminated their pointed headdresses.

The Syrian, Tyrian and Arab dancers, in the costumes of their homelands, agitated weakly while clinking the little bells of their adornments, the medallions in their hair and their glass bracelets and anklets.

Idumeans and Phoenicians accompanied the lascivious dances with their hoarse songs, punctuated by the impacts of tambourines and castanets.

The entire cortege curved in order to pass before the royal throne, which was sheltered by a crimson awning pinned by golden eagles and ornamented with spearheads.

Phédyne, drawn along by the movement, now saw the immense palace behind her, blistered by cupolas, and flanked by apses and transepts, like a stone god with multiple faces and arms. There was an accumulation of edifices, temples, garlanded arches and porticos, decorated with pennants and brightly-colored drapes.

Behind the royal dwelling, the monstrous city of debauches and crimes could be divined, torpid, like a sated beast, in the inaccessible enclosure of its walls.

But the priests, after having filed before the golden throne, were already lighting the sacrificial fires. The dancers arrived in their turn, carrying the image of Mylitta, the goddess of amour.

In their midst, Phédyne gazed with terror at the two individuals who commanded as masters all of the quivering population of dancers, courtesans, slaves, prisoners and executioners.

Where, then, had she seen that russet beard before, expertly undulated and curled in rutilant ringlets? Where had she contemplated that arrogant face, those yellow eyes, caressant and cruel?

Suddenly, she uttered a loud scream, and collapsed at the foot of the throne, while Belsharuzur, with a curt gesture, stopped the cortege.

V

The female star is the planet Venus. But if she is
female when the sun sets, she is male when it rises.
(Chaldeo-Assyrian religious hymn.)

The young woman found herself once again in the large, sad and luxurious chamber where she had groaned and wept so much. Her women surrounded her, on the lookout for her awakening. She would have been able to doubt her senses, believing it to be a feverish vision, a terrible dream, if the pain she experienced in her forehead had not reminded her of her fall in the great garden where Warka was enthroned. But Warka was no longer Warka; he had taken on the face of the baleful tyrant, the enemy of her race, the soulless murderer whom she had sworn to hate until death!

And she recalled with horror her confidence in him, her imprudent words and her unconscious treason. So, she had revealed everything in her weakness of a culpable lover. She had delivered her own people. Smarnis and her brother had doubtless perished by her fault, and she was alive with that crime on her heart, and she conserved sufficient reason to understand all of its atrocity.

Tears flowed down her cheeks; she wrung her hands in anguish.

"Are you in pain, Mistress?" asked one of the women.

She did not reply, but her sobs redoubled.

"Do you desire anything?" asked the slave. "We've been given the order to content all your desires."

She gathered her courage. "I was bought here after my escape?" she interrogated, in a halting voice.

"Yes," said the woman.

"It's the king who ordered you to watch over me?"

The slaves hesitated, and looked at one another fearfully, but one of them said in a low voice: "No, it was the queen."

"The queen?"

"Yes, our beloved sovereign Sahuradha, first wife of Belsharu-zur."

"She knows me, then?"

"We told her your story, and she's interested in your person."

Phédyne shivered; a sharp pain traversed her heart.

"I'd like to see the queen," she said.

"That's impossible."

"Oh, I won't importune her for long, but she's good, she'll have pity."

"It's impossible," repeated the slave, sadly.

The young woman did not interrogate her further, in the fear of learning about the frightful execution that she feared, for she had seen the sacrifices and executioners preparing their instruments of torture. But the doubt was perhaps even more terrible than the certainty; she went on, with a shudder: "And the prisoners?"

"A large number of them were immolated."

"Were they captive warriors or . . ." She dared not continue; her blood was chilled by fear.

"Yes," said the woman, calmly. "Foreign enemies, and also conspirators."

Phédyne uttered a cry of agony.

"The tribe of Juda?"

"Many Jews have perished. Only the chiefs have been reserved for the final days of the fête."

"The chiefs?"

A feeble glimmer of hope penetrated into the darkness of her soul. If those chiefs were Nigabael and Smarnis . . . !

Impetuously, she sat up on the couch.

"I want to see the queen."

"No one can penetrate into the presence of her august Majesty."

But the young woman took off her necklaces, her bracelets and all the jewels that covered her.

"Here," she said to a slave. "Take this and guide me as far as the queen's door. That's not very difficult, and no one will know what you've done, for you'll go away immediately. I'll go in alone, no one will see you with me; the rest is up to me . . . Why hesitate? I repeat that you're not risking anything and that you can save my life, for I'll kill myself in front of you if you refuse to help me . . ."

The slave, very frightened, made no reply. But a young woman who had not spoken until then advanced resolutely. "Follow me," she said. "I'll take you to our beloved sovereign. And as for your jewels, I'll share them with my companions, to buy their silence."

The women held out their hands eagerly, and Phédyne, after having given them her necklaces, her miter and even the embroidered veils that covered her shoulders, drew away on the arm of the servant.

VI

Women are sometimes inspired by the gods.
(Pythagoras.)

Sahuradha was putting on make-up before her silver mirror.

She was very beautiful thus with her large dark eyes, her energetic and passionate features, and the warmly colored complexion of her face. A white robe, embroidered with pearls, enveloped her; her slim feet were playing in light sandals trellised with gold.

Phédyne came swiftly into the large marble chamber where the sovereign was adorning herself and knelt down, trembling.

Sahuradha examined her, surprised. "Who are you?" she demanded, haughtily. "And who permitted you to reach my presence?"

But the young woman had raised her head, and she recognized her. "Oh! I remember now. Yes, you're that Jewess that I saw just now in the palace gardens."

"I'm Phédyne, the sister of Nigabael."

"Nigabael, the king's favorite?"

"Himself."

"But Nigabael is condemned; he's going to die."

Phédyne uttered a cry. "He's still alive?"

"Yes," said the queen. "It's tomorrow that his execution is to take place."

The young woman dragged herself in her knees, and prostrated herself in front of the sovereign.

"You can grant him mercy," she said. "I beg you to have pity, and you'll listen to me, for you're good!"

Sahuradha shook her head sadly.

"I can do nothing against the Master's will. Those he has condemned must perish, you know that very well."

"The king loves you, since he keeps you next to him. I've seen you in glory on his throne. You were like a light star next to the sun. He'll listen to you, I'm certain of it."

"No, the king only listen to his whimsy. I've been able to touch his senses; I can do nothing in regard to his mind."

Phédyne wrung her hands. "Mercy! Mercy!" she moaned. "If you knew what I've done you'd condemn me, but you'd save the innocents that I've doomed."

"What have you done, then?" asked the queen, curiously

"I've betrayed my cause; I've denounced my own people."

"And why have you committed that crime?"

The young woman shivered. "Because . . ."

"Go on, finish, you owe me the whole truth."

"Because I was blinded by passion; because the king lied to me in saying that he was my fiancé."

"Your fiancé?"

"Oh, how I've suffered! How I've wept, while waiting for the man who was my sole reason for living, the man that I loved more than anything! When he was with me, the earth seemed beneficent and sweet, full of scents and murmurs; everything was luminous, everything flowered in order to charm me and numb me delectably . . ."

"How did you meet the king, then? He followed your brother, no doubt?"

"That must be it. He followed Nigabel and he passed himself off as one of ours, Smarnis-Warka, the satrap."

"Yes, I understand . . . he saw you and found you beautiful?"

"Alas," sighed Phédyne. "I'm doomed! Doomed forever! But my existence is very little; I would give it to save my people."

"Nothing can save them."

"Oh, don't say that! Understand that it's me who doomed them, that I indicated the place of their retreat, and that I guided the executioner's weapon! You're as good as you're beautiful! You can speak for the captives. Their death would be too frightful!"

"I can do nothing," repeated the queen, in a melancholy tone. "The king is probably detaching himself from me already and thinking of other amours. His infatuations never last long, and his heart cannot be attached. You know that, anyway, and you know how fickle his caprice is."

Phédyne was in agony. Although very soft, the sovereign's voice was choking her as the string of a bow tightened around her neck would have done.

"Oh, everything is red in this palace! The blood of the tortured has gushed all the way to the walls, all the way to the crimson garments. Everything here respires crime and death. Kill me, then, since you can do nothing for me . . ."

She had put a dagger in the queen's hand, but Sahuradha pushed her away gently and stood up.

"Listen," she said. "It's impossible for me to obtain mercy for your brother, but I can take you to him."

Phédyne shivered.

"Oh! You'll do that?"

"I'll do that . . ."

"But when? Tomorrow, it will be too late! Speak, speak quickly! It's right away that it's necessary to take me into Nigabael's prison. Immediately—the minutes are counted!"

"No, not now—when it's dark."

"You swear it?"

"Yes," said the queen. "Go back to your room, and when the time comes, one of my women will tell you. Go."

Phédyne lifted the hem of Sahuradha's robe to her lips, and went out backwards, so troubled that she did not see, in the shadow of a curtain, Sil-Assur, the chief eunuch, who had been observing them intently for a few moments.

VII

You have learned the things of earth and the things
of heaven. You should not, therefore, withdraw either
from the laws of earth or the laws of heaven.
(Hermes Trismegistus.)

The queen remained thoughtful. So Belsharuzur had doomed that young woman, whom he had already forgotten for other amours. It would have been better to immolate her with the other captives of the tribe of Juda, for her existence henceforth would be nothing but a long martyrdom.

And she remembered the words of the king when he had come to fetch her from the house of her father, a powerful satrap: "Come with me, Sahuradha, I will make you the happiest of terrestrial creatures. To possess you, I would give Babylon and all the riches of my kingdom! To have your love, I would cut off my right hand, I would tear my heart from my breast, my soul from my body, and all my being will be irremissibly submissive to you."

She had given herself, and a week later, he had taken another wife: Ussary, to whom he had addressed the same ardent protestations. Then Amat-Sula, the king's third wife, had also been installed in the palace, in a special lodgment, separated from the harem by the entire breadth of a splendid garden.

Belsharuzur's voice was seductive and passionate; his words had wings to touch feminine souls. To all of them he had made the same lying promises, and they had all forgiven him, because they could not cure the amour that he had put into their being.

Not only had they forgotten the offense—which would have been very little for lovers—but they had made a god out of that man, whom they adored fearfully for his faults, his perfidies, and even his crimes, for the heart of a woman is so made that it is never taken back once it has offered itself.

The man with the somber complexion, the eyes of flame and the proud and robust beauty knew his power. "My wives," he said, "will build me a temple. They will climb up to it with all the people and they will humiliate themselves before my splendor, which they will contemplate in the dust. They will adore me with all the fibers and all the bones of their bodies, as with all their divine faith, all the avid hope of their mind! Nothing will remain in the entire world that is not submissive to me. Am I not the King of Kings, the unique, invulnerable Lord?"

Sahuradha sighed, and her burning breath passed between her dry lips. She took a few steps and lifted the curtain that masked the eunuch, still immobile.

"What are you doing there, Sil-Assur?" she asked, negligently

The man bowed respectfully

"Powerful queen, I have come to announce the visit of your beloved Lord."

"Ah! The king is going to come?"

"Here he is," said the eunuch, bowing very low.

Belsharuzur had taken the young woman's hand. And she recognized in his gaze the somber fire that had animated him for several days.

"May my cherished Master be happy and live forever," she murmured. "His coming fills me with intoxication, and I remain his humble slave."

"Sahuradha," said the king, in a grave voice. "I feel troubled and suffering. As long as the leaders of the conspiracy of Juda have not perished, a dread will remain in my soul. Have the Prophets of the accursed tribe not predicted my imminent death?"

"You cannot die. Who would dare to raise a hand against you?"

"No one, assuredly . . . and yet . . ."

"Are you not the Lord of the world, the omnipotent and glorious Master?"

"Last night, again, I had a sinister dream that Daniel has not explained to me, Daniel no longer responds to my appeal since I have caused his own people to perish, and his hatred is pursuing me."

"That man is an impostor . . ."

"Perhaps. However, his predictions, thus far, have been realized. Daniel is of the enemy royal race. He was one of the captives brought to Babylon by Nabuchodonosor, in the third year of the reign of Joachim. He was only a child then, but his charm and precocious intelligence made him exceptionally distinguished and the king granted him his confidence. Today he's the governor of Babylon and the chief of the Sages of Babylon."

"He could not conspire against you, then!"

Belsharuzur bowed his head. "Oh," he sighed, "that man remains above human creatures; his magical power seems prodigious to me. Has he not also explained the great king's dream?"

"Tell me that dream."

"'You have seen a tree that was very tall and very strong, whose height attained the sky and which seemed to extend over the whole earth; its branches were very beautiful; it was laden with fruits, and all the fruits there were nourishing; the beasts of the land lived beneath it and the birds of the sky roosted on its branches. That tree, O King, is yourself, who have become so great and so powerful, for your grandeur has increased and extended to the extremities of the world. You have also seen, O King, one of the valiant and saintly descend from Heaven and he has said: Fell that tree, cut off its branches, but reserve the stump and the roots, that it might be bound with iron and bronze among the grass of the fields, and that it might be soaked by the dew of the sky and remain with the savage beasts until seven times have passed over it.

"'And this is the interpretation of the decree of the Most High that has been pronounced against my Lord the King: You will be expelled from the company of men and you will live with the animals and the wild beasts; you will eat grass like oxen, you will be soaked by the dew of the sky; seven times will pass over you, until you recognize that the Most High holds all the kingdoms of men under his domination and gives them as he pleases.

"'As for what has been commanded, that the stump and roots of the tree be conserved, that tells you that your kingdom will remain to you after you have recognized that all power comes from Heaven.'"[1]

"Yes," said the queen, "those things were realized."

"The king was expelled from the company of men, he ate grass like an ox, his body was soaked by the dew of the sky, with the result that his hair grew like an eagle's feathers and his fingernails became redoubtable claws. Now, Daniel has predicted punishments even more terrible for me."

"O my beloved Lord," sighed the sovereign, kneeling before the Master, "set the Jewish prisoners free and their malevolent god will grant you mercy."

"They have offended me gravely. If I pardon them I will be accused of weakness."

"What does it matter, if that clemency will save your life?"

But Belsharuzur shook his head proudly. "No one would dare to threaten the Lord of the World. I want to give an extraordinary feast, in order to dazzle the world and strike my enemies with fear!"

"But you will grant mercy to the tribe of Juda? The blood of the Jewish people might poison your days. Fear the Prophet who has never lied. It seems to me that his thought is inspiring me, at this moment, and that I am the echo of his desire."

"I cannot listen to you. Many Jews have already perished."

"But the chiefs are still alive. Pardon Nigabael, the young man that you have loved. Pardon Smarnis, who was a satrap of great value and great power."

"He wanted my death . . ."

"Pardon them for that poor girl who still cherishes you and whom you have doomed . . ."

"What, you know?"

The queen had an adorable smile. "When she fell down like a scythed lily at the foot of the throne, I divined everything. She's a Jewess and you have loved her."

---

1 A paraphrase of *Daniel* 4:20-26.

"Do you think so? I no longer remember that. It's you that I love today."

The young woman replied, with a hint of melancholy "My life belongs to you, O my Master, and I am submissive to your orders. Do as you please, then, but don't forget that the Prophet's malediction is hanging over you, and that if you die, I shall die too."

"Yes," murmured Belsharuzur, "the great voice of Daniel has risen against Babylon."

As he went out, after one last caress for the favorite of the moment, Sil-Assur, the black eunuch, who was waiting for him, let the heavy curtain fall behind him and, walking by his side, whispered a few words in his ear.

"Ah," said the king. "You wish to speak to me?"

"What is happening is grave. But let us go away, for it's necessary that the queen does not . . ."

"Come," said the Master, in a low voice.

The master and the servant drew away on the sonorous paving stones, while the queen, thoughtful and melancholy, let herself fall on to the cushions of her large bed of repose.

VIII

And the high places of Isaac shall be desolate, and
the sanctuaries of Israel shall be laid waste; and I
will rise against the house of Jeroboam with the sword.
(*Amos* 7:9.)

Time passed, and Phédyne, in her retreat, was gnawed by anxiety.

The sovereign had promised to take her to the prisoners. Why had she not come?

The high walls hid the sky from her. She could not even consult the serene night in order to abridge the tedium of the wait with a vision of beyond.

In any case, she was so unaccustomed to hope that she would not have been able to decipher the benevolent signs of the stars. Enveloped in her dolor, in her discouragement of all things, as in a thick veil, the external world no longer touched her. But before disappearing, she would have liked to see her brother, to speak to him, perhaps to save him. Who could tell? They were the same height, with almost the same figure; might not Nigabael, by putting on Phédyne's garments, avoid suspicions and be able to get out of the palace?

Yes, yes, she would attempt that supreme proof. As a punishment for her crimes she would deliver herself to the executioners for the torture.

At that thought, her gaze sparkled and her blood hastened in its flow, animating her face with an ardent redness.

Nigabael, free, would be able to act for the good of the tribe and avenge his brothers.

Oh, to go, to run to the prison! To detach the captive and push him into the great serene night, on the road to happiness and forgetfulness!

With a feverish impatience she bumped into the furniture, wrung her hands and dug her fingernails into her breast.

Suddenly, military music became audible, heavy and measured footsteps resounded under the walls. It was the guard passing by for its habitual patrol. The fanfares came like a final irony to strike the young woman's vibrant nerves. The music, at first loud and close by, soon softened and drew away. Then it no longer reached her ears as anything but an uncertain rumor.

From time to time the wind alone still brought an isolated sound; finally, a lugubrious silence succeeded the harmony, which was lost in space. Phédyne's last hope seemed to be attached to those chords resonating in the distance. It was fleeing with them, drawing further and further away . . .

The young woman fell to her knees, imploring Heaven. Heavy and warm tears fell on the floor, and she also thought about her amour, which she could not forget and which wrung her heart.

She loved, because that was necessary to her, and inevitable. She loved because of the tenderness that persisted in her, and not because of that of others. All great amorous women give themselves thus, without wanting to see the unworthiness of the other. It is in vain that they try to recoil, to emerge from the deadly path, to precipitate into the road built by all the mediocrities and egotisms of life. It is necessary for them to march on the dolorous route of devotion and martyrdom.

Phédyne was still on the ground, inert, when the door opened quietly.

"Come," said a woman's voice.

With a groan, she lifted herself up and rose to her feet.

"The queen has sent you," she said. "You've come on her part?"

"Yes, follow me without making a sound. I'll conduct you faithfully."

Phédyne had enveloped herself in a long veil, which hid her features; she took the woman's hand and allowed herself to be guided. After a rather long trajectory, she found herself in the gardens, at the foot of a small stairway.

Sahuradha was waiting for her, a lamp in her hand. With a gesture, she sent the slave away, and made a sign to Phédyne to follow her in silence.

The damp stairway turned as it plunged underground. Confused rumors rose from the depths of the cellar. It was like a slow and grave song, a sort of funereal psalmody that chilled the bones.

The slope was frightfully steep and slippery. At every instant Phédyne nearly fell, but she retained herself on the projections in the wall, bruising her fingers in her impatient haste.

As they descended, the steps became stickier, and the young woman, having lifted up the hem of her robe, saw that they were full of blood.

Were people murdered even in the prisons, then? An immense disgust made her feel nauseous. She trembled from head to foot.

"We're nearly there," the queen murmured, marching rapidly along a long corridor bordered by massive doors equipped with barred peepholes. "The cells are empty, because the people in them were crucified yesterday."

"Oh!" Phédyne moaned. "That's the fate that awaits the other captives."

Sahuradha did not reply. A man of tall stature loomed up before them, a threat on his lips.

"Who are you? No one can enter here without an order from the king."

"I am the queen," said Sahuradha, raising the lamp to the level of her face,

The jailer stepped back against the wall.

"Open the cell of the chiefs for me."

Meekly, the man caused an enormous door to swing open. "I'm risking my head," he said.

"You're obliged to obey the queen; I'll take all the responsibility."

Phédyne was already launching herself toward Nigabael, who lay in a corner, pale and emaciated, with a rope around his neck and his feet chained.

"Nigabael," she moaned, "don't you recognize me?"

But the young man turned his head away, scornfully

"Oh," she said, "if you knew . . ."

"Listen to her," said a voice nearby. "Perhaps she isn't as culpable as you suppose."

Smarnis had dragged himself on his knees, pulling on the chain that attached him to the wall.

"Who is the generous friend who dared to intervene for me?" she asked, gratefully.

"I'm Smarnis," he said.

"Oh! Smarnis! More than any other, you ought to curse me!"

"No, I feel sorry for you."

"I have done you so much harm, unintentionally. But I loved you without knowing you . . . or, rather, the man who had taken your place."

"Who, then, had taken my place?"

"The king!"

"Oh!" roared the satrap, clenching his fists. "You did not know, then, that he was the king?"

"No," sobbed the young woman. "I swear to you. I knew nothing about him. He pretended to have come on my brother's behalf; he said that he was a Jew like him. Every evening he waited in the shadow, and I supposed that he was the friend, the fiancé of whom Nigabael had spoken to me. Being without suspicion, I loved him and obeyed him blindly. Can you understand my error?"

Nigabael still kept silent, his face pale and his brows furrowed. Smarnis interrogated the young woman avidly.

"He took my name?"

"He called himself Warka, but I assumed that he was adopting that name out of prudence. Do not all our chiefs do the same?"

"She's right," said the satrap, "and we ought to believe her. Why would she lie? It's fatality that pushed her into the monster's arms."

"Listen," said Phédyne, taking Nigabael's hand. "I've come here to save you. Put on my veils and follow the woman who is waiting outside. That woman is the queen. She's kind and merciful, she'll have pity. Hurry up, I beg you!"

"No," said Smarnis. "Nigabael can't accept that sacrifice. We'll die together."

"Yes," repeated the former favorite of the king, slowly, "we'll die together. Life horrifies me!"

"But if you succumb," the young woman groaned, "it's the annihilation of our race. All of our people will be exterminated before long. If you won't do it for me, dear brother, do it for the tribe. Obey me, take my robe, my veil. You resemble me so much that no one will perceive the substitution. Go, I implore you! It's necessary, for the deliverance of Juda."

She had detached Nigabael, and she tried, in spite of his resistance, to pass him her garments.

"It's necessary to go," said the queen, outside. "It would be imprudent to stay any longer."

"Yes," whispered Phédyne, "I'm coming. One more moment, I implore you."

But a strange noise was audible in the corridor. The clink of weapons resonated in the shadows. The impact of a heavy mass beating on the doors resounded like the echo of thunder through the temple and, at every blow struck against the obstacle, a voice rose up, terrible and grim.

"The king," murmured Phédyne. "We're doomed!"

Belsharuzur had just appeared on the threshold of the prison.

IX

The god Bel created me himself; the god Marduk,
who engendered me, deposited the seed of my life
himself in my mother's womb.
(Inscription on the bricks of Babylon.)

The preparations for the feast were completed rapidly in the hanging gardens of Babylon, which were decked with innumerable flags in the midst of trees in flower. All day long prisoners had been massacred, at the entrances to the temples and on the square of sacrifices. Only the chiefs had been set aside for a sensational execution, a special diversion, which was to take place at the end of the meal.

The great banqueting hall at the summit of the gardens was scintillating everywhere like an ardent furnace, and flowery cordons passed between the set tables, snaking between the immense candelabra, hooked on to bronze cups, vessels of gold and silver, and precious ornaments decorated with gems.

Slaves hastened, weaving roses and more roses, and the floor disappeared beneath an embalmed harvest, a thick carpet of shredded corollas.

More than a thousand people were to take their places in the immense hall and drink the wine of glory.

Behind the king's platform stood a colossal gold statue representing Nabuchodonosor in his redoubtable majesty, and other statues of masters and divinities seemed to be watching over the preparations for the feast. There were the twelve great gods of Chaldean mythology. Then, in a corner, Mylitta "the delight of men and gods," the Ishtar of legend, the Venus Astarte who charmed voluptuous Asia, was offered, with the little god Tammuz in her arms.

Jupiter, the master of Olympus, was then called Assur or Bel-Oannes; the fish-god corresponded to Neptune. Ana, the master of the infernal empire, later came to be called Pluto. There was also Vul, the god of the atmosphere, who became Saturn; and Salman or Hea, the ancestor of the Greek Heracles.

The Chaldeans applied the names of their gods to the stars, and astrology reigned as queen on the banks of the lower Euphrates.

Whereas the pharaohs of Egypt commenced their tombs on mounting the throne, preparing their dwelling for centuries to come, the Babylonian kings had sumptuous and fragile palaces built in haste, which the sands of the desert were gradually to cover with a pale shroud. They did not have time to hollow out rock, to traverse the flanks of savage mountains, nor to bring granite for their voluptuous cities. Everything there was kneaded in soft clay, and everything had the same formidable, terrifying and chimerical appearance.

Too splendid, that immense hall, where a thousand people were to drink to the ephemeral glory of a tyrant, seemed an enchanted palace elevated by some ironic djinni. Everything there shone fantastically and immeasurably, everything there provoked alarm rather than the artistic joy of the mind.

And for the third time, Belsharuzur was to wet his lips in the sacred vessels stolen from the temple of Jerusalem.

They were there, those vessels, and their multicolored gems seemed to swarm over the crimson cushions that supported them. Soldiers guarded them grimly, immobile to either side of the table of honor.

In the gardens and around the palace the people of Babylon crowded, a multitude of men and women of somber complexion, with brilliant eyes. All of them had put on their festival clothes in order to witness the final executions of the royal orgy. Their clamors shook the air from one end of the city to the other, chasing away the vultures obstinate in their feast of death.

That rejoicing had taken place every year, but with less magnificence. It was usually called the feast of Saccees; it was celebrated on the sixteenth day of the month of Lous, and lasted for several days, during which, in the capital, slaves commanded their masters under the direction of a chief for the occasion, or Zogamis. That chief was a man condemned to death, who was adorned with the attributes of royalty, and had to perish after his ephemeral glory.

It was already known that Nigabael had been chosen to fill that sad role: Nigabael the fallen favorite, the infidel friend whose execution the ironic crowd demanded.

But the procession was about to commence in the illuminated gardens. A blast of trumpets accompanied the sound of bronze doors rolling formidably to give passage to the host of guests. The guards, in two rows, struck the sand of the pathways with their golden pikes, and women hoisted themselves up on their shoulders in order to get a better view of the cortege.

Syrian women who were to dance during the meal were already entering, to the plucking of the Babylonian asor and the rattle of sistra and castanets. They arranged themselves at the back of the hall, while the chariots and the litters stopped in the gardens in order to permit the guests to see the king pass by.

The priestesses of Mylitta, in loose robes and soft sandals, followed the mimes; then there was the voluptuous battalion of courtesans, with hair tightly bound in golden nets, with veils delicately embroidered with pearls and precious stones. The priests of Bel and Oannes were beating bronze cymbals. They wore white miters, their braided and curled beards came down to the waist. The sacrificers were brandishing hatchets, ropes and irons. A cloth stained with blood covered their knees, for they had just immolated lambs and goats to the beneficent divinities. Others were singing a hymn to the glory of the gods. Colossal sambucas were emitting terrible sounds that sometimes drowned out the stridulations of the small horn flutes, magadis, nabels, lyres and asors.

All the melodies took flight to strange rhythms, which united fortunately nevertheless; the great hall was no more than an enchantment of light, flowers and harmony.

When the priests, the dancers, the courtesans, the singers and the musicians were arranged on either side of the banqueting hall, the royal cortege arrived via the gardens, in the space left free between the guards with the long golden pikes.

Belsharuzur appeared in a robe of trailing silk, whose sleeves hung down, heavy with gems. His golden tiara scintillated in a blaze of rubies, amethysts and emeralds, but a slightly bitter smile creased his features, and his thinned face bore the trace of mysterious alarms.

He guided a chariot with twelve black horses, followed by all the great dignitaries of the court, the senior officers, the satraps, the militia of honor and the palace eunuchs. Chained leopards and lions preceded the litters, carried by black slaves, and carrucas sustained by two wheels ornamented with precious fabrics and cushions. Noisy cavaliers, speaking all languages, made their horses prance with a rattle of spears, fringes and little bells. Sacrificers of Baal led oxen whose heads were garlanded with roses and their horns gilded.

Then there were soldiers carrying naked swords, their shields raised. Others, on their mounts, were displaying golden and silver helmets. Archers and sling-wielders were coiffed with the maw of a lion or tiger. Spear-carriers closed the march, even more sparkling in their gold-encrusted armor and their long crimson cloaks embroidered with royal insignia.

The acclamations of the people departed from all sides under the flamboyance of spears, shields, flagpoles and standards, whose lively movement striped the black sky.

The king had stopped momentarily, superb among all humans, and the entire cortege, like a field of wheat curbed by the wind, had undulated in a movement of profound adoration.

Belsharuzur, upright in his chariot, his brows furrowed and his mouth disdainful, contemplated his prostrate people, and a gleam passed through his yellow gaze.

Certainly, he had the right to be proud, for the glory of his reign filled the world. The renown of Babylon, the capital of the arts and magnificence, rose up radiantly. It was a prestigious ascension that no obstacle could henceforth arrest. The king dominated that crowd, which extended further as he rose above it, and he saw it in the famous hanging gardens, unique in the world, the marvelous gardens that he had opened to the public for the occasion. From the height of his chariot he contemplated the city that was hollowed out beneath him, unfurling the majestic girdle of its ramparts, displaying the multicolored ornaments of its temples and the blue-tinted hole of its submissive river. The human sea with the somber waves of the ever-moving swell extended into the distance, and thousands of gazes remained fixed upon him, as on one unique point in the midst of the furnace of illuminations.

Then, in the face of that quivering immensity, he raised his royal scepter higher, and higher still, while the slaves maintained the chargers of his chariot. He paraded the long sacred stem from one end of the horizon to the other, raising a flap of his crimson cloak at the same time, as if to protect it. He saluted the glorious edifices of Babylon and the devastated blocks of the obscure valleys; he saluted his armies and his people, while a breath of ecstasy passed over heads and things.

An immense rumor rose up into the bright night, celebrating that human celestial body, whose scintillation effaced the stars.

X

> As for their tongue, it is polished by the workman,
> and they themselves are gilded and laid over with
> silver; yet they are but false and cannot speak.
> (*Baruch* 6:8.)

"Put before me," said the Master, "the sacred vessels from the temple of Jerusalem. I desire to wet my lips therein, and all those who understand me will imitate my example."

But the king looked at the redoubtable treasure suspiciously, and, in spite of his words, dared not put his hand upon it. He felt stirred in the depths of his being, anxious and anguished, as in the worst days of his reign.

He no longer had any joy, and those splendors offered him neither consolation nor hope. A somber melancholy troubled his gaze. There was darkness within him, the black of the tempest, which was not traversed by any reparative light.

Nigabael, however, was about to die, and that certainty alone appeased his resentment a little.

Nigabael and Phédyne had repaid his benefits with a frightful ingratitude; it was appropriate that an inexorable punishment should be applied to them. But in the king's heart the sentiments had been whispering and howling since the day before. He had sent Sahuradha away, who had also betrayed his confidence cruelly. However, he had showed himself to be a passionate husband rather than a master; no reproach could attain him, and the bitterness of the fault committed by his wife was all the greater for it.

If he suffered from the deception of the queen, whose imminent maternity filled him with indulgence, he only experienced a grim hatred for Phédyne. The Jewess and her brother would pay for the others, and the torture that he had imagined seemed to him to be scarcely equal to the crime.

✳

Into the crypt of the temple of Mylitta, the young woman had been transported on emerging for the prison. She lay on the ground in the midst of semi-darkness in which mystery shivered. The walls around her were covered with terrifying bas-reliefs; it was already the horror of the tomb, in the depths of which every human creature has to sleep the final slumber.

Women clad in white presented her with the sacred haoma, prepared in accordance with the sacred rites. They sang the praises of the goddess in order to precipitate the madness that was about to take possession of their victim at the moment when the liquid set her veins ablaze. But Phédyne refused to drink, and tears ran incessantly from her eyes like a reparative wave.

Then the priestesses tipped her head back, and forced the green liquid to flow between her teeth, brutally. Then they swayed in cadence, with an increasingly rapid movement, while continuing the sacred hymn. Gradually, their gestures became febrile and disordered, and Phédyne, her temples on fire and her throat dry, drank of her own accord, glad to sense her ideas clouding and her will buckling.

Everything was now dancing before her with the whirling women who were uttering increasingly shrill cries. Some fell on the paving stones, foaming at the mouth, in a convulsive crisis, their limbs twisted and their pupils revulsed.

And Phédyne continued drinking, hoping to die under the action of the inflamed wave that was traversing her being. She had lost all lucid thought and was agitating in an immense insanity.

A strange intoxication gripped her, an increasing annihilation of all her flesh. Above all, she had the profound sensation of being far from the living world, in the depths of the incredible and the superhuman, as if the vault of darkness had become the very barrier of infinity.

She savored an ardent and pleasant drunkenness that drowned her dolorous body. It was like an odor of plants, flowers and warm wax, which inebriated her to the point of vertigo; certainly, it was the commencement of death and the entry into the mysterious abode of souls.

Meanwhile, ardent images passed before her eyes. The hallucinated and convulsive women who surrounded her continued their dances and their clamors in an ever-increasing cerebral excitation, which stimulated her dream.

She saw long caravans laden with fabrics, jewels, gold powder and ivory traversing the land of Israel. She was returning with her brother to the beloved fatherland, the favored country of nearer Asia that covered the ramifications of the Lebanon and offered all the enchantments of a land of election. Beneath its snowy, resplendent summits, the tender pasturelands extended, the delicately nuanced fields of flax, barley and wheat. It really was the blessed country in which milk and honey flowed in streams, where clusters of grapes ripened into enormous amber fruits, and pink figs and brown olives melted.

Phédyne saw once again the cherished images old, and she repeated the words of hope, those that the prophet Jeremiah had addressed to the captives of Babylon:

"Again I will build thee, and thou shalt be built, O virgin of Israel . . . Thou shalt yet plant vines upon the mountains of Samaria . . . Therefore they shall come and sing in the height of Zion, and shall flow together to the goodness of the Lord."[1]

She repeated those predictions, because they were in her memory, but she did not know what she was saying and her soul remained absent.

---

1 *Jeremiah* 4-5 and 12; as usual, the text modifies the verses considerably, but as Phédyne is supposedly quoting I have substituted the A.V. version of the relevant citation.

Her soul was down there, in the light of her native land, in the keen and embalmed morning air. It was the holy city that appeared to her, nested in a deep fold in the terrain, and the oblique rays of the sun outlined in somber lilac its crenellated towers, its crumbling walls, all of its grandiose and venerable ruins.

In the flying golden dust, nothing could any longer be seen but proud ridges, sections of cyclopean constructions sheltering light, fragile houses, which, in the extensive shadow in which they bathed, took on all shades and faded into a pale roseate hue.

Phédyne tried to get up, and fell back on the ground, moaning, for her bonds had bruised her legs and arms.

The vision had disappeared, everything was drowned once again in the darkness of the tomb.

"Come," said the women, and they made her walk between them, dragging her and shivering her into the mysterious subterrains of the temple.

Docile and unconscious, she no longer resisted, obedient to the invincible force of destiny.

XI

MENE: God hath numbered thy kingdom, and finished it.
TEKEL: Thou art weighed in the balances,
and art found wanting.
PERES: Thy kingdom is divided, and given to the Medes
and Persians.
(*Daniel* 5:26-28.)

"Let us drink to the glory of my reign, to the prosperity of Babylon and the annihilation of the enemy army!"

Several times, the king had reached out his hand toward the golden vessels gemmed with rubies, which flourished on the table in the midst of garlands of roses with fading scents, but his tremulous hand had fallen back, inert.

Facing him, Nigabael had been placed, ornamented like him with a royal tiara and a crimson cloak. The young man's eyes were closed, and his face had a sepulchral pallor, for he had already been subjected to torture by fire two hours previously, and his wounds were bleeding.

Smarnis and seven other chiefs condemned to death were waiting at the back of the room under the guard of the executioners. They too had been tortured; dolorous sighs inflated their breasts. However, they did not utter any audible plaint, and their implacable gazes remained fixed upon the tyrant.

The table was covered with gold, amber and jade platters laden with rare fruits, iced delicacies, sugared and spiced dishes, entire birds ornamented with their plumage, large pink fish with silvery fins, game pâtés with trembling jellies, cooked eggs surrounded by pomegranate and olive seeds, acacia and rose creams. The blue wines of Chaldea alternated with the darker wines of Ethiopia and Arabia; and there were cups enriched with precious stones of different colors for each new liquor.

The vehement savor of the dishes and the ardor of the wines excited heads, and the guests were calling out to Nigabael, joking about his royalty of a single night.

"Drink, then," the satrap Ourouka said to him. "Tomorrow your lips will be sealed forever. It's necessary to profit from the good things of life while there's still time."

And Sydilia, the courtesan, leaned over amorously. "Look at these carnal treasures. You won't find similar ones in the realm of shades! Fill your eyes with my voluptuous splendor. O king of the afterlife! I offer you my kiss, without demanding the slightest present in exchange! Is that not an incomparable favor, of which no other can boast?"

Laughter burst forth around the tables, and the dancers, in passing, brushed the young man's pale face with flowers.

Couples were already enlacing, separating and returning to one another among the shredded corollas, to the songs and the dying chords of stringed instruments.

The night was suffocating, one of those profound nights in which the sands seem to fume like volcanic lava. Strange scents, acrid, intoxicating, heavy and tenacious, rose from the ground, plants, animals and humans. The singular effluvia, mingled with the sweet odors of vegetables, flowers, fruits and waves, warmed brains, stretching the nerves to the point of vertigo.

Desires, after amour, called for death, every Babylonian feast having to terminate in blood.

People had been amused by Nigabael's royalty; voices were now demanding his torture. He had committed treason; he had refused to recognize his master's generosity; it was just that he suffer the chastisement of his unworthiness.

All gazes turned toward Belsharuzur, demanding the promised entertainment, the executioner's final game.

"Death! Death!" cried a few women, the most enthusiastic, raising their slender hands charged with rings.

"Death! Death!" repeated the courtiers who had once been jealous of the young man and were now enjoying his humiliation.

"Death! Death!" howled the satraps, impatient to avenge their lord.

Belsharuzur made a sign to the eunuch who was standing behind him and said a few words to him in a low voice. Sil-Assur leapt and disappeared through a secret door in the great hall, while the executioners, who were doubtless about to comply with the king's order, prepared the condemned.

Smarnis could not see or hear anything. He was thinking about Phédyne, who had expiated her sin in coming to offer herself to his cult of amour, to his ardent ecstasy. He had contemplated her in the prison, where she had confessed her error and her unwitting fault.

Oh, if he were only able to see her again, if only for a moment, before dying! Seized by a delirium of amour, he prayed with more fever, more ardor.

And suddenly, his dream seemed to be realized; he uttered a great cry, and extended his arms toward a vision that seemed to him to be radiant with sidereal glory.

Phédyne, entirely clad in white, had just entered, sustained by the priestesses of Mylitta. She was walking slowly, her gaze fixed, strange and supernatural, seemingly obeying a mysterious order.

The executioners had arranged the prisoners against the wall, facing the king, and a great silence now fell in the hall, full of confusion.

"Phédyne," said Belsharuzur, effortfully, "is the sister of Nigabael, the unworthy friend, and the fiancée of Smarnis, the perjured satrap; she is the one who will avenge us for the crime of treason."

A great frisson ran through the audience.

Nigabael had raised his head, his lips quivering, and tears rose to his eyelids. He gazed at the young woman with despair, not understanding yet, but sensing that something was about to happen more horrible than anything he had imagined.

Smarnis remained surprised by the extraordinary beauty that transfigured the face of the woman he had believed to be his fiancée. That woman appeared to him in a splendor of troubling passion, a power of irresistible conquest. Her eyes, above all, her large glaucous eyes, which she usually hid beneath the veil of her eyelids, were burning like divine torches, He understood, and he awaited death with serenity, since she was the one who was to give it to him.

Phédyne continued coming forward, with an automatic step, as if in a dream, and her strange gaze remained fixed upon her brother, whom she did not recognize.

Belsharuzur had rise to his feet.

"Let a large golden pin be placed in her hand," he said, "in order that she can put out the prisoners' eyes before the final torture."

A cry of horror sprang from all mouths.

Those men and women, although habituated to the spectacle of executions, shuddered at the idea of that cruel refinement.

Nigabael paled further, and nothing any longer seemed alive in him but his imploring, tender, dolorous gaze, filled with a limitless stupor and despair.

Meanwhile, Phédyne had taken the golden pin and had approached the young man, close enough to touch him. She had raised her arm, slowly, seemingly obeying an invincible occult force.

Breasts heaved, the lips opening to suck in the stifling air; the flutter of a moth's wing would have been audible . . .

Suddenly, however, the girl dropped the homicidal pin and put her hands swiftly to her forehead. Light sprang forth within her; she woke up from her morbid dream; she saw; she understood.

"Oh!" she cried. "What was I about to do?"

With a great frisson, which shook her from head to toe, she turned round, and her eyes encountered the implacable gaze of the Master, the gaze of the man she had cherished so much.

"You! You!" she said, in a dying voice. "It's you!"

She opened her eyes, took a few tottering steps, and collapsed in front of the great table, in the shredded corollas, and the pools of wine, blood and perfumes.

Belsharuzur was trembling slightly; he ended up no longer being able to distinguish the guests clearly. A great void formed around this thought, and he recalled the prophetic words. Was it necessary to pardon the accursed tribe . . . ?

No, the world does not turn backwards, nations know nothing but the force of conquests. It is cowardly and dangerous to grant mercy, and nothing exists but the human will! Lies, predictions and Propechies! Lies, the laws of duty and forbearance! Lies, sacred oracles that trouble reason and sow fear in hearts!

"Someone pick that woman up and guide her hand," he said. "It's necessary that the torture take place."

"Omnipotent Master, King of Kings," said one of the executioners, "this woman's heart is no longer beating."

But Belsharuzur, with a strident laugh, picked up one of the sacred vessels stolen from the temple of Jerusalem, which was in front of him.

"Let her god resuscitate her!" he shouted. And he filled the cup to the brim with a flame-colored wine, which sparkled sinisterly. "I, Belsharuzur," he continued, effortlessly, "drink to Baal, the master of all verity and all justice, who will always triumph over the god of Israel and all the false divinities of impostor peoples! I drink to new victories, to our triumphs and to the extermination of our enemies! May the entire world tremble before us, and no human or divine force ever annihilate us!"

The king raised the cup to his lips, and immediately, the lights were extinguished and the most profound obscurity fell in the hall. Then a phosphorescent glow ran over the wall facing the table of honor, and Belsharuzur felt an icy chill invade his veins. He staggered, so bewildered by terror that he knelt down in the darkness, groaning.

A hand, now, a monstrous and livid spider, ran over the wall, tracing characters. The tentacles of nightmare agitated in the night and letters appeared, immense letters of fire that the king spelled out in a low voice. A shock ran through his limbs, so frightful that it seemed that his soul was melting in anguish. He was suffering as he had never suffered before, in the irresistible breath of supernatural terror.

And all the guests around him were bewildered, no longer knowing what they were doing.

The livid hand, the hand of death, stopped and disappeared. It had traced on the wall these words in Chaldean characters:

SUTMM
IPKNN
NRLAA

Then the king cried in the night: "Whoever can read that writing and give me an explanation of it will be dressed in crimson like a monarch. He will be the second in the kingdom and I shall put my golden collar around his neck!"[1]

The great voice of Daniel rose up in the tragic silence.

"God," it said, "has counted your reign, which is about to end. You scarcely weigh in the divine balance, and your kingdom already no longer belongs to you."

Belsharuzur had bounded, searching for the great door that opened over the gardens. He had the troubled alarm of an awakening after a nightmare. But the door was closed, and became unbreakable. All the exits were similarly closed, and it seemed that mountains had been raised behind the accursed hall, immuring it for eternity.

Then a fever of flight invaded the people who were there, an indescribable panic that threw them against one another, breathless, bewildered and frantic.

The terrible words were still flamboyant in the darkness, communicating to brains the strange stupor to which miracles give birth and to which the supernatural owes its omnipotence.

---

1 This inscription, and the immediate passage featuring it, are borrowed directly from *Zoroaster* (1885) by F. Marion Crawford. Crawford did not invent it, however, and was undoubtedly familiar with contemporary decodings, which pointed out that the Chaldeans read from right to left and did not insert what they considered to be vowels into written words. If each vertical line is read in turn, starting at the right, treating the two As as punctuation marks, the message reads *MeNe, MeNe, TeKeL UPhaRSIN*. In Crawford's novel, as in the Biblical fable of Daniel, however, it is Darius and not Cyrus who invades Babylon, La Vaudère having made that correction to comply with the historical record.

Then a great din became audible, as if the elements of the earth were returning to the primordial cataclysm. The bronze doors of the garden had just ceded, delivering passage to the triumphant Cyrus, the master of Babylon and its grim king.

CONCLUSION

Thus saith Cyrus, king of Persia: "The Lord, God of Heavens hath given me all the kingdoms of the earth, and he hath charged me to build him a house at Jerusalem, which is in Judah." (Cyrus, King of the Persians.)[1]

Thus perished the master of crimes and debaucheries, in the monstrous city that made the world tremble. Belsharuzur was slaughtered, with all his men, and the country finally respired. The Achaemenids inaugurated a new civilization and a different language, written with the characters that appeared so tragically to the eyes of the Chaldeans during the night of the final orgy.

This is what had happened: Menilok, of the tribe of Juda, had taken the place of Smarnis and joined Cyrus in order to inform and counsel him, for he was well aware of the weakness of the Babylonian city. The height and strength of its walls did not permit an enemy to take it by assault, and it mocked famine, having food stored for twenty years. But Smarnis had had a marvelous inspiration and Menilok, his confidant, had informed the Persian conqueror of it.

During the feast, Cyrus opened a communication between the Euphrates and the two heads of an immense trench established since the last siege. The water flowed into that new bed, and the part of the river that traversed the city became fordable before

---

1 The quotation is taken verbatim from *Ezra* 1:2.

dawn. The enemy then penetrated into the heart of Babylon through the bronze gates, massacring the soldiers guarding them and all those who tempted to oppose their passage.

Nigabael, Smarnis and their brothers of the tribe of Juda had their lives saved, and returned to the holy city, taking with them the body of Phédyne, miraculously recovered among the dead.

Thus was accomplished the vengeful prediction of Iahveh, god of the Jews.